CAPPY RICKS RETIRES

But, in time, Cappy would find her a rich husband.

CAPPY RICKS RETIRES

*But that doesn't keep him from
coming back stronger than ever.*

BY

PETER B. KYNE

AUTHOR OF

**THE PRIDE OF PALOMAR,
KINDRED OF THE DUST,
CAPPY RICKS, ETC.**

ILLUSTRATED BY

T. D. SKIDMORE

GROSSET & DUNLAP
PUBLISHERS   NEW YORK

THE ILLUSTRATIONS

CAPPY RICKS RETIRES

CAPPY RICKS RETIRES

CHAPTER I

IF you have read previous tales of the Blue Star
Navigation Company and the various brisk individuals connected therewith, you will recall one
Michael J. Murphy, who first came to the attention of
Cappy Ricks at the time he, the said Murphy, was chief
kicker of the barkentine *Retriever* under Captain Matt
Peasley. Subsequently, when Matt Peasley presented in
his person indubitable evidence of the wisdom of the old
saw that you cannot keep a good man down, Michael
J. became skipper of the *Retriever*. This berth he
continued to occupy with pleasure and profit to all
concerned, until a small financial tidal wave, which
began with Matt Peasley's purchase, at a ridiculously
low figure, of the Oriental Steamship Company's huge
freighter, *Narcissus*, swept the cunning Matthew into
the presidency of the Blue Star Navigation Company;
whereupon Matt designed to take Murphy out of the
Retriever and have him try his hand in steam as master
of the *Narcissus*.

The same financial tidal wave had swept Cappy
Ricks out of the presidency of the Blue Star Navigation Company—presumably far up the beach to a
place in the sun, where he was to bask for the remainder
of his old age as president emeritus of all his com-

panies. However, if there was one thing about Cappy you could depend upon absolutely it was the consistency of his inconsistency. For, having announced his retirement, his very next move was to bewail his inability to retire. He insisted upon clinging to the business like a barnacle to a ship, and was always very much in evidence whenever any deal of the slightest importance was about to be consummated. Indeed, he was never so thoroughly in command as when, his first burst of enthusiasm anent the acquisition of the *Narcissus* at fifty per cent. of her value having passed, he discovered that his son-in-law planned to order Mike Murphy off the quarter-deck of the *Retriever* onto the bridge of the *Narcissus*, while an unknown answering to the name of Terence Reardon had been selected for her chief engineer.

Cappy listened to Matt Peasley's announcement; then with a propitiatory "Ahem! Hum! Harump-h-h-h!" he hitched himself forward in his chair and gazed at Matt over the rims of his spectacles.

"Tell me, Matt," he demanded presently, "who is this man Reardon? I do not recall such an engineer in our employ—and I thought I knew them all."

"He is not in our employ, sir. He has been chief engineer of the *Arab* for the past eight years, and prior to that he was chief of the *Narcissus*. It was Reardon who told me what ailed her. She's a hog on coal, and the Oriental steamship people used to nag him about the fuel bills. Their port engineer didn't agree with Reardon as to what was wrong with her, so he left. He assures me that if her condensers are retubed she'll burn from seven to ten tons of coal less per day."

"Hum! So you're going to give him the job for telling you something our own port engineer would have told us after an examination."

"No, sir, I'm going to give him the job because he has earned it. He gave me some very valuable information about the wretched condition of her electric-light plant and a crack, cunningly concealed, in the after web of her crank shaft——"

"Oh, by thunder," piped Cappy, "that's worth knowing! Ship a new crank shaft, Matt, and save the Blue Star a salvage bill sooner or later."

"All that inside information will not only save us money in the future," Matt continued, "but it enabled me to drive a closer bargain when dealing with Mac-Candless, of the Oriental Steamship Company. Consequently Terence Reardon gets the job. He's only making a hundred and fifty dollars a month in the *Arab*, and as he is a rattling good man—I've looked him up, sir—I've promised him a hundred and seventy-five a month in the *Narcissus*."

"Oh, you've already promised him the job, eh? Mistake, Matt, serious mistake. You say you looked him up, but I'll bet you a new hat there is one thing about him that you failed to investigate, and that is: What kind of Irish is he?"

"Why, regular Irish, of course—mighty good Irish, I should say. Keen, observing, not too talkative, a hard worker, temperate in his habits and a crackajack engineer to boot."

Cappy settled back wearily in his chair and favored his youthful partner with a glance of tolerant amusement.

"Matt," he announced, "those are the qualifications we look for in an engineer, and it's been my experience that the Irish and the Scotch make the best marine engineers in the world. But when you've been in the shipping game as long as I have, young man, you'll know better than to pick two Irishmen as departmental chiefs in the same ship! I did it—once. There was a red-headed scoundrel named Dennis O'Leary who went from A.B. to master in the *Florence Ricks*. That fellow was a bulldog. He made up his mind he was going to be master of the *Florence* and I couldn't stop him. Good man—damned good! And there was a black Irishman, John Rooney, in the *Amelia Ricks*. Had ambitions just like O'Leary. He went from oiler to first assistant in the *Amelia*. Fine man—damned fine! So fine, in fact, that when the chief of the *Florence* died I shifted Rooney to her immediately. And what was the result? Why, riot, of course. Matt, the Irish will fight anybody and anything, but they'll fight quicker, with less excuse and greater delight, among themselves, than any other nationality! The *Florence Ricks* carried a million feet of lumber, but she wasn't big enough for Rooney and O'Leary, so I fired them both, not being desirous of playing favorites. Naturally, each blamed the other for the loss of his job, and without a word having been spoken they went out on the dock and fought the bloodiest draw I have ever seen on the San Francisco waterfront. After they had been patched up at the Harbor Hospital, both came and cussed me and told me I was an ingrate, so I hired them both back again, put them in different ships, slipped each of them a good, cheerful Russian Finn, and saved funeral expenses. That's what I got, Matt, for not asking those two what kind of Irish they were. Now, then, sonny, once more. What kind of Irish is Terence Reardon?"

"Why, I don't know, I tell you. He's just Irish."

Cappy lifted his eyes to the ceiling as if praying for the great gift of patience.

"Listen to the boy," he demanded of an imaginary bystander. "He doesn't know! Well, stick your head down over his engine-room grating some day, sing The Boyne Wather—and find out! Now, then, do you happen to know what kind of Irish Mike Murphy is? You ought to. You were shipmates with him in the *Retriever* long enough."

"Oh, Mike's from Galway. He goes to mass on Sunday when he can."

"Hum! If he's from Galway, where did he leave his brogue? He runs to the broad *a* like an Englishman."

"That's easily explained. Mike left his brogue in Galway. He came to this country when he was six years old and was raised in Boston. That's where he picked up his broad *a*."

"That doesn't help a bit, Matt. He's Irish just the same, and what a Yankee like you don't know about the Irish would fill a book. You know, Matt, there are a few rare white men that can handle Chinamen successfully; now and then you'll run across one that can handle niggers; but I have never yet met anybody who could figure the mental angles of the Irish except an Irishman. There's something in an Irishman that drives him into the bandwagon. He's got to be the boss, and if he can't be the boss he'll sit round and criticize. But if I want a man to handle Chinamen, or niggers, or Japs, or Bulgarians I'll advertise for an

Irishman and take the first one that shows up. A young man like you, Matt, shouldn't monkey with these people. They're a wonderful race and very much misunderstood, and if you don't start 'em right on the job you'll always be in trouble. Now, Matt, I've always done the hiring and firing for the Blue Star Navigation Company, and as a result I've had blamed little of it to do, considering the size of our fleet; consequently I'll just give these two Harps the Double-O. Have Murphy and Reardon at the office at nine o'clock to-morrow morning and I'll read them the riot act before turning them to."

CHAPTER II

Cappy Ricks was at his office at eight-fifty the following morning. At eight-fifty-two Mr. Terence Reardon, plainly uncomfortable in a ready-made blue-serge Sunday suit purchased on the Embarcadero for twenty-five dollars, came into the office. He was wearing a celluloid collar, and a quite noticeable rattle as he shook hands with Cappy Ricks betrayed the fact that he also was wearing celluloid cuffs; for, notwithstanding the fact that he bathed twice a day, Mr. Reardon's Hibernian hide contained much of perspiration, coal dust, metal grit and lubricating oil, and such substances can always be washed off celluloid collars and cuffs. To his credit be it known that Terence Reardon knew his haberdashery was not *au fait*, for his wife never failed to remind him of it; but unfortunately he was the possessor of a pair of grimy hands that nothing on earth could ever make clean, and even when he washed them in benzine they always left black thumb prints on a linen collar during the process of adjustment. He had long since surrendered to his fate.

At eight-fifty-four Mike Murphy arrived. Murphy was edging up into the forties, but still he was young enough at heart to take a keen interest in his personal appearance, and a tailor who belonged to Michael's council of the Knights of Columbus had decked him out in a suit of English tweeds of the latest cut and in most excellent taste.

"Good morning, captain," Cappy Ricks greeted him. "Ahead of time as usual. Meet Mr. Terence Reardon, late chief of the *Arab*. He is to be a shipmate of yours—chief of the *Narcissus*, you know.

. "Mr. Reardon, shake hands with Captain Mike Murphy. Captain Murphy has been in our employ a number of years as master of sail. The *Narcissus* will be his first command in steam."

"Terence Reardon, eh?" echoed Mike Murphy pleasantly. "That sounds like a good name. Glad to meet you, chief. What part of the old country are you from? The West?"

The wish was father to the thought, since Mike was from the West himself.

"I'm from the Nort'—from Belfast," Mr. Reardon replied in a deep Kerry brogue, and extended a grimy paw upon the finger of which Mike Murphy observed a gold ring that proclaimed Mr. Terence Reardon—an Irishman, presumably a Catholic—one who had risen to the third degree in Freemasonry.

Cappy Ricks saw that ring also, and started visibly. A Knight Templar himself, Terence Reardon was the last person on earth in whom he expected to find a brother Mason. He glanced at Mike Murphy and saw that the skipper was looking, not at Mr. Reardon, but at the Masonic emblem.

"Sit down, chief," Cappy hastened to interrupt. "Have a chair, captain. Mr. Reardon, my son-in-law, Captain Peasley here, tells me you were chief of the *Narcissus* when she was on the China run for the Oriental Steamship Company."

Mr. Reardon sat down heavily, set his derby hat on the floor beside him and replied briefly: "I was."

Captain Murphy excused himself and drew Matt Peasley out of the room. "God knows," he whispered hoarsely, "religion should never enter into the working of a ship, and I suppose I'll have to get along with that fellow; but did you mark the Masonic ring on the paw of the Far-Down? And on the right hand, too! The jackass don't know enough to wear it on his left hand."

"Why, what's wrong about being a Mason?" Matt protested. "Cappy's a Mason and so am I."

"Nothing wrong about it—with you and Cappy Ricks. That's your privilege. You're Protestants."

"Well, maybe the chief's a Protestant, too," Matt suggested, but Mike Murphy silenced him with a sardonic smile.

"With that name?" he queried, and laughed the brief, mirthless laugh of the man who knows. "And he says he's from Belfast! Man, I could cut that Kerry brogue with a belaying pin."

"Why, Mike," Matt interrupted, "I never before suspected you were intolerant of a shipmate's private convictions. I must say this attitude of yours is disturbing."

"Why, I'm not a bigot," Murphy protested virtuously. "Who told you that?"

"Why, you're a Catholic, and you resent Reardon because he's a Protestant."

"Not a bit of it. You're a Protestant, and don't I love you like a brother?"

Matt thought he saw the light. "Oh, I see," he replied. "It's because Reardon is an Irish Protestant."

"Almost—but not quite. God knows I hate the Orangemen for what they did to me and mine, but at least they've been Protestant since the time of Henry VIII. But the lad inside there has no business to be a Protestant. The Lord intended him for a Catholic—and he knows it. He's a renegade. I don't blame you for being a Protestant, Matt. It's none of my business."

Matt Peasley had plumbed the mystery at last. He had been reading a good deal in the daily papers about Home Rule for Ireland, the Irish Nationalists, the Ulster Volunteers, the Unionists, and so on, and in a vague way he had always understood that religious differences were at the bottom of it all. He realized now that it was something deeper than that—a relic of injustice and oppression; a hostility that had come to Mike Murphy as a heritage from his forbears—something he had imbibed at his mother's breast and was, for purposes of battle, a more vital issue than the interminable argument about the only safe road to heaven.

"I see," Matt murmured. "Reardon, being Irish, has violated the national code of the Irish——"

"You've said it, Matt. They're Tories at heart, every mother's son of them."

"What do you mean—Tories?"

"That they're for England, of course."

"Well, I don't blame them. So am I. Aren't you, Mike?"

"May God forgive you," Mike Murphy answered piously. "I am not. I'm for their enemies. I'm for anything that's against England. Ireland is not a colony. She's a nation. Man, man, you don't under-

stand. Only an Irishman can, and he gets it at his
mother's or his grandmother's knee—the word-of-
mouth history of his people, the history that isn't in
the books! Do you think I can forget? Do you think
I want to forget?"

"No," Matt Peasley replied quietly; "I think you'll
have to forget—in so far as Terence Reardon is concerned. This is the land of the free and the home of
the brave, and even when you're outside the three-mile
limit I want you to remember, Mike, that the good ship
Narcissus is under the American flag. The *Narcissus*
needs all her space for cargo, Mike. There is no room
aboard her for a feud. Don't ever poke your nose into
Terence Reardon's engine-room except on his invitation
or for the purpose of locating a leak. Treat him with
courtesy and do not discuss politics or religion when
you meet him at table, which will be about the only
opportunity you two will have to discuss anything;
and if Reardon wants to talk religion or politics you
change your feeding time and avoid meeting him. I've
taken you out of the old *Retriever*, Mike, where you've
been earning a hundred and twenty-five dollars a
month, to put you in the *Narcissus* at two hundred
and fifty. That is conclusive evidence that I'm for
you. But Terence Reardon is a crackajack chief engineer, and I want you to remember that the Blue Star
Navigation Company needs him in its business quite
as much as it needs Michael J. Murphy, and if you
two get scrapping I'm not going to take the trouble
to investigate and place the blame. I'll just call you
both up on the carpet and make you draw straws to
see who quits."

"Fair enough," replied the honest Murphy. "If I can't be good I'll be as good as I can."

At that very instant Cappy Ricks was just discovering what kind of Irish Mr. Terence Reardon was.

The most innocent remark brought him the information he sought.

"Captain Murphy, whom you have just met, is to be master of the *Narcissus*, chief," he explained. "He's a splendid fellow personally and a most capable navigator, and like you he's Irish. I'm sure you'll get along famously together."

Cappy tried to smile away his apprehension, for a still small voice whispered to him and questioned the right of Terence Reardon to call him brother.

Mr. Reardon's sole reply to this optimistic prophecy was a noncommittal grunt, accompanied by a slight outthrust and uplift of the chin, a pursing of the lips and the ghost of a sardonic little smile. Only an Irishman can get the right tempo to that grunt—and the tempo is everything. In the case of Terence Reardon it said distinctly: "I hope you're right, sir, but privately I have my doubts." However, not satisfied with pantomime, Mr. Reardon went a trifle farther—for reasons best known to himself. He laved the corner of his mouth with the tip of a tobacco-stained tongue and said presently: "I can't say, Misther Ricks, that I quite like the cut av that fella's jib."

That was the Irish of it. A representative of any other race on earth would have employed the third person singular when referring to the absent Murphy; only an Irishman would have said "that fella," and only a certain kind of Irishman could have managed to inject into such simple words such a note of scorn

supernal. Cappy Ricks got the message—just like
that.

"Then stay off his bridge, Reardon," he warned the
chief. "Your job is in the engine-room, so even if you
and Captain Murphy do not like each other, there will
be no excuse for friction. The only communication
you need have with him is through the engine-room
telegraph."

"Then, sor," Terence Reardon replied respectfully,
"I'll take it kindly av you to tell him to keep out av
me engine-room. I'll have no skipper buttin' in on me,
tellin' me how to run me engines an' askin' me why in
this an' that I don't go aisy on the coal. Faith, I've
had thim do it—the wanst—an' the wanst only. Begorra, I'd have brained thim wit' a monkey wrench if
they tried it a second time."

"On the other hand," Cappy remarked, "I've had to
fire more than one chief engineer who couldn't cure
himself of a habit of coming up on the bridge when
the vessel got to port—to tell the skipper how to berth
his ship against a strong flood tide. I suppose that
while we have steamships the skippers will always wonder how the vessel can possibly make steerage way,
considering the chief engineers, while the chiefs will
never cease marvelling that such fine ships should be
entrusted to a lot of Johnny Know-Nothings. However, Reardon, I might as well tell you that the Blue
Star Navigation Company plays no favorites. When
the chief and the skipper begin to interfere with the
dividends, they look overside some bright day and see
Alden P. Ricks waiting for them on the cap of the
wharf. And when the ship is alongside, the said Ricks
comes aboard with five bones in his pocket, and the

said skipper and the said chief are invited into the
dining saloon to roll the said bones—one flop and high
man out. Yes, sir. Out! Out of the ship and out of
the Blue Star employ—for ever."

"I hear you, sor. I hearrd you the first time,"
Terence Reardon replied complacently and reached for
his pipe. "All I ask from you is a square deal. I'll
have it from the captain wit'out the askin'."

Thus the Reardon breathing his defiance.

"I'm glad we understand each other, chief. Just
avoid arguments, political or religious, and treat the
skipper with courtesy. Then you'll get along all right.
Now with reference to your salary. The union scale
is one hundred and fifty dollars a month——"

"Beggin' yer pardon for the intherruption, sor, but
the young man promised me a hundhred an' siventy-
five."

"That was before the Blue Star Navigation Com-
pany took over the young man and his ship *Narcissus*.
Hereafter you'll deal with the old man in such matters.
I'm going to give you two hundred a month, Reardon,
and you are to keep the *Narcissus* out of the shop.
Hear me, chief—out of the shop."

"No man can ordher me to do me djooty," said
Terence Reardon simply. "Tell the fine gintleman on
the bridge to keep her out av the kelp, an' faith, she'll
shtay out av the shop. Thank you kindly, sor. When
do I go to wurrk?"

"Your pay started this morning. The *Narcissus* goes
on Christy's ways in Oakland Harbor at the tip of
the flood this afternoon. Get on the ship and stay on
her. It's a day-and-night rush job to get her in commission, and you'll be paid time and a half while she's

repairing. Good-day and good luck to you, chief.
Come in and see me whenever you get to port." And
Cappy Ricks, most democratic of men, extended his
hand to his newest employee. Terence Reardon took
it in his huge paw that would never be clean any more,
and held it for a moment, the while he looked fearlessly
into Cappy's eyes.

" 'Tis a proud man I am to wurrk for you, sor," he
said simply. "Tip-top serrvice for tip-top pay, an'
by the Great Gun av Athlone, you'll get it from me,
sor. If ever the ship is lost 'twill be no fault of mine."

Mr. Reardon's manner, as he thus calmly exculpated
himself from the penalty for future disaster, indicated
quite clearly that Cappy Ricks, in such a contingency,
might look to the man higher up—on the bridge, for
instance.

When Terence Reardon had departed Cappy Ricks
called Mike Murphy into the room.

"Now, captain," he began, "there are a few things
I want to tell you. This man Reardon is a fine, loyal
fellow, but he's touchy——"

"I know all about him," Murphy interrupted with
a slight emphasis on the pronoun. Unlike Mr. Reardon he employed the third person singular and did not
say "that fella," for he had been raised in the United
States of America.

"I have already given the captain his instructions,"
Matt Peasley announced. "He understands the situation perfectly and will conduct himself accordingly."

CHAPTER III

A small army of men swarmed over, under and through the huge *Narcissus* for the next three weeks, and the hearts of Cappy Ricks and Matt Peasley were like to burst with pride as they stood on the bridge with Captain Mike Murphy, while he ran the vessel over the measured course to test her speed, and swung her in the bay while adjusting her compass. She was as beautiful as money and paint could make her, and when Terence Reardon, in calm disregard of orders, came up on the bridge to announce his unbounded faith in the rejuvenated condensers and to predict a modest coal bill for the future, Mike Murphy so far forgot himself as to order the steward to bring up a bottle of something and begged Mr. Reardon to join him in three fingers of nepenthe to celebrate the occasion.

"T'ank you, sor, but I never dhrink—on djooty," Mr. Reardon retorted with chill politeness, "nor," he added, "wit' me immejiate superiors."

A superficial analysis of this remark will convince the most sceptical that Mr. Reardon, with true Hibernian adroitness, had managed to convey an insult without seeming to convey it.

"Isn't that a pity!" the skipper replied. "We'll excuse you to attend to your duty, Mr. Reardon;" and he bowed the chief toward the companion leading

to the boat deck. The latter departed, furious, with
an uncomfortable feeling of having been out-generaled;
and once a good Irishman and true has undergone that
humiliation it is a safe bet that the Dove of Peace has
lost her tail feathers.

"That's an unmannerly chief engineer," Mike
Murphy announced blandly, "but for all that he's not
without his good points. He'll not waste money in his
department."

"A virtue which I trust you will imitate in yours,
captain," Cappy Ricks snapped dryly. "Is Reardon
working short-handed?"

"Only while we're loading, when he'll need just
enough men to keep steam up in the winches. When
we go to sea, however, he'll have a full crew, but the
fun of it is they'll be non-union men with the exception
of the engineers and officers. The engineers will all
belong to the Marine Engineers' Association and the
mates to Harbor 15, Masters' and Pilots' Association."

"He'll do nothing of the sort," Matt Peasley declared quietly. "We have union crews in all our other
steamers, and the unions will declare a strike on us
if we put non-union men in the *Narcissus*."

"Of course—if they find out. But they'll not. Besides, we're going to the Atlantic Coast, so why should
we bring a high-priced crew into a low-priced market,
Mr. Ricks? Leave it to me, sir. I'll load the ship with
longshoremen entirely, and we'll sail with the crew of
that German liner that came a few days ago to intern
in Richardson's Bay until the European war is over."

"I'm not partial to the German cause," Matt Peasley

announced. "So I'll just veto that plan right now, Mike."

"Matt, we're neutral," Cappy declared.

"And it pays to ship those Germans, Matt," Murphy continued. "I confess I'm for the Germans, although not to such an extent that I'd go round offering them jobs just because they *are* Germans. But the minute I heard about that interned boat I said to myself: 'Now, here's a chance to save the *Narcissus* some money. The crew of that liner will all be discharged now that she is interned. However, the local unions will not admit them to membership and they cannot work on any Pacific Coast boat unless they hold union cards. Consequently they must seek other occupations, and as the chances are these fellows do not speak English, they're up against it. Also, they are foreigners who have paid no head tax when coming into the country, because they are seamen. They have the right to land and stay ashore three months, if they state that it is their intention to ship out again within that period; but if they do not so ship, then the immigration authorities may deport them as paupers or for failure to pay the head tax; and in that event they will all be returned to the vessel that brought them here, and the owners of the vessel will be forced to intern them and care for them.' Under the circumstances, therefore, I concluded they would jump at a job in an American vessel, for the reason that under the American flag they would be reasonably safe; and even if the *Narcissus* should be searched by a British cruiser, she would not dare take these Germans off her. Remember, we had a war with England once for boarding our ships and removing seamen!"

"By the Holy Pink-Toed Prophet," said Cappy Ricks, "there's something in that, Matt."

"There's a splendid saving in the pay roll, let me tell you," the proud Murphy continued. "I took the matter up at once with the German skipper and he fixed it for me, and mighty glad he was to get his countrymen off his hands. We get all that liner's coal passers, oilers, firemen, six deckhands and four quartermasters at the scale of wages prevailing in Hamburg. I know what it is in marks, but I haven't figured it out in dollars and cents, although whatever it is it's a scandal! It almost cuts our pay roll in half."

"Do you speak German, captain?" Cappy queried excitedly.

"I do not, sir—more's the pity. But the four quartermasters speak fair English, and I have engaged two good German-American mates who speak German. Reardon has shipped German-American engineers and some of his coal passers and firemen speak fair English. I've got two Native Son Chinamen in the galley and a Cockney steward. We'll get along."

"And a rattling fine idea, too," Cappy Ricks declared warmly. "Mike, my boy, you're a wonder. That's the spirit. Always keep down the overhead, Matt. That's what eats up the dividends."

"Well, I wouldn't agree to it if the *Narcissus* wasn't going to be engaged in neutral trade, or if she was carrying munitions of war to the Allies," Matt declared. "I'd be afraid some of Mike's Germans might blow up the ship."

"Believe me," quoth Michael J. Murphy, "if she was engaged in freighting munitions to England, it'd be a smart German that would get a chance to blow her up. I think I'd scuttle her myself first."

"Well, Mike, if your courage failed you," Cappy Ricks replied laughingly, "I think we could safely leave the job to Terence Reardon."

CHAPTER IV

On that first voyage the *Narcissus* carried general cargo to northern ports on the West Coast. Then she dropped down to a nitrate port and loaded nitrate for New York, and about the time she passed through the Panama Canal the Blue Star Navigation Company wired its New York agent to provide some neutral business for her next voyage. Freights were soaring by this time, due to the scarcity of the foreign bottoms which formerly had carried Uncle Sam's goods to market, and Cappy Ricks and Matt Peasley knew the rates would increase from day to day, and that in consequence their New York agents would experience not the slightest difficulty in placing her—hence they delayed as long as they could placing her on the market.

On the other hand, the New York agents, realizing that higher freight rates meant a correspondingly higher commission for them on the charter, held off until the *Narcissus* had almost finished discharging at Hoboken before they closed with a fine old New York importing and exporting house for a cargo of soft coal from Norfolk, Virginia, to Manila, or Batavia. The charterers were undecided which of these two cities would be the port of discharge, and stipulated that the vessel was to call at Pernambuco, Brazil, for orders. The New York agents marvelled at this for—to them

—very obvious reasons; but inasmuch as the charterers had offered a whopping freight rate and declined to do business on any other basis, and since further the agent concluded it was no part of his office to question the motives of a house that never before had been subjected to suspicion, he concluded to protect himself by leaving the decision to the owners of the *Narcissus*. Accordingly he wired them as follows:

"Blue Star Navigation Company,
 "258 California St., San Francisco, Cal.
 "Have offer *Narcissus,* coal Norfolk Batavia or Manila, charterers undecided, Pernambuco for orders, ten dollars per ton. Shall we close? Answer.
        "SEABORN & COMPANY."

Cappy Ricks was having his afternoon siesta when this telegram arrived. Mr. Skinner, the general manager of the Ricks Lumber & Logging Company, which occupied the same suite of offices as the Blue Star Navigation Company and was so intertwined with the latter company as to be an integral part of it, received the telegram and read it to Cappy, who unfortunately was not so wide awake at the moment as usual. Furthermore, Mr. Skinner had just emerged from a terrible battle with a customer who had tried to crawl out of an order for a cargo of redwood lumber just because the market had slumped fifty cents; in consequence of which the estimable Skinner's mind was on other things as he read the telegram to Cappy.

"Is it all right, Mr. Ricks? Shall I wire them to close?" he queried, wondering all the while if he hadn't made a mistake in insisting upon delivery of that cargo after all. Certainly it did call for a fearful lot of No.

2 boards, 1″ x 8″ and up, and too great a percentage of 4″ x 6″–20′ No. 1 clear. And there were mighty few clear twenty-foot logs coming into the boom these days.

"Well, will a cat eat liver?" declared Cappy Ricks. "I should say we do accept. Why, man, she'll make forty thousand dollars on the voyage, and whether she goes to Batavia or Manila, we're certain to get a cargo back."

"All right, I'll wire acceptance," Skinner replied, and paused long enough to make a notation on the message: "O.K.—Ricks." Mr. Skinner meant nothing in particular by that. He was a model of efficiency, and that was his little way of placing the responsibility for the decision in the event that the wisdom of said decision should, at some future time, be questioned. Mr. Skinner never took unnecessary chances. He always played a safe game.

It is necessary to state here also that Matt Peasley was not in the office when that telegram arrived from Seaborn & Company. If he had been this story would never have been written. He was down at Hunter's Point drydock, superintending the repairs to the steam schooner *Amelia Ricks*, which recently on a voyage to Seattle had essayed the overland route via Duxbury Reef. When Matt reached home that night he found his ingenious father-in-law fairly purring with contentment.

"Well, Matt, old horse," Cappy piped, "I've chartered the *Narcissus*. Norfolk to Batavia or Manila with coal. Got a glorious price—ten dollars a ton. That's what we get for holding off until the last minute."

"That's encouraging," Matt answered pleasantly, and asked no further questions. He was obsessed with the engines of the *Amelia Ricks*. It was going to cost a lot of money to put them in condition again, and he remarked as much to Cappy. Thus it happened that they entered into a discussion of other matters, and the good ship *Narcissus*, having finished discharging her cargo of nitrate, dropped down to Norfolk, where Captain Michael J. Murphy proceeded to let a stream of coal into her at a rate that promised to load her fully in less than four days.

It is worthy of remark, at this juncture, that Mike Murphy and Terence Reardon had, by this time, cast aside all appearance of even shirt-sleeve diplomacy. Diplomatic relations had, in fact, been completely severed. Crossing the Gulf Stream, Murphy had called the engine-room on the speaking-tube and politely queried if Mr. Reardon didn't think he could get a few more revolutions out of her. To this Mr. Reardon had replied passionately that if such a thing were possible he would have done it long ago without waiting to be told. He desired to inform Captain Murphy that he knew his business; whereupon Murphy had replied that he never would have guessed Mr. Reardon was that intelligent, judging by the face of him. In disgust Mr. Reardon had replied: "Aw, go to——" and then tried to close the speaking-tube before the captain would have the opportunity to retort. However, Michael J. knew his own mind, and, like all the Irish, was a marvel at repartee. Quick as was Terence Reardon, therefore, Michael J. Murphy was quicker. Perhaps all of his message had not been delivered before Reardon closed the tube, but the chief got enough of it for all practical purposes.

He caught one word—"Renegade"; a word so terrible that it left the chief engineer speechless with fury, and before he could call the skipper a baboon, the golden opportunity was gone. He closed the tube with a sigh.

CHAPTER V

While the *Narcissus* was loading, the Fates were keeping in reserve for Cappy Ricks, Matt Peasley and Mr. Skinner a blow that was to stun them when it fell. About the time the *Narcissus*, fully loaded, was snoring out to sea past Old Point Comfort, Matt Peasley came across Seaborn & Company's telegram in the unanswered-correspondence tray on his desk. Five times he read it; and then, in the language of the poet, hell began to pop!

Cappy Ricks came out of a gentle doze to find his big son-in-law waving the telegram under his nose.

"Why didn't you tell me?" Matt Peasley bawled, for all the world as if Cappy was a very stupid mate and all the canvas had just been blown out of the bolt-ropes.

"Why didn't you ask me, you big stiff?" shrilled Cappy. He didn't know what was coming, but instinct told him it was awful, so he resolved instantly to meet it with a brave front. "Don't you yell at me, young feller. Now then, what do you want to find out?"

"Why didn't you tell me the *Narcissus* was to drop in at Pernambuco for orders?" roared Matt wrathfully.

Cappy pursed his lips and calmly rang for Mr. Skinner. He eyed the general manager over the rims of his spectacles for fully thirty seconds. Then:

"Skinner, what the devil's wrong with you of late?

It's getting so I can't trust you to do anything any more. Tut, tut! Not a peep out of you, sir. Now then, answer me: Why didn't you tell me, Skinner, that the *Narcissus* was to call in at Pernambuco for orders?"

"I read you the telegram, sir," Mr. Skinner replied coldly, and pointed to the notation: "O.K.—Ricks," the badge of his infernal efficiency. "I read that telegram to you, sir," he repeated, "and asked you if I should close. You said to close. I closed. That's all I know about it. You and Matt are in charge of the shipping and I decline to be dragged into any disputes originating in your department. All I have to say is that if you two can't run the shipping end and run it right, just turn it over to me and I'll run it—right!"

Completely vindicated, Mr. Skinner struck a distinctly defiant attitude and awaited the next move on the part of Cappy. The latter, thoroughly crushed—for he knew the devilish Skinner never made any mistakes—looked up at his son-in-law.

"Well," he demanded, "what's your grouch against Pernambuco?"

"Forgive me for bawling you out that way," Matt replied, "but I guess you'd bawl, too, if somebody who should have known better had placed a fine ship in jeopardy for you. It just breaks me all up to think you may have lost my steamer *Narcissus*—the first steamer I ever owned too—and to be lost on her second voyage under the Blue Star flag——"

"Our *Narcissus*, if you please," Cappy shrilled. "You gibbering jackdaw! Out with it! Where do you get that stuff—lose your steamer on her second voyage! Why, she's snug in Norfolk this minute."

"If she only is," Matt almost wailed, "she'll never be permitted to clear with that German crew aboard. Pernambuco for orders! Suffering sailor! And you, of all men, to put over a charter like that! Pernambuco! Pernambuco! Pernambuco—for—orders! Do you get it?"

"No, I don't. It's over my head and into the bleachers."

"I must say, my dear Matt," Mr. Skinner struck in blandly, "that I also fail to apprehend."

"Didn't you two ever go to school?" Matt raved. "Didn't you ever study geography? Why under the canopy should we waste our time and burn up our good coal steaming to Pernambuco, Brazil, South America, for orders? Let me put it to you two in words of one syllable: The *Narcissus* is chartered to carry a cargo of coal from Norfolk, Virginia, to Batavia or Manila. At the time of charter—and sailing—the charterers are undecided which port she is to discharge at, so they ask us to step over to Pernambuco and find out. Now, whether the vessel discharges at Batavia or Manila, her course in the Atlantic Ocean while en route to either port is identical! She passes round the Cape of Good Hope, which is at the extreme south end of Africa. If her course, on the contrary, was round Cape Horn or through the Straits of Magellan there might be some sense in sending her over to the east coast of South America for orders. But whether she is ordered to Manila or Batavia, the fact remains that she must put in to Durban, South Africa, for fuel to continue her voyage; so why in the name of the Flying Dutchman couldn't the charterers cable the orders to Mike Murphy at Durban? The *Narcissus* is worth a thousand dollars a day, so you waste a few thousand dollars worth of her time, at the very least, sending her to Pernambuco when a ten-dollar cablegram to Durban would have done the business! I suppose all you two brilliant shipping men could see was a ten-dollar-a-ton freight rate. Eh? You—landlubbers! A-a-g-r-r-h! I was never so angry since the day I was born."

While Matt ranted on, Mr. Skinner's classic features had been slowly taking on the general color tones of a ripe old Edam cheese, while at the conclusion of Matt's oration Cappy Ricks' eyes were sticking out like twin semaphores. He clasped his hands.

"By the Twelve Ragged Apostles!" he murmured in an awed voice. "There's a nigger in the woodpile."

"I very greatly fear," Mr. Skinner chattered, "that you are mistaken, Mr. Ricks. Something tells me it's a German!"

"Well, well, well!" Matt Peasley sneered. "Skinner, take the head of the class. Really, I believe I begin to pick up signs of human intelligence in this sea of maritime ignorance."

"Oh, Matt, quit your jawing and break the news to me quickly," Cappy pleaded.

"Haven't you been reading the papers, sir? Australian and Japanese warships have been hunting for the German Pacific fleet for the past few weeks, and the Germans have been on the dodge. Therefore, they've been burning coal. They are only allowed to remain in a neutral port twenty-four hours, and can only take on sufficient coal and stores to enable them to reach the nearest German port. Consequently,

since they have been afraid to enter a neutral port,
for fear of giving away their position, it follows that
they've had to stay at sea—and naturally they have
run short of coal. A few steamers have cleared from
San Francisco with coal, ostensibly for discharge
at Chilean or Mexican ports, but in reality for delivery
to the German fleet at sea, but even with these few
deliveries, there is a coal famine. And now that the
Pacific is getting too hot for it, the general impression
is that the German fleet will try to get through the
Straits of Magellan, for, once in the Atlantic, coal
will be easier to get. More ships, you know; more ship-
owners willing to take a chance for wartime profits—
and they say Brazil is rather friendly to the German
cause. We will assume, therefore, that the German
secret agents in this country realize it is inevitable
that Von Spee's fleet must be forced into the Atlantic;
hence, in anticipation of that extremity, they are ar-
ranging for the delivery of coal to those harassed
cruisers. The agent in Pernambuco is probably in
constant communication with the fleet by wireless; the
fleet will probably come ranging up the coast of South
America, destroying British commerce, or some of the
ships may cross over to the Indian Ocean and join the
Emden, raiding in those waters. So the German secret
agents charter our huge *Narcissus*, load her with ten
thousand tons of coal——"

Matt Peasley paused and bent a beetling glance, first
at Cappy Ricks and then at Skinner.

"Was she to carry soft coal or anthracite?" he
demanded.

"I don't know," Mr. Skinner quavered.

"Search me!" Cappy Ricks piped up sourly.

"I thought so. For the sake of argument we'll assume it's soft coal, because anthracite has not as yet become popular as steamship fuel. Well, we will assume our vessel gets to Pernambuco. If, in the meantime, the German admiral wirelesses his Pernambuco agent, 'Send a jag of coal into the Indian Ocean,' to the Indian Ocean goes the *Narcissus*, and presently she finds a German warship or two or three ranging along in her course. They pick her up, help themselves to her coal, give Mike Murphy a certificate of confiscation for her cargo, to be handed to the owners, who in this case will be good, loyal sons of the Fatherland and offer no objection——"

"I see," Cappy Ricks interrupted. "And if, on the other hand, the German admiral says, 'Send a jag of coal to meet us in a certain latitude and longitude off the River Plate,' and Mike Murphy objects, that German crew on our *Narcissus* will just naturally lock Mike Murphy up in his cabin and take the vessel away from him! When they're through with her they'll give her back——"

"I'm not so certain they'll have to lock him up in his cabin in order to get the ship," Mr. Skinner struck in, a note of alarm in his voice. "Mike Murphy is so pro-German——"

"Ow! Wow! That hurts," Cappy wailed. "So he is! I never thought of that. And now that you speak of it, I recall it was his idea, getting that crew of Germans aboard! He said it would cut down expenses. Holy mackerel, Matt; do you think it was a frameup?"

"Certainly I do, but—Mike Murphy wasn't in on it. You can bank on that. No piratical foreigner will ever climb up on Mike Murphy's deck except over Mike

Murphy's dead body. According to the president emeritus there is more than one kind of Irish, but I'll guarantee Mike Murphy isn't the double-crossing kind."

A boy entered with a telegram. It was a day letter filed by Mike Murphy in Norfolk that morning, and Matt Peasley read it aloud:

"Sailing at noon. Regret your failure take me into your confidence when deciding withdraw vessel from neutral trade. If orders send me to either of ports named in charter party and I am overhauled *en route,* that is your funeral. If orders conflict with charter party, as I suspect they may, that may be my funeral. Regretfully I shall resign at Pernambuco. You know your own business, and I cannot believe you would go it blind; if you change your mind before arrival Pernambuco, cable care American Consul and will do my best for you.

"M. J. M."

Cappy Ricks sprang into the air and tried to crack his aged ankles together.

"Saved!" he croaked. "By the Holy Pink-toed Prophet! Saved! Bully for Mike Murphy! Say, when that fellow gets back, if I don't do something handsome for him——"

Matt Peasley's scowls had been replaced by smiles.

"God bless his old Mickedonian heart!" he said fervently. "He thinks the coal is for that British fleet reported to be *en route* across the Atlantic to give battle to the German Pacific fleet; or for Admiral Craddock's Pacific fleet in case the Germans chase it back into the Atlantic. He knows that we know he is pro-German and for anything that's against England —and if he makes up his mind the coal is for the

British fleet he'll resign before delivering it! By Judas, this would be funny if it wasn't so blamed serious."

"To be forewarned is to be forearmed," Mr. Skinner quoted sagely. "It is most fortunate for us that Murphy's suspicions do us a grave injustice. We know now that he will call on the American consul at Pernambuco and ask for a cablegram."

"Yes, and by thunder! we'll send it," Cappy declared joyously. "Cable him, Skinner, to fire that German crew so fast one might play checkers on their coat tails as they go overside."

"I wish to heaven I could wireless him to put back to New York and ship a new crew," Matt Peasley mourned. "There's just a possibility that German crew of his may take over the ship on the high seas and not put into Pernambuco at all!"

"We can only wait and pray," said Mr. Skinner piously.

Cappy Ricks slid out to the edge of his chair and, pop-eyed with horror, gazed at his son-in-law over the rims of his spectacles.

"Matt," he declared, "you're as cheerful as a funeral. Here we have this thing all settled, and you have to go to work and rip the silver lining out of our cloud of contentment. And the worst of it is, by golly, I think there's something in that theory of yours after all."

"We should always be prepared to meet the worst, Mr. Ricks," Mr. Skinner admonished the president emeritus. "While piracy as a practice practically perished prior to the——"

"Skinner! In the fiend's name, spare us this alliteration and humbug," Cappy fairly shrieked. "You're

driving me crazy. If it isn't platitude, it's your dog-
gone habit of initialing things!" He placed his old
elbows on his knees and bowed his head in his hands.
"If I'm not the original Mr. Tight Wad!" he lamented.
"But you must forgive me, Matt. I got in the habit
of thinking of expense when I was young, and I've
never gotten over it. You know how a habit gets a
grip on a man, don't you, Matt? Oh, if you had only
overruled me when I decided to save money by cutting
out the wireless on the *Narcissus!* I remember now
you wanted it, and I said: 'Well, what's the use? The
Narcissus hasn't any passenger license and she doesn't
have to have wireless—so why do something we don't
have to do?' Skinner, you should have known
enough——"

"I am managing the lumber end of the business, Mr.
Ricks," Skinner retorted icily.

"Never mind what you're managing. You're my
balance wheel. I've raised you for that very purpose.
I've been twenty-five years breaking you in to your job
of relieving me of my business worries—and you don't
do it. No, you don't, Skinner. Don't deny it, now.
You don't. I pay you to boss me, but do you do it?
No, sir. You let me have my own way—when I'm
round you're afraid to say your soul's your own. You
two boys know blamed well I'm an old man and that
an old man will make mistakes. It is your duty to
watch me. I pay the money, but I don't get the service.
When Matt argued with me about the wireless you
sided in with me, Skinner. You've got that infernal
saving habit, too—drat you! Don't deny it, Skinner.
I can see by the look in your eye you're fixing to con-
tradict me. You're as miserable a miser as I am—

afraid to spend five cents and play safe—you penuri-
ous—er—er—fellow! Skinner, if you ever forget yourself long enough to give three hoots in hell you'll want
one of them back. See now what your niggardly policy
has done for us? At a time when we'd hock our immortal souls for a wireless to talk to Mike Murphy and
tell him things, where are we?" Cappy snapped his
fingers. "Up Salt Creek—without a paddle!"

"Come, come," Matt said soothingly. "As Skinner
says, we can only wait and pray——"

"All right. You two do the praying. I'm going to
sit here and cuss."

"Well, we'll hope for the best, Mr. Ricks. No more
crying over spilled milk now. I'll figure out when the
Narcissus is due at Pernambuco and cable Mike to let
his crew go. And you know, sir, even if he should not
receive our cablegram, we have still one hope left.
True, it is a forlorn one, but it's worth a small bet.
The crew of the *Narcissus* is not all German. There
are——"

"Two pro-German Irishmen, two disinterested Native Son Chinamen and a little runt of a Cockney
steward," Cappy sneered. "And she carries a crew of
forty, all told. Matt, those odds are too long for any
bet of mine. Besides, Reardon and Murphy hate each
other. A house divided against itself, you know——"

"They might bang each other all over the main
deck," Matt replied musingly, "but I'll bet they'll fight
side by side for the ship. Of course we haven't known
Terence Reardon very long; he may be a bad one after
all; but Mike Murphy will go far. He's as cunning as
a pet fox, and he may make up in strategy what he
lacks in numbers."

"The Irish are so filled with blarney——" Skinner began, but Cappy cut him short with a terrible look.

"There goes some more of our silver lining," he rasped. "Skinner, what are you? A kill-joy? Now, just for that, I'm going to agree with Matt. A man has got to believe something in this world or go crazy, and I prefer to believe that the ship is safe with those two Hibernians aboard—win, lose or draw. And I want you two to quit picking on me; I don't want the word '*Narcissus*' mentioned in my presence until the ship is reported confiscated by the British, if her coal is for the Germans, or by the Germans, if her coal is for the British—which it isn't—or until Mike Murphy reports at Manila or Batavia and cables us for orders."

"I'm with you there, sir," Matt Peasley declared. "I'm going to bank on the Irish, and refuse to believe it possible for the *Nar*—— for a certain vessel flying our house-flag to be caught by the wrong warship, a couple of thousand miles off her course and with coal, or evidences of coal, in her cargo space. Buck up, Skinner. A little Christian Science here, boy. Just make up your mind no man in authority is going to come over the rail of the—of a certain vessel—and ask Mike Murphy or his successor *pro tem.* for a look at his papers!"

"If she ever is confiscated on an illegal errand," Skinner mourned, "and Mike Murphy has nothing more tangible than a dime-novel tale of coercion as an excuse for being in that latitude and longitude—well, we'll never get our bully big ship back again!"

And for the first time in his life the efficient Mr. Skinner so far forgot himself as to swear in the office!

CHAPTER VI

Throughout the long, lazy days that the *Narcissus* rolled into the South, Captain Michael J. Murphy's alert brain was busy every spare moment, striving to discover, in the incomprehensible charter his owners had made for him, what the French call *la raison d'être.* Not having any wireless, he was unable to keep in touch with the stirring events being enacted in Europe and on the high seas, as news of the said events filtered by him through space. While on the West Coast, where all the newspapers are printed in Spanish, he had been equally barred from keeping in touch with the war, although *en route* through the Panama Canal he did his best to buy up all the old newspapers on the Zone.

Upon arrival in New York with his cargo of nitrate, his anxiety to make a record in his first command in steam caused him to stay on the job every moment the *Narcissus* was discharging, for Cappy Ricks had impressed upon him, as he impressed upon every skipper in the Blue Star employ, the fact that a slow boat is slow paying dividends. Consequently, the worthy captain had had no time to acquaint himself with the movements of the various fleets, and when he sent his day letter to his owners on the morning of the day he sailed from Norfolk for Pernambuco, his action was predicated, not on what he knew, but on what he felt.

The sixth sense that all real sailors possess warned him that his cargo of coal was not destined for Batavia nor yet Manila, but for delivery at sea to the warships of some foreign nation. Devoutly Michael J. hoped it wasn't for the British fleet, since in such a contingency he would be cruelly torn between his love and duty. Consequently he resolved that, should the choice of alternatives be forced upon him, he would steer a middle course and resign his command.

On the other hand, Mike Murphy knew Matt Peasley and Cappy Ricks to be intensely pro-Ally in their sympathies, despite the President's proclamation of neutrality and the polite requests of the motion-picture houses for their audiences to remain perfectly quiet while Field-Marshal von Hindenburg, Sir John French and General Joffre came on the screen and bowed. Under the circumstances, therefore, Murphy found it very difficult to suspect his owners of conspiring to deliver a cargo of coal to the German fleet at sea. No, indeed! Matt Peasley and Cappy Ricks were too intensely American for that; indeed, Cappy was always saying he hoped to see an American mercantile marine established before he should be gathered to the bosom of Abraham.

From whatever angle the doughty skipper viewed it, therefore, the tangle became more and more incomprehensible. Cappy and Matt knew full well the rules of the game as promulgated by their Uncle Samuel, and the dire penalties for infraction. However, granted that they knew they could scheme successfully to evade punishment at the hands of their own government, Mike Murphy knew full well that no man could guarantee immunity from the right of a belligerent

warship to visit and search, or from confiscation or
months of demurrage in a prize court in the event that
his ship's papers and the course the vessel was travelling failed to justify her presence in that particular
longitude and latitude. And with the huge profits to
be made in neutral trade, it seemed incomprehensible
that a sound business man like Cappy Ricks should
assume all these risks for the sake of a little extra
money. Surely he must realize that if he sent her on
an illegal errand her war-risk insurance would not hold.

On the other hand, it appeared to Murphy that the
charter must have been consummated with the full
knowledge and consent of the Blue Star Navigation
Company, for the veriest tyro in the shipping business
could not have failed to be suspicious of that clause
in the charter party, stipulating a call at Pernambuco
for orders. Of course there was the possibility that
this acquiescence had been due to misrepresentation
on the part of the New York agents or rank stupidity
on the part of the Blue Star Navigation Company.
But Seaborn & Company were above a shady deal.
In putting through the charter for the Blue Star Navigation Company it might have occurred to them that
all was not as it should be, but that was none of their
business. If they spread their hand and permitted
Cappy Ricks an unobstructed view, it was up to Cappy
to decide and order them to close or reject the charter.
As for stupidity on the part of the Blue Star Navigation Company, Murphy knew full well that stupidity
was the crime Cappy Ricks found it hardest to forgive.
Even had Cappy overlooked that suspicious clause in
the charter, because of his age, Matt Peasley's youth
and practical maritime knowledge should have offset

Cappy's error; and even if both had erred, there still remained the matchless Skinner, as suspicious as a burglar, as keen as a razor, as infallible as a chronometer.

No, it just didn't seem possible that the Blue Star Navigation Company had gone into the deal with eyes wide open; on the contrary, it seemed equally impossible that they had gone into it with their eyes shut. Consequently Michael J. decided to wake them up— provided they slept on the job—and to give them an opportunity to repent before it should be too late.

He felt very much better after sending that telegram, but as the *Narcissus* ploughed steadily south at the rate of two hundred and thirty miles a day, he began to grieve because he had no wireless to bring him a prompt reply; he berated himself for not waiting at the dock in Norfolk until his owners should have had an opportunity to answer; he abused himself for his timidity in questioning the judgment of his owners, for indeed he had been content to hint when more decisive action was demanded.

How Michael J. Murphy yearned to discuss his problem with some one as loyal and devoted to the Blue Star Navigation Company as himself! His dignity as master of the *Narcissus*, however, bade him refrain from discussing the integrity of his owners with his mates—particularly with new mates, to whom the house-flag stood for naught but a symbol of monthly revenue. In fact, of the forty-one men under him, there was but one with whom he could, with entire dignity, discuss the matter. That man was Terence Reardon. But even here he was barred, for since he had called the chief engineer a renegade, the only possible discussion that could obtain between them now must be anything but academic; in consequence of which Michael J. Murphy was forced to hug his apprehensions to himself until the *Narcissus* steamed slowly into the outer harbor of Pernambuco. Ten minutes after she dropped her big hook the skipper's suspicions were crystallized into certainty.

Just as she came to anchor the steward appeared on deck, vociferously beating his triangle to announce supper—for at sea dinner is always supper.

"Mr. Schultz," the captain called from the bridge, "as soon as your men have had their supper clear away the working boat. I'm going ashore."

"Very vell, sir," Mr. Schultz replied heartily, and the captain went below to supper. He was scarcely seated before Mr. Schultz stuck his head in the dining saloon window and announced that a gentleman who claimed to represent the charterers was alongside in a launch and desired to come aboard and speak with him.

"Let down the accommodation ladder, Mr. Schultz, and when the gentleman comes aboard, show him round to my state-room," the skipper answered. "I'll meet him there in a pig's whisper. It is probable he has come aboard with our orders, Mr. Schultz, so never mind clearing away the boat until I speak to you further about it. Steward, set an extra cover at my right. We may have a guest for supper."

He hurried round to his state-room and donned a uniform coat to receive his visitor. Mr. Schultz came presently, bearing a visiting-card upon which was engraved the name: Mr. August Carl von Staden. Behind the mate a sailor with a bulging suitcase stood at

attention; two more sailors stood behind the first, a
steamer trunk between them, and as Captain Murphy
stepped out on deck to greet his visitor he observed a
tall, athletic, splendid-looking fellow coming leisurely
toward him along the deck. The stranger carried a
large Gladstone bag.

The captain bowed. "I am the skipper of this big
box," he announced pleasantly. "Murphy is my
name."

Herr von Staden shook hands and in most excellent
English, without the slightest trace of a German accent, expressed his pleasure in the meeting. The captain cast a glance of frank curiosity at the bag von
Staden carried and at the baggage the sailors had in
tow. Von Staden interpreted the glance and smiled.

"I have brought you your orders, Captain Murphy.
They are contained in this envelope;" and he handed a
blank envelope to the captain. "However, I happened
to know that one of the orders is to provide a berth
for me. I'm to go with you as supercargo."

"I hadn't heard anything about such a possibility,"
Mike Murphy replied, with just a shade of formality
in his tones. He turned to the first mate: "Mr.
Schultz, will you be good enough to see to it that Mr.
von Staden's baggage is stowed in the owners' suite.
Then tell the steward to see that our guest's quarters
are put in order. Mr. von Staden, will you kindly step
into my stateroom here while I read these orders?"

Von Staden nodded. Entering the captain's room
he sat down on the settee and lighted a gold-tipped
cigarette, while Murphy tore open the envelope. It
contained a cablegram reading as follows:

"Von Staden & Ulrich,—Pernambuco, Brazil,—Ornillo Montevideo.

"BLUESTAR."

The captain reached for his telegraphic-code book. When decoded the message read:

"Instruct captain to proceed to Montevideo and there await further orders.

"BLUE STAR NAVIGATION COMPANY."

The cablegram had been filed at San Francisco two days before. Murphy looked keenly at his guest, who smoked tranquilly and returned the look without interest.

"Mr. von Staden," the captain announced, "these are strange orders, in view of the fact that I cleared from New York for Manila or Batavia, via the Cape of Good Hope. It would be a sure sign of bad luck to the steamer *Narcissus* if a British cruiser should pick her up off the coast of Uruguay."

Von Staden smiled. "You are very direct, captain —very blunt indeed. This is a characteristic more Teutonic than Celtic, I believe, so I shall experience no embarrassment in being equally frank with you. Your cargo of coal is designed for our German Pacific fleet."

"I guessed as much, sir. Nevertheless, my owners did not see fit to take me into their confidence in this illegal undertaking, Mr. von Staden——"

"They did not think it necessary," von Staden interrupted smilingly. "In fact, Captain Peasley assured our people in New York that your sympathies are so overwhelming in favor of our cause we need anticipate no worry as to the course you would pursue. Moreover, in the event of a judicial inquiry it would be an advantage if you could say that you had had no voice in the matter, but had been instructed to obey the orders of the charterers—of whom we are the agents in Pernambuco. Perhaps this cablegram will allay your fears," and he drew an unopened cablegram from his pocket and handed it to Murphy. It was a code cablegram, signed by the Blue Star Navigation Company and addressed to Murphy in care of von Staden & Ulrich. When decoded it read:

"Execute the orders of supercargo if possible. It may lead to further business. Charterers must take the risk. We do not think there is any risk. Please remain."

This cablegram was signed "Matt."

"Well, captain?" von Staden queried politely.

"I don't like this business at all," the captain replied. "My owners may think there is no risk, but I'm afraid. England controls the seas——"

"We are in possession of the secret code of the British Navy, Captain Murphy. We know the approximate location of every British warship in the Atlantic and Pacific—and I assure you there is no risk."

"Well, my boss informs me the charterers assume the risk, so I suppose I shouldn't worry over the Blue Star Navigation Company's end of the gamble. They know their own business, I dare say. Evidently they feared I might want to resign, so I have been asked to remain; and when Captain Peasley says 'please' to me, Mr. von Staden, I find it very, very hard to refuse."

"I am glad, for the sake of our selfish interests, my

dear captain, to find you so loyal to your owners' financial interests," the supercargo replied heartily. "Now that you have decided to remain, I need not point out to you the danger of a resignation at this time. It might lead to some unlooked-for developments which might prejudice your owners, although I think they have covered their tracks very effectually. Nevertheless, it is not well to take the slightest risk——"

"Without being well paid for it," Murphy interrupted sneeringly. "My owners have been well paid for their risk, but where do I come in? I haven't been promised double my usual salary, or a split on the profits of the voyage; and I know if I were to command a vessel loaded with munitions of war I would not be asked to take her into the North Sea at the customary skipper's wages. I'd be offered a large bonus."

"You forget, my dear captain, that your charterers assume all the risks. One of them was the risk that you might resign unless you received adequate compensation. I came aboard prepared to insure that risk," and he touched with his toe the Gladstone bag. "What do you say to $5,000?"

Michael J. Murphy smiled. "It is pleasant, sir," he said, "to be paid $5,000 for doing something one yearns to do for nothing. I am not a hog. Five thousand dollars is sufficient. How do I get it—and when?"

"In gold coin of the United States, or gold certificates of the same interesting country, my dear captain, and you may have it immediately." Again Herr von Staden kicked the Gladstone bag.

"I'll take it in gold certificates. And in order that my dear old father and mother may have the benefit of my rascality in case anything unforeseen should arise to prevent my return, I suggest you hand over the boodle this minute, and I'll go ashore and express it home."

"Captain Murphy, you are a man after my own heart——"

"I am not a born fool, sir," Murphy interrupted. "I'm accepting this money to be a fool, well knowing it is foolish to do it, for still I am taking a risk. I am thirty-eight years old, Mr. von Staden, and a skipper as young as that has his future all before him. Set him down on the beach, however, with his ticket revoked for all time—and his future is behind him."

"In that event," the supercargo replied, "you might accept my assurance, without questioning my authority for such assurance, that you would have no difficulty in procuring a remunerative position ashore. The firm of von Staden & Ulrich could use you very handily."

"Thank you, sir. Consider the matter settled. Will you come ashore with me, sir, and dine, or would you prefer to have supper aboard?"

"I beg of you to be excused from going ashore, captain. I have much to do to-night. The launch which brought me alongside has a knocked-down wireless plant aboard, and I am anxious to have it set up on your good ship *Narcissus*—a task I shall have to oversee personally. I shall probably work all night."

"Praise be!" Michael J. Murphy answered heartily. "We'll have some interest in life now. We can get all the war news, going and coming, can't we? Have you brought along an operator?"

"I am an operator," the supercargo answered. "By the by, can you fix me up with a wireless room?"

"There are two staterooms and a bath in the owners'
suite which you will occupy. You can take your
choice."

"Good. I shall want to sleep close to my instru-
ment."

He opened the bag, counted out five one-thousand-
dollar gold certificates of the United States of America
and handed them to the captain.

"The grand old rag," Michael J. murmured. "How
many rascals fight under the flag of old King Spondu-
lics!"

"I believe you have an Irish chief engineer," von
Staden continued. "While I understand his sympathies are with us, still it seems only right to com-
pensate——"

"Suit yourself, Mr. von Staden."

"What kind of a man is he, captain?"

"I'd hate to tell you. I've had little to do with him,
but that little was enough. We avoid each other as
much as possible and never speak except in the line of
duty. I make no bones of the fact that I think he's a
scrub."

Mr. von Staden nodded sagely. "Perhaps I'd better
wait and get acquainted with him," he suggested, and
closed his bag. Murphy showed him to his quarters,
which the steward, under the first mate's supervision,
was already setting in order; and, having decided to set
up the wireless in the sleeping-room, von Staden accompanied the skipper round to superintend the taking
on board of the wireless plant from the gasoline launch
bobbing alongside. When the equipment was finally
hoisted to the deck of the *Narcissus*, Michael J.
Murphy boarded the launch and was whisked ashore for

the avowed purpose of sending to his aged parents the fruits of his elastic conscience.

Herr August Carl von Staden stood at the head of the accommodation ladder and smiled as the launch disappeared into the tropic twilight. Then he said something in German to Mr. Schultz, who laughed. Evidently it was very good news, for even the quartermaster at the companion ladder smiled covertly. It is possible they would not have felt so cheerful had they known that Michael J. Murphy's "dear old father and mother" had been sleeping in a Boston cemetery some fifteen years, and that their last words to Michael had been an exhortation to remember that manliness and honor must be his only heritage. And as the launch bore him shoreward, he looked back and grinned at the dim, duck-clad figure of von Staden.

"Your agents looked me up, my hearty," he soliloquized, "and if they did their work half well, they told you I was an honest man. Only a crook comes with a bag of gold to talk illegitimate business with an honest man. I'm banking you're as crooked as a bed spring, and that there's something fishy about this enterprise. Cappy Ricks isn't fully informed, otherwise he wouldn't be doing business with a crook!"

CHAPTER VII

Arrived ashore, Captain Murphy hurried to the cable office, registered his cable address, borrowed a code book and sent a code telegram to his owner. Then, having subsidized the operator liberally to rush it, Michael J. Murphy set out for a stroll among the limited attractions of Pernambuco. His cablegram would get through in two hours at the very most, and though the captain figured the Blue Star offices would be closed when the message reached San Francisco, still he was not discouraged. He knew the cable company always telephoned to Mr. Skinner, at his home, all Blue Star and Ricks Lumber & Logging messages arriving after office hours and before midnight. Naturally Skinner could be depended upon to have a copy of the code at home, and if he didn't Murphy knew he would rush down to the office, no matter what the hour, and decode it there. Of course he would cable his reply immediately, in which event it might be that the captain would have an answer shortly after midnight or by breakfast at the latest.

He decided, therefore, to return to the cable office about midnight and await the reply to his cablegram. He had proceeded but a few blocks from the cable office, however, before a disturbing thought struck him with such force as to bring him to an abrupt pause.

His owners had cabled him in care of von Staden & Ulrich, when in the telegram sent just before sailing

51

from Norfolk he had instructed them to cable him in care of the American consul. Murphy's native shrewdness had made him suspicious of von Staden the instant the latter had so nonchalantly offered him a bribe of five thousand dollars, for the proffer of a bribe of that magnitude, without any preliminary bargaining, did not co-ordinate with Michael's idea of business. Certainly if the charterers had his owners "fixed," five thousand dollars was too much money to give their captain, particularly since there were available any number of capable rascals eager to do the job for twenty-five hundred, and the devil take the consequences.

At the time von Staden had handed him the two cablegrams from the Blue Star Navigation Company, no suspicion that they were forgeries had entered the captain's mind; indeed, Matt Peasley's cablegram to him appeared at first blush to be an answer to the telegram which Murphy had sent his owners from Norfolk. In that telegram Murphy had mentioned his suspicions and hinted at unwarranted risks and the possibility of the circumstances attending the delivery of his cargo forcing his resignation. Matt's cablegram handed him by von Staden urged him to remain in the ship and assured him there were no risks; that if there were, the charterers assumed them. For the nonce, therefore, the master's mind did not dwell on any doubts as to the genuineness of the orders he had received, even though he decided instantly as a precautionary measure to confirm them before proceeding to carry them out. This, however, was merely because he was suspicious of von Staden and desired to obviate the possibility of that individual's double-crossing the Blue Star Navigation Company.

Under the circumstances, therefore, he had considered it good policy to appear to fall readily in line, and, the better to disarm von Staden's watchfulness, he had demanded extra compensation. The ease with which the bribe had been secured having crystallized his suspicions, instantly he had cast about in his ingenious brain for a good sound excuse for going ashore and cabling his owners. To demand his bribe in advance and then announce that he would go ashore and express it to those dependent upon him, in case he failed to return and enjoy it himself, seemed to present a reason that would not be questioned and accordingly he had done so.

Michael J. Murphy removed his uniform cap and thoughtfully scratched his head. "Now why," he demanded of the scented night, "did Matt cable me in care of that German firm when he must have known I would call on the American consul in the expectation of finding a cablegram there?" He shook his head. "They've got us winging, Michael," he soliloquized, "so I suppose the only thing to do is to play safe, call upon the American consul immediately if not sooner, and ask if he has a cablegram for us."

And without further ado the worthy fellow sprang into a cab and was whirled away to the residence of the American consul. Yes, the consul had a cablegram for him, but it was at his office. Could Captain Murphy not wait until morning?

Most emphatically Captain Murphy could not. That cablegram was important; it meant a great deal of money and possibly life or death——

Regretfully the consul entered the cab with the captain, drove to the consulate and delivered the cable-

gram to the eager mariner, who swore when he discovered it was in cipher and not code, for this necessitated immediate return to the *Narcissus* in order to
obtain the key to the cipher. He thanked the consul
and sent the latter home in the cab, while he hurried
for the harbor front and the nearest boat landing. He
was filled with apprehension, for indeed there was something radically wrong when his owners cabled him in
the secret cipher of the Blue Star Navigation Company—something the company had, doubtless, never
found occasion to do before. For while each vessel of
the Blue Star fleet had a copy of the A.L. code aboard,
with the cipher key typewritten and pasted on the
second fly-leaf, not a single Blue Star skipper knew
why it had been pasted there or why the company
should have gone to the trouble of getting up any one
of the hundreds of secret ciphers possible to be developed from the A. L. Telegraphic Code. This was a
secret that lay locked in the breast of Mr. Skinner. It
is probable, however, that it had occurred to him in an
idle moment that a secret cipher might come in handy
some day, and Mr. Skinner believed in being prepared
for emergencies.

The captain bade the launch wait for him at the
accommodation ladder, while he hurried round to his
state-room and promptly fell to work on Mr. Skinner's
cipher cablegram. When he had laboriously deciphered
it this is what he read:

"Unaccountably failed note suspicious clause charter.
Something rotten. We are playing square game. Think
plot deliver coal German fleet South Atlantic. Discharge
your German crew immediately, first notifying Brazilian
authorities and American consul. Have help when you

notify them game is off, otherwise may take vessel away from you. They will stop at nothing; fleet desperate for coal. Cable acknowledgment these orders; also cable when orders fulfilled. Very anxious.

"BLUE STAR NAVIGATION COMPANY."

"Ah-h-h!" breathed Michael J. Murphy softly, but very distinctly. "So that's the game, eh?" His big square chin set viciously; subconsciously he clenched his hard fist and shook it at his enemies. "The cunning Dutch devils!" he murmured very audibly, and at that precise instant Herr August Carl von Staden stood in the open doorway. He coughed, and Murphy glanced up from the translation of the cipher message just in time to note a swift shadow pass over the supercargo's face, a shadow composed of equal parts of suspicion, embarrassment and desperation.

"You have returned very promptly, captain," he remarked smoothly, and then his restless glance fell on the cablegram and beside it the scratch pad and the two parallel columns of words scrawled on it. A man of far less intelligence than von Staden possessed would have realized as quickly that the first column was composed of cipher words, while the second column was the translation. From this tell-tale evidence his suspicious glance lifted to the skipper's face, and he read in Michael J. Murphy's black eyes the wild rage which no Irishman could have concealed—which the majority of his race would not even have taken the trouble to endeavor to conceal.

In that glance each learned the other's secret; each realized that the success of his plans depended on the silence of the other; each resolved instantly to procure that silence at any cost. Von Staden reached for his

hip pocket, but before he could draw his automatic
pistol and cover the skipper, Michael J. Murphy had
hurled ten pounds of code book into the geometric
centre of the supercargo's face. It was the first
weapon his hand closed over, and he did not disdain it.
The instant it landed and von Staden reeled before the
blow, Murphy came out of his state-room with a scut-
tering rush and von Staden fired as he came. The
captain felt the sting of the bullet as it creased the top
of his left shoulder; then his right fist came up in a
blow that started at his hip and landed fairly under
the supercargo's heart. Von Staden grunted once, the
pistol dropped clattering to the deck and he folded up
like an accordion. For him the battle was over.

Not so, however, with Mike Murphy. Gone to the
winds now was the caution he would have exercised had
the attack been delayed two seconds longer; forgotten
was the shrewd advice of his owners to have help standing by when the ship cleaning should commence.
Michael J. Murphy thought of nothing but blood, for
the fight had started now and he was loath to have it
cease.

"You bloody murderer!" he growled. "You'd kill me
and steal my ship, would you? And with the reckless
abandon of a sailor he planted the broad toe of a
number nine boot in Herr von Staden's short ribs,
hoping to break a few, for in the process of working
his way up from the bottom Michael had fought under
deep-sea rules too often to be squeamish now. So he
kicked Herr von Staden again, after which a glimmer
of reason penetrated his hot head and he walked to
pick up the supercargo's automatic pistol. Then
something landed on him from above and he went down

backward. His head struck the deck with a resounding thump, and Michael J. Murphy had a through ticket to the Land of Nod and no stop-over privileges.

The something which had thus inopportunely dropped on Michael was Mr. Henckel, the second mate. He had gone up on the bridge to see if the canvas jacket had been dropped over the brightly polished brass engine-room telegraph apparatus at each end of the bridge, in order to protect it from the tropical dew. While thus engaged he had heard the shot which von Staden fired at the captain, and forthwith had run across the top of the house and peered over to discover what was happening on the deck below. Discovering the captain in the act of kicking a distinguished son of the Fatherland in that fragile section of the human anatomy frequently referred to as the "slats," the second mate had stood a moment, immobile with horror, the while he gazed upon the fearful scene. Then the captain walked to a spot on the deck directly beneath the position occupied by his subordinate, and stooped to pick something up.

Even their enemies are proud of the dash and gallantry, the utter contempt for consequences, which animate the German going into battle, and Mr. Henckel, second mate of the S.S. *Narcissus*, was as fine a German as one could find in a day's travel. The instant Michael J. Murphy stooped to recover von Staden's automatic pistol, therefore, Mr. Henckel saw his duty and, in the language of the elect, "he went an' done it"—the which was absurdly simple. He merely leaped down off the house on top of the captain, and forthwith deep peace and profound silence brooded over the good ship *Narcissus*, of San Francisco.

It is worthy of remark here that Mr. Terence Reardon who, had he been present, might have had something to say—not that his action would indicate that he despised Mike Murphy the less, but that he loved his owners more—was unfortunately down in the engine-room. Consequently he failed to hear the shot, and when he came up on deck the victims of the affray had been collected and taken thence, a seaman with a mop had removed the profuse evidence which Mike Murphy's rich red blood had furnished and Mr. Schultz, the first mate, was on the bridge, while Mr. Henckel was up on the forecastle head with his gang, waiting for the order to break out the anchor.

Presently a seaman came up on the bridge and reported that the light in Mr. Reardon's state-room had been out fifteen minutes. So Mr. Schultz waited an hour longer to make certain the chief engineer would be asleep; whereupon commenced a harsh, discordant tune—the music of the anchor chain paying in through the hawse pipe. When it ceased Mr. Schultz stepped to the marine telegraph; a bell jingled in the bowels of the *Narcissus;* an instant later all the lights aboard her went out as the first assistant engineer threw off the switch, and silently in the heavy velvet gloom the great vessel slipped out of Pernambuco harbor and headed south.

CHAPTER VIII

Just about the time the *Narcissus* was kicking ahead at nine knots, in distant San Francisco the cable company was getting Mr. Skinner out of bed to dictate to him over the telephone a message which had just arrived from Pernambuco.

"Ah!" murmured the incomparable Skinner as he donned a dressing gown and slippers and descended to his library to decode the cablegram. "The luck of the Blue Star flag still holds. That belligerent and highly intelligent fellow Murphy has received our cablegram, sent him in care of the American consul, and in accordance with my instructions he is acknowledging its receipt. Hum-m-m! The first word is 'oriana.' Let me turn to 'oriana.' Hum-m! 'I have an order presumably emanating from blank.' Ah, yes, the next word is 'Bluestar,' the cable address of the Blue Star Navigation Company. Well, well, well, the foxy fellow! After wiring us to cable him, he gets our cable and then cables us to confirm it! Caution is a virtue, but this brand is too high-priced. The next word is 'osculo'."

Mr. Skinner turned to "osculo" and discovered that it meant "I am ordered to——." The next word in the cablegram was "Montevideo."

"Good heavens!" Mr. Skinner gasped. "He has received orders, presumably emanating from us, ordering him to Montevideo! Can it be possible that Mr. Ricks or Matt Peasley has sent him a cablegram without my knowledge? I must read further."

He did, and having done so he discovered that, in addition to being ordered to Montevideo, Mike Murphy wanted to know if it was all right and if von Staden and Ulrich—presumably German—were to be trusted; that he would remain in command at the company's request, although he considered such request unreasonable, even if it could be granted without risk. Also, he wanted these instructions confirmed and was anxiously awaiting an answer.

"Well, I'm certain of one thing," Mr. Skinner soliloquized after reading this extraordinary message: "Murphy has not been to the American consul's office for the cablegram I sent him several days ago. Evidently there is mischief afoot. However, there is nothing to be gained by cabling him again in care of the American consul, so I'll just assume that he has registered his cable address with the cable company; hence, if I cable him to his cable address the message will be delivered to him aboard the *Narcissus*. And since he says he is anxiously awaiting an answer, I'll relieve his anxiety with all possible speed and send him an answer immediately."

Whereupon Mr. Skinner wasted several dollars cabling Mike Murphy that the Blue Star Navigation had not, to his knowledge, cabled him any instructions save those sent in care of the American consul; that von Staden and Ulrich were unknown to him, and to be very careful not to lose the ship. This message Mr. Skinner dictated over the telephone to the telegraph office and asked them to rush it. Evidently they did so, for just as Cappy Ricks arrived in the office the following morning, word was received from the telegraph company that owing to the departure of the *Narcissus* from Pernambuco the night before, the Blue Star Navigation Company's cablegram had not been delivered.

"Well, Skinner," Cappy chirped as he sat in at his desk and lighted a cigar, "what's the news around the shop this fine morning? Any word from Murphy?"

"Yes—and no," Mr. Skinner replied, and laid his information before Cappy for perusal. Cappy read it all twice, then slid out to the edge of his chair, placed his hands on his knees and looked at Mr. Skinner over the rims of his spectacles.

"Skinner, my dear boy," he said solemnly, "this is certainly hell! Cable the American consul in Pernambuco and ask him if Murphy received the cablegram we sent in care of the consulate. And, in the meantime, don't whisper a word of this disquieting information to Matt Peasley. Time enough to cross a bridge, Skinner, when you come to it."

Mr. Skinner promptly filed a cablegram to the American consul, and just before the office closed they got about forty dollars' worth of reply, informing them that Captain Murphy had appeared at the consulate greatly excited the night previous; that he had declared the cablegram awaiting him might mean life or death—certainly a large sum of money; that he had been given the cablegram and had gone aboard ship to look up his cipher key. He had not returned and the ship was not in the harbor.

"Let me see the carbon copy of the cablegram you

sent Murphy in care of the American consul," Cappy
demanded. Mr. Skinner with a sinking heart obeyed.

"Skinner," said Cappy, "do I understand you sent
this message in cipher, which necessitated on the part
of our captain a trip back to his ship before he could
decipher it? Why didn't you send him the message
in regular code? He would then have decoded it right
in the consulate, or at best he could have gone to the
cable office and borrowed a code book from them."

"I sent it in our secret cipher," Mr. Skinner faltered.
"It was delicate business—quite—er—an international
complication, as it were, and in the event of unpleasant
developments—Well, how did I know but that some
German might be on the key at the cable office when
the message arrived there for Murphy——"

"Quite right, Skinner, my boy, quite right," Cappy
interrupted sadly. "The only trouble with you, Skinner, is that you're too danged efficient. You look so
far into the future you're always gumming up the
present." He sighed.

"Why, what do you think——" Skinner began, but
Cappy silenced him with an autocratic finger.

"I do not think, Skinner, I know. Had it not been
for your damnable cipher message, Murphy would have
got your warning ashore instead of being forced to go
back to the ship for it. Having got it ashore he
would have taken care to warn the Brazilian authorities
and they would have been on watch and prevented the
ship from leaving. As I view the situation, Mike went
aboard, deciphered your message and got ripping mad.
Von Staden and Ulrich were probably aboard, and hot-
headed Mike probably undertook to throw them overboard single-handed—and failed. His body is doubt-

less feeding the fishes in Pernambuco harbor this minute, and our lovely—big—*Narcissus*—the pride of—
the Blue Star fleet——"

"Shall I tell Captain Peasley?" Mr. Skinner faltered.

"Yes, tell him. He's bound to find out sooner or
later. Skinner, I could stand the loss of the ship, but
what breaks me all up is the thought that after forty
years of honorable business my friends and my enemies
might suspect me of being a filibuster. I, Alden P.
Ricks, whose great-grandfather died at Yorktown,
whose grandfather was killed at Lundy's Lane, whose
father won a medal of honor at Chapultepec—I,
Alden P. Ricks, who had to belong to the Home Guard
because I was such a little runt they wouldn't take me
in the Civil War—to think that I should attain to
seventy years and even be suspected of staining the flag
of my country for the sake of a few dirty dollars—
after all the Ricks blood that has been shed for that
flag! Horrible!"

Mr. Skinner turned away for, man and boy, he had
spent twenty-five years under Cappy Ricks, and he
loved him. He could not bear to see the old man suffer.

CHAPTER IX

When Michael J. Murphy returned to consciousness he found himself in his berth, although for all the effort he made to verify this fact it might have been Mr. Reardon's. For fully half an hour he lay there, gradually straightening out the tangle in his intellect, and presently he was aware that the back of his head was very sore and ached, so he put up his hand to rub it and found a lump as large as a walnut. His right shoulder was numb and he was unable to move it, although this would not have surprised him had he been aware that a hundred and eighty pounds of Teutonic masculinity had landed on that shoulder with both feet and dislocated it. As it was, the skipper wondered vaguely if the ship's funnel had fallen over on him. His right side ached externally, and when he sighed it ached internally. That was a broken rib tickling his lung, for, while he was in blissful ignorance of the reason therefor, the chronicler of this tale can serve no good purpose by concealing the true facts in the case. Immediately upon regaining consciousness, Herr August Carl von Staden had insisted upon returning Michael J. Murphy's kicks with compound interest.

"Holy mackerel!" the skipper murmured. "I feel like I've been fed into a concrete mixer. The only injury I can account for is my left shoulder, where that supercargo shot me."

After spending another half hour in mild speculation on these phenomena he was aware of an added impediment in breathing, so he put his hand up to his nose and found it clogged with blood. His luxuriant black mustache prevented an extended examination of his upper lip, but nevertheless, something told him it was split. A hard foreign substance lying between his right cheek and the inferior maxillary he concluded must be the pit of an olive left over from dinner. Subsequently, however, he discovered it was one of his own teeth. So he swore a mighty oath and felt considerably better.

"This is certainly mutiny on the high seas and punishable by hanging," he soliloquized. "I wonder if Cappy Ricks would know me now;" and he reached up to turn the switch of the electric light over his berth. He turned the switch, but the light did not come on, and while he lay considering this state of affairs, he was aware that something that was not his head was throbbing in the ship. He decided presently that it was her engines. From the steady rhythmic pulsations he realized the vessel was being driven full speed ahead; and since he could not recall having given any orders to that effect, he was not long in arriving at the correct answer to the riddle—whereupon Michael J. Murphy did what every shipmaster does when he loses the ship he loves and finds himself ravished of his reputation as a sane and careful skipper. He wept!

Those who know the breed will bid you beware the Irish when they weep from any cause save grief or sympathy.

CHAPTER X

Cappy Ricks, who claimed to know Mike Murphy's kind of Irish, doubtless would have been extremely gratified had he been granted a peep at the battered, bleeding, weeping wreck of his faithful Michael as the pride of the Blue Star fleet rolled south to meet the grey sea rovers of the Fatherland and deliver the cargo of coal that meant so much to them. The sight might have aroused some hope in Cappy's heavy heart, he being by nature inconsistent and always seeing a profit where others found naught but a deficit. However, though Cappy was variously gifted he was not a clairvoyant, in consequence of which he spent a very sleepless night following the receipt of that windy cablegram from the American consul. He dined at his club, and when it was time for him to leave and his daughter sent her car for him, he lacked the courage to go home and face his son-in-law. So he spent the night at the club and came down to the office about noon, hoping Matt Peasley would have recovered from the shock by that time. The latter was waiting for him, and came into Cappy's sanctum immediately to hold a post-mortem.

"Matthew, my dear boy," said Cappy miserably, "this is terrible."

"I think we should take the matter up immediately with the State Department," Matt replied. "There may be a United States warship in those waters, and she could be instructed by wireless to endeavor to intercept the *Narcissus*. We can prove a clean bill of health with those cablegrams, and get back our ship."

"Yes—from our own Government, of course. But, oh, Matt, if old Johnny Bull ever gets his horns into her we can kiss her good-bye. We can't bring forward any evidence to alibi that German crew on a ship so far off her course and loaded with contraband."

"Well, I know if I were skippering a British warship and picked up the *Narcissus*, her owners would find I was born and bred in Missouri," the honest Matt admitted. "By the way, have you read this morning's papers?"

"No, Matt. I've felt too blamed miserable about this *Narcissus* affair."

"Well, the *Scharnhorst*, the *Gneisenau*, the *Leipzig*, the *Dresden* and the *Nürnberg* met a British fleet under Admiral Craddock, away down off Coronel, Chile. The British were cleaned for fair."

"You don't tell me!"

"I do tell you. And I'll bet my immortal soul that German fleet is heading for the entrance to Magellan this minute. If I were a religious man I'd be praying for clear weather so they'll find the entrance without any trouble."

"I hope they run ashore and drown every man Jack!" cried Cappy fiercely.

"I do not. You will note that our charterers tried to induce Mike to go to Montevideo for orders. That was because they expected to lie snug at Montevideo and be within striking distance of a designated meeting place in the South Atlantic when the German fleet should pass through Magellan from the Pacific. Remember that for several weeks the German fleet has managed to lose itself in the Pacific, but now that the British fleet has stumbled onto it and forced an engagement, the Australian and Japanese cruisers will all be headed for the south coast of Chile to make reprisal. We know the Germans are short of coal; doubtless some of the fleet have suffered in the engagement with Admiral Craddock's ships, so it's a safe bet they'll run into the Atlantic now and raid the Falkland Islands—by the way, a British possession. They will hope to find coal and stores there, which, with the cargo of the *Narcissus,* will enable them to continue raiding.

"Of course they will try to accomplish this before England sends a fleet to avenge Craddock—and I'm hoping the Germans will succeed, for, if they do, they will surely be decent enough to run our *Narcissus* into some South American port and give us an opportunity to get her back again. On the other hand, if the Germans delay their departure from the Pacific, the British will surely get wind of the *Narcissus* waiting at Montevideo; and when she comes out they'll just naturally grab her."

"I guess you're right," Cappy replied gloomily; "so for the present we're pro-German. Still, I find that a hard dose to swallow, in view of the fact that our German crew in the *Narcissus* has evidently taken the vessel away from Mike Murphy."

"I am sure they have done just that, sir; otherwise Mike would have obeyed our orders. We know he received the orders; hence the only reason he did not carry them out was because he wasn't permitted to do so. My only hope is that they haven't killed him, for if he is alive and free, he and Reardon, with the assistance of the cockney steward and the two Chinese cooks, might——"

"Might what?"

"Might steal her back again."

"Matt! It isn't possible, is it?"

"I'll bet Mike Murphy and I could steal her back if we had half a chance. The odds would be forty to two against our succeeding, but a little strategy is sometimes to be preferred to great horsepower. I think I could do it, and I think Murphy will do it—if he only thinks of it."

"How? Tell me how you'd steal her back."

"What's the use?" Matt replied wearily. "I'd have to have help. So will Mike—and I've just remembered Mike Murphy and Terence Reardon are the wrong kind of Irish to have together in the same ship. We did our best to prevent it, but the odds are too long for us; the coal is for the Germans and we hate England, so why worry? I know Mike Murphy will not take that view of it; for my sake he'll fight to the last gasp, but he must have help, and Reardon owes me no such allegiance as Murphy."

"Well, he owes me something," Cappy spoke up. "You promised him a hundred and seventy-five dollars a month and I raised the ante to two hundred. It was an investment, pure and simple. I was buying loyalty, and by the Holy Pink-Toed Prophet, I think I'll get it. Come to think of it, there was a look in Reardon's eyes that I liked, when he took my hand in those greasy paws of his and said he was a proud man to work for me. Matt, that fellow is full of bellicose veins. He may not fight for me, but he'll fight for Mrs. Reardon and the children and that two-hundred-dollar-a-month job, for it's the first he's ever had and if he loses out it'll be the last he'll ever get. He was telling me all about his family and how much the job meant to him, that day we had the *Narcissus* out on her trial trip."

Matt Peasley's face brightened. "By Jupiter, that puts a different face on the situation. If Reardon is alive they might get together for mutual protection."

"Well," Cappy piped up, greatly relieved to discover Matt was facing the tragedy so optimistically, "we might do worse than hope. Wire the State Department, Matt; and in the meanwhile, cheer up, sonny, and trust in the luck of Alden P. Ricks. I remember Captain Noah Kendall—peace to his ashes—used to say to me: 'Mr. Ricks, if you ever fell into Channel Creek at low tide you'd come up with a pearl necklace wrapped round your ankle, and you'd be smelling like a spray of lemon verbena.' Cheer up, Matt! What though the cause be lost, the *Narcissus* is not lost— yet. The Celtic troops remain, and from now on my war cry is going to be——"

"Ireland über Alles," Matt Peasley suggested.

"You're blamed whistlin'!" said Cappy Ricks.

So Mr. Skinner was called into consultation, and he and Matt Peasley and Cappy drew up a heart-rending telegram to the Secretary of State, who consulted with the Secretary of the Navy, who wired the Blue Star Navigation Company that he was sorry but he didn't have as much as a rowboat in the South Atlantic to save their steamer *Narcissus,* and would they please keep still about it, since a noise like that, unless absolutely based on facts—and he understood their wail to be based on suspicion—would tend to create additional friction in an international complication already

strained to the breaking point. Whereupon Cappy
Ricks flew into a rage and immediately dictated a long
letter to his congressman and his senator, urging them
to battle to the last trench in the campaign for a
two-power navy.

Time passed. Then suddenly the world rocked with
the news of the annihilation of the German Pacific fleet
off the Falkland Islands. Cappy Ricks and Matt
Peasley read the horrid tale in the morning papers as
they sat at breakfast, and immediately both lost all
interest in food. Like two mourners about to set out
for the morgue to identify the corpse of a loved one
recently killed by a taxicab, they drove down to the
Blue Star offices, where immediately upon arrival something terrible in Mr. Skinner's face brought on palpi-
tation of Cappy Ricks' heart.

"Skinner, my dear boy," he chattered, "Have you
any news?"

"Not yet, sir," murmured Mr. Skinner brokenly,
"but soon! The British consul wants you to ring him
up. He says he's had a wireless from H.M.S. *Panther*,
off the Falkland Islands, and he thinks it will be of
interest to you."

"Is my *Narcissus* confiscated?" Cappy and Matt
cried in chorus.

"I—I don't know," Skinner faltered. "I just didn't
have the courage to pursue the matter further. The British consul said she was captured but as for con——"

"Idiot! Bonehead!" rasped Cappy. "My *Narcissus*
is gone—gone! Oh, Lord! Matt, you ring up the
British consul—I'm an old man—Skinner, my dear
chap, forgive my harsh language. Have you a little
drop of whisky in the office?"

CHAPTER XI

Capt. Michael J. Murphy's futile tears of rage having dried almost as quickly as they came, he crawled painfully out of his berth and lighted a match, to discover he was a prisoner in his own state-room. He turned another electric switch, but still the room remained in darkness.

"Sneaking out of Pernambuco with the lights doused," he soliloquized. Then he remembered a little stump of candle he kept in his desk for use when heating sealing wax, so he lighted the candle and by its meager rays took inventory of his features in the little mirror over his washstand.

"By the Toe Nails of Moses," he soliloquized, "somebody's sea-boots did that, and if I ever find out who was wearing them at the time there'll be a fight or a footrace. I'm a total wreck and no insurance—yes, thank God! here's the ship's medicine chest."

Having spent the greater portion of an adventurous career far from medical aid in time of bodily stress, Michael J. was, as most shipmasters are, rather adept in rough-and-tumble surgery. His compact little library contained a common-sense treatise on the care of burns, scalds, cuts, fractures and the few minor physical diseases that sailors are heir to, and in accordance with immemorial custom he, as master of the ship, was the custodian of the medicine chest. So he washed the gore from his face, disinfected his split lip and patched himself up after a fashion. The bullet wound in his left shoulder proved to be a flesh wound, high up, so he cleaned that and decided his left wing would be in fair fighting order within a few days. Then he undressed and said his prayers, with a special invocation for help from his patron saint, holy Saint Michael, the archangel. Evidently Saint Michael inclined a friendly ear, for it is a curious fact that no sooner had his namesake risen from his marrow bones than a curious sense of peace and comfort stole over him. As in a vision he saw Herr August Carl von Staden standing on the bridge, bound at ankle, knee and hand and with a rope round his neck. From the supercargo's neck the rope led aloft through a small snatch-block fastened to the end of a cargo derrick and thence to the drum of the forward winch—a device which had been known to hoist with a jerk objects several tons heavier than Herr August Carl von Staden! This picture thus conjured in Murphy's imagination was so real he was almost tempted to recite the litany for the dying!

" 'Twould have been better for them had they killed me dead and hove my carcass overboard," he decided. "The fact that they didn't, but took the trouble to carry me to my own bed and lock me in, is proof that they'll not murder me now—so I'll not worry. I'll have every beer-drinking, sausage-making son of a seacook begging me for mercy before the week is out. I'll just lie low and rest up a bit, and by the time we're off Rio I'll drop on them like a top-mast in a typhoon. Then with the help of the two Chinamen, the steward and Reardon 'twill not be hard to run her into Rio. I wonder if that pirate frisked me of my five thousand." He searched through his clothing and was amazed to discover that the bills were still in his possession.

"I'll give them back in the morning," he concluded. "I had a pistol in the drawer of my desk and a rifle in that locker;" and in the wild hope that his luck still held, he searched eagerly for both. They were gone.

Nevertheless, Michael J. Murphy smiled as he wrapped a wet towel round his throbbing head, for he had already decided upon his plan of campaign for regaining command of his ship, a *coup* for which he required no weapon more formidable than his native intelligence. As he sank groaning into the arms of Morpheus, however, even a Digger Indian would have realized that for the next two weeks the master of the *Narcissus* would be unable to defend himself against an old lady armed with a slipper. Nevertheless, the indomitable fellow, with the amazing optimism of his race, had already decided to attack and subdue, within four days, thirty-six husky male enemies; which lends some color to the oft-repeated declaration that an Irishman fights best when he is on his back with his opponent feeling for his windpipe.

When Michael J. Murphy awoke it was broad daylight and Herr August Carl von Staden was standing over him. The supercargo was clad in an immaculate suit of white flannels and was looking as fresh as new paint.

"Can it be possible?" Murphy queried in amazement. "Upon my word, friend pirate, I had flattered myself I'd tucked you away for a couple of days at least."

"The excellent Mr. Henckel tells me I was out for ten minutes from that solar-plexus blow you landed," Mr.

von Staden replied in tones of mingled admiration and friendliness. "And of course you cannot see how sore my ribs feel. I take it rather ill of you to have kicked me."

"Kicked you! I wish I'd killed you! And, speaking of kicks, somebody certainly kicked me. Who was it?"

"Upon recovering consciousness," the supercargo replied with some embarrassment, "I was overcome with fury. You were lying on the floor of your stateroom, where Mr. Schultz and Mr. Henckel had hurriedly tossed you—so I came in and kicked you."

"I never kicked you in the face," Murphy complained.

"No, but you flattened my nose with your code book."

"Well, I'll admit a good smack on the nose does make a man mad. But you shot me in the shoulder. By the way, do your lungs hurt when you breathe, Dutchy?"

"No. Do yours?"

"A slight tickle. I think you caved in my superstructure. Who jumped on me from the top of the house?"

"The second mate."

"He dislocated my shoulder. I can wiggle my fingers, so I know it isn't a fracture. Suppose you take off your shoe, sit at the foot of my bed, put your foot under my right armpit and press, and at the same time pull on my right arm."

"Delighted, I'm sure," declared Herr von Staden in his charming Oxford accent, and forthwith snapped Michael J. Murphy's shoulder into place with great dexterity.

"Thank you," the skipper answered, and wiped the beads of agony from his white face. "If you'll frisk my trousers over there on the settee you'll find the five thousand dollars you gave me to sell out my owners. I don't want it. I never intended to keep it. I was suspicious of you and your confounded cablegrams, and I had to have a reasonable excuse to go ashore and cable my owners for confirmation. The bribe furnished that excuse. I suppose you thought I'd fallen for your game."

"I must confess your attitude completely deceived me."

"Thanks for the compliment. And now, if you don't mind, suppose you tell me something: Was it a German agent who put the bug in my ear about hiring the crew of that interned German liner in San Francisco?"

"I greatly fear it was," von Staden answered smilingly. "There is an old man who presides over the destinies of the Blue Star Navigation Company——"

"You mean Cappy Ricks?"

"I believe that is the name. He has a reputation for being at once the most reckless spendthrift and the most painstaking money saver in the world. He is always preaching economy——"

"And well I know it. If he hadn't preached it, Captain Peasley would never have stood for this rabble your friends wished on me."

The supercargo chuckled. "We wanted the largest vessel we could find," he explained; "and when it was reported to us that the Blue Star Navigation Company's *Narcissus* was going from San Francisco to the West Coast and thence to New York with nitrate, we decided to get her. We investigated you. Your

name is Michael J. Murphy; naturally we knew you
were Irish; and the Irish—your kind of Irish—are not
sympathetic toward the cause of Merry England.   The
same held true of your chief engineer, Mr. Reardon.
We knew of the passion of this interesting person,
Cappy Ricks, for cutting down expenses.   We knew
you and Reardon were new to your jobs and would
be likely to consider any reasonable plan for eliminating expense in your respective departments, in the
hope of pleasing your employer.   So the suggestion
that you ship our people was made to you and Reardon, and you accepted it with alacrity.   The rest was
very easy.   We got in touch with your New York
agents through some friends of ours in very good
standing there, and they were enabled to charter the
ship merely by offering an extraordinary freight rate.
They purchased the cargo of coal and sold it to us at
a nice profit, and we depended on your national ani-
mosity and racial sympathy, seasoned with a liberal
cash subsidy, to enable us to deliver it.   We preferred
to do the decent thing, but in the event that you
proved unreasonable, we concluded it would be wise to
have our own people aboard and take the vessel away
from you.   I admit we tried to trick you with the
cablegrams.   Why attempt to conceal the fact now?
That was unsportsmanlike.   However, if the fat is in
the fire, as you Americans would say, you have put it
there by forcing my hand."

"Very cleverly done," quoth Michael J. Murphy.
"I always admire brains wherever I find them."

"Men in my line of endeavor are trained to provide
for all conceivable emergencies, captain.   I think I
provided for all of them in the case under discussion.

Who, for instance, would conceive that you would have taken the trouble to call upon the American consul for the cipher message that has caused all this unpleasant row and facial disfigurement?"

"You have read the translation, of course?"

"Naturally."

"It is self-explanatory. You intend delivering my cargo somewhere off the south coast of Uruguay. May I be pardoned for expressing some curiosity as to your plans thereafter, my piratical friend?"

"Please do not call me your piratical friend."

"Well, you're a pirate, aren't you?"

"Legally—yes. Morally—no. In times of national necessity one's patriotism—one's duty to one's country—excuses, in the minds of all fair men, the commission of acts which ordinarily would bring about the deepest condemnation. I assure you that if we had had the faintest hope of doing business in a businesslike way with your owners, we should have been happy to pay almost any price for their ship, for she carries ten thousand tons of coal; and you surely must realize, Captain Murphy, how limited is the number of ships suitable for our purpose under the American flag. We were desperate——"

"I believe Bethmann-Hollweg said something of the same nature with regard to Belgium," Murphy replied blandly. "A nation fighting for its life is a law unto itself, eh?"

"Self-preservation is the first law of human nature," the supercargo replied.

"All right. Then we understand each other. While I decline to terminate the war between August Carl von Staden and Michael Joseph Murphy, nevertheless

under the law you have just cited I believe I'm entitled
to breakfast. I'm starved. I figured on having supper
ashore last night, but after I received that cablegram
from my owners I forgot all about food. Now I'm remembering. I wish you'd send the steward in with
about forty dollars' worth of spoon victuals. My
grinders are very loose."

"Captain Murphy," his jailer declared, "do you
know you are a very wonderful man?"

"All the Murphys are. It runs in the blood, like a
wooden leg."

"I really regret that you are such a wonderful man.
If you were not I'd give you the liberty of the ship.
As it is, I crave your pardon for keeping you a prisoner
in your state-room. The exigencies of war, you know."

"Don't mention it, Dutchy. For the second time I
ask you: When you have delivered this cargo of coal,
what do you intend to do with my ship?"

"We will, in all probability, give you a new crew,
and the present crew of the *Narcissus* will go aboard
one of our warships and thus remove themselves from
the reach of a possible indictment for piracy and
mutiny on the high seas."

"Where will you get a new crew for me?"

"Our fleet has sunk a few British tramps in mid-
ocean during the past sixty days. Naturally they removed the crews first. These prisoners are in our
way, and the admiral will welcome an opportunity to
load them all aboard the empty *Narcissus,* for even
prisoners of war must eat, and the stores aboard our
fleet are more valuable than these captured seamen.
In obedience to that first law of human nature they

will not object to working the *Narcissus* into the
nearest South American port."

"Well, that's comforting; but for heaven's sake don't
be too much of a hog with my cargo. Leave me enough
of it to carry my ship to the nearest port. She burns
about thirty-five tons a day—you might get the statis-
tics from Reardon."

"By all means, captain. Our capture of the *Narcissus* is merely a deplorable national necessity. We
would not lose her for you for anything."

"How about a British cruiser picking her up before
we make connections with your fleet?"

Herr von Staden shrugged. "That," he replied,
"would be the fortune of war."

"It would look like the picture of misfortune to me.
And how about the freight on this cargo you've stolen?
Don't my owners get something out of this deal to
help pay expenses? You're going to play as fair as
you can with me, aren't you, Dutchy?"

"By all means. However, you are evidently in doubt
as to the real situation. Your charterers are responsible to your owners for the freight money. If they
do not pay it Mr. Cappy Ricks can sue them. As
for the cargo, we have not stolen it, since one cannot
steal that which one owns. We paid cash for this cargo
before you cleared from Norfolk, for our go-between
would take no risks whatsoever."

"I see. Well, I suppose I'll have to grin and bear it.
By the way, don't forget to take back your blood
money. It's in my trousers pocket."

Von Staden was genuinely distressed. "Are you
quite certain you want me to do that?" he queried.
"Five thousand dollars is quite a sum for a poor sea

captain to toss aside so contemptuously. Why not accept it as compensation for that broken rib, and that bullet I put through your left shoulder, the dislocated right shoulder, the loose teeth and the split lip? In fact, I am so certain five thousand dollars will not cover your personal injuries I am willing to be a sport and add something to the sum."

Michael J. Murphy grinned—rather a horrible grin it was, owing to his swollen lip and jaw.

"Dutchy," he said, "listen to me: All the money in the world couldn't make me be untrue to my salt. And if you have any lingering notion that I'm not going to collect a million dollars' worth of satisfaction for the way you've acted aboard my ship, I can only say that as a fortune-teller you'll never earn enough money to keep yourself in cigarettes. You say you have been trained to provide for all conceivable emergencies, so I'm advising you, as a friend, to brace yourself for the surprise of your life before you're a week older. Have you pondered the possibility of sudden death aboard the S.S. *Narcissus?*"

"Certainly. Should we be overhauled by a British cruiser I should take a short cut to eternity. One naturally dislikes the thought of being hanged for a pirate. It would be a reflection on one's family. As for sudden death by violence at the hands of any member of the crew of this steamship, I should be willing to risk quite a sum of money that no such tragedy will be enacted."

"Just why?"

"Well, you'll be safe in this stateroom until I am ready to turn your command back to you, and a man with two shoulders in the condition of yours is hardly likely to try battering down this stout state-room door."

"Correct. And I'm a trifle too thick in the middle to think of crawling through the state-room window."

"And if," the supercargo continued, "you have any idea of calling the engine-room on that speaking tube and soliciting aid from Mr. Reardon, please be advised that for the present Mr. Reardon has been relieved from duty in the engine-room."

"So you've got Reardon locked up, too?" Murphy queried. "Well! Well! I'd hate to think of being locked up and that man Reardon free. However, you need not have worried. I'd die before I'd ask that fellow for help—and he'd die before he'd give it."

"So I understand from the first mate. However, I thought it prudent to guard against a temporary truce and an alliance for the common interest."

"Dutchy," said the skipper, "you're pretty smart."

Von Staden smiled most companionably. "I also took the precaution to remove some weapons from your apartment."

"Take anything from me, Dutchy, except my honor, my pipe and tobacco, and my ship. Take any one of those four, however, and may the Lord have mercy on your soul. Please hand me that book entitled *Backwood's Surgery* till I see what's good for a broken rib; then send the steward for my breakfast order. After that—well, after that you might make your will, Dutchy."

"I did that in Pernambuco," the delightful Herr von Staden replied, "so your advice is wasted."

He handed the skipper the book on surgery and went out, carefully locking the door behind him. He returned presently and stood beside the steward, who thrust his head through the state-room window and desired to know the captain's choice of breakfast.

"A bowl of mush and milk, three soft-boiled eggs and a pot of coffee. No toast. Hurry!"

When the steward returned with the order he was accompanied by Mr. Schultz, the first mate. The sight of the traitor threw Mike into a furious rage.

"Mr. Schultz," he said ominously, "the things I'm going to do to you would make the devil blush."

"So?" Mr. Schultz replied soothingly.

"I'm going to hang von Staden. He's a pirate, and the rule of the Seven Seas is that a skipper hangs a pirate whenever he can lay hands on him. And you know me, Mr. Schultz. I'm a devil for etiquette aboard ship. As for you, you're only guilty of mutiny, so I'll content myself with tricing you up to the shrouds and flogging you with a cat soaked in brine."

And so on, *ad libitum, ad infinitum.*

Mr. Schultz was frankly mystified. Being a German, he did not understand the Irish, although in view of the fact that during the war he had room in his head for but one thing—the Fatherland—perhaps the skipper might have pardoned his mate the glance of contempt and utter disgust which the latter now bent upon him. Here was a man, Mr. Schultz told himself, who, having stipulated his price and struck a bargain, had demonstrated beyond cavil that he was not a gentleman, for he had refused to stay bought. More, he had basely attacked his benefactor.

"So?" he repeated.

"Out, you blackguard, and leave me alone!" Murphy yelled.

"It iss an order dot I stay und see dot der steward shall mayg no conversations vatsoefer," Mr. Schultz declared firmly.

"Verboten, eh?" sneered the skipper. He had once been to Hamburg, and naturally he had acquired the word most commonly used in the German language.

"*Ja*," Mr. Schultz replied placidly, but with an air of finality that left no room for further argument.

CHAPTER XII

In the course of the afternoon, having chewed the bitter cud of reflection and reviewed his situation from every possible angle, Mike Murphy came to the conclusion that, for all Terence Reardon's religious backsliding, he might be fairly honest in money matters and possessed of a sense of loyalty where his owners' interests were concerned. Also, having found Herr von Staden bluffing in one instance it occurred to the captain he might be discovered bluffing in another—so he resolved to investigate. Accordingly at an hour when he knew Terence should be in the engine room he took up the speaking-tube at the head of his bed and blew into it. But no shrill whistle signalled his desire in the engine room, and though Michael blew until he was red in the face and his lips hurt him cruelly, reluctantly he came to the conclusion that Herr August Carl von Staden had the situation very well in hand and Terence Reardon in the latter's state-room under lock and key.

He was right in one particular: von Staden had the situation very well in hand, but he did not have Terence Reardon under lock and key. Murphy had been balked in making connections with the unsuspecting Terence for the reason that a little ball of cotton waste had very carefully been tucked into the engine-room howler a few inches at the back of the whistle at the chief's end of the tube. Hence, in the event that one sought to whistle

85

up the other, he merely wasted his breath. Having learned, on the very excellent authority of both men in the case, that they despised each other and were not on speaking terms, von Staden decided that the chance of Terence Reardon's listening to Michael J. Murphy's tale of piracy and mutiny was so vague as to be almost negligible. However, he was painstaking and careful in all things and never ran any unnecessary risks; consequently, just to be on the safe side, he had instructed the first assistant to plug the speaking-tube leading to the skipper's room. And in order to discourage the captain from seeking an interview with the chief, von Staden had told the former that the chief was a prisoner.

Mr. Reardon was too important a personage to be deprived of his liberty when nothing was to be gained by such action. If he could be kept in ignorance of the state of affairs aboard the *Narcissus,* he would continue to attend to business; if the worst came to the worst his friendship would be a better asset than his hatred. If he grew suspicious and demanded a showdown, Herr von Staden would give it to him without reservation and stuff his mouth with gold; then, if the chief declined to listen to reason, it would be time enough to lock him up. While the supercargo would not hesitate to sacrifice his life, his liberty, or his honor for his country, he was nevertheless desirous of being a gentleman if accorded the opportunity. And it must be admitted he had found Mr. Reardon amusing and vastly entertaining, for the very first night aboard, after Mr. Schultz had introduced him to the chief and he had presented the latter with a good cigar, Mr. Reardon, under the spell of the witchery cast by the sea and the night, had sat on deck and told the German wonderful tales of the fairies in Ireland—this while the skipper was ashore. In particular he told von Staden the tale of the fairy queen with the iron hand.

"Her hand," said Terence, "was as beautiful as ye'd find in a day's thravel, an' 'twas herself that'd dhrive men crazy afther wan look at her. An' she was good to the poor, but divil a bit av love did she have for a redcoat. Whin she'd take human form an' a bowld buck av a British dragoon would come making love to her, 'tis herself would say to him: ' Captain, alannah, would ye oblige me wit' a dhrink av wather?' An' whin he turrned to dhraw the wather, she'd breathe on her hand—like that—an' immejiately 'twould turn to iron an' wit' wan blow she'd knock his brains out. Sure they found the bodies all over Ireland, but divil a man, woman, or child could they ever convict av the murrder. For why? Why, sure, the minute she'd killed a redcoat she'd breathe on her hand ag'in, an' immejiately 'twas flesh an' blood ag'in!"

No, decidedly it would not do to imprison this excellent fellow. Von Staden had read fairy tales as a boy, but never had he met a man who could tell them like Terence Reardon. A hard-headed, highly intelligent chief engineer of a big tramp steamer telling tales of the fairies! Von Staden couldn't understand it. It was so childish—and yet there was nothing childish about Terence Reardon. The German wondered if Terence Reardon believed in the fairies and finally he asked him point-blank if he did; whereupon Terence turned a solemn eye upon him and replied:

"Why, av course I do not. Do you think I'm a blubber-jack av a bhoy? But isn't it pleasant to talk about thim whilst wan has nothing betther to do? Sure, whin I'm lonely at night I think up new fairy tales to tell to the childhren whin I come home from a v'yage."

So that was the Irish of it! Strangely enough it did not occur to the practical German that an individual with an imagination like that, on such an expedition as the present, was the most dangerous person imaginable to be given the freedom of the ship.

So passed twelve days and nights. Mr. Schultz kept in his pocket the key to the captain's state-room, and consequently was always present when the little cockney steward brought the prisoner his meals, tidied up the state-room and made up the captain's bed. The captain spent most of his time lying on his uninjured side and remained very quiet, for the fractured rib, which had received no attention, was causing him a great deal of suffering. Neither did the bullet wound in his shoulder heal cleanly, for the reason, unknown to the captain, that the bullet had carried with it into the muscle a fragment of Michael J.'s undershirt.

However, his physical sufferings were as nothing compared with those he experienced mentally. He had hoped to be in fair fighting condition within a week at the latest. Wrapped in paper and tucked away in the back of the ship's safe he had a silver-hilted stiletto he had taken away from a cutthroat who had tried to rob him once in Valparaiso—and with this weapon he had planned to cut away the lock on the state-room door. And once outside——

What Michael J. Murphy did not know was that when one has dislocated one's shoulder one will do very little wood-carving during the three subsequent weeks. It almost broke the skipper's heart to think he had

made a threat in good faith and was balked from
making it good.

During this entire period Mr. Reardon was going
about his duties as usual, in absolute ignorance of
the state of affairs about the ship, for he was an innocent, trustful sort of fellow, and to a born romanticist
like Terence the fairy tale which Mr. Schultz had spun
at breakfast the morning after leaving Pernambuco was
not at all difficult of assimilation. It appeared—according to Mr. Schultz—that the skipper had gone
ashore for a night of roystering, and upon returning
to the ship about midnight, in a wild state of intoxica-
tion, had become involved in an altercation with the
launchman over the fare. In the resultant battle the
skipper, in his helpless condition, was being terribly
beaten by the vicious Pernambucan; hence one could
scarcely blame him for drawing a pistol and shooting
the launchman—fatally, according to Mr. Schultz.
Of course, after that, to have lingered longer inside
the three-mile limit would have been sheer insanity, so
Mr. Schultz, taking matters into his own hands, had
uphooked and skipped with doused lights from the
jurisdiction of the Pernambuco police.

"And how did the skipper come out of all this?" Mr.
Reardon had inquired anxiously.

"He iss in rodden shape," Mr. Schultz had declared.
"Von of hiss angles vos brogen, und he vos cut mid
a knive—preddy deeb, but noddings to worry aboud.
Der only drouble iss der dooty of navigading der shib
falls double on der segond mate und me."

"Make him pay ye over-time out av his own wages,
the wurthless vagabone!" Mr. Reardon had urged.
"May he walk wit' a limp for the rest av his days—

bad cess to him! I've a notion, Misther Schultz, that
lad'll never comb his hair grey."

Mr. Schultz nodded lugubriously; then he glanced
up and caught the little cockney steward staring at him
so balefully, that he realized he must have speech in
private with the steward. Consequently he lingered at
table until Mr. Reardon finished his breakfast and went
below; whereupon Mr. Schultz intimated to the steward,
in his direct blunt fashion, that for the remainder of
the voyage, Riggins—for that was the steward's name—
was to consider himself deaf, dumb and blind; the
penalty for reconsideration within the hearing of Mr.
Reardon being a swift and immediate excursion, personally conducted by Mr. Schultz, to Davy Jones's
locker! Following this earnest exhortation, Riggins,
never a robust person mentally or physically, came
abruptly to the conclusion that this was one of those
occasions where silence, if not exactly golden, was at
least to be preferred to great riches.

CHAPTER XIII

It may appear strange that during the days and nights Michael J. Murphy lay on his bed of pain Terence Reardon did not once pass the little open window of the skipper's state-room. Not, however, that the latter watched for him, for he did not. He believed that Reardon, like himself, was a prisoner; although, had the chief passed the window and had the captain observed his passing, the complacence of Herr von Staden and his patriotic company would have received a jar much earlier in the voyage.

Unfortunately, however, for Murphy's plans, the chief's stateroom was located in the after part of the house and on the side opposite the skipper's, and following their brief spat through the speaking-tube, Terence Reardon had confined himself exclusively to his engine-room and that portion of the ship along which he must of necessity pass when going to and from his state-room. He told himself it was the part of wisdom for one of his ferocious temper to avoid the occasions of sin. Certainly it would be hard to pass the skipper's state-room without looking in, particularly since in these warm latitudes the door would probably be open; for should the skipper be within at the time, they would peradventure scowl at each other, and he is a fool indeed who cannot foretell the future when a thousand generations of natural enemies exchange "the black look." Terence remembered his boy Johnny, a youth

who, according to Mrs. Reardon, should never be a
marine engineer, but the finest lawyer that ever pouched
a fat fee. And there was Mary Agnes and Catherine
Bertram. Next year they would begin taking piano
lessons, and in the fullness of time, no matter how hard
the pull, both should go to the state university and
acquire the education made to fit their father's head,
but by force of circumstances denied him. And at
the thought Terence looked at his hard black hands and
set himself resolutely to face a life sentence of rattling
ash hoists, roaring furnaces and the soft sucking
sounds of the pistons. Two hundred dollars a month—
and the union scale was a hundred and fifty! Ah, no,
he dared not trifle with that job. He must, at all
hazard, avoid friction with the skipper, for what would
Mrs. Reardon say if Cappy Ricks forced him to roll
the bones with Mike Murphy—one flop and high man
out? Mr. Reardon could close his eyes and see Mike
Murphy roll out a "stiff," while with trembling hand
the Reardon rolled five sixes!

The *Narcissus* had been out of Pernambuco harbor
four days before Mr. Reardon, upon comparing the sun
—which all are agreed rises in the east—with the direction in which the ship was headed, and then extracting
the cube root of the resultant product, and subtracting
it from the longitude and latitude of the Cape of Good
Hope, decided that there must be something wrong with
Mr. Schultz's navigation. So he spoke to Mr. Schultz
about it, and was laughingly informed that they were
traveling on a great circle. Thereupon Mr. Reardon
remembered that at sea a ship traveling on the arc of
a great circle, for some mysterious reason repudiates
the old geometrical theorem that a straight line is the

shortest distance between two points. He recalled that
vessels plying between San Francisco and Yokohama
describe a great circle which brings them well up toward
the Aleutian Islands. So he was satisfied with the explanation, this being his first voyage into the South Atlantic anyhow; but he continued to observe the sun each
morning, and still the vessel's head held far to the south.
A suspicion that all was not as it should be slowly
settled in Mr. Reardon's head, and though he said
nothing, he used his eyes and ears. A dozen times a
day, as the ship rolled steadily south, he was tempted
to take down the speaking tube and confide his suspicions to the master, confined in his state-room by reason
of deep—but not serious—knife wounds. Each time
he was on the point of yielding, however, he remembered
that Mike Murphy had called him a renegade—so he
refrained.

The installation of the wireless plant and the presence aboard the ship of Herr von Staden had failed
to arouse his suspicions the first day out. True, the
wireless could not have been connected with the electric
light plant below without Mr. Reardon's knowledge
and consent, but when he asked Mr. Schultz about it the
latter replied that Cappy Ricks must have changed his
mind about installing wireless on the *Narcissus,* for he
had cabled to the agents of the charterers in Pernambuco to have a wireless plant and a competent operator
waiting for the vessel upon arrival. It was Mr.
Schultz's opinion that the owners had evidently arrived
at the conclusion that it was wise to have a wireless
aboard during war times. Personally, Mr. Schultz approved of the innovation.

So did Terence Reardon, for that matter. He found

the new wireless operator a charming fellow, possessed
of talents far superior to those of the young men
who ordinarily pound the brass at sea. Indeed, after
the second day out, Mr. Reardon would have been
heartbroken had anything happened to that wireless.
For Herr August Carl von Staden sat at the key almost continuously, eavesdropping on the war news, and
Mr. Reardon never came to the wireless room that the
operator did not have some news of an overwhelming
British defeat!

As the voyage proceeded, however, and Mr. Reardon's mind grew a trifle uneasy, reluctantly he began
to view Herr von Staden and the wireless with apprehension. He asked the affable operator how much the
Marconi company charged the *Narcissus* for his services and the rental of the wireless plant, and von
Staden, momentarily stumped, replied that the tariff
was two hundred dollars a month; whereupon Reardon
knew he lied, for the charge is one hundred and forty.
The German, realizing instantly that he was not on
the target, added: "That is, for a first-grade operator
and a plant like this. Of course we furnish cheaper
operators and less powerful plants, Mr. Reardon."

"Oh! So that's the way av it?" the chief replied,
and immediately went to his state-room for the purpose
of thinking it over. Eventually he came to the conclusion that all was not as it should be, but that, nevertheless, it was no affair of his. He was paid to obey
signals given him from the bridge.

" 'Tis no business av mine, afther all," he soliloquized. "For why should I be puttin' dogs in windows?
He's paid to navigate the ship, an' didn't Cappy Ricks
tell me to mind me own business? And yet, there's

something wrong in this ship. I feel it in me bones."

He felt it with a force that was almost violent when Mr. Schultz called down through the speaking-tube late one afternoon and told him to put her under a dead-slow bell. That meant they were practically heaving to, and steamers only heave to at sea in fine weather when they have reached a certain longitude and latitude and plan to keep an appointment. On the instant there was a strong odor of rat in Terence Reardon's engine room, but his "Very well, sir," contained no hint of his surprise and suspicion. He gave his orders to the firemen to bank the fires, and when this had been done he informed his engine-room crew that they might all go on deck for five minutes and get a breath of fresh air. Nothing loath, they scrambled up the steel stairway—and the instant the last man was out of earshot Terence Reardon sprang to the speaking-tube to whistle up the skipper in his room.

Now, undoubtedly the cool and calculating Herr August Carl von Staden had been carefully trained to take into consideration, when planning his strategy, every conceivable contingency that might possibly arise. It is probable that the German secret service never turned out a more finished graduate than Herr von Staden; but the fact remains, nevertheless, that there are certain contingencies over which no human being has control. One of these is Newton's law of gravitation; another, an equally immutable law to the effect that water will seek its own level; a third, the vindictiveness of an outraged Irishman; and a fourth, the very natural tendency of any man, not excepting Mr. Terence Reardon, to be profoundly surprised and intensely curious when certain phenomena, which we shall now proceed to explain, take place in the engine room where he is chief.

Michael J. Murphy, having only the day before again essayed the task of whistling up the engine room, and having, by reason of the ball of cotton waste with which the tube had been plugged by the first assistant engineer, again failed to receive the courtesy of a reply from any one, had, to put it mildly, been annoyed.

"Very well, my bullies," he soliloquized as he hung up the tube, "you wouldn't speak to me when I wanted to speak to you; so now the first time one of you wants to speak to me I'll hand you a surprise, and I'll hand it to you right in the mouth." And forthwith Michael J. had carefully poured down the speaking tube the contents of the basin in which he had just made his morning ablutions! He longed to do something nasty, and he succeeded admirably.

As we have already remarked, water seeks its own level. It ran down the speaking-tube until it encountered the cotton waste plug; whereupon, due to the hydrostatic pressure, the plug gave way and was forced down to the tightly closed mouth of the tube, and the suds backed up behind it. It was pretty warm in the engine room, and most of the water had evaporated by the time Terence Reardon took down the looped tube and opened it for the purpose of putting his lips to the mouthpiece and blowing heartily through it. However, there was about a gill of water left in the tube.

Now, as everybody knows, water running down a slope of seventy-five or eighty degrees comes rather fast. Consequently Mr. Reardon had no time to dodge.

Why be squeamish? He got a mouthful and was

very nauseated for half a minute. Also he cursed, we regret to record, and was very, very angry. Carefully he drained the devilish tube, wiped it clean with some fresh waste, and racked his brain for the right thing to say to Michael J. Murphy. Finally he hit upon something he concluded would about fill the bill, so he put his lips to the mouthpiece once more and whistled up the skipper. To his surprise, however, his breath didn't seem to get anywhere: in fact, it was directed back in his face rather forcefully; so he investigated and discovered the mouthpiece was only half open. Upon endeavoring to open it fully he sensed an obstruction in the back of it, so he unscrewed the mouthpiece and drew forth a ball of dirty, sour-smelling cotton waste.

He gazed a moment in speechless wonder. Then: "I'll whistle that dirrty Tomfool, until he answers me in self-defense," he announced to the main motor, and forthwith blew a mighty blast. Almost instantly Michael J. Murphy yelled: "Hullo!"

"Murphy," Terence Reardon announced calmly and very distinctly, "you're a contimptible dhrunken ape!"

"Holy Moses! Reardon, is that you?" the astounded Murphy demanded.

"It is—as you'll discover whin you're able to come on deck an' give me the satisfaction I'll demand for the dirrty dab av wather an' cotton waste you put in the tube, knowin' that the firrst time I took it down to spheak to you, ye blackguard, in the line av djooty— which is the only reason I would spheak to you—I'd get it full in the mouth. Ye dirrty, lyin', schamin', dhrunken murrderer!"

He paused to let that stream of adjectival opprobrium sink in. Silence. Then:

"I poured the contents of my washbasin in the tube, I'll admit, but I did not plug it with cotton waste. One of your assistants did that, chief, and as for the water, as God is my judge, I didn't intend it for you——"

"Who else would ye be afther insultin' if it wasn't me? Are ye not friendly wit' me assistants?"

"Forgive me, Reardon, and listen to what I'm going to tell you."

And then the tale was told. When it was done Terence Reardon grunted.

"I knew it!" he said. "I knew it! I felt in me bones there was something wrong aboard this ship. An' so ye were not dhrunk an' disordherly at Pernambuco?"

"The liars! Did they tell you that? Reardon, it's only the mercy of heaven they didn't murder me. I'm lying here, helpless and crippled in my state-room, with the key turned in the lock. They've stolen my ship from me, and I can tell by the roll of her she's practically hove to under a dead-slow bell this minute. We've reached the rendezvous—we're waiting for the German fleet to deliver the coal; and oh, man, man, if we're caught by a British cruiser we'll lose the ship! They'll confiscate her, chief. Wirra! Wirra!" he cried, breaking into the forgotten wail of his childhood. "How can I ever face Matt Peasley and Cappy Ricks after this? Reardon, man, they'll think we stood in with the Germans and let them do it. We're both Irish —they know we're both pro-German——"

"What's that you said?" Terence demanded sharply. "Me pro-German. Me? I *was* pro-German—yis— wanst!"

Fell a silence.

Now, for the benefit of the uninitiated, be it known that there is a certain curse employed by the Irish and by no other race on earth. Whenever you hear an Irishman employ it, you know instantly—provided, of course, you are Irish yourself—just what kind of Irish that Irishman is. You cannot mistake it. There is no possible chance. It is only brought forth with the dust of the centuries on it, so to speak, to grace a fitting occasion. Terence Reardon felt that such an occasion was now at hand. As naturally, as inevitably, therefore, as the suds ran down the speaking-tube, that curse climbed up it—softly, distinctly, and with a wealth of feeling in the back of it:

"God put the curse av Crummle on thim!"

Mr. Reardon, of course, referred to the late Oliver Cromwell. Any one who has ever read the sorry history of Erin knows what the amiable Oliver did to the Irish. Consequently such an one will have no difficulty in estimating the precise proportions of bad luck Terence Reardon prayed might be the immediate heritage of the crew of the S.S. *Narcissus*.

Michael J. Murphy blinked rapidly, for all the world as if Mr. Schultz had entered at that moment and struck him a terrific blow on top of the head. A more dazed Irishman than he never threw an ancient egg or a defunct cat at an alleged Celtic comedian with green whiskers. He was absolutely staggered—but not for long. The Irish come back very quickly.

"Shame on you, Terence Reardon!" he declared. "And you with a Masonic ring on your finger."

"Glory be!" cried the delighted Terence. "Sure are you wan av us?"

"One of you!" Mike Murphy fairly shrieked. "The minute I'm out of this room you'll apologize or fight for thinking I'm a renegade."

"*Naboclish!*" laughed Terence Reardon, slipping into the Gaelic and out again. "The divil a Mason am I! Sure that ring ye saw on me finger that day in the office av the owners belonged to me second assistant in the *Arab*. He'd lost it in the engine room, an' a mont' afther he'd left I found it. Not knowin' what ship he was in, 'twas me intintion to take the ring over to the Marine Engineers' Association an' lave it for him wit' the secreth'ry; and to make sure I wouldn't forget it I put it on me finger——"

"Well, you knew, Terence, that with the likes of me round you'd not be liable to forget it," Mike Murphy laughed.

"As for you, ye divil," Terence continued, "faith, what wit' yer English tweeds an' the fancy cut av thim, an' yer lack av the brogue an' the broad *a* av ye, I thought, begorra, ye were a dirrty Far Down! God love ye, Michael, but 'tis the likes av you I'm proud to be ship-mates wit'."

"But you said you were from Belfast, Terence."

"So I am. I was borrn there, but me parents—the Lord 'a' merrcy on their sowls—moved back to Kerry."

"Terence!"

"What is it, Michael, me poor lad?"

"Do you ever drink on duty? I don't mean with your superiors——"

The chief chuckled. He knew what Murphy was alluding to.

"I do," he replied, "wit' me equals."

" 'Tis a pity, Terence, that man Schultz has the

key to my state-room in his pocket. Now if you could manage to tap that Dutchman on the head with something hard and heavy, take the key out of his pocket and throw him overboard, you could let me out of this purgatory I'm in. Then I wouldn't be surprised if the sight of me and the absence of Mr. Schultz would put a bit of heart in that little cockney steward—and maybe he'd bring a drink to hearten you for what's ahead of you this night."

"An' what might that be, avic?" Terence demanded.

"I want you to steal the ship back from them, Terence."

"Very well, Michael. 'Tis not a small thing ye ask me to do, but the divil a more willin' man could ye find to ask. Have ye figured out the plan av campaign? Sure what wit' the suddenness av it all I'm all in a shweat wit' excitement."

"You may be cold enough before morning, Terry, my boy."

"Bad luck to you, Michael! Dyin' is wan thing I cannot afford to do, although be the same token they tell me ould Ricks has a kind shpot in the heart av him for the widow an' the orphan—particularly av thim that dies in his service! As I say, I cannot afford to get kilt, but in back av that ag'in I cannot afford to lose the best job I ever had. An' afther all, 'tis a poor man that won't fight for a fine, kind gentleman——"

"Damn the fine, kind gentleman! It serves him right for letting us get into this fix. He can afford the loss of the ship, but you and I, Terence Reardon, cannot afford the loss of our honor and self-respect. For the sake of the blood that's in us we can't afford to let a lot of Dutchmen steal our ship and cargo."

"Whist!" Reardon warned. "Hurry up. Me crew is comin' below ag'in."

"Make it a point to pass by my state-room window after dark. You'll find a scrap of paper on the sill. Help yourself to it."

"Faith, I will," Mr. Reardon promised fervently, and the tube closed with a click.

CHAPTER XIV

Terence Reardon's preparations for the night's work began the instant he hung up the speaking-tube. The *Narcissus* carried three assistant engineers, in consequence of which Mr. Reardon was not required to stand a watch unless he so elected; although from force of habit acquired in the days when he had been chief of the *Arab*—a little three-thousand-ton tramp—and perforce had to stand a regular watch, he found it very difficult not to spend at least eight hours in every twenty-four in the engine room. When, eventually, he came to a realization that his job was not to make the engines behave, but to see that they behaved properly, he spent more of his time on deck, and put in only a few hours below during the watch of the third assistant engineer—the third assistant being a young man in whom the chief reposed exactly that degree of confidence a chief engineer should always repose in a third assistant. Mr. Reardon, therefore, was at liberty to leave the engine-room whenever he felt so disposed; and following his illuminating conversation with the captain he felt very much disposed to leave immediately.

He went first to his state-room, where he bathed, changed into new under-clothes and socks, donned a freshly laundered suit of faded dungarees—old, faded, well-washed dungarees, by the way, always appearing neater and cleaner than new ones—and shaved; for if

103

Providence willed it that he should die to-night, Mr.
Reardon was resolved to be in such a highly sanitary
condition that "those upon whom should devolve the
melancholy duty of laying him out"—which phrase,
in the Hibernian sense, means those who should dispose
his limbs, close his eyes, tie up his black jowls with
a towel and fold his hands—alas, so white in death,
at last! across his still breast—might be moved to remark that, notwithstanding the nature of the de-
ceased's vocation, they could not recall ever having
seen a cleaner corpse.

Having attended to his pre-dissolution toilet, Mr.
Reardon next sat in at his littered desk, swept a space
clear of tobacco crumbs, ashes, pipes and some old
copies of the *Cork Eagle*, and sat down to write a
farewell letter to his wife, hoping that, even though
his enemies should slay him, yet would they have sufficient respect for the dead to mail that letter to Mrs.
Reardon. And, in order that he might not anger his
posthumous benefactors, he mentioned nothing of the
state of affairs aboard the ship. He merely stated
that she might never see him again, in which event
she was to call upon the owners and ask them to invest
for her the proceeds of his life insurance policy, since
they could and would invest it to better advantage
than she. Then he spoke of his grief at the thought
of the children being forced to forego their college education and suggested that she ask Cappy Ricks to give
Johnny a place in his office; also, should the owners
offer anything as compensation for the loss of her
husband, she was to accept it, for, as God was his
judge, she would be entitled to it! This last sentence
Terence underscored for emphasis; that was as close

as he came to saying that if he died it would be in defense of his owner's interest. Then he commended her to the comfort of her religion and subscribed himself: "Your loving and devoted husband, Terence P. Reardon, Chief Engineer S.S. *Narcissus*."

Having set his small affairs in order against a hasty exit from this vale of hatreds, Mr. Reardon, in unconscious imitation of all the condemned men who had preceded him on the voyage across the Styx, repaired to the dining saloon and partook of a hearty meal. He realized he had undertaken a contract that would require the employment of weapons more formidable than his hard fists, and devoutly he wished that, like the fairy queen, he had but to breathe on them to metamorphose them into pig iron. He pictured the slaughter aboard the *Narcissus* when he should wade into the conflict. Finally he made up his mind that, in lieu of an iron hand or two, he would use his favorite monkey wrench, for he had no firearms whatsoever; although, had somebody presented him with a one-man machine gun with full directions for using, Mr Reardon would have recoiled in horror from it. Firearms were highly dangerous. They killed so many people!

He left the table long before the others had finished. There was no one on deck as he emerged from the dining saloon, so he walked leisurely round past the captain's cabin, whistling the "Cruiskeen Lawn" to let Mike Murphy know who was coming. Evidently Michael assimilated the hint, for there was an envelope on the little window sill as Terence hove abreast of it. He snatched it swiftly away and continued round to his own state-room.

The envelope contained Michael J. Murphy's plan

for campaign worked out to the most minute detail,
by reason of his absolute knowledge of the customs
aboard the ship.   Mr. Reardon read the remarkable
document and sat lost in admiration; a twinkle leaped
to his eyes and a cunning, rather deadly little smile came
sneaking round the corners of his broad chin.

"Arrah, but 'tis a beautiful schame," he soliloquized.
"Who but that lad could have t'ought av it?   An' here
I've been shpendin' the past two hours borrowin' trouble."

He read and reread the plan of attack, in order to
familiarize himself with the details; then he held a
match to the document and destroyed it.   He considered a moment, and then performed a similar service
to his farewell letter to Mrs. Reardon, for the chief
engineer of the S.S. *Narcissus*, of San Francisco, had
made up his mind not to die—to-night!

CHAPTER XV

Mr. Schultz, the first assistant, and Mr. von Staden were engaged in coffee and repartee when Terence Reardon thrust his head in at the dining saloon window. He was mildly excited.

"Be the Great Gun av Athlone!" he declared. "I've just been bit be a bedbug—an' I t'ought there wasn't a bedbug in the ship!"

Mr. Schultz looked up, horrified. "Chieve," he said, "dot is rodden news. Bedbugs! *Ach!*"

"An' well you may '*Ach*,' Misther Schultz. Let a colony av bedbugs move into the *Narcissus* an' Terence P. Reardon will move out. There's only wan thing to do, Misther Schultz, an' that is to tackle the divils before we're overwhelmed be the weight av numbers. Have ye a bit av sulphur in yer shtore-room, Misther Schultz—the kind that comes in balls an' is used to burrn in shtate-rooms to kill bedbugs?"

When Terence Reardon put that innocent query to the first mate he knew very well Mr. Schultz would reply in the negative—which he did—for the reason that Michael J. Murphy had privately informed Mr. Reardon that the little cockney steward, Riggins, had charge of the bedbug ammunition. Riggins, who had been standing with his back against the wall, eyeing Mr. Schultz sourly, now spoke up and said he had some sulphur.

"More power to ye, Riggins!" Mr. Reardon declared

107

heartily. "Then do ye, like the good lad, give me two or three balls av it. I'll burn them in me shtate-room to-night, wit' the door an' window locked, an' be morrnin' sorra bedbug will be left alive."

"Very well, sir," Riggins replied. "Might Hi arsk, Mr. Reardon, where you hintend passin' the night?"

"I'll shleep in me auld aisy-chair abaft the house an' next the funnel, where I'll be snug an' warrm," Mr. Reardon replied, for he desired an excuse to be on deck all night without arousing the suspicions of Mr. Schultz or von Staden.

The steward, having finished serving those who ate in the dining saloon, stepped out on deck and started for his own room. Mr. Reardon remained by the window a minute, discoursing on the curse of bedbugs aboard a ship, and then with a sigh followed the steward leisurely. Mr. Schultz appeared undecided whether or not to accompany him in the capacity of censor, but finally concluded to remain and finish his coffee, for if Riggins had decided to enlighten the chief as to the real reason for the skipper's indisposition he had had frequent opportunity to do so during the past ten days. It did not seem likely, therefore, that he would run any risks at this late date. To Mr. Schultz, Riggins appeared to be a man who could be depended upon to remember which side his bread was buttered on and who supplied the butter.

Arrived at the steward's state-room, Mr. Reardon helped himself to the entire box of bedbug exterminator and addressed Riggins very briefly:

"Riggins, ye're a child av Johnny Bull, are ye not?"

Riggins, without the slightest trace of embarrassment, admitted his disgrace.

"An' bein' what ye are," Mr. Reardon continued, "would ye do somethin' av great binifit to England?"

Riggins replied that inasmuch as he had lost two brothers at the Battle of the Marne, that ought to indicate bally well where the Riggins tribe stood on the subject of defense of the realm.

"Good!" Mr. Reardon murmured. "Even if misguided in their pathriotic motives, shtill yer brothers were brave min, an' for that I respect thim. Now, thin, Riggins, ye rabbit, listen to me: In a momint av surpassin' innocince Captain Murphy an' mesilf swallowed a cute suggestion from a lad whose back I'll break in two halves whin the *Narcissus* gets back to San Francisco. 'Why not save expinse,' says he, 'an' ship the crew av this German liner that's interned over in Richardson's Bay?' Riggins, to make a long shtory short, we have thim this minute, an' the dear God knows that even if shipped at the German scale av wages that gang'll prove a dear crew to the Blue Star Navigation Company if you an' I, Riggins, fail to do our djooty. They've half murdered the captain, shtolen the ship an' cargo from him, an' run her t'ousands av miles off her course to deliver the coal to the German fleet."

"Oh, my bloody ol' Aunt Maria!" gasped the horrified Riggins.

"What I want to know from you, Riggins, is this: Will ye help me shteal the ship back to-night? We're runnin' almost due south, an' that good-for-nothin' von Staden has been in communication wit' the fleet all day long. I feel it in me bones. If we get the ship back we'll head due west for the coast av South America an' hug the three-mile limit—an' the devil

scoort them thin. Riggins, ye gossoon, what for the
cause av Merry England? They wouldn't take ye for
a gift in the British Arrmy, for I doubt if ye'd weigh
ninety pounds soakin' wet an' a rock in yer hand, but
for all that, here's an iligant opporchunity for ye to
serrve yer counthry, an' should worrd av yer brave
action reach the king—bad cess to him—he may call
ye Sir Thomas Riggins an' make ye consul-general av
the Cannibal Islands.

"Out wit' it, Riggins. Yer king an' counthry calls
ye, an' be the same token so do Michael J. Murphy an'
Terence P. Reardon. What'll ye give, Riggins, to
preserve the seas to Britain?"

"Me 'eart's blood, that's wot!" Riggins replied
quietly.

"I accept the sacrifice in the name av His Majesty,
King Jarge! Be on deck at ten o'clock sharp, waitin'
close undher the shtarboard companion leadin' to the
bridge. Whin I come out on the shtarboard ind av
the bridge an' whistle 'O'Donnell Abu,' do ye——"

"S'help me, chief, I never 'eard of the blighter before," Riggins interrupted.

"God forgive me!" Mr. Reardon murmured *sotto
voce*. "I'll have to do it. Well, thin, Riggins, whin I
come out on the shtarboard ind av the bridge an'
whistle 'God Save the King'—troth, I'll gamble that's
one blighter ye've hearrd tell av—do ye run up into the
pilot-house an' take the wheel. I'll not whistle until we
have the deck to ourselves, wit'out fear av intherruption, an' ye must come quick an' take the wheel, else
the vessel'll fall off into the trough av the sea an'
commince to wallow—which same'll wake up the second
mate an' bring him an' von Staden on deck to see

what's wrong wit' her.   An' until I'm ready to call on
those lads I'm not wishful to have them call on me!
Remimber, Riggins: Wan jump an' ye're into the
pilot-house; then howld her head up to the sea—an'
lave the rest to me.   Gwan wit' ye now, or that skut,
Schultz, will be gettin' suspicious av us."

When Mr. Schultz came along ten minutes later he
found Mr. Reardon very busy calking with oakum the
cracks round the door and window of his state-room,
through which little wisps of yellow smoke were curling.
Mr. Schultz was so completely deceived that he hurried
round to his own quarters and pawed over his own
mattress and bedding in a vain search for bedbugs.

CHAPTER XVI

At eight o'clock Mr. Schultz relieved the second mate on the bridge, and five minutes later Terence Reardon, for the first time invaded that forbidden territory. "Bad cess to me!" he complained plaintively. "I'm the picthur av bad luck. I've a leaky connection below an' divil a bit av red lead. Could ye lind me a dab av red lead from yer shtore-room, Misther Schultz?"

Mr. Schultz marvelled that any man could force his mind to dwell on red lead, leaky pipe connections, sulphur and bedbugs in a ship like the *Narcissus* at a time like this. He had met a few innocents in his day, but this Irish engineer was most innocent of all.

"Sure, Mike!" he replied, and grinned at his feeble play on words. "*Und* as I gannot leave der bridge yet, here iss der key to der store-room. Helb yourself, mine *Freund, und* den gif me der key back."

"Ye addle-pated son of sin!" Mr. Reardon soliloquized as he took the key and departed. "Faith, a booby birrd has more sinse nor you! D'ye suppose I didn't wait until ye were on djooty before axin' ye, well knowin' ye'd lind me the key an' I'd be alone in yer shtore-room!"

Mr. Reardon was in the store-room less than two minutes. When he emerged he carried a daub of red lead on an old spoon, as Mr. Schultz, looking down on the dimly lighted main deck, observed. What he did not observe, however, was the chief's action in tossing

112

the spoon overboard the instant he passed beyond the range of Mr. Schultz's vision. It is probable, also, that the mate would have been disturbed could he have seen Mr. Reardon in his state-room, with the door locked, removing from beneath his dungaree jumper several fathoms of light, strong, cotton signal halyard, two five-foot lengths of half-inch steel chain, and a strip of canvas. His pockets also gave up two pad-locks, with keys to fit. This loot Mr. Reardon very carefully hid in the space under his settee, after which, with due thanks, he returned the key to Mr. Schultz.

The remainder of the evening until nine-thirty Ter- ence spent in the wireless room with Herr von Staden. Then he retired, very low in spirits, to his state-room, to make his preparations for wholesale assault with a deadly weapon—possibly wholesale murder! He cut the signal halyard into short lengths; then he cut the piece of canvas into strips about two inches wide and secreted the halyard and canvas strips here and there about his person. Then he descended to the engine room and selected his monkey wrench from the tool rack on the wall, helped himself to a handful of cotton waste, and returned to his state-room mournfully keening "The Sorrowful Lamentation of Callaghan, Greally and Mullen, killed at the Fair of Turlough- more."

"Wirra," he murmured presently, "but 'tis a terrible thing to hit an unsuspectin' man wit' a monkey wrench! An' that divil von Staden, for all his faults, is not a bad lad at all at all. An' I'd give five dollars—yes, seven an' a half—if he were bald an' shiny on any other shpot save an' exceptin' the shpot I have to hit him. Ochone!

" 'Come tell me, dearest mother, what makes me father
    shtay
  Or what can be th' reason that he's so long away?'
  'Oh, howld yer tongue, me darlin' son, yer tears do grieve
    me sore,
  I fear he has been murdhered in the fair av Turlough-
    more!'

"Sure, I haven't got the heart to dhrive the head av
this monkey wrench into that bald shpot. If he'd hair
there I wouldn't mind." Mr. Reardon sighed dismally.
"I'll have to wrap a waddin' av waste around me
weapon, so I'll neither kill nor mangle but lay thim out
wit' wan good crack——

" 'It is on the firrst av August, the truth I will declare,
  Those people they assimbled that day all at the fair,
  But little was their notion that evil was in shtore,
  All by the bloody Peelers at the fair av Turloughmore.'

"I must practice crackin' the divils! Sure, 'twould
be an awful thing to have the sin av murrder on me
sowl—not that 'tis murrder to kill a Dutchman that's
a self-confessed pirate into the bargain. Shtill, 'tis
a terrible t'ought to carry to the grave——"
Wham! Mr. Reardon brought his padded wrench
down on his defenseless bed. "Too harrd," he told
himself. "Sure a blow like that on top av the head
would knock out the teeth av the divil himself! Less
horse-power, Terence!"
Wham! He tried it again, this time with better
results. For five minutes he beat the bedclothes; then
his spirits rose and, like the mercurial Celt that he was,
he chanted blithely a verse from "The Night Before
Larry Was Stretched":

" 'Though sure 'tis the best way to die,
    Oh, the divil a betther a-livin'!
For sure whin the gallows is high,
    Your journey is shorter to heaven;
But what harasses Larry the most,
    An' makes his poor sowl melancholy,
Is to think av the time whin his ghost
    Will come in a sheet to sweet Molly!
    Oh, sure, 'twill kill her alive!' "

He slipped the short, heavy monkey wrench up his right sleeve, walked out on deck and stood at the corner of the house, smoking placidly and gazing down on the main deck forward. The look-out on the forecastle head was not visible in the darkness, but Mr. Reardon was not worried about that. "For why," he argued to himself, "should I go lookin' for the skut whin if I wait a bit he'll come fluttherin' into me hand?"

He did. At five minutes after ten Mr. Schultz hailed the look-out in German, and although Mr. Reardon spoke no German, yet did he understand that order. Mr. Schultz, a victim of habit, desired the look-out to go to the galley and bring up some hot coffee for him and the helmsman. It was the custom aboard the *Narcissus,* as it is in most Pacific Coast boats, for the cook, just before retiring, to brew a pot of coffee, drain off the grounds and leave it to simmer on the galley range where, at intervals of two hours during the night, the watch could come and help itself.

Terence Reardon knew that the look-out, after heating the coffee and bringing a few cups up on the bridge, would return to the galley and partake of a cup and a bite himself.

The man came down off the forecastle head, crossed

the main deck and disappeared in the galley. In about ten minutes Mr. Reardon saw him climb up the port companion to the bridge; a minute later he came down. Mr. Reardon waited until he was certain the fellow was sipping his coffee in the galley; then with the utmost nonchalance he went up on the bridge and hailed Mr. Schultz, who was standing amidships blowing on a cup of coffee.

"Begorra," he complained, "Divil a wink can I shleep to-night. I've been sittin' wit' the wireless operator all evenin', an' now, thinks I, he's weary listenin' to me nonsinse, so I'll go up on the bridge an' interview Misther Schultz. If I——be the Rock av Cashel! What was that?"

"Vot? Vere?" Mr. Schultz exclaimed, and set down his cup of coffee. He was all excitement, for he had been looking for the flash of a searchlight for the past hour and he wondered now if the unsuspecting Reardon had seen it first.

"Over that way." Mr. Reardon pointed off the port bow. "Did ye not see that light?"

"A light. *Gott im Himmel!*"

"Ye can't see it now," Mr. Reardon replied soothingly. He stepped round to the back of the mate and permitted his trusty monkey wrench to slip down into his hand. "But if ye continue to look in that direction, Misther Schultz, ye'll see not wan light but several."

"*Donnerwetter!* I gannot see dem," Mr. Schultz protested, wondering if there might not be some defect in his eyesight.

"Have no fear. Keep lookin' that way an' ye'll see thim," Mr. Reardon reassured him. "Ha-ha, ye divil!" he crooned—and struck.

"I'll gamble ye saw the lights I promised ye," he breathed into the ear of the unconscious mate as he deftly caught the falling body and eased it noiselessly to the deck to avoid calling the attention of the helmsman to the interesting tableau going on behind him. Quickly he gagged Mr. Schultz with a strip of canvas; then he tied his hands behind him and bound him at ankle and knee with the short lengths of signal halyard. As a final attention he "frisked" the mate and removed his keys and a heavy automatic pistol.

"Lie there now, me jewel," he said, and trotted out to the starboard end of the bridge, whistling shrilly "God Save the King." When the swift patter of feet along the deck warned him that the steward was coming, he walked back amidships and opened the little sliding trap in the roof of the pilot-house, which on the *Narcissus* was set just below the bridge. The quartermaster's head was directly beneath the trap. "Oh-ho, me laddybuck!" Mr. Reardon murmured, and dropped his padded monkey wrench on that defenseless head. Instantly the quartermaster staggered and hung limply to the wheel.

"Bad luck to me, I'll have to hit ye agin," Mr. Reardon complained—and did it. Then he slid through the trap into the pilot-house, steadied the wheel with one hand and unlocked the pilot-house door with the other to admit the steward.

"Strike me pink!" that astounded functionary exclaimed as he gazed at the quartermaster lying beside the wheel.

"I will—if ye don't take howld av this wheel an' do less talkin'," Mr. Reardon replied evenly. "Bring her round very slowly, me lad, an' in the intherval I'll wrap up me little **Baby Bunting** on the floor forninst ye."

When the quartermaster had been duly wrapped *à la* Mr. Schultz and dragged clear of the wheel, Mr. Reardon returned to the bridge and with brazen impudence set the handle of the marine telegraph over to full speed ahead. He hummed "Colleen Dhas Cruthin Amoe" as with a light heart he skipped down to the galley and found the look-out eating bread soaked in coffee. Mr. Reardon nodded and said "Good nicht, *amigo*," for his voyages had taken him to many ports and he was naturally quick at picking up foreign languages. The fellow, concluding Mr. Reardon desired a cup of coffee also, turned to the rack to get him a cup.

"How dare ye ate up the owners' groceries in this shameful manner?" Mr. Reardon demanded. "Do ye not get enough at mess that ye must be atin' between meals? Shame on you——"

One tap did the trick. " 'Tis a black way to repay a kind t'ought," Mr. Reardon observed to his victim as he bound and gagged him; "but war is war, an' a faint heart an' a weak stomach never shtole a ship back from forty German pirates!"

He closed the galley door on the unfortunate look-out and climbed up on the boat deck to get Michael J. Murphy out of prison. Cautiously he unlocked the state-room door with the key taken from Mr. Schultz, and the skipper came forth. Mr. Reardon led him under an electric light and gazed upon him wonderingly.

"Begorra, Michael, me poor lad," he whispered, "be the look av the white face of you I'm thinkin' ye ought to be in bed instid av out raisin' ructions."

"I'm weak; I have a fever," Murphy replied. "Still,

half that fever may be plain lunatic rage. Did you find a gun on the mate?"

"I did. Take it, Michael, I'll have nothin' to do wit' it."

The skipper grasped the weapon eagerly. "The ship is headed due west undher full speed," Terence explained, "an' the mate, the quarter-master an' the look-out have all received evidence av me affectionate regard. Next!"

"Von Staden. He kicked me and broke my ribs, Terence."

"Wit' the greatest joy in life, Michael. The skut's busy in the wireless room."

So they went to the wireless room. Von Staden was taking a message as they entered; at sound of their footsteps he turned carelessly and found himself looking down the muzzle of the captain's automatic.

"Will ye take it peaceably, ye gossoon, or must I brain ye wit' this monkey wrench?" Mr. Reardon queried fiercely.

"And take your hand off that key, you blackguard. No S O S," Murphy ordered.

The supercargo stared at them impudently. "This," he said presently, "is one of those inconceivable contingencies."

"Your early education was neglected, Dutchy. However, don't complain and say I didn't give you warning. Terence!"

"What is it, Michael?"

"All well-regulated ships carry a few sets of hand-cuffs and leg irons. If you will put your hand in my right hip pocket, Terence, lad, you'll find a pair for present emergencies. They were in my desk and I concluded to bring them along."

"An' a pious t'ought it was, Michael."

So they handcuffed Herr August Carl von Staden and gagged him, after which Mr. Reardon, leaving the skipper to guard his prisoner, ran round to his own room and got the two lengths of chain and the padlocks. When he returned, Michael J. Murphy kicked his unwelcome supercargo to the mate's store-room and Mr. Reardon locked him in among the paint pots, pipe, old iron and other odds and ends which accumulate in a mate's store-room.

They went next to the door of the forecastle. It was open—and, what was better, it opened inward. Also, it was of steel with a stout brass ring on the lock, this ring taking the place of what on a landsman's door would have been a knob.

Terence Reardon and Michael J. Murphy listened. From within came a medley of gentle sighs, snores and the slow, regular breathing of sleeping men. Softly Mr. Reardon closed the door, turned the ring until the latch caught, drew a section of chain through the ring in such a manner as to prevent the latch from being released, passed the ends of his chain round the steel handrail along the front of the forecastle and padlocked them there.

"Now, thin," Mr. Reardon announced, "that takes care av the carpenter, the bos'n, four seamen, two waiters an' the mess bhoy. Do ye wait here a minute, Michael, lad, whilst I run up on the bridge and give that unmintionable Schultz the wanst over."

The weak, half-dead Murphy sat down on the hatch coaming and waited. The chief was away about ten minutes and the captain was on the point of investigating when Mr. Reardon appeared.

"That unfortunate divil had come to, an' was lookin' an' feelin' cowld whin I wint up on the bridge," he explained, "so I wint to me room an' got a pair av blankets to wrap round him where he lay. It's wan thing to tap a man on the head, but 'tis another to let him catch his death av cowld."

Captain Murphy smiled. Ordinarily he would have laughed at the whimsical Terence, but he didn't have a good laugh left in him. His lung was hurting, so he suspected an abscess.

They returned to the boat deck, and with his rule Mr. Reardon carefully measured the exact distance between the ship's rail and the center of the doors of the state-rooms occupied by the mates and assistant engineers. This detail attended to, they went to the carpenter's little shop and cut two scantlings of a length to correspond to the measurements taken, and in addition Mr. Reardon prepared some thin cleats with countersunk holes for the insertion of screws. He worked very leisurely, and it was eleven o'clock when he had everything in readiness.

"There's nothin' to do now until midnight, whin the watch in the ingine room is changed," Mr. Reardon suggested, "so lave us go to the galley. Wan av me brave lads is in there, an' if he's not dead intirely, faith, I'm thinkin' I might injoy a cup av coffee!"

So they went to the galley and found the look-out glaring at them. He made inarticulate noises behind his gag, so Mr. Reardon, much relieved, found seats for each of them and poured coffee. Then he filled his pipe, crossed his right leg over his left knee and puffed

away. He was the speaking likeness of Contentment.
And well he might be.

The first assistant engineer had been driving the
Narcissus for an hour at full speed at right angles to
the course he believed she was pursuing. He would,
being totally ignorant of the change of masters, continue to drive her at full speed until midnight, when he
would come off watch, tired and sleepy, and go straight
to his state-room. The second assistant would *go*
direct from his state-room to duty in the engine-room
and continue to drive the *Narcissus* at full speed
until four o'clock, and inasmuch as it would be quite
dark still when the third assistant came on at four
o'clock to relieve the engineer on watch, there was
not the slightest doubt in the minds of Murphy and the
chief but that the deception could go on until breakfast. However, that would interfere with their plans.
Long before that hour the men locked in the forecastle
would have discovered their plight, and the noise of the
discovery might reach below decks and bring up, to investigate, just a few more husky firemen and coal
passers than even the redoubtable Terence Reardon
could hope to cope with successfully.

"By four o'clock we'll be more than fifty miles off the
course Schultz was holding her on," the captain suggested. "In all likelihood the German admiral wirelessed his last position and the course he was steering,
and von Staden gave Schultz his course accordingly."

"Faith, we're not a moment too soon at that," Mr.
Reardon replied. "Schultz was lookin' for searchlights
whin I tapped him. Be the Toe Nails av Moses ye're
right, Michael. We'll be so far off that course be daylight they won't even see our shmoke. D'ye think that

little handful av bones, Riggins, can manage the wheel until we've claned up the ingine-room gang? We can relieve him wit' wan av the Chinamen then."

"Tell him he'll have to stick it out. And by the way, Terence, come to think of it, you had better run forward and remove the sidelights; then unscrew all of the incandescent lamps on deck until the contact is lost. You can screw them in again just before the watch is changed, so they won't suspect anything, and unscrew them again after we have the watch under lock and key. The fleet may be too far away to see our smoke by daylight, but they may be close enough to see our lights to-night! Tell Riggins to darken the pilot-house. The binnacle light is enough to keep him company."

"Thrue for ye," Terence replied, and hurried away to carry out Murphy's instructions.

CHAPTER XVII

At twelve o'clock the second assistant engineer, hurrying along the deck to relieve the first assistant on watch, found Mr. Reardon leaning over the rail meditatively puffing his old briar pipe. In answer to the former's query as to what kept the chief up so late, the latter replied that he was burning sulphur in his room to kill bedbugs.

"The good Lord forgive me the lie," he prayed when a few minutes later he was called upon by the first assistant, hurrying off watch, to repeat the same tale.

The first assistant and his watch had a shower-bath and turned in. They were not interested in the workings of the deck department in the dark; they could not know that the vessel's course had been changed; they thought only of getting to sleep. Mr. Reardon waited until one-thirty A. M. to provide against possible sleepless ones, and then crept aft on velvet feet. The *Narcissus* had very commodious quarters in her stern, where her coolie crew had been housed in the days when she ran in the China trade; and when the Blue Star Navigation Company took her over these quarters had been fitted up to accommodate the engine room crew. In the same manner, therefore, that he had imprisoned the men of the deck department in the forecastle, Mr. Reardon now proceeded to imprison the men of the engine department in the sterncastle. This delicate mission accomplished, he went up top-side and measured

124

the diameter of the ventilators, in order to make certain that the thinnest of his German canaries could not fly the cage via that difficult route. Having satisfied himself that he had no need to worry on this score, he made his way forward again.

"Well, Michael, me poor lad," he announced as he rejoined the skipper, "I'll tell you wan thing—an' it isn't two. The crew av the *Narcissus* off watch at this minute will never come on watch ag'in—in the *Narcissus*."

The skipper smiled wanly. "I'm sorry you must take all the risks and do all the work, Terence," he replied.

"Gwan wit' ye, Michael. Sure if I had a head on me like you, an' a college edication in back av that ag'in, I'd be out playin' golf this minute wit' Andhrew Carnegie an' Jawn D. Rockefeller—ayther that, or I'd have been hung for walkin' away wit' the Treasury Buildin'."

They discussed the remaining details of that portion of the ship cleaning still before them. "Remember, Terence," Mike Murphy warned the chief, "when the blow-off comes at four o'clock and the uproar commences fore and aft, we have the means to keep them quiet. I'll go forward and you go aft. When we threaten to throw burning sulphur down the ventilators and suffocate them, they'll sing soft and low!"

Mr. Reardon chuckled. "An' Schultz t'ought I was afther bedbugs whin I asked the shteward for the sulphur," he replied. "Shtill an' all, Michael," he added, a trifle wistfully, "I could wish for a bit more excitement, considerin' the size av the job."

"Don't worry, Terry, you may get it yet. I'm dizzy and weak, chief; I'm fearful I'll not be able to last out the night—and these Germans are desperate. Suppose we go forward now, while I'm able, and awaken Mr. Henckel. It's high time he relieved Mr. Schultz, and he'll be waking naturally if we let him oversleep much longer."

The subjugation of Mr. Henckel was accomplished without the slightest excitement or bloodshed. Mr. Reardon rapped at his door and Mr. Henckel replied sleepily in German. The skipper and the chief merely lurked, one on each side of his state-room door, until he stepped briskly out; whereupon the captain jabbed him with the gun while Mr. Reardon shook the monkey wrench under his nose. Indeed, Mr. Reardon had the gag in the second mate's mouth even while it hung open in surprise. They bound him hand and foot, and Mr. Reardon picked him up and tucked him gently in his berth, for, as the chief remarked to him, he was as safe there as anywhere and far more comfortable, although Mike Murphy objected and was for putting him in the mate's store-room with von Staden, whom they had put in the dirtiest and most unwholesome spot aboard the *Narcissus*, for two reasons: In the first place, he had kicked Michael J. Murphy and shot him through the shoulder; and in the second place, he was the cleanest German and the most wholesome pirate they had ever seen, and they figured the contrast would annoy him. Mr. Reardon, however, objected to this plan. He argued that von Staden would be glad of Mr. Henckel's company, and was it not their original intention to keep that laddybuck von Staden in solitary confinement? It was. They closed the state-room door on Mr. Henckel, and left him to meditate on his sins while they repaired to the carpenter's little shop,

to return to the boat deck presently with the scantlings
and cleats Mr. Reardon had prepared.

With the scantling the chief shored up the doors
to the state-room occupied respectively at the time by
the first and third assistant engineers; then he screwed
the cleats into place at top and bottom, so the scantling could not slip. Not for worlds would he have used
a hammer to nail them into place, for that would have
spoiled the surprise for the objects of his attentions.
Throughout the entire operation he was as silent as a
burglar, although by way of additional precaution the
captain stood by with drawn pistol.

"Now thin, Michael," Mr. Reardon whispered as they
pussy-footed away, "there are six fine Germans below in
the ingine room, an' two Irishmen an' half an Englishman on deck. The Chinee cooks don't count, for sure
the poor heathens would only get excited and turrn
somebody loose if we asked them to do anything desperate. And, as ye know, wan good Irishman—and bad
luck to the man that says I am not that—can keep
a hundhred Germans from comin' up out av that ingine
room. Go to yer bed, Michael, an' lie down until I
call ye."

"Better take this automatic," Murphy suggested,
and showed him how to use it.

But Mr. Reardon resolutely refused to abandon his
monkey wrench, although he consented to carry the
automatic to Riggins in the pilot-house. The estimable
Riggins had been steering a somewhat erratic course,
for he found it impossible to keep his eye on the lubber's
mark while the bound quartermaster glared balefully at
him from the floor. Indeed Riggins had been pondering
his fate should that husky Teuton ever get the upper

hand again; hence, when he found himself in a state of preparedness and was informed that he must stick by the wheel until relieved, the prospect did not awe him in the least. The present odds were counterbalanced by the strategic position held by the minority, and Riggins was content.

On his way back to his state-room, there to rest until the final call to arms, Michael J. Murphy concluded it would be well to search the quarters of the second mate and Herr von Staden for contraband of war. So he did, with the result that he unearthed in von Staden's room the rifle and revolver which belonged to the *Narcissus*, and under the second mate's pillow he found another automatic pistol. He confiscated all three weapons by right of discovery, and hid the rifle in the galley, the last place anybody would think of looking for it.

In the meantime Mr. Reardon proceeded further to strengthen his position by closing the port entrance to the engine room and shoring up the door with a stout scantling, cleated at top and bottom to hold it securely in place. Then he donned Mr. Schultz's heavy watch-coat, dragged round from the lee of the house the upholstered easy-chair Mrs. Reardon had insisted upon his taking to sea with him for use in his leisure moments, placed this chair on deck just outside the starboard entrance to the engine room, loaded his pipe, laid his trusty monkey wrench across his knee and gave himself up to the contemplation of this riot we call life. He resembled a cat watching beside a gopher hole. By half-past three o'clock he had finished figuring out approximately the amount of money Mrs. Reardon would have in the Hibernia Bank at the end of five years—figuring on a monthly saving of fifty dollars and interest compounded at the rate of four per cent. So, having satisfied himself that Johnny would yet be a law-yer and the girls learn to play the piano, Mr. Reardon heaved a sigh and reluctantly went to call Michael J. Murphy for the final accounting.

CHAPTER XVIII

At ten minutes to four Mr. Uhl, the second assistant, a man of some thirty years and ordinarily possessed of a disposition as placid as that of a little Jersey heifer, ordered one of his firemen to go and call the watch to relieve them. Mr. Reardon, his monkey wrench firmly grasped in his right hand, knew that at exactly ten minutes to four Mr. Uhl would issue that order—so he was on the spot to receive the fireman as the latter came leisurely up the greasy steel stairway. As the fellow emerged on deck he paused to wipe his heated brow with a sweat rag and draw in a welcome breath of cool fresh air. He did not succeed in getting his lungs quite full, however, for Michael J. Murphy, lurking beside the door, thrust the barrel of his gun in the fireman's ribs, effectually curtailing the process of respiration practically at once. From the other side of the door the chief engineer stepped out and wagged his bludgeon under the fireman's nose.

"*Ach!*" Mr. Reardon coughed, and grimaced pleasantly. "*Schmierkase und Sauerkraut,* ye big shtiff! *Vat wilse du haben,* eh? *Zwei bier?* Damn the weather, as Misther Schultz would say."

He laid his finger on his lips, enjoining silence; then with the same finger he pointed sternly onward, and the fireman took the hint. In the clear space aft the

house and next to the funnel Mr. Reardon bound and
gagged him and laid him tenderly on his back to await
developments.

"Now thin, Michael," he said to the skipper, "lave us
go back an' see can we catch another. At four o'clock,
whin this lad fails to return, Misther Uhl, the omad-
haun, will sind up another man to see what the divil ails
the firrst man."

And it was even so. This time it was the oiler.

At five minutes after four a coal passer came up the
stairs, and he was swearing at the delay in being relieved. Something told Mr. Reardon this fellow would
make trouble, so without warning he hit the coal passer
a light rap "to take the conceit out av him." Two
minutes later the coal passer had joined his fellows
beside the funnel.

At a quarter after four Mr. Uhl scratched his head
and said something very explosive in German. He
started up the stairs, got halfway up—and came down.
It had occurred to him very suddenly that three men
had already gone up the stairs and had failed to return. He called a fireman and gave him some very ex-
plicit orders in German; whereupon the man disappeared in the shaft alley. Five minutes later he returned, pop-eyed with excitement and the bearer of a
tale that caused Mr. Uhl to arch his blond eyebrows
and murmur dazedly "*So?*"

Ten minutes passed. Mr. Reardon glanced inter-
rogatively at Michael J. Murphy. "I think the divils
are suspicious," he whispered. "We should have had
another be now. Have a care now, Michael. Whin
they come they come wit' a rush an'——"

A pistol shot echoed through the ship. It came up

from forward. Three more followed in rapid succession
—a scream—a shout!

"May the divil damn me!" Terence Reardon cried in
a horrified voice. "I clane forgot the little companion
hatch at the ind av the shaft alley. They've crawled
down the shaft alley an' up on deck at the very sterrn
av the ship!"

He dashed aft towards the spot where his prisoners
were laid out close to the funnel. As he turned the
corner of the house he observed that the electric lamp
which he had so carefully screwed out of its socket
had been screwed in again, and by its light Terence
beheld no less a person than Mr. Uhl cutting the halyards that bound the oiler. The fireman had already
been cut loose, but the potent effects of Terence Reardon's blow with the wrench still remained; though conscious, the man was unfit for combat. The coal passer,
evidently the first man to be rescued by Mr. Uhl, was
standing by.

"Gower that, ye divils!" Mr. Reardon shrieked, and
charged, swinging his monkey wrench with all his horse-
power. He missed his first stroke at Mr. Uhl, who
very deftly stabbed him high up on the hip for his
carelessness; then the chief swung again, and Mr. Uhl
was out of the fight.

Not so the big coal passer, however. He planted
in Terence Reardon's face as pretty a left and
right—hay-makers both—as one could hope to see
anywhere outside a prize-ring; whereupon the chief
took the count with great abruptness. The fireman
reached for the monkey wrench—and at that instant
the weak, pale-faced skipper lurched around the corner
of the house and his automatic commenced to bark.

It was not a time for sentiment. Michael J. Murphy glanced once at Terence Reardon's bloody, upturned face, and the glazed eyes thrilled him with horror. The chief engineer was dead! That meant that Michael J. Murphy would soon be dead, too. Well, they had fought a good fight and lost, so nothing now remained for him to do save slaughter as many of the enemy as possible and go to his accounting like a gentleman.

He turned his back on the heap of bloody, prostrate men, stepped over a little rivulet of gore that ran rapidly toward the scupper as the ship heeled to port, then hesitated and started back as she heeled to starboard. He was vaguely conscious that Mr. Uhl had shut down his engines before coming on deck and that in consequence the ship had lost headway and was beginning to wallow. In his weak state her plunging caused him to stagger like a drunken man. As he crossed to the port side of the ship and gazed down the deck he noticed that the incandescent lamps had all been screwed back in their sockets, and by their brilliant light he beheld one of the firemen in the act of removing the scantling from before the first assistant's door. Just as the door swung open the captain fired, but evidently missed, for the man sprang nimbly into the state-room for safety.

If the great European War has proved nothing else to date, it has demonstrated one comforting thing about the German people: one does not grow impatient waiting for them to carry the fight to him. The fireman had no sooner entered the first assistant's stateroom than the first assistant came out. He was wearing his pajamas and a piece of young artillery, and without the slightest embarrassment he commenced shooting at Michael J. Murphy, who, not to be outdone in politeness while he could stand and see, promptly returned the compliment.

The first assistant's first shot nipped a neat little crescent out of Mike Murphy's large red right ear; his second ripped clean through the inside of the skipper's left leg.

"High and then low," was the thought that capered through Mike Murphy's brain. "God grant he don't get me through the middle! That's what comes of fast shooting—so I guess I'll go slow."

The electric lamp over his head was shattered and the fragments scattered round him as he leaned against the corner of the house and took careful aim at the first assistant, who missed his next shot by a whisker and died in his tracks with two cartridges still in his gun.

Dazedly Michael J. Murphy advanced along the deck, stepped over the body and entered the state-room. In the corner the fireman crouched, hands uplifted in token of surrender, so the skipper closed the door and shored it up again with the scantling. Mechanically he picked up the first assistant's huge revolver, broke it, removed the cartridges and threw them overboard. Then he slipped a clip of seven cartridges into his automatic and staggered round to Mr. Henckel's state room.

The door was open. The bird had flown.

Michael J. Murphy went in and sat down on Mr. Henckel's settee, for he was very weak and dizzy; and at least nobody could shoot at him in there. "Come, come, Michael," he croaked, "no going out this voyage. You have work ahead of you. Pull yourself together and let us count noses. Now then, there were two firemen, two coal passers, one oiler and Mr. Uhl on watch. Terence killed Mr. Uhl with the monkey wrench, I killed the big coal passer, I think I killed the oiler, and one fireman was out of the scrap from the beginning. Then I killed the first assistant and locked the other fireman in his room. That leaves Mr. Henckel and a coal passer to be reckoned with. Now there was some shooting up forward and somebody was hit. That means Riggins shot somebody or somebody shot Riggins. The second mate probably went forward to let the men out of the forecastle, while the fireman went aft to let the engine-room gang out of the sterncastle. They haven't had time to do it yet; they'll have to pry those rings out of the door with a crowbar. I'll go aft and drive the fireman forward; when I have them bunched I'll argue with them."

He arrived at the break of the house and looked down on the deck aft. The lights had been turned on and a man was just raising a short crowbar to attack the door, from behind which came shouts and cries of anger and consternation.

Mike Murphy rested his automatic on the deck rail and fired twice at the man in front of the sterncastle door. The fellow fled at once dashing along the deck, zigzag fashion, to distract the skipper's aim, and disappeared in the dark entrance to the starboard alleyway. So Michael J. Murphy slid down the companion and followed into the alleyway, firing two shots for luck as he came.

Scarcely had he disappeared into the murk amidships when Terence Reardon rolled groggily down the companion after him. Terence had no means of ascertaining which alleyway the skipper had charged into—and he did not care. Blind with fury he lurched into the port alleyway; in consequence of which the fugitive, fleeing ahead of the captain down the starboard alleyway and thinking to turn down the port alleyway and double back to complete his labors at the sterncastle door, bumped squarely into the chief engineer.

Mr. Reardon said no word, but wrapped his arms round the man and held the latter close to his breast.

Thus for a moment they stood, gripping each other, each wondering whether the other was friend or foe.

Then Mr. Reardon decided that even if his nose was bloody he could not possibly be mistaken in the odor of a fireman just come off watch. He had lost his monkey wrench in the *mêlée* on the upper deck— the defunct Mr. Uhl having fallen upon it, thereby obscuring it from Mr. Reardon's very much befogged vision, but his soul was still undaunted, for Mr. Reardon, in common with most chief engineers still in their prime, firmly believed that he could trounce any fireman he saw fit to employ. He bit suddenly into the fireman's cheek just where the flesh droops in a fold over the lower jaw, and was fortunate enough to secure a grip that bade fair to hold; then he crooked his leg at the back of his opponent's and slowly shoved the fellow's head backward. They came down together, Mr. Reardon on top, content for once to hold his man helpless—and rest—while his enemy's shrieks of pain and rage resounded through the ink-black alleyway.

Michael J. Murphy heard that uproar and halted.

After listening a few seconds he came to the conclusion that a German was in deep distress, and that hence it was no part of his business to interfere. Besides, he had business of his own to attend to. He could hear a chain rattling up forward, and while it was too dark to see who or what was doing the rattling, he found Mr. Henckel guilty on mere suspicion, and fired at the sound; whereupon somebody said "*Ach, Gott!*" in tones of deep disgust, two little flashes of fire cut the dark, and two bullets whispered of death as they flew harmlessly down the alleyway.

Instantly Mike Murphy returned the salute, firing at the other's flashes; then he fell to the deck and rolled over into the scupper to escape the return fire, which was not slow in coming.

"I wonder where the devil he got that gun," was Murphy's comment. "Mr. Uhl must have had it in his pocket and lent it to him."

There was profound silence within the forecastle, and pending the destruction of his attacker Mr. Henckel judged it imprudent to make any further attempts at a delivery. He required time to formulate a plan of attack, and in the interim he desired shelter. Mike Murphy heard the patter of feet, the patter ceasing almost as soon as it commenced—and he smiled grimly.

"He's hiding," the captain soliloquized. "Now, where would I take shelter if I were in his fix? Why, back of the hatch-coaming, of course—or the winch." He had a sudden inspiration and called aloud:

"Riggins! Riggins! Answer me, Riggins. This is Captain Murphy calling you."

" 'Ere, sir," came the voice of Riggins from the pilot-house above. The voice was very weak.

"Climb out of the pilot-house, Riggins, to the bridge, turn on the searchlight and bend it down here on the deck till I get a shot at this scoundrel. Don't be afraid of him, Riggins. It's Henckel and he can't shoot for beans. Get the light fair on him and keep it on him; it'll blind him and he won't be able to shoot you."

"The dirty dawg!" snarled Riggins wearily. " 'E come up on the bridge a while—ago—an' I drove 'im off—but 'e plugged me, sir—through the guts, sir—an' me a married man! Wot in 'ell'll my ol' woman—say——"

And that was the last word Riggins ever spoke. True, he managed to crawl out of the pilot-house and up the short companion to the bridge; he reached the searchlight, and while Mr. Henckel and Mike Murphy swapped shots below him he turned on the switch.

"Bend it on the deck, Riggins. On the deck, my bully, on the deck," Mike Murphy pleaded as the great beam of white light shot skyward and remained there; nor could all of Murphy's pleading induce Riggins to bend it on the deck, for Riggins was lying dead beside the searchlight, while ten miles away an officer on the flying bridge of H.M.S. *Panther* watched that finger of light pointing and beckoning with each roll of the ship.

"Something awf'lly queer, what?" he commented when reporting it to his superior.

"Rather," the cuperior replied laconically. "It can't be the *Dresden* and neither is it one of ours. We'll skip over and have a look at her, Reggie, my son."

CHAPTER XIX

Michael J. Murphy had two shots left in his automatic, and he was saving those for daylight and Mr. Henckel's rush, when a searchlight came flickering and feeling its way across the dark waters. Slowly, slowly it lifted and rested on the big blunt bows of the *Narcissus*, hovered there a few seconds and came slowly aft, and as it lighted up the main deck Mr. Henckel rose from behind the hatch-coaming.

"*Deutschland über Alles!*" he yelled joyously—and rushed.

Terence Reardon, having pounded his fireman into insensibility, had crept down the port alleyway, and, unknown to Captain Murphy and Mr. Henckel, he had, from the opposite side of the deck, watched the flashes of their pistols as they fired at each other.

"I'll have to flank that fella an' put a shtop to this nonsense," Mr. Reardon decided presently, and forthwith crept across the deck on his hands and knees until he reached the hatch-coaming. Mr. Henckel lurked just round the other corner of the coaming, so close Mr. Reardon could hear him breathing. And there the crafty chief had waited until Mr. Henckel rose for his charge—whereupon Mr. Reardon rose also.

"Ireland upper always, ye vagabone!" he yelled, and launched himself at Mr. Henckel's knees. It was a perfect tackle and the second mate went down heavily.

In an emergency such as the present all Terence

Reardon asked was good fighting light. Fighting in
the dark distressed him, he discovered, for while polish-
ing off the fireman in the black alleyway he had missed
one punch at the fellow's head, and had been reminded
to his sorrow and the ruin of his knuckles, that the deck
of the *Narcissus* was of good Norway pine. However,
H.M.S. *Panther* was scarcely three cable lengths distant now, and the officer on her flying bridge could see
that some sort of a jolly row was in progress on the
deck of the *Narcissus;* so he kept the searchlight on
the combatants while Mr. Reardon bent Mr. Henckel's
back over the hatch-coaming, took his automatic away
from him, and proceeded to take a cast of the mate's
features in the vulcanite butt of the weapon. And
vulcanite is far from soft!

When Terence Reardon had completed his self-
appointed task he stood up, hitched his dungarees, spat
blood on the deck, and stood waving from side to side
like a dancing bear. His face was unrecognizable; his
dungarees, so neat and clean when he donned them the
night before, were now one vast smear of red, and he
grinned horribly, for he was war mad!

"Next!" he croaked, and turned to the master for
orders.

But Michael Joseph Murphy was out of the fight.
He lay prone on the deck, conscious but helpless, and
because his broken rib was tickling his lung the froth
on his lips bore a little tinge of pink. Only his eyes
moved—and they smiled at Terence Reardon as the
triumphant exiles of Erin faced each other.

Terence Reardon turned and shook his battered fists
full into the rays of the searchlight. He was mag-
nificent for one brief instant; then the war-madness

left him, and again he was plain, faithful, whimsical,
capable, honest Terence P. Reardon, chief engineer of
the S.S. *Narcissus*, who considered it a pleasure to dis-
course on the fairies when he had nothing more important to do. Now that the fight was over and the
German fleet had overhauled them at last, he had time
to think of Mrs. Reardon and the children and his best
job gone for ever—tossed into the discard with his
honor as a faithful servant.

He sat down very suddenly on the hatch-coaming
and covered his terrible face with his terrible hands.

"Ah, Norah! Norah!" he cried—and sobbed as if
his heart must break.

CHAPTER XX

When Captain the Hon. Desmond O'Hara, of H.M.S. *Panther*, boarded the steamer *Narcissus* via the Jacob's ladder Mr. Reardon hove overside at his command, he paused a moment, balanced on the ship's rail, and stared.

"My word!" he said, and leaped to the deck, to make room for a pink-and-white middy. The pink-and-white one stared and said "My aunt!" Then he, too, leaped to the deck, and a stocky cockney blue-jacket poked his nose over the rail.

"Damn my eyes!" said this individual. " 'Ere's a bloomin' mess!"

"Who is that person?" Captain Desmond O'Hara demanded, pointing to the semiconscious Mr. Henckel, who was moaning and saying things in his mother tongue.

"That," said Mr. Reardon with a familiar wink, "was a fine, decent Gerrman until I operated on him!"

"So I observed. And who might you be?"

"Me name is Terence P. Reardon, an' I'm the chief engineer av the United Shtates steamer *Narcissus*, av San Francisco."

"Ah! An Irish-American, eh?"

Mr. Reardon looked down at the deck, smiled a cunning little smile and looked up at Captain O'Hara. "Well, sor," he declared, "I had me hyphen wit' me

142

whin I shipped; as late as yestherd'y afthernoon 'twas
in good worrkin' ordher; but what wit' the exertion av
chasin' our Gerrman crew round the decks, faith I've
lost me hyphen, an' I'm thinkin' the skipper's lost his
too. That's him forninst ye. For the prisent he's in
dhrydock awaitin' repairs, which leaves me in command
av the ship. And since he's in no condition to go to
his shtate-room an' unlock the ship's safe, an' sorra
wan av me knows the combination, the divil a look will
ye have at our papers. I'll save time an' throuble for
us all be tellin' ye now that we've ten t'ousand tons av
soft coal undher deck, that we cleared from Norfolk,
Virginia, for Manila or Batavia, Pernambuco for
ordhers, an' that we're a couple av t'ousand miles off
our course. So confiscate the ship an' be damned to
ye! Only I'm hopin' ye'll not be above takin' a bit av
advice from wan who knows. There's a Gerrman fleet
not far off, an' if ye shtop to monkey wit' us, faith ye
may live to regret it—an' ye may not."

Captain the Hon. Desmond O'Hara smiled sweetly.
"Divil a fear," he said, in no way cast down. "We met
the beggars off the Falklands yesterday and sunk them
all but the *Dresden*. She slipped away from us in the
dark, making for the mainland, and we were looking
for her when we saw your searchlight cutting up such
queer didoes, so the *Panther* dropped behind to investigate. Had it not been for your searchlight we would
have missed you."

"An' be the same token a little dead Englishman
signalled ye." Mr. Reardon gave another hitch to his
dungarees. "Sor," he said doggedly, "I never t'ought
I'd live to see the day I'd want to cheer a British
victh'ry—but I do." He glanced down at his right

hand and shook his head. "Englishmen that ye are," he continued, "I'll not offer ye a hand like that—much as I want to shake hands wit' ye."

"Faith, don't let that worry you, Mr. Reardon. I'm not an Englishman."

"In the divil's name, you're not an—an——"

"I'm an Irishman! My name is Desmond O'Hara."

Mr. Reardon was fully aware that here was a grand specimen of the kind of Irish he had been taught to despise—the Irish that take the king's shilling, the gentlemen Irish that lead the king's cockneys into battle. And yet, strange to say, no thought of that entered his head now. He stepped up to Captain O'Hara, looked round cautiously as if expecting to be overheard, winked knowingly and whispered, as he jerked a significant thumb toward the unhappy Mr. Henckel: "Sure 'tis the likes av us that can take the measure av the likes av thim."

"It is," replied Captain O'Hara, and reached for Terry Reardon's awful hand. "It is!"

Together they lifted Michael J. Murphy into a bos'n's chair, the jackies unslung a cargo derrick, Mr. Reardon went to the winch, and the skipper was hoisted overside into the *Panther's* boat and taken aboard the warship for medical attention. Just before Mr. Reardon hoisted him he drew the chief's ear down to his lips.

"About von Staden," he whispered. "I thought I wanted to see him hung. Legally he's a pirate; but, Terence, he was raised wrong; you know, Terence— *Deutschland über Alles.* These Dutch devils thought it was all right to steal our ship—national necessity, you know. Let von Staden out of the mate's store-room and tell him the English have us—that his fleet is gone. Then turn your back on him, Terence."

Mr. Reardon followed orders. "Captain Murphy ordhered me to let ye out," he explained to the supercargo, "an' towld me to turrn me back on ye."

"Please thank him for me," von Staden replied gently. "I scarcely expected such kindness at his hands. You may turn your back now, Mr. Reardon."

So Mr. Reardon turned his back, and, despite the rush of the British jackies to stop him, Herr August Carl von Staden reached the rail. *"Deutschland über Alles!"* he shouted defiantly—and jumped. He did not come up.

Captain the Hon. Desmond O'Hara removed his cap. "They die so infernally well," he said presently, "one hates to fight them—individually. Yesterday the *Nürnberg* fell to us. We outranged her, and when she was out of action and sinking, with her men swimming and drowning all round her, the *Panther* was stripped of life preservers in two minutes. Some of my lads went overboard to help the Boche."

Mr. Reardon remembered he had wrapped waste round the head of his monkey wrench and curtailed his indicated horse-power when tapping individuals; yet, when he fought them in bulk, with what savage joy had he struck down Mr. Uhl, a poor, inoffensive devil and the victim of a false ideal of national honor! Mr. Reardon was quite sure he despised Englishmen; yet the tears came to his eyes when the jackies carried poor little Riggins away from the searchlight, and he prayed for eternal rest for the soul of his late assistants, for he had learned in a night, as he fought with tooth and fist and monkey wrench, what those who fight with tongue and typewriter will never learn—that racial and religious animosities are just a pitiful human bugaboo—in bulk. Only that valiant minority that sheds its blood for the heartless majority can ever know this great truth—and the pity of it—that warriors never hate each other.

They are too generous for that.

CHAPTER XXI

Capt. Matt Peasley, with his heart in his throat, called up the British consul at San Francisco. Cappy Ricks, looking very pale and unhappy, sagged in his chair, while Mr. Skinner stood by, gnawing his nails and looking as if he would relish being kicked from one end of California Street to the other.

"Hullo!" Matt Peasley began. Cappy Ricks shuddered and closed his eyes. "Is this the British consul's office? . . . This is Captain Peasley, of the Blue Star Navigation Company . . . Yes . . . About our steamer *Narcissus* . . . You say the consul is on his way down to our office . . . Thank you . . . Goodbye."

Cappy Ricks sighed like an old air-compressor. "I hope I live till he gets here," he declared feebly. "Deliberate race, the British. No pep. Never get anywhere in a hurry."

As if to give the lie to Cappy's criticisms, the British consul was admitted at that moment.

"Gentlemen," he announced as the heart-broken trio gathered round him, "I have some very grave news for you." His voice was vaguely reminiscent of that of the foreman in a quarry who calls upon a lady to inform her that her husband has just been caught in a premature blast and that the boys will be up with the pieces directly. "Your steamer *Narcissus*, loaded with ten thousand tons of coal, has been captured a hundred miles north-east of the Falkland Islands by His Majesty's cruiser *Panther*. In view of your vessel's clearance——"

A low moan broke from Cappy Ricks.

"Tightwad!" he reviled. "Old Alden P. Tightwad, the prince of misers! He thought he'd add a couple of ten-dollar bills to his roll, so he encouraged his skipper to hire a lot of interned Germans to work his ships in neutral trade! He was penny-wise and pound-foolish, so he cut out the wireless to save a miserable hundred and forty dollars a month. Bids are invited for the privilege of killing the damned old fool—Skinner! What are you looking at?"

"N-n-nothing!" stammered Mr. Skinner.

"I won't be looked at that way, Skinner. I have my faults, I know——"

"Ssshh!" Matt Peasley interrupted.

"And I won't be 'sshh-ed' at either. I lost the ship. I admit it. I O.K.'d the charter, and Murphy did his best to save her for us and couldn't. I'm the goat, but if it busts me I'll reimburse you two boys for every cent you have lost through my carelessness——"

"I beg your pardon, Mr. Ricks," the consul interrupted. "Pray permit me to proceed. The circumstances attending this case are so very unusual——"

"My dear Mister British Consul, I shall not argue the matter with you. You're too bally deliberate, and, besides, what's the use? The ship is gone. Let her go. We'll build another twice as big. Of course I could give you an excuse, but if I did you'd think I was old Nick Carter come to life. We'll just have to take it up through our State Department, present our alibi, and try to win her back in the prize court."

"She will never be sent to a prize court, Mr. Ricks. It doesn't require a prize court to decide the case of the steamer *Narcissus*. The evidence is too overwhelming. There could not possibly be a reversal of the decision of our admiral."

Mr. Skinner sat down suddenly to keep from falling down. The consul continued: "The commander of the *Panther*, Captain Desmond O'Hara—by the way, an old schoolmate of mine—has sent me a long private report on the affair; by wireless, of course, and in code. It appears that in Pernambuco harbor your German crew overpowered the captain——"

"What?" cried Cappy, Matt and Skinner in chorus. "You admit that?"

"We do, Mr. Ricks. And last night your chief engineer, Mr. Terence Reardon, with the aid of the steward, one Riggins—a British subject and unfortunately killed in the affray—and Captain Murphy overpowered the German crew——"

"Oh, Mr. Ricks!" gasped Skinner.

"Oh, Matt!" shrilled Cappy Ricks.

"Oh, Cappy!" yelled Matt Peasley.

"Oh, nonsense," laughed the British consul. "They stole her back, gentlemen, and when Captain O'Hara found her rolling helplessly and boarded her, she was a shambles. Dead men tell no tales, Mr. Ricks—yet it was impossible for any fair-minded man to doubt the testimony of the dead men aboard your *Narcissus!* Her killed, wounded and prisoners formed a perfect alibi. In the meantime, Mr. Reardon and Captain Murphy are aboard the *Panther*, receiving medical attention, and will be returned to duty in a few weeks;

the *Narcissus* is proceeding to meet the other ships of our fleet. She will coal them at sea."

"Then you've confiscated her cargo?" Matt Peasley demanded.

"We should worry about the cargo if they give us back our vessel," Cappy Ricks declared happily. "We haven't received our freight money, of course, but by the time I get through with the charterers they'll pay the freight and ask no questions about the coal."

"We confiscated it, Mr. Ricks," the British consul continued, "for the reason that it was German coal. The supercargo who boarded the vessel at Pernambuco told your captain his people had paid cash for it to the charterers. But we're going to give you back your vessel because we haven't any moral right to keep her, since her owners have committed no breach of international law. The supercargo left fifteen thousand dollars behind him when he jumped overboard, but Captain O'Hara declined to confiscate that. At Captain Murphy's suggestion it will be forwarded to the widow of the man Riggins. Captain O'Hara especially requested that I call upon you and inform you that you have two of the finest Irishmen in the world to thank for your ship."

"Thank you, Mister Consul. By the way, can you reach Captain O'Hara by wireless? If you can, I should be glad to pay for a message if you will send it."

"I shall be delighted indeed."

"Then tell him the Blue Star Navigation Company thanks him for the courtesy of his message, but that it does not agree with his statement that we have two Irishmen to thank for our ship. We think we have three! I know the Irish. The scoundrels never go back on each other in a fight."

The consul laughed.

"By the way," he said, as he took up his hat preparatory to leaving, "your ship is now equipped with wireless—a fine, powerful plant such as they use in the German Navy. The supercargo brought it aboard at Pernambuco."

Matt Peasley, the Yankee, came to life at that. "Has that been confiscated, too?" he queried.

"No, captain. However, we have confiscated that German crew of yours——"

"Hallelujah!" yelled Cappy Ricks.

"—— and loaned you a crew of British seamen from the tramp *Surrey Maid*. The *Scharnhorst* torpedoed her off the coast of Chile, and we found her crew on board one of the German transports when we captured them after the fleet was destroyed. You're all fixed up, from skipper to cabin boy——"

"Wireless operator, too?" Matt Peasley cried.

The consul nodded. "He's got a steady job," the youthful president declared, and turned to Cappy Ricks for confirmation of this edict. But Cappy, the pious old codger, had bowed his head on his breast and they heard him mutter:

"O Lord, I thank Thee! All unworthy as I am, Lord, thou loadest me with favors—including a wireless plant, free gratis!"

CHAPTER XXII

Long after the British consul had departed Cappy Ricks sat alone in his office, dozing. Presently he roused and rang for Mr. Skinner.

"Skinner," he said, "Matt reports that the late Riggins made an allotment of his wages to his wife when he shipped aboard the *Narcissus?*"

"Yes, sir."

"Riggins's wages hereafter shall constitute a charge against the *Narcissus* while Mrs. Riggins lives and while the Blue Star Navigation Company can afford to give up seventy dollars every month. Attend to it, Skinner. Another thing, Skinner."

"Yes, sir."

"We ought to do something for Murphy and Reardon. Now then, Skinner, you've never had a chance to be a sport heretofore, but you're a stockholder in the Blue Star Navigation Company now, and as such I feel that I should not use my position, as owner of a controlling interest in the stock of the company, to give away the property of the company in an arbitrary fashion. So I'm going to leave it up to you, Skinner, to suggest what we shall do for them. I believe you will agree with me that we should do something very handsome by those two boys."

"Quite so, sir, quite so. Well, to start off with, Mr. Ricks, I think we ought to pay their hospital bills, if

any. Then I think we ought to give each of them a
handsome gold watch, suitably engraved and with a
small blue star—sapphires, you know—set in the front
of the case."

"You feel that would about fill the bill, eh, Skinner?"

"Well, next Christmas I think we ought to give them
each a month's salary."

"Hum! You do?"

"Yes, sir. I think that would be a very delicate
thing to do."

Cappy sighed. Poor Skinner! Victim of the saving
habit! Decent devil—didn't mean to be small, but just
couldn't help it. A bush-leaguer—Skinner. Never
meant for big company——

"In addition——" Skinner began.

"Yes, Skinner, my boy. Go on, go on, old horse.
Now then, in addition——"

"It seems like the wildest extravagance, Mr. Ricks,
but those men have fought for their ship and I—remember, Mr. Ricks, this is only a suggestion—I think
it would be a very—er—tactful thing to do to—
er——"

"It'll choke him before he gets it out," Cappy soliloquized. Aloud he said: "Go on, Skinner, my dear
boy. Don't be afraid."

"At a time like this, when freights are so good and
vessel property pays so well, it seems to me—that is,
if you and Matt have no objection—that we ought to
give Mike and Terence a—er—a little piece of the
Narcissus—the ship—er—they love—say—er—a—
ten-thousand-dollar interest—each——"

"God bless you, Skinner! You came through at last,

didn't you? The president emeritus agrees with you, Skinner, and it is so ordered.

"Now skip along and wireless the glad news to Mike and Terence. Tell them when they have the coal out to proceed to Rio and load manganese ore."

CHAPTER XXIII

IN due course Captain Michael J. Murphy and Mr.
Terence Reardon came off the dry dock, the sole
visible evidence of that unrecorded second naval engagement off the Falkland Islands being a slight list
to starboard on the part of the Reardon nose, and a
notch in Murphy's right ear. Mr. Skinner had had
a local jeweler prepare the presentation watches
against the day of the home-coming of the warriors
of the Blue Star, and on a Saturday night Cappy
gave a banquet to Mike and Terence, and every employee of the Ricks' interests who could possibly attend, was present to do the doughty pair honor and
cheer when the awards for valor were duly made by
Cappy and congratulatory speeches made by Mr.
Skinner and Matt Peasley. It was such a gala occasion that Cappy drank three cocktails, battened
down by a glass or two of champagne, and as a result
was ill for two days thereafter. When he recovered,
he announced sadly and solemnly that he was about to
retire—forever; that nothing of a business nature
should ever be permitted to drag him back into the
harness again. Then he bade all of his employees a
touching farewell, packed his golf clubs, and disappeared in the general direction of Southern California.
He was away so long that eventually even the skeptical
Mr. Skinner commenced to wonder if, perchance, the

age of miracles had not yet passed and Cappy had really retired.

Alas! On the morning of December 24th, Cappy suddenly appeared at the office, his kindly old countenance aglow like a sunrise on the Alps. Immediately he cited Mr. Skinner to appear with the payrolls of all of the Ricks enterprises and show what cause, if any, existed, why there should not be a general whooping up of salaries to the deserving all along the line. The Ricks Lumber & Logging Company had already declared a Christmas dividend; the accounts of every ship in the Blue Star fleet had been made up to date and a special Christmas dividend declared, and, in accordance with ancient custom, Cappy had appeared to devote one day in the year to actual labor. Christmas dividend checks and checks covering Christmas presents to his employees were always signed by him; it was his way of letting the recipients know that, although retired, he still kept a wary eye on his affairs.

He had writer's cramp by the time he finished, but while the spending frenzy was on him he would take no rest; so he seized a pencil and, while Mr. Skinner called off the names of the deserving and the length of time each had spent in the Ricks service, Cappy scrawled a five, a ten or a twenty beside each name. Thus, in time, they came to the first name on the Blue Star pay roll.

"Matthew Peasley, president; salary, ten thousand dollars a year; length of service, four months," Mr. Skinner intoned. "How about a raise for Captain Matt?"

Cappy laid down his pencil and looked at Skinner over the rims of his spectacles.

"Skinner," he said gravely, "you're only drawing twelve thousand a year, and you've been with me twenty-five years! And here I'm giving this boy Matt ten thousand a year and he's been on the pay roll only four months. Why, it isn't fair!"

"Remember, he was three years in the Blue Star ships that——"

"Can't consider that at all when raising salaries. The salaries of ship's officers are fixed and immutable anyhow, and when considering raises for my employees I can take into consideration only the length of time they've been directly under my eye. Cut Matt's salary to five thousand a year and let him grow up with the business. His dividends from his Ricks L. & L. and Blue Star stock will keep him going, and he hasn't any household bills to keep up. He and Florry live with me, and I'm the goat."

"I fear Matt will not take kindly to that program, Mr. Ricks—particularly at this time, when every ship in the offshore fleet is paying for herself every voyage."

"Why?" Cappy demanded.

"Well," Mr. Skinner replied hesitatingly, "perhaps I have no business to tell you this, because the knowledge came to me quite by accident; but the fact of the matter is, Matt is going to build himself an auxiliary schooner——"

"Good news!" Cappy piped. "That's the ticket for soup! An auxiliary schooner with semi-Diesel engines, four masts and about a million-foot lumber capacity would be a mighty good investment right now. Every yard in the country that builds steel vessels is filled up with orders, but our coast shipyards can turn out wooden vessels in a hurry; and, with auxiliary power, they'll pay five hundred per cent on their cost before this flurry in shipping, due to the war, is over. I don't care, Skinner—provided he builds a ship that's big enough to go foreign——"

"But this isn't that kind," Mr. Skinner interrupted.

"No other kind will do, Skinner."

"This is to be a schooner yacht——"

"A what!" Cappy shrilled.

"A yacht—eighty-five feet over all——"

"Eighty-five grandmothers! Why, what the devil does that boy want of a yacht? How much money does he intend to put into her?"

"I do not know, Mr. Ricks; but we can be reasonably certain of one thing; Matt Peasley will not build a cheap boat. She'll have a lot of gewgaws and gadgets, teak rail, mahogany joiner-work—at the very least, she'll cost him thirty thousand dollars."

"Skinner," Cappy declared solemnly, "he might as well put the money in a sack, go down to Clay Street Wharf and throw the money overboard! The other night I saw a couple of soldiers having a pleasant time in a shooting gallery, but what the president of the Blue Star Navigation Company wants with a thirty-thousand-dollar yacht beats my time. Why, he has more than thirty good vessels to play with all week, and yet he wants a yacht for Sunday! Skinner, my dear boy, that is wild, wanton extravagance."

"Well, I dare say Matt thinks he can afford the extravagance."

"Skinner, no man can afford it. Extravagance may reach a point where it becomes sinful. And I say it's a crime to put thirty thousand dollars into a yacht when the same thirty thousand, invested in a good vessel, will yield such tremendous returns. Skinner, my boy, how did you find out about this yacht nonsense?"

"I was looking through Matt's desk for a letter I had given him to read, and I ran across the plans. Thinking they were Blue Star plans, I looked them over; there was a letter from the naval architect attached——"

Cappy threw down his pencil.

"By the Holy Pink-Toed Prophet," he cried in deep disgust, "I thought I was going to have a Merry Christmas—and now it's spoiled! Good Lord, Skinner! To think of a man throwing away thirty thousand dollars, not to mention the upkeep and interest after he's thrown it away——"

"You've just this very day thrown away about thirty thousand dollars you didn't have to," Mr. Skinner reminded him.

"I do have to. I've got to keep all my boys happy and satisfied and up on their toes, or what the devil would happen to us? They're my partners when all is said and done, and how am I going to face my Maker if I don't give my partners a square deal? There's a vast difference between justice and extravagance. Skinner, you don't suppose Matt's like every other shellback of a skipper? Why, he's only twenty-five years old; and if he's got the blue-water fever again, after a year ashore, there'll be no standing him at thirty."

"Well, he's got it, sir," Mr. Skinner opined firmly. "Did you ever see an old sailing skipper that didn't get it? You remember Burns, who had the *Sweet Alferetta?* His father died and left him a million dollars, and five years later he came sneaking in here one day, told you he was tired clipping coupons and that if you wanted to save his life you'd give him back the *Sweet Alferetta* and a hundred dollars a month to skipper her! He sold his interest to his successor for two thousand dollars when he fell into the fortune—and five years later he bought it back for three thousand, just so he could have a job again."

"Yes," Cappy admitted; "they all get the blue-water fever—after they've left blue water. I never knew a sailor yet who wouldn't tell you sailoring was a dog's life; but I never knew one who quit and quite recovered from the hankering to go back. I think you're right, Skinner. This yacht is just a symptom of Matt's disease. He realizes his business interests tie him to the beach; but if he has a sailing yacht that he can fuss round with on week-ends in the bay, and once in a while make a little cruise to Puget Sound or the Gulf of Lower California, he figures he'll manage to survive."

Mr. Skinner nodded.

"Speaking of yachts," Cappy continued, "the case of old Cap'n Cliff Ashley suggests a cure for this boy Matt. Cap'n Cliff was a Gloucester fisherman, with the smartest little schooner that ever came home from the Grand Banks with halibut up to her hatches. He couldn't read or write and he'd never learned navigation; but he'd been born with the instincts of a homing pigeon, and somehow whenever he pointed his schooner toward Gloucester he managed to arrive on schedule; and any time he got a good fair breeze from the west, like as not he'd run over to England and sell his catch there.

"Like most of his breed, Cap'n Cliff had to have a fast boat; he had to keep her as immaculate as a yacht in order to be happy, and he was never so happy as when he'd meet a squadron of the New York Yacht Club out on a cruise and sail circles round the flagship with his little old knockabout fish schooner. On such occasions old Cap'n Cliff would break out a long red burgee with M. O. B. Y. C. in white letters on it. On one of his trips to England he hooked up with a big schooner wearing the ensign of the Royal Yacht Club and dassed 'em to race with him.

"Well, sir, it happened that the late King Edward was aboard his yacht that day, and you know what a sport he was in his palmy days. Cap'n Cliff cracked on everything he had in the way of plain sail and, after holding the King even for a couple of hours, he put his packet under gaff topsails and fisherman's staysail and broke out the balloon jib, bade Edward good-bye in the International Code—and flew! About six hours after Cap'n Cliff came to anchor, the King loafed up in his yacht, dropped anchor, cleared away his launch, and came over to visit Cap'n Cliff and shake hands with him.

" 'My dear sir,' says Edward, pointing aloft to the red burgee with M. O. B. Y. C. on it, 'pray to what yacht club do you belong?'

" 'My own bloomin' yacht club, your majesty,' says Cap'n Cliff; and if he hadn't been a Yankee fisherman the King would have knighted him on the spot!

"And that remark, Skinner, my dear boy, clears the atmosphere in the case of our own dear Matthew. He shall have his own blooming yacht club, only his yacht shall carry cargo and pay her way."

"You mean——"

"I mean I'm going to send him to sea for one voyage, once a year, which will break up that blue-water fever and save Matt thirty thousand dollars as an initial investment, and about ten thousand a year upkeep and interest. All that boy needs to cure him, Skinner, is the old *Retriever*, totally surrounded by horizon and smelling of a combination of tarred rope, turpentine, wet canvas, fresh paint, green lumber and the stink of the bilge water. Lordy me, Skinner, it puts them to sleep and they wake up feeling perfectly bully! Where's the *Retriever* now, Skinner, and who is in charge of her destinies?"

"She's due on Puget Sound from the West Coast. Captain Lib Curtis has her."

"Good news! Well, now, Skinner, you listen to me: The minute he reports his arrival you wire Lib to put the old harridan on dry dock and slick her up until she looks like four aces and a king, with everybody in the game standing pat. Can't have any whiskers on her bottom when Matt takes her out, Skinner, because if the boy's to enjoy himself she's got to be able to show a clean pair of heels. Then write Lib to wire his resignation and give any old reason for it. Have him resign just before the vessel is loaded and ready for sea, and tell him to insist on being relieved immediately. Of course, Skinner, Matt will get busy right away, looking for the right skipper to relieve Captain Curtis —and about that time the president emeritus will shove in his oar and ball things up. Every doggoned skipper Matt recommends for the job is going to have his application vetoed by Alden P. Ricks, and—er—ahem! Harumph-h-h!"

"Yes, Mr. Ricks."

"And you stick by me, Skinner. Follow all my leads and don't trump any of my aces; and just about the time Matt begins to get good and mad at my doggoned interference—you know, Skinner, my boy, I'm only a figurehead—you cut in and say: 'Well, for heaven's sake! You two still squabbling over a skipper for the *Retriever?* Matt, why don't you save the demurrage and take her out yourself—eh?'" And Cappy winked knowingly and prodded his general manager in the ribs.

"I guess that plan's kind of poor—eh, Skinner? I guess it won't work—eh? Particularly when I come right back and say: 'Well, he might as well, for all the use he is round this office. Here I go to work and appoint him president of the Blue Star and he won't stay in the office and 'tend to the president's business. Yes, sir! Leaves all that to you and me, Skinner, while he degrades himself doing the work of a port captain.'"

"All of which is quite true, Mr. Ricks," Mr. Skinner affirmed. "He will not stay in the office—and he's getting worse. Two-thirds of his time is spent round the docks."

"Well, two-thirds of his time in 1915 will not be spent round the docks, Skinner. Play that bet to win! We're going to have a busy old year in the shipping game in 1915, and a busier one in 1916 if that war in Europe isn't over by then. A voyage in the *Retriever* will fix the boy up, Skinner, and he'll stick round the office and put over some real business. Yachts! Hah! What does a business man want of a yacht?"

"You overlooked one very important detail, Mr. Ricks," Skinner ventured.

"I overlook nothing, Skinner—nothing. His wife shall accompany him on the voyage. I shall implant the idea in her head, beginning this very night as soon as I get home. I'll just tell her she isn't and never will be a true sailor's true love until she takes a voyage with her husband. Romantic girl, Florry! She'll about eat that suggestion, feathers and all, Skinner. She'll do the real work for us. Always remember, my boy, that an ounce of promotion is worth enough perspiration to float the *Narcissus*."

"But what shall we do for a port captain?"

"I've ordered Mike Murphy—via Matt, of course—to take a vacation under full salary and recover from the wounds he received walloping that German crew on the *Narcissus*. About the time Matt leaves in the *Retriever*, Mike will be ready to go to work again or commit murder if we don't give it to him; so we'll slip him a temporary appointment as port captain. I'm going to make it permanent some day, anyhow. I suppose you've noticed that Mike Murphy has a crush on your stenographer; and I don't see how he's going to put anything over if he never gets a chance to see the girl!"

"I really hadn't noticed it, Mr. Ricks."

"If it was a ten-cent piece you'd notice it," Cappy retorted. "And now that matter is settled, how about this port steward? Is he a grafter? If not, raise him five dollars a month. He's been with us only a year."

Late that afternoon, after Cappy had made the rounds of his office, distributing his checks and wishing all hands the merriest of Christmases, he paused at last at Mr. Skinner's desk and laid a thousand-dollar check thereon.

"Not a peep out of you, Skinner—not a peep!" he cautioned his general manager. "No thanks due me. You've earned it a thousand times over—and then some. Hum-m! Ahem! Harumph-h-h! By the way, Skinner, my dear boy, I forgot to mention to you another little idea that's in the back of my head."

"You mean about sending Matt to sea for a voyage?"

"Exactly. The sea is a wonderful institution, Skinner—wonderful! It promotes health and strength; and—er—damn it, Skinner, my dear boy, have you ever observed that there isn't a married skipper in our employ that hasn't been lucky? Many well-known authorities prescribe a sea voyage——"

"What for, Mr. Ricks?"

Cappy thrust his thumb into Skinner's ribs, winked, bent low, and whispered:

"Too slow, Skinner; too slow. I'm getting old, you know—I can't wait for ever. And if the experiment succeeds—Skinner, my dear boy, you're next! You've been married more than a year now——"

"I fail to comprehend——"

"Grandson!" Cappy whispered. "Grandson!"

"Oh!" said Mr. Skinner.

CHAPTER XXIV

One of the remarks most frequently heard on California Street was to the effect that whenever Cappy Ricks girded up his loins and went after something he generally got it. His scheme to get Matt Peasley to sea for one voyage, accompanied by Florry, worked as smoothly as a piston; and on the fifteenth of January the Peasleys went aboard the *Retriever* at Bellingham and towed out, bound for Manila with a cargo of fir lumber. Matt made the run down in sixty-six days, a smart passage, waited a week in Manila Bay before he could secure a berth and commence discharging, discharged in a week, loaded a cargo of hemp, with a deckload of hardwood logs, and was ready for the return trip to San Francisco on April twenty-fourth, on which day he towed out past Corregidor.

His wife, however, was not with him on the return voyage. Following a family conference, it was decided that Florry should return home on the mail steamer—which action Cappy Ricks considered most significant when Matt apprised him of it by cable, but failed to state a reason. The president emeritus, immediately upon receipt of this information, trotted into Mr. Skinner's office and laid Matt Peasley's cablegram on the latter's desk.

"Well, Skinner, my dear boy," he piped, rubbing his

hands together the while, "what do you know about that?"

"Do you—er—suspect—er—something, Mr. Ricks?"

"Suspect? Not a bit of it. I know! Neither Florry nor Matt would dream of permitting the other to come home alone if there wasn't a third party to be considered. Paste that in your hat, Skinner. It isn't done."

Cappy was right, for the same steamer that bore his daughter home carried also a brief letter from his son-in-law conveying the tidings of great joy. The old man was so happy he went into Mr. Skinner's office and struck his general manager a terrible blow between the shoulders, after which he declared it was a shame that his years and reputation for respectability denied him the privilege of chartering a seagoing hack and painting the town red!

The *Retriever* crept slowly up the China Sea on the first of the southwest monsoon. At that period of the year, however, the monsoon is weak and unsteady; and after clearing the northern end of Luzon the *Retriever* kicked round in a belt of light and baffling airs for a week. Then the monsoon freshened somewhat and the *Retriever* once more rolled lazily away on her course, with young Matt Peasley humming chanteys on her quarter-deck and pondering the mystery that confronts all mankind in their first adventure in fatherhood. Would it be a boy or a girl? He was expressing to himself for perhaps the thousandth time the hope that it would be a boy, when from the poop he saw something he did not relish.

It was the ship's cat coming across the deckload toward him, in his yellow eyes a singularly pleased expression and in his mouth a singularly large rat.

Matt Peasley stepped below, found an old glove and drew it over his right hand, after which he returned to the quarter-deck.

"Come, Tommy!" he called; and pussy came, to be seized by the tail and, still holding fast to his prey, cast overboard.

"It's bad luck to do that to a black cat, sir," the mate informed him.

Matt Peasley's eyes were blazing.

"And it's worse luck still for any mate aboard my ship who neglects to put the rat-guards on the lines when the vessel is lying at the dock," he growled. "You lubberly idiot!"

"But I did put the rat-guards on the lines," the mate protested.

"Yes, I know you did; but I had to remind you of it," Matt replied. "You didn't get them on in time—and now the Lord only knows how many rats we have aboard. Ordinarily I don't mind rats, but an Oriental rat is something to be afraid of."

"Why, sir?"

"Because they carry the germs of bubonic plague, you farmer!" And Matt very carefully removed his glove and cast it overboard after the cat. "And it's a cold day when you can't find an occasional case of plague in the Orient. The cat caught the rat and mauled it round; hence the cat had to go, because I never permit in my cabin a cat that has been on intimate terms with an Oriental rat. And now I bet I know what's wrong with that fo'castle hand that went into the sick bay the day before yesterday. He complained of swelling in the glands of his neck and groins."

The cook left the forward deckhouse and came aft over the deckload. At the break of the poop he paused.

"Captain Peasley," he announced, "Lindstrom is dead."

"Tell everybody to keep away from him," Matt ordered. He turned to the mate. "Mr. Matson," he announced, "the first duty of a murderer is to get rid of the body. Go forward and throw Lindstrom's body overboard; then stay forward. If you come aft until I send for you I'll blow your brains out!"

CHAPTER XXV

When the *Retriever* was out from Manila seventy days Cappy Ricks remarked to Mr. Skinner that Matt would be breezing in most any day now. On the eightieth day he remarked to Mr. Skinner that Matt was coming home a deal slower than he had gone out. The efficient Skinner, however, cited so many instances of longer passages from Manila to San Francisco that Cappy was comforted, although he was not convinced. "You make me a type-written list of all those vessels and their passages, Skinner," he cautioned; "and when you can't think of any more authentic cases fake up a few. Florry's beginning to worry. She knows now what it means to be a sailor's wife, and if that doggoned Matt doesn't report soon I'll know what it means to be a sailor's father-in-law. I wish to Jimminy I hadn't sent Matt out with the *Retriever*."

Ninety days passed. Cappy commenced to fidget. A hundred days passed, and Cappy visited the hydrographic office and spent a long time poring over charts of the air currents in the China Sea, along the coast of Asia and in the North Pacific.

"Skinner, my dear boy," he quavered when he returned to the office; "I'm a most unhappy old man."

Mr. Skinner forgot for an instant that he was a business man and, with a sudden, impulsive movement, he put his long, thin arm round the old man and squeezed him.

170

"If you didn't think so much of him, sir," he comforted Cappy, "you'd worry less. She really will not be overdue until she's out a hundred and twenty days."

"Skinner," Cappy piped wearily, "don't try to deceive me. I've been in the shipping game for forty-odd years, boy. I know it's about six thousand miles from San Francisco to Manila, and if a vessel averages ninety miles a day she's making a smart passage. Matt made it down in sixty-six days, and he ought to come back in sixty, because he has fair winds all the way. Skinner, the boy's a month overdue; and if he never shows up—if he stays out much longer— Florry'll break her heart; and my grandson—think of it, Skinner!—think of the prenatal effect on the child! Oh, Skinner, my dear, dear boy, I want him big and light-hearted and sunny-souled like Matt—and to think this is all my doing—my own daughter! Oh! Oh, Skinner, my heart is breaking!"

Mr. Skinner fled to his own office and did something most un-Skinner-like. He blinked away several large bright tears; and while he was blinking them the telephone bell rang. Mechanically Mr. Skinner answered. It was Jerry Dooley, in charge of the Merchants' Exchange.

"Mr. Skinner," said Jerry, "I've got some bad news for you."

"The—the—*Retriever*——" Skinner almost whispered.

"Yes, sir. I thought I'd tell you first, so you could break it to the old man gently. The Grace liner *Ecudorian* arrived at Victoria this morning and reports speaking the *Retriever* eight hundred miles off the coast of Formosa. The vessel was under jib, lower topsail, foretopmast staysail, mainsail and spanker. She was flying two flags—an inverted ensign and the yellow quarantine flag. The *Ecudorian* steamed close alongside of her, to windward. Captain Peasley was at the wheel——"

"Thank God!" Mr. Skinner almost sobbed. "What was wrong with her, Jerry? Hurry up, man! Hurry up! Tell me!"

"He was alone on the ship, Mr. Skinner. Bubonic plague! Killed the entire crew! Matt was the only man immune, and he's sailing the *Retriever* home alone!"

Mr. Skinner groaned.

"Good gracious Providence! Why didn't the *Ecudorian* take him off?"

"Credit them with offering it," Jerry replied. "He wouldn't come. He declined to jeopardize the people aboard the steamer and he wouldn't abandon the *Retriever* with her full cargo; so what could they do? They had to sail away without him."

Gently Mr. Skinner broke the news to Cappy Ricks; for, of course, the United Press dispatches had carried it to the later afternoon editions and it would be useless for Mr. Skinner to attempt to lie kindly. Cappy, with bowed head, heard him through; when finally he looked up at Skinner his eyes were dead.

"Quite what I expected of him, Skinner," he said dully. "And I'd rather have him die than dog it! This report from the *Ecudorian* helps some, Skinner. It will do to keep hope alive in my Florry—and every two weeks until the boy is born we'll—we'll——Oh, Skinner——"

"Yes, sir; I'll attend to it. Leave everything to me,

Mr. Ricks. I'll have wireless reports and telegrams and cablegrams from every port on earth telling of ships' having spoken the *Retriever*, with the skipper well and hearty, and sending messages of good cheer to his wife."

"You—you won't be—er—stingy, Skinner? You'll send out the *Tillicum* to find him and tow him in, won't you? And you'll have real telegrams—spend money, Skinner! I'll have to bring those messages home to Florry——"

"Everything, Mr. Ricks. And I'll start right in by slipping fifty dollars to each of the waterfront reporters on all the papers. They're good boys, Mr. Ricks. I'll tell them why I have to have the service. Mrs. Peasley must have our fake reports confirmed in the papers——"

"For work like that the marine reporters should have more money," Cappy suggested wearily. His old hand reached out gropingly, closed over Mr. Skinner's and held it a moment childishly. "You're a very great comfort to me, Skinner—very great indeed! And you'll come home with me to-night, won't you, Skinner? I'm a little afraid—I want you near me, Skinner—in case I can't get away with it to Florry."

His dry, dead eyes studied the pattern in the office carpet.

"Two mates, a cook and ten A. B.'s!" he murmured presently. "One man, even a Matt Peasley, cannot do the work of thirteen men. No, Skinner; it isn't done. One man simply cannot sail a barkentine."

But Mr. Skinner was not listening. He was on the long-distance phone calling the master of the *Tillicum*, just about finishing discharge of a cargo of nitrate at

San Pedro. And presently Cappy heard him speaking:
"Mr. Ricks, listen! Grant, of the *Tillicum*, says
Matt would go up the China Sea on the southwest
monsoon . . . Yes, captain. You say—ah, yes; quite
so . . . Grant says he'd edge over until he got into
the Japan Stream, and that would add a knot or two
an hour to his speed . . . Yes, Grant. Speak up!
. . . Grant says, Mr. Ricks, that about the middle of
September or the first of October Matt would run out
of the southwest monsoon into the northeast monsoon
—that's it, Grant, isn't it? He'd get them about off
Formosa, eh? . . . Yes, Grant. Then he'd run into
the prevailing westerly winds and run north on a great
circle about five hundred miles below the Aleutian
Islands—I see, Grant. All right! Fill your oil tanks
and take an extra supply on deck, head into the North
Pacific . . . Yes; use your own judgment, of course.
Mine's no good . . . Yes; and bring a lot of disin-
fectants and a doctor, so it'll be safe to put a few men
aboard when you find her and put your hawser on her
. . . Yes, Grant. If you find her you'll not have
reason to regret it. Good-bye! Good luck!"

"While the *Tillicum* is on this wild-goose chase,
Skinner," Cappy said wearily, "she is chartered by the
Blue Star Navigation Company to Alden P. Ricks
personally, at the prevailing rates. The stockholders
mustn't pay for my fancies, Skinner. You'll see to
that, won't you?"

CHAPTER XXVI

*Excerpt from the log of Captain Matt Peasley
relief skipper of the American barkentine Retriever; Manila to San Francisco.*

May Third.—Seaman Olaf Lindstrom died today, following an illness of thirty-six hours.
He was taken with chills and fever on the morning of
the second, complained of a severe headache and
vomited repeatedly. Removed him from the forecastle
to a spare room in the forward house, which on the
Retriever has always been used as a sick bay. While
being supported along the deck he collapsed, and when
the mate undressed him and put him to bed he complained of soreness in his groins. I examined them
and found them slightly swollen. Treated him for
ague—calomel, salts, quinine and whisky, and one-
fortieth-grain strychnine hypodermic solution to keep
up his heart action when the fever registered one
hundred and four and higher. He grew steadily worse.
Could not find anything in my Home Book of Medicine
that exactly described his symptoms, and was at a loss
to diagnose Lindstrom's case until I discovered the
ship's cat with a rat it had just killed.

There were no rats aboard the *Retriever* when she
left San Francisco. I recalled that the first night we
tied up to the dock in Manila a dirty little China Coast
tramp lay just ahead of us; and as I passed her on

my way uptown I saw a rat run down her gangplank.
She had rat-guards on her mooring lines. We had just
tied up to the dock and I returned immediately and
instructed the mate to be sure to put the rat-guards on
our mooring lines, and not to use any sort of gangplank. When I returned to the vessel later that night
I found that the mate had neglected to put on the rat-
guards and logged him for it. Before we left the dock
a Chinaman died of bubonic plague aboard that tramp,
and the port health authorities put the vessel in quarantine immediately and prevented further spread of the
disease.

When I saw the ship's cat with a rat, therefore, I
knew we had some of that rotten China Coaster's
plague rats aboard. Accordingly threw cat and rat
overboard just as the cook announced Lindstrom's
death. Upon looking up the information on plague, I
am now convinced we have it aboard—that Lindstrom
died of it. First Mate Olaf Matson wrapped himself in
my old bathrobe, gloved his hands and threw Lindstrom's body overboard, following it with the gloves
and bathrobe.

I am, in a measure, prepared for plague. When I
learned we had lain close to a vessel with a case of
plague aboard I laid in some plague medicine, on general principles and just to have an anchor out to
windward. At the English drug store on the Escolta
I bought a tiny bottle of Yersin's Antipest Serum and
another of Haffkine's Prophylactic Fluid. It was all
they had on hand and it wasn't much; but—it is enough
to save me—and I intend to be saved if possible. I
cannot afford to die now. I do not know how old the
Haffkine's Fluid is; and the older it is, the longer it

takes to render one immune. The antipest serum will render me immune immediately, but the duration of the immunity thus granted lasts, at the most, only fifteen days. I must, therefore, first take a hypodermic injection of antipest serum to render me immune immediately and the next day follow with an injection of Haffkine's Fluid, which gives permanent immunity, but not for a week or longer when used alone.

There is this devilish thing about it to be considered, however: I may at this moment be inoculated with plague, for the period of incubation is from three to seven days—and I've fondled that cat every day since we left Manila. If I am already infected and do not know it, and while in that condition take an injection of the antipest serum, the book says the serum will immediately bring on a fatal and virulent attack of the plague! On the other hand, if I am not inoculated and take the antipest serum I am safe.

The question before the house, therefore, is: Shall I take it or shall I not? And if I do take it shall I be saving my life or committing suicide? I am like the fellow in the story who was forced to drink from one of two glasses of wine. He knew one of them contained poison, but he didn't know which one it was! I shall make my will and flip a coin to decide the issue.

May Fourth.—Two a.m. Mate reports another sick man in the forecastle. Wish I had some formaldehyde gas. Have told mate to sprinkle chloride of lime in Lindstrom's bunk and to dust the walls and floors of the forecastle and sick bay with it. That is the only disinfectant I have aboard in quantity.

At midnight I flipped the coin—heads I'd take it; tails I wouldn't. The coin fell heads—and I took it.

Four a.m.—Mustered the crew and gave them a lecture on bubonic plague. I have sufficient antipest serum for four men. After explaining that it was Hobson's choice, I asked the men to draw matches, held in the hand of the first mate, to see who should be the lucky ones. They all decided to take a chance and go without it, with the exception of two seamen and the mates, who, learning that I had taken it, decided to follow suit. Accordingly I inoculated them with the antipest serum.

Five p.m.—Inoculated myself with Haffkine's Fluid.

Seven-thirty.—Seaman Ross died. Mr. Matson threw the body overboard. No services.

Midnight.—Mr. Matson is down with it.

May Fifth.—Mr. Matson very ill and delirious. Cook moping round like a drunken man; complains of severe headache. Wind blowing lightly from southwest. Everything set. Inoculated second mate and the two seamen with Haffkine's.

May Sixth.—Mr. Matson died at noon today. Cook down with it; also another seaman, and Mr. Eccles, the second mate. Have altered ship's course and am running for Hongkong. Winds light and baffling. Have not made thirty miles today. Calm at midnight. Mr. Eccles died just as the watches were being changed. I now feel that I have escaped; so examined Mr. Eccles' body. He went so fast I am curious. No swelling of the glands at all. Am inclined to think his was pneumonic or septicæmic. Threw him overboard myself.

May Seventh.—Light and baffling airs all day; monsoon blowing in weak puffs. Another seaman ill. So ends this day.

May Eighth.—Cook died at noon. No buboes on him either. He turned kind of black. I was chief undertaker. No airs to speak of. Ship barely making steerage way. So ends this day.

May Ninth.—Seaman Peterson died early this morning. Do not know exact hour. Found him dead in his berth. Another funeral; no services. Monsoon freshening. Made forty-eight miles today. Two more seamen on sick report; and, to add to my worries, they are the very two I inoculated with the antipest serum and Haffkine's. Is this stuff worthless?

May Tenth.—Seamen Halloran and Kaiser died within an hour of each other this evening—Halloran at nine-thirty and Kaiser at ten-eighteen. Put both bodies overboard immediately.

I have four seamen left, and am doing the cooking, navigating, nursing and undertaking. Wind freshening hourly. Made seventy-two miles today. Glad Florry and Cappy Ricks cannot see me now, although, for some fool reason, I have a notion I shall see them again. If I were going to get plague it would have developed before now. I feel quite safe, but most unhappy and worried.

Midnight.—Seaman Anderson down with it. Jumped overboard to save me the bother of throwing him overboard about the day after to-morrow, which is a courtesy I did not expect of Anderson. I am obliged to him. I am exhausted and so are my three remaining seamen. We cannot handle the canvas now, so have taken in the foresail, royals, and topgallant sails, hauled down the flying jib and got the gaff topsail off her, leaving her under the jib, fore-topmast staysail, upper and lower fore-topsails, main-topmast staysail, mainsail and spanker. Hove her to and turned in.

May Eleventh.—After a horrible breakfast, which I cooked, got under way again. Monsoon blowing nicely, but under the small amount of canvas I am forced to carry cannot make more than six miles an hour. Have decided not to run to Hongkong. If I am to lose my three remaining seamen I shall have lost them long before I sight land, and the tug or steamer that hooks on to me off Hongkong will stick me with a terrific salvage bill. If I'm going to be stuck I prefer to be stuck closer to home, and if I manage to keep these three men the four of us can sail her home. I'll take a chance and run up the coast of Asia with the Japan Stream until I reach the northeast monsoon. I'm certain to be spoken and can send word to Florry. In a pinch, at this season of the year, I can sail her home alone.

May Fifteenth.—I am alone on the ship. Into the Japan Stream, monsoon blowing the sweetest it ever blew. Lucky thing for me I had the forethought to trim her down; otherwise I should have had to cut away a lot of canvas. And how Cappy Ricks would scream at the sail bill later on! We were hove to over-night when Borden and Jacobsen died, on the thirteenth. McBain complained of a headache and vertigo on the morning of the fourteenth; so I laid to until he died, last night. I was not with him when he passed. What good would it have done? I had breakfast; and after breakfast I found him in his berth, dead. I tossed him overboard, and every last rag of clothing, dunnage and blankets aboard, with the exception of those in my own cabin. Then I burned sulphur in the forecastle, the galley, the cook's room and the stateroom formerly occupied by the mates, closed the doors, and hoped for the best. Slept a lot that day and night; and at eight this morning slacked off my spanker and main sheets, checked in my foreyard and topsail by taking the the braces to the donkey engine, and was off for home.

Have established my commissary in the lee of the wheel box. Set up a small kerosene stove I found in the storeroom, and get along nicely. It is quite an art to fry eggs with one hand and steady the wheel with the other, but I managed it three times today. To-morrow I will cook enough at breakfast to last me for luncheon and supper; hence will only have to heat some coffee.

Logged fifty-one miles by eight o'clock; then lashed the wheel and let her take care of herself while I got steam up in the donkey and hauled in my spanker and mainsail; then I slacked off my foreyard and topsail yards, hove her to on the port tack, hung three red lights on the forestay to show she wasn't under command, set my alarm clock and turned in. I have to smile at the ease with which one man—provided he is a sizable man and able to stand strain—can sail a barkentine before the wind in fair weather. I am not worried. I am not going to have bubonic plague. It is horribly lonely, but I am due for fair winds—and I should worry.

Even if I should get a blow and have to take the lower topsail off her, I can lower the yard by the topsail halyards until it rests on the cap; then I'll skip aloft and run a knife along the head of the topsail and let it whip to glory. After that it may blow and be damned! All the clothes the old girl is wearing now will never take the sticks out of her. I've trimmed her down to jib, lower topsail, fore-topmast staysail, mainsail and spanker. Wish I dared carry the foresail. However, I must play safe. It is awful, though, to be in a ship as fast as the *Retriever* and have to crawl the way I'm crawling. Crawl all day and sleep all night! Well, sometimes I can crawl all day and night and sleep half a day. We shall see. I used to be able to stand considerable before I hit the beach and got soft. The necessity for firing the donkey every night would soon exhaust my fuel supply; but I have a deck-load of hardwood logs!

CHAPTER XXVII

Four months had passed since the *Ecudorian* had spoken Matt Peasley off the coast of Formosa; during that period no further news had been received in Cappy Ricks' office, although the diligent Skinner, aided and abetted by the waterfront reporters, managed to have a piece of cheering information for Florry about every two weeks. And, in order to forestall any possibility of some garrulous girl friend, with a male relative in the shipping business, "spilling the beans," as Cappy expressed it, the old man had taken a house in the country, and came to the office only twice a week to mourn for his lost Matthew and glean what little comfort he could from the empty words of hope Mr. Skinner dispensed so lavishly.

"If we can only keep Florry buoyed up with hope until the baby comes!" Cappy would groan. "She's worried; but, strange to say, Skinner, she hasn't the slightest idea he's in any danger. Those fake cablegrams and reports of ships speaking Matt—each time closer to home—have done the trick, Skinner. Of course the boy's dead, and I killed him; but Florry— well, she took a trip on the *Retriever* and knows how safe she is, and I've had a lot of old sailing skippers down to visit me, and primed them to tell her just how they would get away with such a proposition as Matt's —and how easy it would be. Besides, she knows Matt had some plague prophylactic aboard——"

"Yes; and I've told her she mustn't show the white feather—for your sake," Mr. Skinner interrupted; "and I think she's sensible enough to know she mustn't permit herself to show it—for the baby's sake."

Cappy bowed his head and shook like a hooked fish.

"When the baby's two weeks old I'll tell her," he moaned. "Oh, Skinner, Skinner, my dear boy, this is going to kill me! I won't last long now, Skinner. All my fault! I had to go butting in. That girl's heart is breaking with anxiety. When she comes down to breakfast, Skinner, I can see she's been crying all night."

"Horrible!" Mr. Skinner murmured. "Horrible! We can only hope."

On the twelfth of September Florry's baby was born. It was a boy, and a bouncing boy at that; and Cappy Ricks forgot for the moment he had rendered that baby fatherless, and came up to the city to report the news to Skinner.

"Well, Skinner, my dear boy," he announced with just a touch of his old-time jauntiness, "little Matthew just arrived! Everything lovely."

Mr. Skinner was about to formulate suitable phrases of congratulation when the telephone bell rang. It was Jerry Dooley up at the Merchants' Exchange; and he was all excitement.

"Hey, Skinner," he cried. "The *Retriever* is passing in!"

"No!" Mr. Skinner shrieked. "It isn't possible!"

"It is! She's coming in the Gate now—she's right under the lookout's telescope; and there's only one man on deck——"

Mr. Skinner turned to Cappy Ricks, put his arms

round him and jerked the old man from one end of the
office to the other.

"He's safe, he's safe, he's safe, he's safe!" he howled
indecorously. "Matt's sailing her in. He's sailing
her in——"

"You scoundrel!" Cappy shrilled. "Be quiet! Is
she sailing in or towing——"

"She's sailing in."

Cappy Ricks slumped down in his chair, his arms
hanging weakly at his sides.

"Yes, Skinner," he barely whispered, "Matt's alive,
after all. Nobody else would have the consummate
crust to sail her in but him. Any other skipper under
heaven would have hove to off the lightship and sent in
word by the pilot boat to send out a tug. Oh, Lord, I
thank Thee! I'm a wicked, foolish, bone-headed old
man; but Lord, I do thank Thee—I do, indeed!"

Half an hour later Cappy Ricks and Mr. Skinner,
in a fast motorboat, came flying up the bay and caught
sight of the *Retriever* loafing lazily past Fort Mason.
On she came, with a tiny bone in her teeth; and suddenly, as Cappy peered ahead through the spray that
flew in over the bows of the launch and drenched him
to the skin, the *Retriever's* mainsail was lowered rapidly. The vessel was falling off by the time the mainsail was down and Cappy and Mr. Skinner saw Matt
run aft, steady the wheel and bring the vessel up on
the wind again. She was now under spanker and the
headsails. Matt lashed the wheel and again ran forward, pausing at the main-topmast-staysail halyards
to cast them off and permit the sail to come down by
the run.

On to the topgallant forecastle Matt Peasley leaped,

praising his Maker for patent anchors on the *Retriever*. With a hammer he knocked out the stopper; the starboard anchor dropped and the red rust flew from her hawsepipe as the anchor chain screamed through it. With his hand on the compressor of the windlass, Matt Peasley snubbed her gently to the forty-five fathom shackle, cast off his jib halyards to let the jib slide down the stay by its own weight, raced aft, and gently lowered the spanker as the American barkentine *Retriever*, with the yellow flag flying at the fore, swung gently to anchor on the quarantine grounds, two hundred and twenty-one days from Manila.

Cappy Ricks turned to his general manager.

"Pretty work, Skinner!" he said huskily. "I guess there's nothing wrong with that boy's health. Damn! The quarantine boat will beat us to it! Matt's throwing the Jacob's ladder over the side for them."

"We can't board her until she passes quarantine——" Mr. Skinner began; but Cappy silenced him with a terrible look.

"The word can't, Skinner, was eliminated from my vocabulary some fifty years ago. We can—and I will! You needn't; but I've simply got to! Hey, you!"—to the launchman—"kick her wide open and show some speed."

Despite the warning cries from the quarantine officers in the health boat, the launch ran in along the *Retriever's* side; Cappy Ricks grasped the Jacob's ladder as the launch rasped by and climbed up with an agility that caused Mr. Skinner to marvel. As his silk hat appeared over the *Retriever's* rail a wind-bitten, bewhiskered, gaunt, hungry-looking semi-savage

(Excerpt from the log of Cap't Matt Peasley:)

"I am alone on the ship—all the rest are now dead"—

reached down, grasped him under the arms, snaked
him inboard and hugged him to his heart.

Silence for a minute, while Cappy Ricks' thin old
shoulders shook and heaved as from some internal
spasm, and Matt Peasley's big brown hand patted
Cappy's back. Presently he said:

"Well, father-in-law——"

From somewhere in Matt Peasley's whiskers Cappy's
voice came plaintively:

"Not father-in-law, sonny. New title—this morning—six o'clock—nine—pounds—grandfather! Eh?
Yes; grandfather! Grandpa Ricks!"

"Boy or girl?" Matt Peasley roared, and shook the
newly-elected grandfather.

"Boy! Florry—fine—never lost hope!"

A port health officer came over the rail. He shook
an admonitory finger at Cappy Ricks.

"Hey, you! Old man, you're under arrest—that is,
you're in quarantine, and you'll have to stay aboard
this ship until she's fumigated. Yes; and we'll fumi-
gate you, too. Whadje mean by coming aboard ahead
of us?"

"Cappy," Matt Peasley said, "tell that person to go
chase himself! Why, there hasn't been any plague
aboard the ship in nearly five months!"

Cappy looked up and wiped the tears of joy out of
his whiskers.

"Scoundrel!" he cackled. "Infernal young scoundrel! What do you mean by risking my *Retriever*, sailing her through the Gate with a crew of one man?"

"Take a look at me!" Matt laughed. "I'm all hands!
And didn't I prove I'm enough men to handle her? The
pilots wouldn't board me, and by sailing her in myself

I saved pilotage and salvage claims. I lost the lower topsail and the consignees are going to find a shortage in those hardwood logs; but that's all—except that I haven't had a decent meal in God knows when. Say, Cappy, what does he look like? A Peasley or a Ricks?"

"Both," Cappy chirped diplomatically. "Matt, are you all over the blue-water fever?"

"You bet!" he declared. "No more relief jobs for me. I've had plenty, although it might have been worse. It was lonely and sometimes I thought I was going crazy. Used to talk out loud to myself! I had some awful weather; but I just tucked her head under her wing and let her roll, and after I ran into the northeast monsoon, and later into the westerly winds, I had it easier and got more rest. You know, Cappy, when a ship is sailing on the wind, if you lash her helm a little bit below amidships she'll steer herself. Slow work, but—I got here; and, now that I'm here, I'm going to stay here.

"Of course, Cappy," he added, "I've just got to have something with sails to play with; but no more offshore sailing in mine—that is—well, I'm going to stay home for a long time—after a while, maybe—and meantime I'm going to build a little schooner yacht——"

"For the love of Mike, do!" Cappy pleaded. "I'll be stuck in quarantine with you for a couple of days and we'll kill time drawing up a rough set of plans. And when that schooner yacht is ready, Matt, I'll tell you what I want you to do."

"What, Cappy?"

"Send the bill to grandpa, Matthew!"

"If I hadn't been a case-hardened old fool I'd have

cheered you on when you wanted to build that schooner yacht last year. I'd have saved myself a world of grief."

He placed his hand gently on Matt's shoulder and his face was ineffably sad as he continued: "Of course, with you away and your fate undecided, as it were, Matt, that infernal Skinner wasn't worth two hoots in a hollow. Why, the boy flopped around the office like a rooster with its head off, and as a result I've had to come out of my retirement and keep an eye on things. Thank God, I can let go now. Really, Matt, you have no idea how I long to separate myself from the hurly-burly of California street. What I want is peace and seclusion——"

"You can have my share of that commodity for the remainder of my natural life," Matt laughed happily, "I want noise and people. I want screaming and yelling and fighting and risks and profits and losses and liars and scoundrels and honest men all inextricably mixed." He tossed his great sun-tanned arms above his head. "Lord, I want Life," he half shouted.

Cappy sighed. These young pups! When they grow to see life as old dogs——

"Well, Matt, all I've got to say is that the first man that butts into my private office and starts unloading a cargo of grief on me, is going to get busted between the eyes with a paper weight. I'm through with grief and woe. I don't give a hoot what happens to the world or anybody in it. I want peace and a rest. I can afford it and wouldn't I be a first-class idiot not to take it while the taking is good, Matt?"

"No more mixing in the shipping end, eh?" Matt asked hopefully.

Cappy raised his right hand solemnly. "Never again, Matt. I'm through with ships and sailors and cargoes and the whole cussed Blue Star fleet can sink and be damned to it, but I'll not lift a hand to save it. I'm THROUGH."

CHAPTER XXVIII

ALAS! Man proposes, but God disposes. Cappy had smoked his post-prandial cigar next day and was in the midst of his mid-afternoon siesta, when the buzzer on his desk waked him with its insistent buzzing. He reached for the telephone.

"My dear," he reproved his private exchange operator, "how often have I told you not to disturb me between two and three o'clock?"

"I knew you wouldn't mind being disturbed this afternoon, Mr. Ricks. Your old friend Mr. Gurney, of New York, is calling."

"Old Joe Gurney? By the Holy Pink-Toed Prophet! Show him in." Cappy was at the door to meet his visitor when the latter entered. Mr Joseph Gurney, senior partner of the firm of Gurney & Harlan, was, like Cappy Ricks, a shipping man and a Down-Easter. He and Cappy Ricks had been boyhood friends in Thomaston, Maine, and Gurney & Harlan were the agents and controlling owners of the Red Funnel Line plying between New York and ports on the West Coast.

"Well, Joe, you doddering old pirate!" cried Cappy Ricks affectionately. "Come in and rest your hands and feet. I'm tremendously glad to see you. When did you drift into town?"

He shook hands with Gurney and steered him toward a chair.

"Ten minutes ago, Alden, my boy. Delighted to see you again, and particularly pleased to see how carelessly you carry your years. I'm three months younger than you—and I feel like the last rose of summer."

"You look it, Joe. Take a leaf out of my book and let the young fellows 'tend to business for you. Don't let worry ride over you in the shank of your old age, my boy. I never do. Haven't paid a bit of attention to business in the last ten years, and that's why at my age I'm looking so fit."

"You'll live to be a hundred, Alden."

Cappy smiled.

"Well," he declared, "I'm going to live while I have the time. I never expect to be a walking corpse just stalling round in an effort to defer settlement with the undertaker, and I won't be a dead one until the neighbors hear a quartet singing Lead Kindly Light out at my house—Joe you look worried. Anything gone wrong with you, old friend? Need some money? Have you married a young wife?"

"It's Joey," Gurney confessed miserably.

"What? My godson, little Joey Gurney?"

"He's big Joey Gurney now."

"Yes, and a fine boy, Joe—no thanks to you. His mother's influence was strong enough to counteract any impulses for crime he might have inherited from his father."

Gurney smiled sadly at Cappy Ricks' badinage.

"He is a fine boy, Alden, but—he's only a boy, and I'm afraid he's going to make hash of his young life before it's fairly started."

"Booze?"

"No."

"Well, then where did he first meet this woman?"

Joe Gurney, Senior, hitched his chair close to his friend's and laid an impressive hand on Cappy's knee.

"Alden," he said feelingly, "you and I have been friends, man and boy, for about sixty-five years. I believe we were five years old when we robbed Deacon Follansbee's beehive and got stung to death."

"Yes, and we've both been getting stung more or less ever since, only somehow we still manage to recover and be none the worse for the experience. At least, Joe, we learned about bees. When it comes to boys, however, I've still got my experience coming. My little chap died when he was twelve, you know. I've never quite gotten over his loss; in fact, Joe, I was dreaming of him a minute ago when you called."

"You had him long enough, Alden, to realize how I feel about Joey."

Cappy nodded. "Let's see," he answered, reflectively pulling his whiskers, "Joey must be about twenty-four years old now, isn't he?"

"Twenty-four last Tuesday; and at twenty-five he comes into his mother's fortune. I've managed his little nest egg pretty well, Alden; invested it all in the vessel property of Gurney & Harlan, and since the war started I've swelled what originally was a quarter of a million to about a million and a half. His stock in the Red Funnel Line is worth a million at the very least, and the remaining half million is represented by cold cash in bank and bonds that can be converted into cash overnight."

"Hum-m-m! Harumph-h-h! Quite a fortune for a youth of twenty-five to be intrusted with. I'll bet somebody will take it away from him before he's thirty."

"That's a safe bet, Alden. He has a candidate for his money on his trail right now."

"And he doesn't realize it?"

"Alden, he's only twenty-four years old. What does a boy know at twenty-four?"

"Well, Joe, you and I had accumulated a heap of experience and hard knocks at that age, and I seem to remember we each had a little money we'd managed to save here and there. I don't agree with you at all on this twenty-four-year-old excuse. My son-in-law, Matt Peasley—you remember the Peasleys of Thomaston; Matt's a nephew of Ethan, who was lost off the main yard of the *Martha Peasley*—was holding a master's ticket for sail, any ocean and any tonnage, before he was twenty-one. He's not much older than your Joey right now, but, nevertheless, he's president of the Blue Star Navigation Company and worth a million and a half, every dollar of which he has made by his own energy and ability."

"Well, of course, Alden, there are exceptions to every rule."

"Not if you raise 'em right and you've got the right kind of stock to work on and the boy is healthy and normal. Now I know your Joey comes from the right stock; I know his mother raised him right until he was sixteen when the good Lord took her away from you both; and I know he is healthy and normal. Hasn't he proved that by falling in love? The only conclusion I can draw, therefore, is that you've made a monkey out of him, Joe Gurney."

"Perhaps I have, Alden; perhaps I have," Gurney replied sadly.

"No 'perhaps' about it. I know you have. You sent

him to college and gave him ten thousand dollars a
year to spend. If you wanted to give him a fine education and turn out a man and a gentleman you might
have gotten him into the Naval Academy at Annapolis,
where he would have learned something of ships and
graduated with a master's ticket; after serving a few
years and getting the corners knocked off him he could
have resigned and you would have had a sane, depend-
able man to sit in at your desk when you're gone.
By the Holy Pink-Toed Prophet, Joe Gurney, you
make me sick! You're like every other damphool American father who accumulates a few million dollars in
excess of his legitimate needs and then gets all puffed
up with the notion he's got to give his son all the so-
called advantages his own parents were too poor to
afford him—or too sensible. The result is you turn out
an undeveloped or over-developed boob, too proud to
work and not able to take a real man's place in the
world because he hasn't been taught how. And in the
course of time he marries a female boob who has been
raised according to the same general specifications, and
nine times out of ten she's too refined to be bothered
with a family. And presently there's a trip out to
Reno and the little squib in the paper and—er—
ahem! Drat your picture, Joe, you're the responsible
party. You created a ten-thousand-dollar-a-year par-
asite on the body politic while your boy was still in his
teens, and now you want to know what the devil to do
about it, don't you?"

"That's exactly what I want to know, Alden," Gurney confessed miserably, "and I've crossed the con-
tinent to get your advice. I haven't very many real
friends—the kind I can open my heart to——"

"Tut, tut, Joe. Enough of vain repining. Now then, old friend, let's get to the bottom of this thing and see if we can't buy this wreck in from the underwriters, salvage it and put it in commission again. Never say die, Joe! Where there's a will there's a lawsuit or a heartache—particularly if the estate makes it worth while. Now then, Joe, you must realize that it's the fashion nowadays, when a fellow has to consult a specialist, to give his personal and family history for three generations back before receiving treatment. So if I am to diagnose Joey's case I'll have to have a history of Joey. Now then! He graduated from college at the age of twenty-two did he not?"

"He didn't graduate, Alden. He was requested to leave."

"Hum-m-m! I didn't know that. What for?"

"General uselessness and animal spirits, I suppose. It wasn't anything dishonorable. The main contributory cause was an alleged poem lampooning some individual they called Prexy."

"Hum-m-m! And since leaving college what has he done?"

"I've had him in my office."

"Joe, answer my question. I know you've had him in your office. But what has he done? Has he earned his salary?"

"I'm afraid he hasn't, Alden. Somehow golf and tennis and week-end parties and yachting and big-game hunting in Alaska and tarpon fishing in Florida sort of interfere with business."

"Well, that isn't much of a crime, Joe. I never had time to do those highly enjoyable things and I couldn't afford them. When I could afford them and had time

to do them I was too old. You say the boy is fond of
yachting?"

"It's his greatest hobby. In his taste for salt water
he at least resembles his ancestors. The Gurneys were
all sailors and shipping men."

"Is he a good yachtsman, Joe?"

"He has a schooner that's a hundred and six feet
over all and he seems to win pretty regularly with her.
I never knew him to get worse than second place in
all the races he has entered."

"Too bad," Cappy Ricks murmured sadly. "A
noble ambition absolutely misdirected. He would have
been a skipper and, lastly, a good shipping man if you
had only managed him like a sensible father should.
Now about this girl he's in love with?"

"That happened about three months ago. He met
her at one of those roof-garden, midnight cabaret,
turkey-trot palaces in New York——"

"Yes, I know. I always take in the sights when I
go to New York, but the last time I was at that one up
near Fifty-fourth Street the noise bothered me. And
the show was very poor; in fact, after seeing it I
made up my mind I was off cabaret stuff for keeps."

"You ancient scalawag! What were you doing in a
place like that?"

"Seeing life as it ought not to be, of course. Your
boy Joey took me up there, by the way. In-fer-nal
young scoundrel! He showed me the town and we had
quite a time together."

Joe Gurney's old eyes popped with amazement.

"You went batting round with my Joey—an old ruin
like you?"

"Why not? We behaved ourselves, and besides I

always trot a heat with the young fellows whenever
I get a chance. It keeps me young. I enjoyed Joey a
heap, although I could see he was a jolly young jackass.
Moreover, I'm his godfather, and I guess it was all
right for me to tag along and see to it that my godson
didn't get into deep water close to the shore, wasn't
it? Don't you ever step out with Joey and get your
nose wet?"

"Certainly not!"

Cappy Ricks smiled wistfully.

"If I had a son I'd pal up with him," he declared.
"I'd want to get out with him and raise a little digni-
fied hell once in a while, just to be a human being and
keep him from being a mollycoddle. Ahem! Harumph.
So he flagged this damsel in the leg show, eh?"

Joe Gurney nodded miserably.

"Have you given her the once over?" Cappy demanded.

"Yes, I went up there one night. I was afraid somebody would see me, so I took along Joey's aunt, Matilda. We saw the young woman. She does a dance
specialty—an alleged Hawaiian hula-hula. It's fake
from start to finish."

"You show a guilty technical knowledge of the hula,
Joe," Cappy reminded him. "But passing that, what's
the latest report on the situation?"

"Horrible, Alden, horrible!" replied Joe Gurney.

"Careful, Joe, careful! Many a wheat-straw skirt
and sharks'-teeth necklace may conceal a pure and
honest heart."

"Well, she's been married twice and divorced once,
to begin with, and——"

"That's a-plenty, Joe."

"And she has just completed her contract in the show and gone out to Reno to acquire a six months' residence in order to get rid of husband number two so she can take on Joey."

"Who told you all this?"

"I found it out—by asking."

"Have you told Joey?"

"No."

"Does he know it?"

Gurney nodded.

"I had one of his young friends, whom I can trust, tip him off in confidence. The news didn't make any difference to Joey. He asked her about it, and she explained it all away to his entire satisfaction."

"I dare say. And you haven't given any indication to your son that you're on to him and his love affair?"

"I thought best to pretend ignorance, pending my arrival at a solution of the difficulty."

"Therein you showed a gleam of real intelligence. Having humored your boy all his life you could not expect to cross him in his first love affair and get away with it. No, sir-ree! The thing to do is to put the skids under Joey and his lady love before they know you know it. Tell me more about her, however, before I begin making skids and skid grease."

"She is thirty-one years old——"

Cappy Ricks threw up both hands.

"Farewell, O my countrymen!" he murmured.

"She has two children—one by her first husband and one by her second. They're living with her mother. She supports them from the proceeds of her hula dancing."

"Score a white mark for her, Joe. Is she a good looker?"

"A brunette, Alden, and Joey's Aunt Matilda admitted against her will that she was a beauty. My lawyer tells me, however, that she hasn't an ounce of brains, and proclaims the fact by laughing loudly when there is nothing particularly worth laughing at."

"I imagine you've had a detective agency investigating her."

"I have. She has little education and no refinement; her people are very ordinary. Her father is a whitewing in Philadelphia and is separated from her mother, who keeps a boarding house in Muncie, Indiana."

"I'm afraid, Joe, she won't do for your daughter-in-law," Cappy Ricks opined slowly. "But don't worry, my boy. You've come all the way from New York to confide in me and get my advice, and somehow I have a sneaking notion you've come to the right shop. If there's anybody calculated to put a crimp in love's young dream, I'm that individual."

"I knew Joey and you were good friends, and besides, you're his godfather. He thinks a lot of you, Alden, and I kind of thought maybe you might come East with me, see the boy, get him to confide in you and—er—sort of advise him in the way he should go. I'm—er—well, Alden, I'm afraid I feel too badly about this to talk to Joey. I might lose my temper, and besides—besides, he's all I have and he reminds me so much of his mother that I——"

"Yes, yes, I understand, Joe. Leave it to me and I'll advise with him. Yes, I will—with an ax handle! And I'll go East with you and tie knots in his tail—

only he won't know anything about it. It may cost you a little money, but I assume expense is no object."

"It would be cheap at a million."

"Where that boy and your money are concerned you're such an ass, Joe, I'm almost tempted to charge you a million extra for the operation. However, considering Deacon Follansbee's beehive, and Joey's mother and my godson——"

Old Joe Gurney took Cappy Ricks' hand in both of his, that trembled so with age and anxiety.

"Dear old Alden," he declared. "I knew you wouldn't fail me."

CHAPTER XXIX

For a long time after old Joe Gurney had terminated his visit Cappy Ricks sat in the position which with him always denoted intense mental concentration. He had sunk low in his swivel chair and swung his old legs to the top of his desk; his head was bowed on his breast and his eyes were closed.

Suddenly he started as if snake-bitten, sat up at his desk and reached for the telephone.

"Get me the West Coast Trading Company," he ordered the private exchange operator, "and tell Mr. J. Augustus Redell I want to speak to him.

Redell answered presently.

"Gus, my dear young friend," Cappy began briskly, "I want you to do me a favor, and in so doing I think you'll find you are going to perform one for yourself also."

"Good news, Cappy. Consider it done."

"Thank you, my boy, but this particular favor isn't done quite so quickly. I want you to tell that Peruvian partner of yours, Live Wire Luiz Almeida to dig up a specification for a cargo of fir to be discharged on lighters at some open roadstead on the West Coast, and the more open the port and the more difficult it is to discharge there; and the harder it is to get any sane shipowner to charter a vessel to deliver a cargo there, the better I'll be pleased. Surely, Gus, you must have a customer down on the West Coast in some such

202

port as I describe, who is actually watering at the mouth for a cargo of lumber and is unable to place it with a mill that will guarantee delivery? Look into the matter, Augustus, and see what you can do for me."

"Do you want to furnish such a cargo from one of the Ricks Lumber & Logging Company's northern mills and freight it in one of your Blue Star Navigation Company vessels?"

"No, I don't *want* to do it," Cappy replied; "but in this particular case the acceptance of such a cargo and the freighting of it via a Blue Star windjammer, even though the usual demurrage at such discharging ports will cause the vessel a loss, is a consummation devoutly to be wished. Ordinarily, if you made such a proposition to me I'd call in the boys from the general office and tell them to throw you out, but—well, in this case I'm willing to stand the loss, Augustus."

"Yes, you are—not. Somebody else will recompense you for any loss, Cappy Ricks, never fear. Do you want the West Coast Trading Company to give you a bonus for accepting our order?"

"No, my boy. I'll make Skinner sell you the lumber at the regular base price at the mill, plus insurance and freight to point of discharge. And I won't stick you too deep on the freight, even in wartime."

"There's something wrong with you this morning, Cappy," Redell declared, highly mystified. "You're too obliging. However, I'm not to be outgamed. I have a specification for a cargo of half a million feet for delivery at Sobre Vista, Peru; I've been trying for a month to place the order and nobody will accept it because nobody wants to guarantee delivery. On the other hand, the purchasers have been unable to get any

ship owner to charter them a vessel to go to Sobre
Vista without a guaranty of a perfectly prohibitive
rate of demurrage per diem; consequently I had just
about abandoned my efforts to place the order."

"Fine business, Gus. And is Sobre Vista a rotten
port at which to discharge?"

"It's vile, Cappy. It's an open roadstead and the
vessel lies off-shore and discharges into lighters. About
four days a week the surf is so high the lighters cannot lie alongside the ship or be run up on the beach
without being ruined, and to complicate the situation
they only have two or three lighters at the port. Labor
is scarce, too, and the few *cargadores* a skipper can
hire have a habit of working two days and staying
drunk for the remainder of the week on the proceeds
of those two days of labor. So you can see for yourself that discharge in Sobre Vista is very hard on
the skipper's nerves, and that if he can work two days
a week he's in luck. And when we deduct from those
two days all the national holidays and holy days and
saints' feast days that have to be duly celebrated, not
to mention the three hundred and sixty-five days in the
year the populace doesn't feel like exerting itself—well,
Cappy, I couldn't give you anything worse than Sobre
Vista if you paid me for it."

"May the good Lord bless you, Augustus! Come
down and do business with Skinner on the cargo. Get
him to quote you a price f.o.b. ship's tackles at the
mill dock and tell him you'll furnish the tonnage when
the cargo is ready for delivery. There's no sense
in worrying poor Skinner until his worries are due, and
when I send a Blue Star schooner to load your cargo
for Sobre Vista I'm going to have to fight him and my

son-in-law, Matt Peasley. But leave it to me, Gus. I'll guarantee the tonnage."

"This is certainly wonderful," the grateful Redell observed. "Thank you, Cappy. What I'll do to those Peruvian customers of mine on price will be a shame and a disgrace. Are you going to stick me for any demurrage on the vessel, Cappy? Because if you are, I'll have to stick my customers in order to get out clean."

"No demurrage, Gus, not a penny."

"Bully! Then I'll stick my customers anyhow. It makes the profit all the greater, and since they expect to pay a reasonable demurrage I see no reason why I should disappoint them."

When Redell had hung up Cappy summoned into his presence Captain Matt Peasley.

"Matt," he queried, "what schooners have you got due at any one of our northern mills within the next thirty days?"

Matt Peasley pondered and counted on his big fingers. "The *Tyee* will be in from Valparaiso about that time," he answered.

"Have you got her chartered?"

"Oh, no. We're using her in our own trade. Skinner will have a cargo ready for her by the time she gets back, although we don't know yet where we will send her."

"Well, Matt, you tell Skinner he can't have her and to look around for some other vessel to take her place. I may give her to him at the last minute, but then again I may not. When she arrives at the mill, Matthew, my boy, tie her up to the mill dock to await my pleasure."

"Why, what the devil are you going to do with the *Tyee?*" Matt demanded, astounded beyond measure.

"I might want to take a cruise for my health and use the *Tyee* as a pleasure boat," Cappy answered enigmatically. "They tell me she's as fast as a yacht in a breeze of wind."

"The longer I'm acquainted with you, father-in-law," Matt Peasley declared, "the less I know you. You can have your *Tyee*, but for every day she is held awaiting your pleasure your personal account will be charged with something in three figures. I'll figure out her average profit per day for the last five voyages and soak you accordingly."

"Fair enough," quoth Cappy Ricks.

CHAPTER XXX

Three weeks later Alden P. Ricks arrived in New York. After he had been driven to his hotel and had removed the stains of travel he telephoned the office of Gurney & Harlan and got Gurney, Senior, on the line.

"Well, I'm here, Joe," he announced. "Have you followed my instructions and cut Joey off at the pockets?"

"I have, Alden. He's rather desperate as a result, and has been trying to borrow money by hypothecating the inheritance due him on his twenty-fifth birthday. You see, I didn't give him a second's notice; just told him he was spending too much time in play and too much money for pleasure, and that until he came into his private fortune he would have to earn any money he desired to spend. I have been very firm."

"That's the stuff, Joe. And is he trying to earn it?"

"Yes, I think so. He's sticking round the office at any rate."

"Hum-m-m! That's because it costs money to go anywhere else. Has he succeeded in raising a loan by assigning an interest in his inheritance?"

"No, not yet. I blocked him at all the banks and with my old friends, and I do not think he can borrow as much as he needs from any of his friends. They, like him of course, are dependent on their fathers' generosity."

"Fine way to raise a boy! Bully. Well, I'll be down to your office in about an hour and take you and Joey to luncheon at India House. You haven't forgotten what I wrote you, Joe? You know your part, don't you? . . . Well, see that you play your hand well and we'll save that boy yet."

Two hours later the Gurneys were lunching with Cappy Ricks at the one New York club to which Cappy belonged—quaint old India House in Hanover Square, haunt of shipping men and shippers, perhaps the best and least-known club in New York City. Joey had been unaffectedly glad to see his godfather; so much so, indeed, that Cappy rightly guessed Joey had designs on the Ricks pocketbook; for after all, as Cappy admitted to himself, he is a curmudgeon of a godfather indeed who will refuse to loan his godson a much needed twenty-five thousand dollars on gilt-edged security. In expectation of an application for a loan before the day should be done, however, Cappy was careful not to be alone with Joey for an instant, for something told him that only the presence of Gurney, Senior, kept Gurney Junior from promptly putting his fortune to the touch.

"Well, Joey, you young cut-up," Cappy began as the trio settled in the smoking room and the waiter brought the coffee and cigars, "I see you're getting to be quite an amateur sailor. Your Dad tells me you won your last race with that schooner yacht of yours in rather pretty fashion."

"It was a bully race, Mr. Ricks. I wish you could have been aboard with me," Joey declared enthusiastically.

"Hum-m-m! Catch me on a yacht!" Cappy's tones were indicative of profound disgust.

"Ricks, you're a kill-joy," old Gurney struck in. "All you think of is making money, and you've made so much of it I should think the game would have palled on you long ago. I tell Joey to go it while he's young —while he has the capacity for enjoyment."

"Joe, I tell you now, as I've told you before, you're spoiling this boy. When he's twenty-five years old he comes into a fortune and you're not even preparing him for the task of handling that money wisely. You bought Joey that schooner yacht, didn't you?"

"I bought her cheap," old Joe Gurney protested lamely.

"They cost a fortune to maintain, Joe. Now if Joey wanted some salt-water experience you should have sent him to sea as quartermaster on one of your own Red Funnel liners; presently he would have worked up to second mate; then first mate, and finally skipper. By that time he would have known the salt-water end of his father's business, after which he could sit in at a desk and learn the business end. Somehow, Joe, when I see a shipping man's son fooling away his time on a pleasure yacht instead of learning the shipping business, I feel as if I'd just taken a dose of ipecac."

"Godfather is out of sorts," Joey soliloquized sagely, and resolved to wait a day or two before broaching the subject of a loan. Cappy Ricks surveyed the young fellow severely.

"Joey," he began, "I've no doubt you're quite a sailor on your handsome yacht, in your yachting uniform, with all the real head work to be done by your sailing master——"

"Not a bit of it," Joey protested. "I'm not that kind of a yachtsman. I'm the captain tight and the midshipmite, and the crew take orders from me, because I don't employ a sailing master."

"Do you mean to tell me that when you go on a cruise to the West Indies you navigate the yacht yourself— lay out your own courses and work out your own position?"

Joey smiled patronizingly.

"Certainly," he replied. "That's easy."

"Sure. Play is always easy. But let me tell you, young man, if you had command of a big three-legged windjammer, with a deckload of heavy green lumber fresh from the saws, and ran into a stiff sou'-easter such as we have out on the Pacific coast, you'd know what real sailoring is like."

"Joey could handle her like that," old Gurney declared with pride, and snapped his fingers.

"Could you, Joey?" Cappy Ricks demanded. "I have my doubts."

"Why, I think so, Mr. Ricks. I might be a little cautious at first——"

"Well, I don't think you could," Cappy interrupted.

"Well, I do," old Gurney declared with some warmth. "I've been out with Joey on his yacht and I know what the boy can do."

"Bah! You're a doddering old softy, Joe. Yachting is one thing and sailoring is another. I have an old lumber hooker on Gray's Harbor now, loading for a port in Peru, and I'd certainly love to see Joey with her on his hands. I'll bet fifty thousand dollars he couldn't sail her down to Sobre Vista, discharge her and sail back inside of six months." The old schemer chuckled. "Lordy me," he continued, "I'd like to see Joey trying to make her point up into the wind! She'd break his heart."

"Look here, Alden," Old Joe Gurney commenced to bristle. "Are you serious about that or are you just making conversation bets? Because if you're serious I'm just shipping man enough to call you for the sheer sporting joy of it."

"By the Holy Pink-Toed Prophet, you're on!" Cappy Ricks almost yelled. "Put up or shut up—that is, provided Joey is as big a sport as his father and will undertake to sail my schooner *Tyee* to Sobre Vista and back."

"Oh, she's a schooner!" There was relief in Joey's voice. "Why, I'll sail any vessel with a fore-and-aft rig. I thought perhaps you were trying to ring in a square-rigger on me, and I'm not familiar with them. But a schooner—pooh! Pie for little Joey!"

"She's got three legs, and with a deck-load of lumber she's cranky and topheavy. I'm warning you, Joey. Remember he is a poor ship owner who doesn't know his own ship."

Joey got up and went to a map laid out on a table, with a piece of plate glass over it, to compute the sailing distance from Gray's Harbor to Sobre Vista. He could not find Sobre Vista on the map.

"Figure the distance to Mollendo and you'll be close enough for all practical purposes," Cappy called to him, and winked at the boy's father. "A little pep, here, boy," he whispered to Gurney, "and we'll snare him yet."

Joey came back from his study of the map.

"I'd have the nor'west trades clear to the Line," he

remarked to his father. "After that I'd be liable to
bang round for a couple of weeks in the doldrums, but
in spite of that—did you say I couldn't do it in six
months, Mr. Ricks?"

"That's what I said, Joey."

"Take the bet, dad," said Joey quietly, "and I'll take
half of it off your hands. I'll give you my note, secured
by an assignment of a twenty-five-thousand-dollar interest in mother's estate to secure you in case Mr. Ricks
should win and call you for his winnings—but he
hasn't a chance in the world."

"Money talks," Cappy Ricks warned him and got out
his check book. "Joe, I'll make a check in your favor
for fifty thousand dollars and you make one in my
favor for the same amount. We will then deposit both
checks with the secretary of the club, who will act as
stakeholder——"

" 'Nuff said, Alden P. Ricks. I accept the dare.
Sonny, if you're a worse sailor-man than you appear to
be, you're liable to cost your father a sizable wad.
However, I can't resist this opportunity to put a nick
in the Ricks bank roll." Gurney snickered. "Alden,"
he declared, "you'll bleed for a month of Sundays.
Really, this is too easy! For old sake's sake, I'll
give you a chance to withdraw before it is too late."

"Let the tail go with the hide, Joe. I don't often bet,
but when I do I'm no piker. Joey, there's just one
little condition I'm going to exact, however. I'm going
to send one of my own skippers along with you on the
Tyee, because your license as master only permits you
to skipper pleasure boats up to a hundred tons net
register; so in order to comply with the law I'll have
to have a sure-enough skipper aboard the *Tyee*. But

he shall have orders from me to be nothing but a companion to you, Joey. Once the tugboat casts you off, you are to be in supreme command until you voluntarily relinquish your authority, when of course he will take the ship off your hands. Any relinquishment of authority, however, will be tantamount to failure, and you will, of course, lose your twenty-five thousand."

"That's a reasonable stipulation, godfather. I accept if father does—that is, provided dad lets me in on half the bet."

"Better let the young feller in, Joe," Cappy suggested. "If you don't he might throw the race."

"Well, I don't like to encourage the habit of betting, least of all with my own son, but in view of the fact that this is a friendly little bet and—er—well, you can have half, Joey."

"Thank you, sir," said Joey. "Mr. Ricks, when do I start?"

Cappy Ricks glanced at his watch.

"The sooner the better," he replied. "The *Tyee* is loading now, but I'll wire them you're coming and to hold her for you. You have time to arrange your affairs, pack a trunk and catch the Lake Shore Limited for Chicago at five o'clock. From Chicago you take the——"

"Never mind. I know the quickest route. Dad, I'll need some money before I go."

"How much, son?"

"Oh, a couple of thousand, just to play safe. And I'll have to leave you a batch of bills to settle for me."

"All right, son, I'll settle them. Here's your two thousand. You can pay me back out of your winnings on the voyage. And never mind about your note or

the assignment of an interest in your inheritance. If
I cannot take my own son's word of honor I don't deserve a son. Just take care of yourself, Joey, because
if anything should happen to you it would *go* rather
hard with your old man."

He wrote Joey a check for two thousand dollars and
took an affectionate farewell of his son.

"Now listen to me, my dear young Hotspur," Cappy
Ricks commanded him as he shook Joey's hand in farewell. "The schooner's name is *Tyee* and you'll find her
at the Ricks Lumber & Logging Company's mill dock
in Aberdeen, on Gray's Harbor, Washington. And
don't be afraid of her. She was built to weather anything. The skipper's name is Mike Murphy, and if
you can't get along with Mike and learn to love him
before you're in the ship a week, there's something
wrong with you, Joey. Just don't start anything with
Mike though, because he always finishes strong, and
whatever he does is always right—with me. When
you get out there he'll show you the orders I will have
telegraphed him and you have my word of honor, boy,
that there'll be no double-crossing and no interference
unless you request it."

"Right-o!" cried Joey, and was off to earn twenty-
five thousand dollars of the easiest money he had ever
heard of.

"Like spearing a fish in a bathtub," murmured
Cappy Ricks dreamily, and tore up the fifty-thousand-
dollar check he had just written. "Joe, if your boy is
such easy game for a pair of old duffers like us, just
think what soft picking he must have been for that
nimble-footed lady with the raven hair, the pearly teeth
and the eyes that won't behave!"

"But she's coarse and brainless, Alden. I can't imagine a boy like my Joey falling in love with a woman like that. He ought to know better. Just remember how he was raised."

"Fooey! Joey isn't in love. He only thinks he is, and the reason he thinks it is because she has told him so a hundred times. Can't you just see her looking up at Joey with her startled-fawn eyes and saying: 'Oh, you do love me, don't you, Joey?' As if the fact that Joey loved her constituted the eighth wonder of the world! And she's probably told Joey she'll die if he ever ceases to love her; and he's kind and obliging and wouldn't hurt a fly if he could avoid it. Why, Joe, you old idiot, you mustn't feel that Joey has disgraced himself. Isn't he planning to marry the woman? Only a decent man—a born idealist—could hold that designing woman in such reverence. Blamed if it isn't kind of sweet of the boy, although I *would* love to give him a kick that would jar all his relations—including his father!"

Old Joe Gurney gazed at Cappy in admiration.

"Alden," he declared, "you have a singularly acute knowledge of women."

"I employ about fifteen of 'em round my office; I had several narrow escapes in my youth; I have had a sweet and wonderful wife—and I have a replica of her in my daughter. And I do know young men, for I have been young myself; and I know old fools like you, Joe, because I've never had a son to make an old fool of myself over."

"Well, now that you've hooked Joey for a six months' voyage, what's next on the program?" Gurney asked after a brief silence.

Cappy smiled—a prescient little smile.

"Why, I'm going to pull off a wedding," he declared. "I'm going to marry Joey to the sweetest, nicest, healthiest, prettiest, brainiest little lady of twenty summers that ever threatened to put the Ricks organization on the toboggan. She's my private secretary and I've got to get rid of her or some of the young fellows in our office will be killing each other."

"Here, here, Alden, my boy, go slow! I ought to be consulted in this matter. Who is this young lady and what are her antecedents?"

"Say, who's running this layout?" Cappy demanded. "Didn't you come to me squealing for help? Joe, take a back seat and let me try my hand without any advice from you. The girl's name is Doris Kenyon and she's an orphan. Her father used to be the general manager of my redwood mill on Humboldt Bay, and her mother was a girlhood friend of my late wife's; so naturally I've established a sort of protectorate over her. She has to work for a living, and any time there's a potentially fine, two-million-dollar husband like Joey lying round loose I like to see some deserving working girl land the cuss. As a matter of fact, it's almost a crime to steer her against Joey in his present state. But," Cappy added, "I have a notion that before Joey gets rid of that hula-hula girl he's going to be a sadder, wiser and poorer young man than he is at present."

"Your plan, then, is to give Joey six months away from his captor in order that he may forget her?"

"Exactly. Absence makes the heart grow colder in cases like the one under discussion, and the sea is a great place for a fellow to do some quiet, sane, uninterrupted thinking. The sea, at night particularly, is

productive of much introspection and speculation on
the various aspects of life, and in order to make Joey
forget this vampire in a hurry all that is necessary is
to have a real woman round him for a while. The first
thing he knows he'll be making comparisons and the contrast will appall him."

"You don't mean——"

"You bet I do. Joey's future wife accompanies him
on the voyage, and my bully port captain, Mike Murphy, and his amiable sister go along to chaperone the
party and make up a foursome at bridge. I've had a
naval architect at work on the old cabin of the *Tyee*,
putting in some extra staterooms, bathrooms, and so
on, and in order to make a space for the passengers I
subsidized the two squarehead mates into berthing with
the crew in the fo'-castle. Doris always did want to
take a voyage in one of the Blue Star windjammers,
and I had promised to send her at the first convenient
opportunity."

"You deep-dyed, nefarious old villain!"

"Old Cupid Ricks, eh? Well, it's lots of fun, Joe,
this butting in on love's young dream. And I'm just
so constituted I've got to run other people's affairs
for them or I wouldn't be happy. I do think, however,
that this house party on the old *Tyee* is about the
slickest deal I have ever put over. Joe, they're going
to be right comfortable. I've shipped a maid for the
girls, and the cook this time is several degrees superior
to the average maritime specimen, for there's nothing
like a couple of days of bum cooking to upset tempers—
and I'm taking no chances. Also, just before I left
I gave your future daughter-in-law her quarterly dividend—you see, when her father died I had to sort of

look after the family, and I ran a bluff that **Kenyon**
had some Ricks Lumber & Logging Company stock—
you know, Joe. Proud stuff! I had to hornswoggle
them. Well, as I say, I gave her the money, and my girl
Florry went shopping with her. Sports clothes? Wow!
Wow! White skirts, blue jersey, little sailor hat—
man—oh, man, the stage is set to the last detail! I
even had them ship a piano. Doris plays the guitar
and has a pleasing voice, and just for good measure
I threw in a crackajack cabinet phonograph and a
hundred records with enough sentimental drip to sink
the schooner."

Joe Gurney stared at his old friend rather helplessly
and shook his head. Such finesse was beyond his comprehension.

"You see, now," Cappy continued, "the wisdom of
my course? I insisted that you cut off Joey's allowance and get him hungry for money. You did—and he
got hungry. He would have been posted at his clubs in
thirty days; it is probable he owed a few bets here and
there; his tailor may have needed money. Consequently,
by the time I arrived on the scene he was ripe for any
legitimate enterprise that would bring him in the need-
ful funds; we arranged the enterprise and he promptly
smothered it. Right off, Joe, your son said to himself:
'It will be almost a year before I come into my inheritance, and in the interim I'm going to get married, and
a married man who lives on the scale my wife will expect me to assume is going to need a lot more money
than a clerkship in his father's shipping office will bring
him. Now, there's Tootsy-Wootsy out in Reno with a
five months' sentence staring her in the eye before she'll
be free to marry me, and I can't very well go out to

Reno to visit her without running the risk of incurring
my father's displeasure or the tongue of gossip. Consequently, I have five months' time to kill, also, and how
better can I kill it than by a jolly sea voyage in a bally
old lumber hooker? I can easily win twenty-five thousand dollars from my godfather, and that twenty-five
thousand will carry us along until dad turns over my
mother's estate to me. Fine business! I'll go to it.'
And, Joe, he's done gone! Of course I'm going to
win his twenty-five thousand bet because he doesn't
know what it means to discharge a vessel in Sobre Vista,
and Mike Murphy has orders from me to hire all the
available stevedores there to do something else while
Joey is trying to hire them to discharge the *Tyee*.
Don't worry, Joe! The country is safe in the capable
hands of Mike Murphy."

"I see. And the twenty-five thousand dollars you will
win from Joey——"

"Will reimburse me for the extraordinary expense
I've been to in saving your son. If Joey's end of the
bet doesn't cover I'll nick you, Joseph, although I figure
Joey's end of it will pay the fiddler. He won't miss it
out of his two millions. Besides, I've noticed that the
only experience worth while is the kind you pay real
money for—and Joey has to buy his experience the
same as the rest of us."

Five days later Cappy Ricks dropped into the Red
Funnel Line and laid a telegram on old Joe Gurney's
desk.

"Read that," he commanded, "and see if you can't
work up a couple of cheers."

Gurney read:

"Aberdeen, Wash., June 3, 1916

"Alden P. Ricks

"Waldorf-Astoria Hotel, New York

"Joey arrived bung up and bilge free. Had loaded and hauled into stream, waiting for him. Came out in launch, climbed Jacob's ladder and stood on rail, sizing up ship. Saw Doris and almost fell face down on deck. He says Doris is a dream, she says Joey is a dear. Take it from me, boss, it is all over but the wedding bells.

"M. CUPID MURPHY."

Old Joe Gurney took Cappy Ricks' hand in both of his and shook it heartily.

"My worries are over, Alden," he declared. "You have, indeed, been my friend in need."

"My troubles and Joey's are just commencing, however," Cappy retorted blithely. "However—'never trouble trouble until trouble troubles you' is my motto. Where's that hundred-and-six-foot schooner yacht of Joey's?"

"She's at her moorings in Greenpoint Basin. Why?"

"I want to borrow her for a cruise to San Francisco, via the Panama Canal. Joey and his bride can sail her back. May I have her, to do what I please with, Joe?"

"Alden, don't ask foolish questions. Take her and God bless you! Joey owns her, but I pay the bills; so her skipper takes orders from me."

Two days later Joey's schooner *Seafarer* was standing out to sea past Sandy Hook, but Cappy Ricks was not aboard her, for that ingenious schemer had boarded a train and gone back to San Francisco and his lumber and ships.

CHAPTER XXXI

Cappy Ricks' meditations were interrupted by a knock at the door of his private office.

"Come in," he piped, and his son-in-law, Captain Matt Peasley, stuck his head in.

"The *Tyee* is sailing in, Cappy," he announced. "The Merchants' Exchange has just telephoned."

"It's an infernal lie," Cappy shrilled excitedly. "It can't be the *Tyee*. If it is, she's two months ahead of her schedule, and by the Holy Pink-Toed Prophet, I fixed up that schedule myself."

Matt Peasley grinned.

"Perhaps Joey didn't like your schedule and rearranged it to suit himself," he suggested.

"Impossible! That infernal young scoundrel put it over me? Preposterous! Why, Mike Murphy was on the job. Get out, Matt, and don't come in here again today throwing scares into the old man."

Nevertheless, Cappy's confidence in human nature was badly jarred when Captain Michael J. Murphy was announced two hours later. Indeed Cappy could scarcely credit his sense of sight when the redoubtable Michael entered the room. He glared at the worthy fellow over the rims of his spectacles for fully a minute while Murphy stood fidgeting just inside the doorway.

"Well," said the Blue Star despot presently, "all I've got to say to you, Mike Murphy, is that you're certainly a hell of a seaman to stand idly by and

221

see that young Joey do me up like this. Give an account of yourself!"

"They're engaged," Murphy protested valiantly.

"That's my work, Mike, not yours. Don't take any credit that isn't coming to you. I want a report on your end of this deal. How does it happen that this boy harpoons me for twenty-five thousand dollars? Have the *cargadores* at Sobre Vista gone on the water wagon? Did Joey out-bid you for their services? Have they added a lot more lighters to their lighterage fleet? Has the surf quit rolling in on the beach? Have the inhabitants of Sobre Vista been converted to the Mohammedan faith and declined to celebrate saints' days and holy days? Is there smallpox in the town, that the quietus has been put on fiestas and fandangos, and has Peru been annexed by Chile and the celebration of the national holidays forbidden?"

"No, Mr. Ricks. It's the same old *mañana* burg. The trouble was that Joey is a better sailorman than he appeared to be. He cracked on all the way down and made a smashing voyage, and, of course, as soon as we got there he went ashore. Two other schooners were there ahead of us. One was loading general cargo and the other was discharging it, and when Joey heard they had been there a month he investigated conditions and saw where you had him. Mr. Ricks, he came back as mad as a hatter. Of course I saw he would have to wait until the other schooners were out of the way before he could begin discharging, because they had first call on the lighters; so in view of the situation and the fact that Miss Murphy and Doris were a bit tired of the ship and wanted to go ashore and see the back country, I organized a trip for them."

"You left Joey aboard the *Tyee,* of course."

"Yes, sir. And there's where I made my fatal break.
The minute my back was turned the son of a pirate
got busy. It appears there was a six-inch waste pipe
leading from the crew's lavatory out under the stern
of the ship, and this pipe had rusted away and broken
off at the flange just inside the skin of the ship some-
time during the vessel's previous voyage. Of course
it happened while she was homeward bound in ballast,
and was standing so high out of the water that this
vent where the pipe was broken was above the water-
line; consequently not enough of a leak developed to
be noticeable. At the mill dock, however, after we got
her under-deck cargo aboard, the vessel had settled
until this vent was under water, and immediately she
developed a mysterious leak. In fact, due to the enormous pressure, the water came in faster than the pumps
could handle it. Fortunately, however, we discovered
where the leak was, though it was then too late to mend
it. To do so we would have had to take out the under-
deck cargo again. So I just whittled out a six-inch
wooden plug, fastened it to the end of the boat hook,
ran it down the narrow space through which the broken
pipe led, found the vent, hammered the plug home,
stopped the leak, pumped out the well, finished taking
on cargo and sailed for Sobre Vista."

"A small leak will sink a great ship," Cappy Ricks
murmured. "I think I anticipate the blow-off, Mike;
but proceed."

"Unfortunately for us that cargo of lumber we
had was for the Peruvian government. They were
going to use it in the construction of barracks or a
new customhouse or something—and Joey knew this.

And he knew about that plug. So the minute my back was turned he pulled out the plug and the water came in and trickled all through the cargo and the ship commenced to settle. But Joey didn't care. He knew a little salt water couldn't hurt the lumber. When the top of the *Tyee's* rail was flush with the water he plugged the hole again, got his crew busy with the pumps, and by judiciously plugging and unplugging that leak he kept the crew pumping all day and all night without raising the vessel an inch, and the people ashore could see the streams of water cascading overside and the crew pumping like mad. And presently Joey gave up, went ashore, sought the captain of the port and put up a hard luck story about a leak in his ship—a leak he couldn't find anywhere—a leak that was getting away from him, because his men were too exhausted to do any more pumping. And he said his ship would get water-logged and settle until the surf began to break over her. And presently the deck lashings would part under the battering of the surf and the deck load would go by the board. Half of it would drift out to sea, and the other half would pound on the beach and get filled with sand, which would dull the saws and planes of the carpenters when they came to cut it up. Also, the ship's cabin would be sure to go, and unless he had help he would have to abandon the vessel and she would lie there, submerged, at anchor, a menace to the navigation of the port."

"The scoundrel! The in-fer-nal young scoundrel!" cried Cappy Ricks.

"Well, he got away with it, sir. Remember our cargo was for the Peruvian government and they'd had the devil's own time getting it; consequently they couldn't afford to lose any part of it and have their anchorage ground menaced by a derelict. So the captain of the port took it up with the commandant of the local garrison, and the commandant, as Joey expressed it, heard the Macedonian cry and got busy. He commandeered all the lighters the other schooners were using; the soldiers rounded up the *cargadores* at the point of the bayonet, and they started discharging the American schooner *Tyee*, with the spiggoty soldiers swelling Joey's crew at the pumps and Joey doing business with that wooden plug according to the requirements. Fortunately there weren't any surf days that week, and the way the cargo poured out of the *Tyee* was a shame and a disgrace. And when it was all out Joey plugged the leak again, pumped out the ship, and wired me at Mollendo to hurry back with the ladies or he'd sail without me. So you can see for yourself, Mr. Ricks, it was a hard hand to beat. And his luck held. He cracked on all the way home and, as you know, sir, the *Tyee* is fast in a breeze of wind, and you told me not to interfere unless he asked me to."

Despite his disappointment Cappy Ricks lay back in his chair and laughed until he wept.

"Oh, Mike," he declared, "it's worth twenty-five thousand dollars to know a boy who can pull one like that. What do you think of him, anyhow?"

"He'll do. His father has spoiled him, but not altogether. I think a heap of him, sir. Remember I've been shipmates with him a trifle over four months, and that's a pretty good test."

"Very well, Mike. I forgive you, my boy. I hope Miss Murphy enjoyed the trip. Tell her——"

The door opened and Joey Gurney, accompanied by Miss Doris Kenyon entered unannounced.

"Hello, godfather," yelled Joey joyously. He jerked the old man out of his chair and hugged him. "I'm back with your schooner, sir. She was easy to navigate, but that was a cold deck you handed me in Sobre Vista——"

"Glad to see you, Joey, glad to see you," Cappy interrupted. "Ah, and here's my little secretary again. Miss Kenyon, this is a pleasure——"

"Mr. Ricks," Joey interrupted him, "the lady's name is no longer Miss Kenyon. She is now Mrs. Joseph K. Gurney, Junior. The minute we got ashore at Meiggs' wharf and could shake the Murphys, who stood out till the last for a church wedding, we chartered a taxicab, went up to the City Hall, procured a license, rounded up a preacher—and got married. What do you know about that?"

"You're as fast as a second-story worker, Joey. I shall kiss the bride." And Cappy did. Then he sat down and stared at the fruit of his cunning labors.

"Well, well, well!" cried Joey. "Kick in, godfather, kick in. You owe me twenty-five thousand dollars, and if I'm going to support a wife I'll need it."

Cappy summoned Mr. Skinner, who felicitated the happy pair and departed pursuant to Cappy's order, to make out a check for Joey.

"And now," said Cappy, as he handed the groom his winnings, "you get out of here with your bride, Joey, and I'll telephone Florry and we'll organize a wedding supper. And to-morrow morning, Joey, I'd like to see you at ten o'clock, if you can manage to be here."

Joey promised, and hastened away with his bride.

CHAPTER XXXII

True to his word he presented himself in Cappy's lair promptly at ten next morning. The old gentleman was sitting rigidly erect on the extreme edge of his chair; in his hand he held a typewritten statement with a column of figures on it, and he eyed Joey very appraisingly over the rims of his spectacles.

"My boy," he said solemnly, "sit down. I'm awfully glad you cabled that hula-hula girl of yours in Reno that the stuff was all off."

Joey's mouth flew open.

"Why—why, how did you know?" he gasped.

"I know everything, Joey. I'm that kind of an old man."

Joey paled.

"Oh, Mr. Ricks," he pleaded, "for heaven's sake don't let a whisper of that affair reach my wife." He wrung his hands. "I told her she was the only girl I had ever loved—that I'd never been engaged before— that I—oh, godfather, if she ever discovers I've lied to her——"

"She'll not discover it. Compose yourself, Joey. I've seen to all that. I knew you'd give Doris the same old song and dance; everybody's doing it, you know, so I took pains to see to it that you'll never have to eat your words."

"I must have been crazy to engage myself to that woman," Joey wailed. "I don't know why I did it—

227

I don't know how it happened—Oh, Mr. Ricks, please believe me!"

"I do, Joey, I do. I understand perfectly, because at the tender age of twenty-four I proposed marriage to a snake-charmer lady in the old Eden Musee. She was forty years old if she was a day, but she carried her years well and hid the wrinkles with putty, or something. Barring a slight hare-lip, she was a fairly handsome woman—in the dark." He reached into a compartment of his desk and drew forth a package of letters tied with red ribbon. "You can have these, Joey," he announced; "only I shouldn't advise keeping them where your wife may find them. They are your letters to your Honolulu lady."

Joey let out a bleat of pure ecstacy and seized them.

"You haven't read them, sir, have you?" he queried, blushing desperately.

"Oh, yes, my boy. I had to, you know, because I was buying something and I wanted to make certain I got value received. Pretty gooey stuff, Joey! Read aloud, they sound like a cow's hoof settling into a wet meadow!"

"I'm so glad she took it sensibly," Joey announced, for he was anxious to change the topic of conversation. "I suppose she saw it was the only way."

"No, she didn't, my son. Don't flatter yourself. On your way out West to join the *Tyee* you wrote her every day on the train. You told her about your bet with me, and who I was and all about me. Lucky for you that you did, and doubly lucky for you that you cabled her the jilt from Sobre Vista, or she would not have come to me with her troubles. Joey, that must have taken courage on your part. It's mighty hard for a gentleman to cable a lady and break an engagement. That's the lady's privilege, Joey."

"I—I was desperate, Mr. Ricks. I had to. I had to have her out of the way by the time I got back, or Doris might have found it out. You see, I wanted to clear the atmosphere."

"Well, you clouded it for fair! You see, Joey, in all those letters it appears that you never once mentioned the words marriage or engagement. But your cablegram was an admission that an engagement existed, and the lady was smart enough to realize that. It appears also that about a week after you cleared for Sobre Vista her annoying husband was killed by a taxicab in New York, so that saved her any divorce proceedings; and when your cablegram reached her she was a single lady who had been heartlessly jilted. The first thing she did was to hire a lawyer, and the first person that lawyer called on was Alden P. Ricks, the old family friend. It appears a suit for breach of promise was to be instituted unless a fairly satisfactory financial settlement could be arrived at."

"How much did she want?" Joey barely whispered the words.

"Only a million."

"How much did you settle for? I'll pay it out of my inheritance, Mr. Ricks. Don't worry! I won't see you stuck, for you've stood by me through thick and thin."

"Why, I didn't give her anything, Joey. I just had her lawyer bring her on to San Francisco for a conference. Of course when lunch time came round and I hadn't heard any proposition I felt I could submit to your father, I invited Miss Fontaine and her lawyer to luncheon with me in the Palace Hotel Grill, and while we were lunching, who should come up and greet me but my old friend, the Duke of Killiekrankie, formerly Duncan MacGregor, first mate of our barkentine *Retriever*. Mac is an excellent fellow and for some time I had felt he merited promotion. So I made him a duke.

"Well, the duke was awfully glad to see me, and being a gentleman I couldn't do less than introduce him to the lady and her lawyer. He only stayed at our table a minute and then rejoined his friends, but all during the meal I could see Betsy Jane's mind wasn't on her breach-of-promise suit. She asked me several questions about the duke, and I told her I didn't know much about him except that he was sinfully rich and a globe-trotter, and that we'd met in Paris. Lies, Joey, but pardonable, I hope, under the circumstances.

"Well, Joey, it seems that she and the duke were registered at the same hotel and I'll be shot if his lordship didn't meet her—by accident, of course—in the lobby that afternoon. He lifted his hat and she smiled and they had a chat. The next day she cut an engagement with her lawyer and me to go motoring with the duke in my French car, and Florry's chauffeur driving, for, of course, the duke was an expensive luxury and I was trying to save a dollar wherever possible. That night the duke gave a dinner party in honor of the lady —and he gave it aboard his yacht, the *Doris*, formerly the *Seafarer*, right out here in San Francisco harbor——"

Joey went up and put his arm round Cappy's shoulders.

"Oh, Cappy Ricks, Cappy Ricks!" he cried, and then his voice broke and his eyes filled with tears.

"Yes," Cappy continued, "I had sort o' suspected she

might pull that breach-of-promise stuff on you,
Joey——"

"What made you suspect it?"

"Why, I sort of suspected you were going to marry
Doris Kenyon——"

"You planned to get us together on the same
ship——!"

"Only place I could think of where you were safe
from the Honolulu lady and couldn't run away from
Doris, Joey. Well, as I say, I had sort of suspected
she might sue you and disgrace you and break the heart
of that little girl I'd picked out for you long before
you ever met her—so I started to get there first and
with the heaviest guns. I borrowed your yacht for the
duke and had him sail her round himself, so he'd have
her here to give the dinner party on. Then I got a
Burke's peerage and told MacGregor who he was and
had him study up on his family history and get acquainted with his sister, Lady Mary, and his younger
brother, the Honorable Cecil Something-or-other—in
particular he was not to forget to rave about the grouse
shooting in Scotland."

Cappy paused and puffed his cigar meditatively for
half a minute.

"Joey," he continued, "any time you run a bluff,
run a good one. If you're starring a globe-trotting
duke, have his ancestry all straightened out in advance,
because he's bound to break into the newspapers and
the motto of the newspaper editor is 'Show me.' And
the yacht—just one of the props of the comedy, Joey;
and with a little cockney steward in livery to say
'Your ludship'; and the name of the yacht changed in
case she'd ever heard you speak about the *Seafarer;*

and the cabin done over in white enamel with mahogany trim; and a new set of dishes with your family crest and the name of the yacht on every piece in case you had ever had her aboard; and a private secretary—borrowed him from my general manager, Skinner, by the way—we were certainly there when it came to throwing the ducal front. And we got away with it, for MacGregor's accent is just Scotchy enough, and he comes of good family and has excellent manners. Yes, I must say Mac made a very comfortable duke. Skinner's young man tells me it would bring tears of joy to your eyes to see him kiss the lady's hand.

"Well, Joey, the upshot of it was that after paying violent court to the lady for two weeks—Mac said he could have pulled the stunt the night of the dinner, for she fell for the title right way, but I told him to make haste slowly—the duke received a cablegram calling him home from his furlough. Oh, yes, Joey, I had him in the army. Any young unattached duke that doesn't join the British army these days doesn't get by in good society, and I had my duke on a six months' furlough to recover from his wounds. Fortunately a bunch of cedar shingles had fallen on Mac's foot recently and he was dog lame, which strengthened the play.

"Of course the duke was up in the air right away. In a passionate scene he confessed his love for that damsel of yours, Joey, and laid his dukedom at her feet. Would she marry him P. D. Q. and help him sail the yacht home? Would she? 'Oh, darling, this is so sudden!' she cried, and almost swooned in his arms. From a cabaret to a dukedom. Some jump! Sail the yacht home to England through the mine fields and

submarines? Perfectly ripping, by Jove! I give you
my word, Joey, she tacked on one of those New York
British accents for the duke's special benefit. There
was a lot of beam to her *a*'s, Mac told me, but blamed
little molded depth to her mentality. So they were
married in haste, and after the duke had seen his bride
in the elevator bound for their rooms at the hotel, he
excused himself to get a highball. And I guess he got
the highball, because I find it in this expense account
he turned in to me."

"It sounds like a fairy tale," Joey murmured in an
awed voice. "What did the duke do next?"   .

"Came right down to this office and informed me he
was plumb weary of the life of a bon vivant and was
anxious to get to sea again. So I made him master of
a new steamer we acquired recently, and he's gone out
to Vladivostok with munitions for the Russians."

"But didn't you give him some money, Mr. Ricks?"

"No. Why should I? Didn't I give him command
of a steamer? You can slip him a fat check if you feel
that way about it, but I never coddle my skippers,
Joey, until I'm sure they're worth while. I think, however, that Mac will make good. He's very thorough."

"Wha—what became of Ernestine?"

"Oh, by Godfrey, that's a sad story, Joey. It seems
she waited at the hotel for the duke to come back and he
didn't come, so the following morning she went down
to the water front looking for the yacht—and the
yacht was gone. During the night I'd had it towed
over to Sausalito; consequently the launchman she
hired couldn't find it down in Mission Bay, and back
to the beach she came. After a couple of days had
passed, however, she commenced to smell a rat, so she

came down to my office and asked me if I'd seen any-thing of the duke.

" 'Why, yes, I have,' I told her. 'The old duke came in here yesterday afternoon, soused to the guards, and complaining he'd been cruelly deceived into marrying a two-time loser with a couple of youngsters, and inas-much as he was certain the family wouldn't receive her he was leaving the United States immediately, never to return.

" 'And this morning the justice of the peace who per-formed the ceremony mailed him the license, which has been duly recorded in the office of the Secretary of State in accordance with law; and inasmuch as the license was sent to him in my care I am holding it in our safe until he calls for it.'

"Well, Joey, she looked at me and she knew the stuff was all off. She'd married the duke; I had the license to prove it, and of course she realized her breach of promise suit and claim for a million dollars' worth of heart balm would be laughed out of court if she had the crust to present it. So she did the next best thing. She abused me like a pickpocket and ended up by get-ting hysterical when I told her how I'd swindled her. When she got through crying I lectured her on the error of her ways and suggested that inasmuch as she had had one divorce already, another wouldn't be much of a strain on her, and I'd foot the bill for separating her legally from John Doe, alias the duke, on a charge of desertion. Then I offered her a thousand dollars and a ticket back to New York for the surrender of all your letters to her and that infernal cablegram and a release of all claims against you. I guess she was broke for she grabbed it in a hurry, Joey. The atmosphere is now clear, my son, and nothing further remains to be done in the premises, save settle the bill of expense. Fortunately the *Tyee* made money on that fast voyage under your command, but the cost of bringing the yacht round from New York, doing over the cabin, buying the new dishes with the crest, and settling with the lady should rightfully be borne by you. As I say, the duke was expensive, for the rascal certainly rolled 'em high. Skinner has made me up a statement of the total cost, with interest at six per cent to date, and it appears, Joey, that you owe your godfather $12,143.18. On the day you come into your inheritance, add six per cent to that sum and send me a check."

"But the twenty-five thousand dollars I won from you——" Joey began, but Cappy held up a rigid finger, enjoining silence.

"I am going to stick your dub of a father for that, as a penance for his sins of omission, Joey; for by the Holy Pink-Toed Prophet, if ever a boy won a bet and was entitled to it, you're that young man. In-fer-nal young scoundrel! Keep it and split fifty-fifty with your wife. You won a straight bet from a crooked gambler, and if I haven't had a million dollars' worth of fun out of this transaction I hope I may marry a hula-hula woman—and I've passed my three score and ten and ought to know better!"

"But about this man MacGregor——"

"Don't worry about him. The Scotch are a hardy race and Mac is a sailor. Joey, I know sailors. The scoundrels have a wife in every port!"

CHAPTER XXXIII

DURING the period when Joey Gurney was busy doing all that Cappy Ricks desired him to do and some things that were slightly off Cappy's program, the president emeritus of the Blue Star Navigation Company and allied interests was discovering that it is one thing to declare for the simple life and quite another to live it. The Great War challenged so much of the Ricks interest that he could not bear to live far from morning and evening editions—and he wanted them red hot off the presses. Things were doing in the shipping world. The most inconceivable trades were being consummated daily, freights were soaring, lumber prices had reached an unprecedentedly high level and promised to go higher; there was something doing every minute and not enough minutes in a working day to accommodate half of these somethings. What more natural, therefore, than that Cappy presently should find himself caught in the maelstrom, even though he told himself daily that, come what might *he* would keep out of it.

The first indefinite evidence that he was about to be engulfed came in the form of a newspaper story, ex the steamer *Timaru*, from Sydney, via Tahiti. There it was, as big as a church—a paragraph of it, tucked away in a column-and-a-half story of the bombardment of Papeete by the German Pacific fleet early in September of 1914:

"An incident of the bombardment was the sinking of the German freight steamer *Valkyrie* by shells from the German fleet. The vessel had been captured by the French gunboat *Zeile* some weeks previous and was at anchor in the harbor, under the guns of the *Zeile,* when the German squadron appeared off the entrance. The gunboat immediately was made the target for the German guns, and sunk. During the attack, however, a wild shell missed the *Zeile* and struck the *Valkyrie,* tearing a great hole in her hull and causing her to sink in ten fathoms at her anchorage."

Ten fathoms! Sixty feet! Why, at that depth Cappy should have known that her masts and funnel would be above water; that in all probability she carried war-risk insurance; that she was so far from anywhere the underwriters would have abandoned her, even had she not been a prize of war, since there are no appliances in Papeete for salving a vessel of her size; that she could be raised if one cared to spend a little money on doing it; that one projectile probably had not ruined her beyond repair; that she was a menace to navigation in Papeete Harbor and hence would have to be gotten out of the way, either by dynamite or auction; that—well, any number of thats should have occurred to Cappy Ricks to suggest the advisability of keeping track of the wreck of the *Valkyrie.* However, for some mysterious reasons—his resentment against the German cause, probably—the golden prospect never appealed to him, for when he had finished reading the article he merely said:

"Well, what do you know about that? Skinner, it's a mighty lucky thing for that German admiral that I'm not the Kaiser, for I'd certainly make him hard to catch. The idea of sinking that fine steamer—and a German steamer at that! Here was the little old French gunboat, about as invulnerable as a red-cedar shingle; and instead of moving into proper position and raking her with their light guns—instead of calling on her to surrender—these Germans had to go to work in a hurry and inaugurate a campaign of frightfulness. The minute they were off the harbor—Zowie! Blooey! Bam! It was all over but the cheering, and they'd chucked an eight-inch projectile through a ship that was worth four of the gunboat.

"Skinner, that's what I call spilling the beans. Why they didn't take their time, recapture that freighter and give her skipper a chance to hustle across to San Francisco or Honolulu and intern, is a mystery to me. The idea! Why, for that German fleet to waste ammunition on that Jim-Crow town and a hand-me-down gunboat was equivalent to John L. Sullivan whittling out a handle on a piece of two-by-four common fir in order to attack a cockroach!"

Cappy was so incensed that he growled about the Germans for an hour. Then he forgot the *Valkyrie*, notwithstanding the fact that the press jogged his memory again when the German fleet, deciding that prudence was the better part of valor, fled from the Pacific to escape the Japanese, only to be destroyed in the South Atlantic by the British fleet. A résumé of the operations of the German squadron in the Pacific brought forth mention of the destruction of the *Zeile* and the *Valkyrie*. However, Cappy's mind was not in Tahiti now, but off the Falkland Islands, for he was very much pro-Ally and devoted more thought to military and naval strategy than he did to the lumber and shipping business.

However, the climax of Cappy's indignation over the disaster to the *Valkyrie* was not attained until a few months later when, in conversation on the floor of the Merchants' Exchange with the skipper of the schooner *Tarus*, who happened to have been in Papeete at the bombardment, he learned he had done the German admiral a grave injustice. He came back to his office, boiling, declaring the French were a crazy nation, and that, after all, he could recall meeting one or two fine Germans during the course of a fairly busy career. He summoned Mr. Skinner and Matt Peasley to hear the sordid tale.

"Remember that steamer *Valkyrie* the Germans were supposed to have sunk by accident in the harbor of Papeete during the bombardment in September of 1914?" he queried.

"I believe I read something about it in the papers at the time," Mr. Skinner replied.

"What about her?" Matt Peasley demanded.

"Why, the Germans didn't sink her at all, Matt! The Frenchmen did it," Cappy shrilled. "The crazy, frog-eating jumping-jacks of Frenchmen! The tramp wasn't flying the German flag—naturally the Frenchmen had hauled it down; so the Germans didn't investigate her. Besides, they were in a hurry—you'll remember the Japs were on their trail at the time; so they just devoted forty minutes to shooting up the town, and beat it. I don't suppose they ever knew they hit the *Valkyrie*; perhaps they figured that, having sunk the gunboat, the *Valkyrie* could up hook and away at her leisure, since there was nothing left to prevent her.

"Huh! Makes me sick to talk about it; but the skipper of the *Tarus* was there at the time and he tells me that, though the *Valkyrie* was pretty well down by the stern, her bulkheads were holding and she wouldn't have sunk if those blamed Frenchmen, fearful that the German fleet was coming back after her, hadn't gone aboard and opened her sea cocks! Yes, sir. Rather than risk having her recaptured, they opened her sea cocks and sunk her! And, at that, they didn't have sense enough to run her out to deep water. No! They had to do the trick as she lay at anchor; and there she lies still, a menace to navigation and a perennial reminder to those Papeete Frenchmen that he who acts in haste will repent at leisure."

To this outburst Mr. Skinner made some perfunctory remark, attributing the situation to a lack of efficiency, while Matt Peasley went back to his office and grieved as he reflected on the corrosive action of salt water on those fine, seven-year-old engines.

CHAPTER XXXIV

Time passed. Mr. Skinner developed a pallor and irritability that bespoke all too truly an attack of nerves, from overwork, and sore against his will was hustled off to Honolulu for a rest while Cappy Ricks had the audacity to take charge of the lumber business. Whereupon Mr. J. Augustus Redell, of the West Coast Trading Company, discovered the unprotected condition of the Ricks Lumber & Logging Company and promptly, in sheer wanton deviltry, proceeded to sew Cappy Ricks up on an order for a million grape stakes.

A word here regarding the said J. Augustus Redell. He was a blithe, joyous creature, still in the sunny thirties, and what he didn't know about the lumber business—particularly the marketing of lumber products—could be tucked into anybody's eyes without impairing their eyesight. Mr. Redell had fought his way up from office boy with the Black Butte Lumber Company to lumber broker with offices of his own. He had owned a retail yard in which business he had gone "bust" for more money than the world appeared to contain. But he had fought his way back and paid a hundred cents on the dollar, including some hundred and forty thousand dollars he had owed the Ricks mills at the time of his collapse. Because he was young and fine and good-natured and brave and brilliant, Cappy had always admired J. Augustus Redell, but after the

241

latter had so splendidly re-established his credit and
formed a partnership with a Peruvian gentleman, one
Señor Luiz Almeida, known locally as Live Wire Luiz,
Cappy found that he had for the genial J. Augustus
an admiration that amounted to affection. The West
Coast Trading Company, under which title Live Wire
Luiz and J. Augustus Redell did a lumber brokerage
business with Mexico, Central American and South
American countries principally, had Cappy Ricks' entire confidence, although he would have died rather
than admit this. Live Wire Luiz he ignored and always
dismissed as a factor in the affairs of that company,
but whenever Redell had a deal on that was too heavy
for his financial sinews, Cappy could always be depended upon to lend a helping hand. On his part,
Redell revered Cappy Ricks as only an idealistic and
naturally lovable rascal of a boy can revere an idealistic and lovable old man. To J. Augustus Redell little,
old, naïve, whimsical, gentle, terrible, brilliant, cunning,
generous, altruistic, prudent, youthful old Cappy
Ricks was a joy forever. With the impishness of his
tender years, Mr. Redell could conceive of no greater
joy than picking on Cappy Ricks just to see the latter
fight back.

Quite early in their friendship, the astute Redell
discovered a rift in Cappy's armor—two rifts, in fact.
The first was that Cappy feared and loathed old age
and fiercely resented even the most shadowy intima-
tion that with age he was, to employ a sporting phrase,
"losing his punch." The second weakness that lay
exposed to Redell was Cappy's passion for wringing
a profit, by ingenious means, from apparently barren
soil where no profit had ever hitherto burgeoned. At

heart Cappy was a speculator; only the fact that he was a prudent and careful speculator had conduced to enrich him rather than impoverish him.

Now, Cappy was fully convinced, from optical evidence, that J. Augustus Redell was a gambler. He admired Redell's genius for business, the soundness of his decisions, the alertness of his mind and the brilliance of his financial *coups*, but—he deprecated the younger man's daring. Cappy called it recklessness. By degrees the old gentleman had come to assume a proprietary interest in Gus Redell and the latter's affairs, for the younger man frequently sought counsel from Cappy and not infrequently, a loan! Cappy knew his young friend to be the soul of manly honor, but—he was young! Ah, yes! He was young. Ergo, he was foolish. True, his foolishness had not as yet been discovered, but Cappy was certain it would come to the surface sooner or later. The boy was reckless— a gambler. Cappy abhorred gambling. He never gambled. Occasionally he speculated! What more natural, therefore, than that little Cappy should presently arrogate to himself the privilege of stabbing young J. Augustus to the vitals from time to time, just to impress upon the boy the knowledge that this is a hard, cold, cruel world with a great many bad men in it!

Nothing could possibly have delighted Redell more. Whenever Cappy stabbed him, forthwith he set about to stab Cappy in return, and thus had developed a joyous business feud. These best of friends spent an hour and a half daily, at luncheon, "picking" on each other, telling tales on each other, eternally "joshing" for the edification of a coterie of their lumber and shipping friends who always lunched in a private dining room at the Commercial Club and who were known within that organization as the Bilgewater Club.

Early in 1915 Redell had seen an opportunity for inducing Cappy Ricks to speculate in grape stakes—to his financial hurt and humiliation. There was to be an election that fall—a special election to see whether California should "go dry" or "stay wet," and for some reason not quite apparent to Mr. Redell, a great many people believed the state would "go dry." Among the people who so believed, Redell discovered, were the woodsmen who, during the winter of 1914, would, under normal conditions, have split from redwood trees sufficient grape stakes to support such new vineyards as would come into bearing in the fall of 1915. Fearing that there would be no market for their grape stakes when the making of wine should be prohibited by law, these woodsmen had made no effort to supply the demand; wherefore the Machiavellian J. Augustus Redell, taking advantage of Mr. Skinner's absence from the office of the Ricks mills, cleverly managed to inculcate in Cappy Ricks the idea that it would be a splendid and profitable venture if he, the said Cappy, should wade into the grape stake market and corner it. The idea appealed to the speculative part of the old gentleman's nature and he had gone to work in a hurry, only to discover, after he had accepted orders from the West Coast Trading Company for a great many carloads of grape stakes for future delivery, that, when the day of reckoning should come, he would not be enabled to pick up enough grape stakes to fill his orders, for the very sufficient reason that nobody had manufactured grape stakes for that year's market, and they were not available at any price!

It had been a cruel blow and Cappy's weakness had been exposed without mercy to the members of the Bilgewater Club by Mr. Redell, who thereafter kept both eyes wide open, knowing that sooner or later Cappy would retaliate.

Retaliation was, of course, inevitable. Cappy realized this. For the first time in his career as a lumber and shipping king the sly old dog realized he had been out-thought, out-played, out-gamed and man-handled by a mere pup. And, though he had taken his beating like the rare old sport that he was, nevertheless the leaves of memory had a horrible habit of making a most melancholy rustling; and for two weeks, following his ignominious rout at the hands of J. Augustus Redell, Cappy's days and nights were entirely devoted to scheming ways and means of vengeance. Curiously enough, it was the West Coast Trading Company that accorded him the opportunity he craved.

Having massacred Cappy in the grape-stake deal and established an unlimited credit thereby, the West Coast Lumber Company, per Señor Felipe Luiz Almeida, alias Live Wire Luiz, decided to purchase a little jag of spruce from the Ricks Lumber & Logging Company. Cappy Ricks looked at the proffered order, saw that it called for number one clear spruce, and promptly accepted it at a dollar under the market. He was to bring the spruce in to San Francisco on one of his own schooners, lay her alongside the *City of Panama* and discharge it into her, for delivery at Salina Cruz, Mexico.

Cappy knew, of course, that Live Wire Luiz handled exclusively the West Coast Trading Company's Mexi-

can, Central and South American business. He knew,
also, that there were many points about the lumber
business that the explosive little Peruvian had still to
learn; so he decided to stab the West Coast Trading
Company, through the innocent and trusting Señor
Almeida, with a weapon he would not have dreamed of
employing had J. Augustus Redell placed the order.
Live Wire Luiz knew the Ricks Lumber & Logging
Company always sold its output on mill tally and inspection; that Cappy Ricks' grading rules were much
fairer to his customers than those of his competitors;
that when he contracted to deliver number one clear
spruce he would deliver exactly that and challenge
anybody to pick a number two board out of the lot.
But what Live Wire Luiz did not know was that there
are two kinds of number one spruce on the Pacific
Coast.   One grows in California and the other in
Oregon and Washington—and Cappy Ricks had both
kinds for sale.

"Aha!" Cappy murmured as he glanced over Live
Wire Luiz's order after the latter had gone. "Number
one clear spruce, eh? All right, sir! Away down in
my wicked heart I know you want some nice number
one stock from our Washington mill, at Port Hadlock;
but unfortunately you have failed to stipulate it—so
we'll slip you a little of the California product and
teach you something you ought to know."

Whereupon Cappy sent the order to his mill on
Humboldt Bay, California. Though this plant manufactured redwood lumber almost exclusively, whenever
the woods boss came across a nice spruce or bull-pine
tree among the redwood he was wont to send it down
to the mill, where it was sawed and set aside for trust-

ing individuals like Live Wire Luiz. When seasoned
this spruce was very good stock. Unfortunately, however, experts differ in their diagnosis of California
spruce. There are those who will tell you it is not
spruce, but a bastard fir; while others will tell you it
is not fir, but a bastard spruce. Cappy Ricks had no
definite ideas on the subject, for he didn't own enough
of that kind of stumpage to grieve him. All he knew
or cared was that when such outlawed stock was billed
as spruce no judge or jury in the land could say it was
fir; also, that in its green state it possessed an
abominable odor!

The lumber was delivered to the *City of Panama* in
due course and, as Cappy had suspected, Live Wire
Luiz failed to come down to her dock and take a smell.
This was a privilege left intact for the consignee at
Salina Cruz; and he, according to Mexican custom,
which only demands a ghost of an excuse to seek a rebate, promptly wired a protest and declared himself
swindled to the extent of five dollars a thousand feet,
gold.

Also, having been similarly outraged once before, he
demanded to know why he had been sent California
spruce; whereupon Live Wire Luiz called up Cappy
Ricks, abused him roundly and sent him a bill for six
dollars a thousand, rebate! Unfortunately for the
West Coast Trading Company, however, it had already
discounted Cappy's invoice; so the latter could afford
to stand pat—which he did.

CHAPTER XXXV

Shortly after noon on the day of his small triumph over the West Coast Trading Company, Cappy Ricks bustled up California Street, bound for luncheon with the Bilgewater Club.

On this day, of all days, Cappy would not have missed luncheon with the Bilgewater Club for a farm. As he breezed along there was a smile on his ruddy old face and a lilt in his kind old heart, for he was rehearsing his announcement to his youthful friends of how he had but recently tanned the hide of a brother! He almost laughed aloud as he pictured himself solemnly relating, in the presence of J. Augustus Redell and Live Wire Luiz, the tale of the ill-favored spruce, excusing his own mendacity the while on the ground that he wasn't a mind reader; that if the West Coast Lumber Company desired northern spruce they should have stipulated northern spruce; that, as alleged business men, it was high time they were made aware of the ancient principle of *caveat emptor*, which means, as every schoolboy knows, that the buyer must protect himself in the clinches and breakaways. And lastly, he planned to claim it the solemn duty of the aged to instruct the young and ignorant in the hard school of experience.

Judge, therefore, of his disappointment when, on entering the lobby of the Merchants' Exchange Building, on the two top floors of which the Commercial

Club is situated, he encountered Redell and Live Wire Luiz leaving the elevator.

The West Coast Trading Company had offices in the same building and, as Redell carried a plethoric suit case, while Live Wire Luiz followed with a small hand bag, Cappy realized they were bound for parts unknown. In consequence of which he realized he had rehearsed to no purpose his exposé of the pair before the Bilgewater Club. He halted the partners and secured a firm grip on the lapel of each.

"Cowards!" he sneered. "Running out on me, eh? By Judas Priest, I just knew you didn't dast to stay and hear me tell the boys about that spruce. Drat you! The next time you'll know the difference between attar of roses and California spruce!"

Redell put down his suit case, pulled out his watch, glanced at it and then at his partner.

"Shall I tell him, Luiz?" he queried.

Live Wire Luiz thereupon consulted his watch, scratched his ear and said:

"Friend of my heart, do you theenk eet ees safe?"

"Oh, yes. He isn't a bit dangerous, Luiz. He's lost all his teeth and all he can do now is sit and bay at the moon."

Live Wire Luiz shrugged.

"I theenk maybe so you are right, *amigo mio*. The steamer she will go to depart in half an hour, an' that ees not time for thees ol' high-binder to do somet'ing. Eet ees what you call one stiff li'l' order. I admit thees spruce bandit ees pretty smart, but—" again Live Wire Luiz shrugged his expressive shoulders—"he ees pretty ol', no? I theenk to myself he

have lose—what you call heem? ah, yes, he have lose
hees punch!"

"I fear he has, Luiz; so I'll tell him. At least the
knowledge will gravel him and take all the joy out of
that stinking little spruce swindle of his."

" 'Twon't neither!" Cappy challenged. "I stung
you there—drat your picture!—and I'm glad I did it.
I rejoice in my wickedness. Cost you five hundred
dollars for making a monkey out of the old man in
that grape-stake deal, Gus."

"Why," said Redell wonderingly, "I thought you'd
forgiven me that, Cappy."

"So I have; but I haven't forgotten. Expect me to
lose my self-respect and forget about it? No, sir!
When I go into a deal and emerge in the red, I take a
look at my loss-and-gain account and forget it; but
when I'm ravished of my self-respect—wow! Look
out below and get out from under! In-fer-nal young
scoundrel! If I don't show you two before I die that
I haven't lost my punch I'll come back from the grave
to ha'nt you. Go on and spin your little tale, Augustus. You can't tell me anything that'll make me mad.
What you got on your mind besides your hair, Gus?
Out with it, boy; out with it! I'm listening."

And Cappy came close to Redell and inclined his
head close to the young fellow's breast; whereupon
Redell put his lips close to Cappy's ear and answered
hoarsely:

"I'm going to Papeete to bid in that sunken German
steamer, *Valkyrie*."

Cappy nodded.

"Huh!" he said. "Is that all? Well, when you re

turn from Papeete you're going to take another journey right away."

"Where?"

"Into the bankruptcy court first, and then up to
the Home for the Feeble-Minded. On the level, boy,
you're overdue at the foolish farm."

"I'll take a chance, Cappy. All you old graybeards
can do is sit on the fence and decry the efforts of the
rising generation. You just croak and knock. Of
course I admit that once on a time an opportunity
couldn't fly by you so fast you wouldn't get some of
the tail feathers; but that was a long time ago."

He paused and glanced at his partner. Sorrowfully
Live Wire Luiz tapped his forehead with his brown,
cigarette-stained forefinger.

"Senile decay!" Redell murmured.

"Sure; I bet you, Mike!" Live Wire Luiz answered.

He wagged his head lugubriously, turned aside and
affected to wipe away a vagrant tear with his salmon-
colored silk handkerchief.

"Look here!" Cappy rasped. "This thing is getting
personal. Never mind about my years, you pup! If
my back is bent a trifle it's from carrying a load of experience and other people's mistakes. And never mind
about my noodle! It may have a few knots and shakes
in it, but they're tight and sound, and it's free of pitch
pockets, wane and rotten streaks; so this old head
grades as merchantable timber still.

"As for your head, Gus, and that of this human
firecracker with you, both have streaks of sap round
the edges, and I'll prove it to you yet. No; on second
thought I don't have to prove it. You've already done

that yourself! You're going to Papeete to try to bid
in the *Valkyrie,* and she's junk!"

"Partly," Redell admitted. "She's been under water
about two years and I suppose the teredo have digested
her upper works by now; but they can be rebuilt quickly
and without a great deal of expense."

"How about her boilers? You'll have to retube
them."

"I don't think so. I was talking with Captain
Hippard, of the Morrison-Hippard Line. They had
the steamer *Chinook* under water a year in Norton
Sound, but they raised her and brought her to San
Francisco under her own steam. You know, Cappy,
it's the combination of water and air that makes iron
and steel rust. It seems that when a boiler is under
water and not exposed to the air it rusts very slowly;
also, the rust is like a soft film—it doesn't pit and
scale off in great flakes. And a couple of years under
water will not do any appreciable damage to the *Valkyrie's* boilers. The *Chinook* is running yet, notwithstanding the fact that fifteen years ago she was submerged
for a year."

"Huh!" Cappy grunted.

"The same condition, of course, holds true with
regard to her hull, only more so," Redell continued.
"The paint will protect the hull perfectly. Of course
if, after getting her up, she is permitted to lie exposed
to the air, the soft film of rust will promptly harden
and scale off and she'll go to glory in a few months.
However, nothing like that will happen, because the
minute she's up she'll be thoroughly cleaned and
scrubbed and painted. Of course the asbestos cover
will have peeled off her boilers, but even at that I'll

bring her to San Francisco under her own steam. She'll just be ungodly hot below decks and a hog for coal until the boilers are re-covered."

Cappy sighed. He was not prepared to combat this argument, for he had a sneaking impression Redell was right. However, he returned undaunted to the attack.

"She's shot full of holes," he declared.

"She has one hole through her, and when she's loaded light that hole is above water line. The wrecking vessel that goes down to salve her will have steel plates, tools and mechanics aboard, and new plates can be put in temporarily. And if that cannot be done those holes can be patched with planking and cemented over."

"Well, all right. Grant that. But think of her engines, Gus. Think of those fine, smooth bearings and polished steel rods all corroded and pitted by salt water. The water may not have a disastrous effect on the boilers and hull, but an engine can't stand any rust at all and still remain one hundred per cent efficient. I tell you I know, Gus. I had my *Amelia Ricks* submerged on Duxbury Reef for a week; then I hauled her off and she lay on the tide flats in Mission Bay another three weeks until I could patch her up and float her into the dry dock. Do you know what it cost me to make her engines over again? Thirteen thousand dollars, young man—and, at that, they're nothing to brag of now."

"Quite right; but that's because you didn't employ a German engineer and tell him you were going to put the *Amelia Ricks* on Duxbury Reef. Are you familiar with the characteristics of German engineers, Cappy?"

Cappy threw up both hands.

"I'm neutral, Gus. Between them and the French it's a case of heads I win, tails you lose."

"No, no, Cappy. You're wrong. The Germans are a careful, thrifty, painstaking, systematic race, and the chief of the *Valkyrie* was the flower of the flock. When that little French gunboat captured her this chief engineer looked into the future and saw himself and the *Valkyrie* interned indefinitely—and he didn't like it. It just broke his heart to think of a stranger messing round among his engines; so the instant he got into Papeete and blew down his boilers he did a wise thing. He knew the war risk insurance would probably cover the *Valkyrie's* loss as a war prize, but there was a chance that her German owners might send one of their hyphenated brethren down to Papeete to buy her in the prize court; and if that happened the chief wanted them to have a good ship. Perhaps, also, he figured on getting his old job back after the war. At any rate he got out a barrel of fine heavy grease and slobbered up his engines for fair."

It was too much. Cappy Ricks was too fine a sport not to acknowledge a beating; he was too generous not to rejoice in a competitor's gain.

"You lucky, lucky scoundrel!" he murmured in an awed voice. "Not enough salt water will get through that grease to hurt those engines. Gus, how did you find this all out?"

"Well, you can bet your whiskers, Cappy, I didn't depend on hearsay evidence and water-front reporters to dig it up for me. The minute I heard her sea cocks had been opened and that her funnels and masts were sticking up out of the harbor I concluded I was interested; so I sent Bill Jinks, of our office, down to

Papeete to get me some first-hand information. The chief of the *Valkyrie* is interned there, of course."

"May mad dogs bite me! Why in the name of all that's sweet and holy didn't I have sense enough to do that?" Cappy mourned.

"You have lose the punch!" chirped Live Wire Luiz, and Cappy glared at him.

"She's an honest vessel, Cappy."

"An' what you s'pose she have in her?" Live Wire Luiz demanded. "Oh, notheeng very much, Señor Ricks. Just two t'ousand tons of phosphate."

"Worth ten or twelve dollars a ton, Cappy."

"An' t'irteen hundred tons of the good coal to bring her to San Francisco. *Ai,* Santa Maria!" Live Wire Luiz blew a kiss airily into space and added: "I die weeth dee-light!"

"You haven't got her yet," Cappy snapped viciously.

"No; but we'll get her all right," Redell declared confidently.

"How'll you get her?"

"We've only one real competitor to buck—an Australian steamship company. They're crazy to get her; and as there are no French bidders on this side of the world, naturally and in view of the present condition of world politics the French authorities in Papeete are pulling for the Britisher. Jinks is now in Papeete and I'm about to start for there at one o'clock. Two bids, Cappy; I'll be the dark horse and file my bid at the last minute, after I've sized up the lay of the land. But, before I do so, I'm going to take the representative of that Australian steamship company into my confidence and find out what he's going to bid. For instance, now, Cappy, if you were bidding against me, how high would you go?"

"She's a long way from nowhere," Cappy replied thoughtfully. "It means sending a wrecking steamer down there with a lot of expert wreckers, divers, mechanics and carpenters; it means lumber for coffer dam and pontoons; it means donkey engines, cables, pumps, the stress of wind and wave——"

"She lies in a protected cove, Cappy; the mean rise and fall of the tide, so close to the equator, is about eighteen inches, and the water is so clear you can always see what the divers are doing. Forget the stress of wind and wave."

"Forty thousand dollars would be my top figure if I were the Australian bidder," Cappy declared, and added to himself: "But, as Alden P. Ricks, seventy-five might not stagger me in view of the present freight rates."

"Just what I figured," Redell answered. "She'll cost us two hundred thousand dollars before we get her in commission again. I figure the Australian people will not go over forty thousand dollars. They won't figure Jinks as a heavyweight. I told him to create the impression that he was a professional wrecker—a sort of fly-by-night junk dealer, who would buy the vessel if he could get her at a great bargain. Then I'll drop quietly into Papeete, and at the eleventh hour fifty-ninth minute I'll slip in a bid that will top the Australian's. If by any chance Jinks' bid should also top the Australian's I'll just forfeit the certified check for ten per cent of my bid, run out and leave the ship to Jinks, the next highest bidder. The chances are I'll make a few thousand dollars at that."

"How do you purpose raising her—provided you are the successful bidder?"

"Well, she has four hatches and she lies on an even keel. I'll build a coffer dam on her deck round these four hatches and pump her out. If we have enough pumps we can pump her out faster than the water can leak in under the coffer dam. When I've lightened her somewhat I'll kick her into the shore, little by little, until she lies in shallow water with her bulwarks above the surface. Then I'll patch the holes in her, pump her out—and up she'll come, of course."

"You say that so glibly," Cappy growled, "one would almost think you could whistle it."

"Don't feel sore, Cappy. Do you know what a vessel of her age and class is worth nowadays? Well, I'll tell you. About sixty dollars a ton, dead weight capacity—and the *Valkyrie* can carry seven thousand tons; that's four hundred and twenty thousand dollars——"

"If you can get her up," Cappy interrupted.

"If I bid her in I'll get her up. Don't worry."

"It'll clean you of your bank roll to do it."

"Of course. Luiz and I aren't millionaires like you; so we'll just form a corporation and call it the S. S. Valkyrie Company and sell stock in our venture. I have you down right now for a ten-thousand-dollar subscription at the very least, though you can have more if you want it."

"Gus," Cappy pleaded, "if you bid that boat in for forty thousand dollars I'll give you ten thousand dollars for your bargain and reimburse you for all the expense you've been put to."

"Nothing doing, Cappy."

"I'll make it—let me see—I'll make it twenty thousand."

"You waste your breath. She'll pay for herself the first year she's in commission."

"I'll furnish the sinews of war, Gus, for a half interest in her. Let me add her to the Blue Star Fleet and you'll never regret it."

"Sorry, Cappy; but Luiz and I are ambitious. We want to get into the steamship business ourselves."

"Well, then, I've offered to do the fair thing by you two lunatics," Cappy declared with a great air of finality. "So now I'll deliver my ultimatum: I'm going to keep the *Valkyrie* and not give you two as much as, one little piece of her. Yes, sir! I'm going to send a representative to Papeete and match you and that Australian chap for your shoe-strings. Gus, you know me! If I ever go after a thing and don't get it, the man that takes it away from me will know he's been in a fight."

"Indeed, I know it, Cappy—which is why I kept this information carefully to myself. However, I guess you'll not get in on this good thing."

"Why?"

"You're too late for the banquet."

"Not one leetle hope ees left for you, Cappy Reeks," Señor Almeida asserted. "The *Moana*, on which my good partner have engaged passage to-day, ees the last steamer which shall arrive to Papeete before the bids shall be open. The next steamer, Capitan Reeks ees arrive too late."

"Yes; and the *Moana* sails in just twenty-five minutes, Cappy. If you're thinking of sending a man down to bid against me you'll have to step lively."

Cappy Ricks was now beside himself; this gentle, good-natured heckling had made of him a venerable Fury.

"I'll cable my bid!" he shrilled.

"No you won't Cappy, for the reason that there is no cable to Tahiti."

"Then I'll wireless it!"

"Well, you can try that, Cappy. Unfortunately, however, the only wireless station in Tahiti is a little, old, one-cat-power set. It can receive your message, but it can't send one that will reach the nearest wireless station—and that's at Honolulu. And until the bank in Tahiti can confirm drafts by wireless I imagine it will not pay them on presentation."

Cappy surrendered. He couldn't stand any more.

"Good-bye, Gus," he said. "Good luck to you! If you get that vessel you'll deserve her, and when you're forming the S.S. Valkyrie Company I'll head the list of stock subscribers with a healthy little chunk. You know me, Gus! I'm the old bell mare in shipping circles; a lot of others will follow where I lead."

"I forgive you the spruce deal, Cappy. You're an awful pirate; but, for all that, you're a grand piece of work. God bless you!" And Redell put his arm round the old man affectionately. "Good-bye."

And, followed by Live Wire Luiz, who was going to the dock to see his partner aboard the *Moana*, Redell disappeared into California Street.

"Dammit!" Cappy soliloquized bitterly. "**I can't eat lunch now. One bite would choke me.**"

CHAPTER XXXVI

And he turned toward the entrance to the Merchants' Exchange, being minded to enter a telephone booth and notify the Bilgewater Club he would not be present that day. As he walked through the gate into the Exchange, however, he was accosted by a heavy, florid-faced man carrying a thick woolen watch coat over his arm. This individual was Captain Aaron Porter, one of the San Francisco bar pilots, and he greeted Cappy with a respectful query after the old gentleman's health.

"I don't feel very well," Cappy replied wearily. "I'm getting old, captain—getting old."

Then he noted the watch coat the pilot was carrying and decided subconsciously that there could be no connection between it and the sultry August weather prevailing at that moment; consequently it informed the observant Cappy, as plainly as if it had a tongue and had spoken, that Captain Aaron Porter expected shortly to be exposed to the chill northwest winds outside as he piloted a vessel to sea. In the manufacture of sheer inane conversation, therefore, Cappy tugged the coat and said:

"Going to take a ship out this afternoon, captain?"

"Yes, sir. I'll be responsible for the *Moana* until we cross the Potato Patch——"

"The *Moana!*" Cappy cried, and pulled out his

watch. "You'd better be stepping lively, then. She sails at one, and you have twenty minutes to get to Greenwich Street Pier."

"Oh, there's no hurry, Mr. Ricks. She'll be delayed from half to three-quarters of an hour waiting for the Australian mail. The mail train from the East is late, and of course the *Moana* cannot sail till——"

"You will pardon me, captain," Cappy Ricks interrupted politely, "but I've just thought of a very important matter. I must run and telephone."

As J. Augustus Redell had just pointed out, twenty minutes was scarcely ample time in which to decide on the right emissary to send to Papeete, get into communication with the said individual and induce him to go. In addition, such a person would have to have time to pack some clothing; also, to procure a letter of credit at the bank and purchase a ticket, not to mention the time requisite to receive his instructions and get to the steamer's dock. But with almost an hour—well, a wide-awake man can accomplish much in an hour, and Cappy Ricks was a natural leader of forlorn hopes. In the brief interval required to accomplish the journey from the door of the Merchants' Exchange to a telephone booth a flock of bright ideas capered through Cappy's ingenious head like goats on a tin roof.

"Main 2000!" he barked, and in five seconds he had the connection. "Put Skinner on the line!"

Cappy's own private exchange operator had the temerity to inform him that Mr. Skinner was out at luncheon.

"The in-fer-nal scoundrel—just when I need him! Put Captain Matt Peasley on the line, and be quick about it. Matt! Matt, listen! This is the old man speaking. Get an earful of what I'm going to tell you now, and don't ask any questions—just obey! Do you remember that big German freighter—the *Valkyrie*—sunk in Papeete Harbor?"

"Yes, sir."

"She's a prize, Matt. I've just been given a low-down on her condition. Gus Redell is leaving on the *Moana* to bid her in at the government sale—the young scoundrel told me all about it and twitted me because we were asleep on the job and let the good thing get away from us. The *Moana's* supposed to sail at one o'clock, but the Eastern mail is late—she won't get away from the dock until about one-thirty; but when she does——"

"When she does we'll have a man aboard her to beat Redell to the German steamer," Matt Peasley interrupted. "I've got the message. Where are you, father-in-law?"

"At the Merchants' Exchange."

"You attend to the funds and I'll do the rest."

"Confound you!" rasped Cappy Ricks. "You're so headstrong, you'll jam things up yet if you don't listen to me."

"But you'll have to send somebody Redell doesn't know."

"That doesn't matter at all. Now, son, will you listen to me? I'll attend to the money and I'll also frame this entire deal. Is Miss Keenan in the office— you know—Skinner's stenographer?"

"Yes, sir."

"She's been wanting to go on a vacation. When I heard about it I asked her how she'd like a cruise to

Alaska—remember we have the *Tillicum* leaving at
six to-night for St. Michael's. She said that would
be fine; so I gave her a pass and the owner's suite
on the *Tillicum*."

"So I hear. Her trunk was sent to the *Tillicum's*
dock this morning and she has her suit case in the
office. She planned to work today and go aboard the
Tillicum after office hours."

"Good! Then she's all ready 1or a voyage to
Tahiti. Have the private exchange operator phone our
wharf office instantly and tell them to load Miss
Keenan's trunk on the first wagon handy and rush it
over to the *Moana.* Give Miss Keenan fifteen hundred
dollars and tell her she's to go to Papeete. If she kicks
about clothes tell her to get along with what she has
and buy what she needs on arrival."

He waited while Matt Peasley gave the necessary
instructions to the exchange operator. Then:

"It's all right, sir. Miss Keenan will go. She'll
be on her way in five minutes. I've told her to go
aboard and buy her ticket from the purser or from
the ticket agent at the gang plank."

"Fine business! Now who else have we in our employ
that I can send? I want a man—and a rattling smart
one."

"Mike Murphy, the skipper of the *Narcissus*," Matt
suggested.

"The very man! He's discharging at Union Street
Wharf. Phone the wharfinger's office and tell him he'll
not regret taking a message down to the dock to Captain Murphy. Murphy will probably be at lunch
aboard. Tell the wharfinger to tell him to throw a few
clothes into a suit case—that he's to go to Papeete on

mighty important business—and to meet me at the head
of Greenwich Street Dock at one-twenty, without fail,
for his orders and his money. Having phoned these
orders, Matt, take the office automobile and scorch
to the water front to see that they're carried out.
Take Miss Keenan with you. Good-bye."

And Cappy Ricks dashed out of the Merchants' Exchange as though the devil was at his heels walloping
him at every jump. It was four blocks to the Marine
National Bank, but the California Street cable car took
him there in four minutes. Gasping and perspiring
Cappy trotted into the cashier's office, where for ten
precious seconds he stood, open-mouthed, unable to
say a word.

"Well, Mr. Ricks," the cashier greeted him, "if you
can't talk make signs."

Cappy flapped his hands and made three rapid
strokes with his index finger, like a motion-picture
actor writing a twelve-line letter; then the words came
in a veritable cascade.

"Letters of credit," he croaked—"two." The cashier
picked up a pencil and a scratch pad. "One, twenty-
five thousand, favor Michael J. Murphy; one, favor—
oh, what in blue blazes is that girl's first name? Oh,
dear! Oh, dear! I never heard her first name—she's
just Miss Keenan. Oh, the devil! Call her Matilda—
that's it—Matilda Keenan—fifty thousand dollars for
her; and——"

"You appear to be in a terrific hurry for them, Mr.
Ricks, so I'll get them started immediately," the cashier
interrupted, and turned his memorandum over to an
underling, with instructions to give Mr. Ricks' letters
of credit precedence over all other business.

"Now write—check—your favor—seventy thousand. I'll sign it—hope Skinner has enough cash on deposit; if he hasn't—my personal note, you know."

"A mere trifle, Mr. Ricks. We will not worry over that." The cashier filled in the check and Cappy signed it with a trembling hand. "And now," the cashier continued, "we will have to have Miss Keenan and Mr. Murphy come to the bank to register their respective signatures——"

"Nothing doing!" Cappy piped. "Give me the cards and I'll have 'em write their signatures on them aboard the steamer and send them ashore by the pilot. None o' your efficiency monkey business, my son! I guarantee everything."

He dashed to the telephone and yelled into the receiver: "Taxicab! Taxicab!"

"One of the cars belonging to the bank is at the curb, Mr. Ricks. The chauffeur will take you wherever you desire to go," the cashier suggested.

"Bully for you!" Again Cappy commenced to flap his hands. "Stenographer—where's the stenographer? Oh, Judas Priest, nobody helps me! Bless your sweet heart, my dear, here you are, aren't you? Yes, and I'll not forget you for it either. No, no, no! No notes. Just stick piece of paper in the typewriter—now then! Ready! Dictation direct to machine. Er—ah! Harumph-h-h! Oh, suffering sailor! What's the name of the French bank in Papeete? I don't know. I'm a director and vice president of this infernal bank—and I don't know I'm alive! Man, man, I want it—a thing —a what-you-may-call-'em—a——Oh, the devil! Why do I deposit in this dratted bank? Eureka! I have it! I want a notice."

"You mean an advice, Mr. Ricks."

"Bully boy! An advice. That's it. Holy mackerel, how I love a man that's fast on his feet! A notice to the bank in Papeete, Island of Tahiti, that you've given Captain Michael J. Murphy a letter of credit for twenty-five thousand dollars—only one notice for one letter of credit. I'm up to skullduggery. Man, man, why don't you dictate? Usual courtesies—good customer of your bank—you know; usual flubdub. No advice regarding Miss Keenan's letter of credit—just Murphy's."

The cashier good-naturedly shouldered Cappy Ricks aside and dictated to the bank's correspondent in Papeete a brief note to the effect that the Marine National had that day issued to Captain Michael J. Murphy a letter of credit in the sum of twenty-five thousand dollars; that it understood Captain Murphy was proceeding to Papeete on some matter of business and took this occasion to commend him to their kindly offices.

"Stick that in an envelope—address envelope, seal it, and write outside: 'Kindness purser S.S. *Moana.*' The mail to Papeete is closed, but I'll see that the *Moana's* purser delivers it to the bank," Cappy ordered.

CHAPTER XXXVII

Ten minutes later Cappy dashed up to the entrance of Greenwich Street Pier and found Matt Peasley waiting for him, with Captain Murphy. Miss Keenan had already gone aboard the *Moana*, the huge funnel of which, as Cappy noted with a thrill, was still sticking up over the roof of the dock. He crooked his finger and Michael J. Murphy leaped up on the running board of his car.

"Mike," said Cappy solemnly, "listen to me! Here's a letter of credit in your name for twenty-five thousand dollars, and an advice to the bank in Papeete from our bank here stating that the letter of credit has been issued. Give this letter to the purser, together with a good-sized bill, and ask him to deliver it to the Papeete bank when the *Moana* arrives there. Here, also, is a letter of credit for Miss Keenan in the sum of fifty thousand—and the bank in Papeete has no notice of it! Remember that! It's important. Keep it to yourself. Miss Keenan has the expense money for both of you; tell her to split the roll with you. Tell her, also, that her name from now until she gets back is Matilda Keenan, and to sign her drafts that way.

"Here are the signature cards. You sign yours and have her sign hers; then you give both to Captain Porter, the pilot, when he leaves the ship, and ask him

to deliver them to me. I, in turn, will deliver them to
the bank. Tell Miss Keenan she is absolutely under
your orders; that she's to forget she ever heard of the
lumber and shipping business. Both of you are to keep
away from a man by the name of J. Augustus Redell.
He's aboard and he's our enemy, captain. He's going
to bid forty thousand dollars on the German steamer
Valkyrie; so you bid forty thousand and five dollars—
and take her away from him. At the very last minute
have Miss Keenan put in a bid for thirty thousand—
in case—you know, Mike—we might catch it going
and coming. It might pay to have you fall down on
your bid—you know, Mike! She's the dark horse—the
reserve capital. "Papeete—one-horse town, Mike.
Everybody knows the other fellow's business—principal competitor for the steamer is an Australian
steamship company. Considering condition world
politics today, and no French bidders, naturally
Frenchmen will pull for the Britisher. Expect bank
will leak and tell 'em you only arrived with twenty-five
thousand—you know, Mike! Can't be too careful.
Trust nobody—and remember this man Redell is the
smartest young man in the world and the trickiest
scoundrel under heaven. Don't hold him cheap. He's
a holy terror! He'd pinch the gold out of your wisdom
teeth while you'd be laughing at him."

"How high am I to go—if it becomes necessary to
bid more than——"

"Shoot the piece!" Cappy ordered. It is to be re-
gretted that the Bilgewater Club, cut off from the
house rules in a private dining room, had a habit of
shooting craps occasionally after luncheon, and Cappy
Ricks had picked up the patois of the game. "Seventy-

five thousand is the limit; but satisfy yourself she's worth the limit before you go to it."

"And Redell is going to bid forty thousand, sir?"

"That's his limit. He told me so in confidence when he felt certain I couldn't possibly be a competitor— told it to me, and kidded me for a dead one at twenty minutes of one, when he knew I couldn't possibly have time to act. But he forgot the mail—it was delayed——"

"I get you, sir. There's more to this job than merely acquiring the ship," retorted the astute Murphy.

"There's a million dollars' worth of satisfaction in it for me if I can beat Gus Redell to that steamer. He says I've lost my punch."

But Captain Murphy was off down the dock, suit case in hand, while Cappy dismissed his borrowed car and climbed into the office car with Matt Peasley. Five minutes they waited at the head of the dock—and then four huge motor trucks, laden with mail, lumbered through the dock gate. Cappy beamed into Captain Matt Peasley's face.

"I guess this is a rotten day's work for the president emeritus, eh?" he chuckled. "President emeritus! By the Holy Pink-Toed Prophet, if I waited for you and Skinner to get wise to all the good things that are lying round loose, the Blue Star Navigation Company would be in the hands of a receiver within the year. Matt, if you expect to manage the Blue Star you'll have to wake up. You're slow, boy—s-l-o-w-w! For heaven's sake, don't force me back into the harness! You know I've been wanting to retire for years."

"Well, our messengers are aboard, so let's get out

of here. I'm hungry; I haven't had any lunch," Matt replied.

"Come to think of it," Cappy answered cheerfully, "I believe I could eat a little something myself. However, I still have one small duty to perform, Matthew. I've got to send a wireless."

"To whom?"

"That scoundrel Redell, of course. Think I'm going to swat him and leave him in ignorance of the fact?"

Immediately upon arrival at the Commercial Club, Cappy sent the following message:

"J. Augustus Redell,
        "Aboard S. S. *Moana.*
    "Augustus, my dear young friend, I have known men who grew rich by keeping their mouths closed!
                                                "CAPPY."

"There!" said Cappy, as he dispatched this simple declarative sentence. "I'll wager one small five-cent bag of smoking tobacco our friend Gus Redell will not sleep to-night. He'll just lie awake wondering what in Sam Hill I meant by that."

When he got back to his office he found an aërogram, which read as follows:

"Alden P. Ricks
        "258 California Street
        "San Francisco
    "Everything lovely. After getting aboard decided to bluff; went to Redell, told him I was your representative. He went green clear back of the ears; said he had observed delay in sailing. Told him he'd better quit and go ashore with pilot; that I had bank roll choke hippopotamus. Your wireless handed him that moment! Would hesitate repeat his language. Have agreed pay him for his first-class

ticket. All first-class cabins sold out; had to have it for Matilda. Steerage an awful place for a skipper, but will have to make the best of it.

                                                    "MURPHY."

Mr. Skinner, alarmed at the shrill screams emanating from Cappy Ricks' office, rushed in and found the president emeritus rolling round in his swivel chair, beating the air and stamping on the floor.

"Good gracious, Mr. Ricks!" Skinner cried. "What's the matter? Are you hurt?"

"Hurt!" Cappy shrilled. "Hurt? Well, I should say so! Skinner, my boy, if you ever lose your punch you'll know just how much I'm suffering. As Live Wire Luiz would say: 'I die weeth dee-light!'"

CHAPTER XXXVIII

Three months later Cappy Ricks sat alone in his office, his feet on his desk, his old head bowed on his breast. Apparently he was having a gentle snooze. Suddenly he sat up with the suddenness of a jack-in-the-box and stepped to the door leading to Mr. Skinner's office.

"Skinner, my dear boy," he said, "do you remember that stinking Humboldt spruce I sawed off on Live Wire Luiz one day when you were out to lunch?"

Mr. Skinner nodded.

"They claimed a rebate of six dollars a thousand on it," he declared; "and we declined to allow the claim. Well, I've decided to allow it, Skinner. Tell Hankins to draw a check for the rebate in full and bring it in to me. Send in a stenographer."

Cappy clawed his whiskers as the stenographer took her seat at his desk.

"Ahem! Hum! Harumph-h-h!" he began. "Take letter."

"Mr. J. Augustus Redell
   "President West Coast Trading Co.
      "Merchants' Exchange Building, City.
   "My dear Gus: Having waited for several weeks in the hope of meeting you at the Bilgewater Club, to which, due to some mysterious reason, you appear to have been excessively disloyal of late, I despair of the delight of a personal interview and am accordingly writing you.

"You will recall that jag of odoriferous spruce your excitable partner was chump enough to buy from the Ricks Lumber & Logging Company. On the receipt this morning of a communication from my exceedingly capable representative in Papeete I came to the conclusion that I could afford to allow the rebate claimed by the excessively sour-balled Señor Almeida, and accordingly I am inclosing herewith, to the order of your company, the Ricks Lumber & Logging Company's check for $536.12.

"I also beg to tender you my assurance that if I have seemed in the past to cherish an unchristian resentment of that little deal in grape stakes, the memory of the outrage no longer rankles in my bosom. For you, my dear young friend, I entertain the kindliest, the most paternal of feelings. I have not only forgiven, but I have also forgotten; for my honor is clear again and I figure I can pretty blamed well afford myself the luxury.

"Regarding that steamer *Valkyrie,* please be advised that the next steamer to Australia, via Papeete and Raratonga, will carry a Blue Star flag and my instructions to our representative to have it tacked to the main truck of the *Valkyrie* as she dies submerged in the harbor. Since I assume you will be interested in learning the details of our acquisition of the steamer in question, and since, further, I cannot see that I have anything to lose by withholding this interesting information, please be advised that we bought her in for twenty-two thousand five hundred dollars.

"I fear you will be inclined to doubt this and accuse me of romancing for the purpose of dropping more salt in a wound still fresh and bleeding; but I assure you such a suspicion would be a grave injustice to an old man whose portion from you should be pity, not opprobrium.

"To begin, it was very easy—after we had you out of the way. Like a sensible man, you knew you were licked and threw up the sponge to save yourself unnecessary punishment. It has been my experience that only a very wise man has sense enough to do that; consequently, despite your youth and impetuosity, I seem to see the glimmer of a very brilliant commercial future for the West Coast Trading Company.

"However, to the story: When Mike Murphy got down to Papeete he found a couple of broken-down junk dealers hanging round—the kind of fellows who would have been glad to bid in the vessel at a couple of thousand dollars for the privilege of breaking her up for junk and gutting her of her cargo. A little reflection convinced Captain Murphy that he could eliminate these small fry and centre his attention on the Australian steamship company; and he was aided in arriving at this conclusion by your Mr. Jinks, whom he found glooming at the dock on the arrival of the *Moana* minus your handsome self. By the way, Mr. Jinks' action in aiding and abetting Murphy, after discovering that his own company was out of the running, was so sportsmanlike that, if you will kindly advise me of the expense to which you were put in sending him to Papeete, we will gladly send you our check to cover.

"It took the capable Murphy about an hour and a half to get the lay of the land—and then he started to play his little game. In the rather restricted society of Papeete Murphy played the fool. Every little while he would apparently acquire a small jag and get very confidential. He told everybody his business—in confidence—and everybody in Papeete knew just how much he was going to bid on the wreck. Finally, the day before the bids were to be opened—Murphy was waiting till the last minute before filing his—the captain of the port got a wireless from some adventurer down in Nouméa, asking him to withhold the opening of the bids till he could get up to Papeete and make a bid. Murphy had already fooled away three weeks in Papeete and if the captain of the port hearkened to the request from the man from Nouméa it would mean a wait of another three weeks. Consequently he awaited the next move with interest.

"Well, Augustus, the captain of the port had the temerity to delay the opening of the bids, and Murphy noticed that his competitor hired an attorney and made a bitter and formal protest against the delay. However, it looked to Murphy like they had made just a little bit too much noise—so he hired an attorney and made a lot of noise himself. The captain of the port overruled both protests, however; and about that time Murphy decided to put over a dirty Irish trick. He announced he could see very clearly there was a move on to double-cross the legitimate bidders and that he wasn't going to hang round any longer. The *Timaru* was due the next day, so he and Jinks engaged passage to San Francisco on her; and, just before he left, Murphy went up to the bank and drew eighteen thousand dollars on his letter of credit.

"He got a certificate of deposit in his own name, and that same afternoon his attorney filed a sealed bid with the captain of the port.

"Now I had suspected there might be a leak from that French bank in favor of the Australian; so I had taken care to have it advised by the Marine National here that the latter bank had issued a letter of credit for twenty-five thousand dollars to Captain Murphy. Therefore, the Papeete bank very naturally concluded that twenty-five thousand dollars was all the money Murphy had with him! And when he drew eighteen thousand dollars on it they thought they knew the exact amount of his bid; they thought, also, he had made a bid, in view of the fact that his attorney filed one the same afternoon. At any rate, the news reached the Australian and he withdrew his bid and substituted another. Since he was the possessor of straight inside information as to the amount of his single competitor's bid, he saw no reason why he should waste money; so he bid four thousand pounds, or approximately

nineteen thousand five hundred dollars. They say he felt
pretty sore when the bids were opened and the *Valkyrie*
went to Miss Matilda Keenan for twenty-two thousand five
hundred dollars.

"Miss Keenan, by the way, is Skinner's stenographer.
Murphy was only the decoy. She carried the real bank
roll and nobody suspected her; in fact, Murphy was so
certain of his prey he didn't even bid! He tells me the
Valkyrie is really a gift, and that, at the widest possible
estimate of salvage cost, the Blue Star Navigation Company has purchased, for two hundred thousand dollars, a
four-hundred-and-fifty-thousand-dollar ship — thanks to
you!

"With kindest regards, and again assuring you of the
pleasure I have always taken in our friendship—a friendship which, I trust, nothing will ever disrupt—I am

"Cordially and sincerely ———"

Cappy paused and gazed at the stenographer appraisingly.

"Read that over again, my dear young lady," he
commanded.

The girl complied and Cappy nodded his satisfaction.

"You and Mr. Skinner get along all right?" he
queried.

"Oh, yes, sir."

"I'm very glad to hear that. You've been substitut-
ing for Miss Keenan, haven't you?"

"Yes, sir."

"Well, you can have the job for keeps if you want
it. You suit me. Take letter: 'Miss M. Keenan—'
I called her Matilda, but her name's Mary; so let it
go at that.

"My dear Miss Keenan: Captain Murphy arrived on the *Timaru,* with the information that he had taken a chance and left our affairs in the laps of the gods and the capable hands of his understudy. It has been pretty tough sledding waiting for the next Australian steamer, but, thank God! she made port yesterday and your report of the success of your mission is before me. I thank you. You're a good girl, and I am very happy to learn of your engagement to Captain Murphy. He is a splendid fellow and I am sending him back to Papeete in command of our *Amelia Ricks,* which has been fitted up as a wrecker, to raise the *Valkyrie.* You had better wait in Papeete and marry him there, as I am opposed to long engagements among my employees; and Michael will do better and faster work if he settles all his personal worries before tackling those of the Blue Star Navigation Company.

"On his return with the *Valkyrie* I shall make him port captain of the Blue Star Fleet, which job will keep him home nights. And since, by his ingenuity, he succeeded in purchasing for twenty-two thousand five hundred dollars a piece of property for which I was prepared to pay as high as seventy-five thousand dollars, for your wedding present I shall allot you and Captain Murphy a ten-thousand-dollar piece of the *Valkyrie.* It should earn you thirty per cent and make you independent in your old age.

"Very sincerely ——"

Cappy Ricks ceased dictating and clawed his whiskers reflectively.

"Yes," he murmured irrelevantly; "I guess that's considerable of a knock-out from an old fogy who's lost his punch!"

Then, to the stenographer:

"That will be all, my dear. As you pass through the general office tell those fellows out there that I've

gone into executive session with myself and am not to
be disturbed unless it's something very important. I've
got to decide which one of our skippers to promote
into the *Valkyrie* when we get her up and I must think
up a new name for her. I think I'll call her the J. H.
Skinner. Skinner's a little slow on his feet, but he
means well and he's old enough to have a ship named
after him."

CHAPTER XXXIX

THE practical theft from the West Coast Trading Company of the German steamer *Valkyrie*, had, to Cappy's mind, atoned for the loss and humiliation he had suffered in that grape stake deal. His honor was clean again and for weeks he taunted Redell with the latter's inefficiency, insufficiency and general business debility, until, having extracted the last shred of triumph from the affair, a vague sympathy for Redell commenced to surge up in Cappy's kindly heart and he commenced casting about for an opportunity to do the former a favor.

Redell had enjoyed his beating, for he was, indeed, a rare sport. However, he would have to retaliate. The feud must go on. Unless he could mix a modicum of fun with his profits, J. Augustus would not have regarded the fight worth while, so accordingly he kept his eyes and his ears open for a handy weapon with which to jab Cappy through that same old rift in his armor—his passion for a large profit through an adroit and ingenious deal in a commodity where even a very modest profit was not discernible to ordinary mortals.

Finally Redell found the opportunity he sought. He was so proud of his formula that he could not forbear remarking casually to Live Wire Luiz one bright day that, granted good health and the approval of Providence for one week, he would knock Cappy Ricks for a goal. And he narrated his scheme.

"Friend of my heart!" the little Peruvian cried excitedly, and held out his arms to Redell, inviting a fraternal embrace. "I love you! Damn eet! I say eet! You are one wezard weeth the money-making schemes!"

Mr. Redell cautiously compromised on a hearty handshake; to avoid a kiss he was careful to keep the table between himself and Live Wire Luiz.

"Shall we empty the corporate sock and climb aboard for every cent we can beg, borrow or steal?" he demanded.

"Sure, I bet you!" Live Wire Luiz cried; for, though a featherweight physically, he was possessed of the courage of an Alexander.

J. Augustus Redell put on his hat, took from a pigeonhole in his desk the last trial balance of the West Coast Trading Company's books and departed for a conference with his banker. Half an hour later he returned, and the expectant Luiz promptly noted a cloud on Mr. Redell's sunny countenance.

"I can't arrange for a loan," he reported disgustedly. "The limit, in view of our present obligations, has been reached."

"On the margin of ten cents," suggested Live Wire Luiz, "take a chance, *amigo*. Thees is not speculation. It ees what you call the ceench weeth the copper reevets."

"I figure it that way; nevertheless, copper-riveted cinches sometimes aren't properly cinched and Fortune backs out of the packsaddle. I dare not take a long chance on this, Luiz. If something went wrong we'd

be sadly embarrassed. We dare not take a chance up
to the limit of what money we have on hand, because
we need those funds for other things."

Live Wire Luiz swore mournfully in Spanish. Redell
nodded and retired to his own office, where for an hour
he sat with his head in his hands, searching his agile
brain for a bright idea that would lead him out of his
dilemma. Suddenly he leaped to his feet, tossed his
hat to the ceiling and caught it again as it came down.

"Cappy Ricks is my meat," he declared aloud. "Besides, I owe Cappy one for making a monkey out of
me on that last deal. He hoisted me on my own petard.
Now I'll hoist him, and incidentally annex a profit for
the West Coast Trading Company."

He rushed out into California Street and for the
major portion of the day was very busy among various
shipping offices. When he returned, late in the afternoon, to the offices of the West Coast Trading Company, his alert young face wore a pleased and confident
smile. Live Wire Luiz noted this and took heart of
hope.

CHAPTER XL

Cappy Ricks was, for the thousandth time since his voluntary retirement from active business some ten years previous, overwhelmed with his ancient responsibilities. Mr. Skinner had, under the insistent prodding of his wife, consented grudgingly to a vacation and had gone up into the Sierras to loaf and fish.

Scarcely had Skinner departed when one of the Blue Star steamers ran ashore on the Southern California coast, and Captain Matt Peasley left immediately for the scene of the disaster to superintend the work of floating the stranded vessel. This left Cappy riding herd on the destinies of the Blue Star ships, with Mr. Hankins, Skinner's understudy, looking after the lumber.

Prior to boarding the train, Matt Peasley had ventured the suggestion that Mr. Skinner be ordered by wire to return to town at once; but this veiled hint that the Blue Star ships could not be managed by the man who had built up the Blue Star Navigation Company had been received very coldly by the president emeritus of the Ricks interests.

"Young feller," Cappy informed his son-in-law testily, "I'll have you know I was managing the Blue Star Navigation Company quite some years before you quit wearing pinafores; so I guess, while you and Skinner are away from the office, we can manage to stagger along after a fashion."

He always shouted when telephoning.

"But I don't like to have you worried with business after you've retired——"

"Retired!" Cappy hooted. "Swell chance I've got to retire! I'll die in the harness whether I want to or not. Tut, tut, my boy! Don't be afraid to put me in as a pinch hitter for this organization. The worst I can do is to single—and I might clout a home run."

"But Skinner has been away two weeks——"

"Enough! It would be a bad thing to obsess Skinner with the notion that we can't get along without him. Then he never would take a rest; and I don't want any martyrs or neurasthenics round my office. You got anything on the fire that's liable to burn or boil over before you get back?"

"Nothing to worry about, Cappy," Matt answered. "Our five-masted schooner *Mindoro* is the only vessel requiring immediate attention. She arrived at Sydney yesterday with lumber from Gray's Harbor, and as yet I haven't been able to get a satisfactory return cargo for her."

"What have you been holding out for?"

"I want to get a cargo for delivery in San Francisco if possible. The vessel will be ready to go on dry dock by the time she gets back here; and besides, I'm planning to put a semi-Diesel-type engine in her."

"Not by a jugful! She wasn't built with a shaft log, and I won't have you weakening my *Mindoro* by cutting away her deadwood——"

"Tish! Tush! You're a back number, Cappy. They don't cut through the deadwood any more. They run the shaft out over her quarter and hang it on struts."

"She'll carry a helm——"

"She'll not; but if she does, let her. It'll give the helmsman something to do."

Cappy subsided, fearful that if he persisted he might be given new evidence of the fact that times had changed a trifle, here and there, since he had—ostensibly—gone on the retired list.

"Well, I'll take care of the *Mindoro*," he assured his son-in-law. "Early in life I adopted the woodpecker as my patron saint. Ever since, whenever I want anything I keep pecking away, and pretty soon I bust through somewhere."

The following morning, bursting with a sense of responsibility, Cappy came bustling down to the office and got on the job at eight-thirty. After looking through the mail he called up all the freight brokers in town and urged them to make a special effort to line up a San Francisco cargo for the *Mindoro;* then he summoned Mr. Skinner's stenographer and was busy dictating when Mr. J. Augustus Redell was announced by a youth from the general office. Cappy went to the door to welcome his beloved young friend and business enemy.

"Come in, Gus, my dear boy," he chirped, "and rest your face and hands." He turned to the stenographer. "That will be all, my dear, for the present. I can't dictate business secrets in the presence of this— ahem—harumph-h-h!—er——"

His desk telephone rang. Cappy took down the receiver and grunted.

"J. O. Heyfuss & Co. are calling you, Mr. Ricks," his private exchange operator announced.

Cappy smiled and nodded. J. O. Heyfuss & Co. were ship, freight and marine insurance brokers.

"Something doing for my *Mindoro*," he soliloquized aloud.

"Mr. Ricks?" a voice came over the wire.

"Hello there!" Cappy replied at the top of his voice. For some reason he always shouted when telephoning. "Ricks on the job! Whatja got for my *Mindoro*, Heyfuss? . . . Zinc ore? Never carried any before. Don't know what it looks like. . . . Yes; that freight rate is acceptable. We should have more, but God forbid that we should be considered human hogs . . . Yes. . . . Sure it's for discharge in San Francisco? . . . All right. Close for it. . . . Good-bye! . . . Hey there, Heyfuss! Don't close in a hurry. See if you can't get the charterers to pay the towage over to her loading port. If they won't pay all, strike 'em for half."

He hung up without saying good-bye.

"Well, that's out of the way," he declared with satisfaction. "Just closed for a cargo of zinc ore from Australia to San Francisco ex our schooner *Mindoro*. Matt Peasley's been hunting wild-eyed for a cargo for her—scouring the market, Gus—and nothing doing! And here the old master comes along and digs up a cargo while you'd be saying Jack Robinson. By the Holy Pink-Toed Prophet, if you can show me how the rising generation is going to get by——"

He paused suddenly, leaned forward, and pointed an accusing finger at his visitor.

"Gus," he charged, "you're up to something. I can see it in your eyes. You look guilty."

Mr. Redell hitched his chair close to Cappy and with

his index finger tapped the old gentleman three times on the right knee—three impressive taps.

"Alden P. Ricks," he began with equal impressiveness, "I have a scheme——"

Cappy chuckled and slapped his thin old thigh.

"I knew it! By the Holy Pink-Toed Prophet! Gus, if you ever come into my office and fail to unload a scheme on me I'll think you aren't enjoying your usual robust health. What are you going to start now? A skunk farm for cornering the market on Russian sable?"

"Cut out the hilarity. This is serious business, Cappy. I can show you where you and I can waltz into the Chicago Pit, make a killing on December wheat, and escape with a sizable wad before our identity is discovered."

Cappy, caught off his guard, blinked at the enormity of the prospect; but, remembering his dignity as a business man, he shook his head sadly and replied:

"Wheat! Wheat, eh? A lumber and shipping man monkeying with wheat? Not for little old Alden P. Ricks! No, sir! When I go speculating I stick to my specialties—lumber and ships. Did you ever hear of a gambler, winning a fortune at faro, who didn't drop his winnings on the ponies?"

"But this is a beautiful layout."

"I don't know anything about wheat and I'm too old to learn. Besides, I don't trust you, Gus. You're an infernal scoundrel; and experience has taught me that any time I take your tip and go in on a deal I have to step lively to keep from being walked on."

"But this time I'm free from guile. I won't stab you, Cappy."

"No use! The last boat just left, Augustus."

Mr. Redell, however, was made of rather stern stuff. He was a young man who never took "No" for an answer. Persistence was his most striking characteristic.

"Now listen," he implored. "Let the dead past bury itself. I give you my word of honor, Cappy, that this deal is on the level. Just let me put all my cards on the table while you take a look; then, if you don't want to come in, all I ask is your word of honor that you'll stay out while I round up a partner with red blood in his veins."

Cappy pricked up his ears at that. He saw that Redell was serious; he knew that once the latter passed his word of honor he never broke it. Still, Cappy did not wish to appear precipitate in his surrender; so he said weakly:

"I am against speculation."

"You mean you're against foolish speculation," Redell corrected him. "I take it, however, that you have no objection to playing a sure thing."

"Well," Cappy admitted, "in that event I might be persuaded. Nevertheless, I'm afraid of you. There's a fly in the ointment, even if I cannot see it. You owe me a poke, and you'll never rest until you've squared the account between us."

Mr. Redell held up his hands in abject distress.

"Cappy," he pleaded, "don't say that. You wrong me cruelly. It is in my power to stand idly by and let you assimilate a poke right now; but, just to show you I haven't any hard feelings, I'll do something nice for you instead."

"What do you mean—nice?"

"I'll save you money—not only today but for years to come; and I'll save your self-respect."

"Shoot!"

"Call up J. O. Heyfuss & Co. and tell them to take their cargo of zinc ore in bulk for your schooner *Mindoro* and go to the devil with it!"

"But, good gracious, boy, I have to get something for her homeward trip!"

"In this case nothing is better than something. Do you know anything about zinc ore?"

"Yes; as much as an Eskimo knows about the doctrine of transubstantiation."

"I thought so. Well, I'll enlighten you. Zinc ore is blamed near as heavy as lead, and it's as fine as cement. Load it in a ship in bulk and, what with the pitching and rolling of a vessel on a long voyage, she opens up every seam and crack in her interior; then this powdered ore sifts into the skin of the ship and down into her bilge, and you'll never be able to get it out without tearing the ship apart. Why, after a vessel has freighted a cargo of zinc ore there may be as much as fifty tons left in her after she's supposed to be discharged; and, of course, thereafter she'll carry that much less cargo than she did before. Besides, the consignees are liable to send you a bill for the shortage; you can gamble your head they'll deduct it from the freight bill."

"Holy sailor!" Cappy was appalled.

"Why," Redell continued, "I'm surprised at your ignorance, Cappy!"

"And I'm amazed at your intelligence! Where did you get all this zinc-ore dope?" Cappy challenged. "How do you know it's true?"

"I got it from Captain Matt Peasley. I heard him give it to J. O. Heyfuss on the floor of the Merchants' Exchange two weeks ago, when Heyfuss tried to sneak up on his blind side and hang that cargo of zinc ore on him. I guess they weren't importing much zinc ore when you were active in business, Cappy, or you'd have known all about it. You see the plot, don't you? As soon as Heyfuss learned that Matt Peasley and Skinner had gone away, leaving a defenseless old man on the job, he organized himself to spear you."

"The shameless son of a sea cook! By gravy, Gus, you're my friend!"

"Need any more proof?"

"Not a speck."

"Then I'll give you some. Call up Heyfuss and declare that ore cargo off; after you've done that I'll tell you where you can get something better. Moreover, you can close the deal yourself and save the brokerage."

CHAPTER XLI

Cappy Ricks called up J. O. Heyfuss and in a few terse sentences told that individual where to head in.

"Now, then——" he began, facing round on Redell once more.

Again Redell's index finger tapped Cappy's knee. Dramatically he pronounced a single word:

"Wheat!"

"Wheat?"

"Wheat!"

"What kind of wheat?" In his amazement Cappy was rather helpless.

"Number One white Australian wheat."

"You jibbering jackdaw! Wheat? Don't you know blamed well that wheat is one of the commodities Australia never exports to these United States? Why? Because we don't need her doggoned wheat! We grow all the wheat we need and a lot more we don't need; we export that, and it's just as fine wheat as you'll find anywhere. Moreover, any time our crop is a failure, our next-door neighbor, Canada, is Johnny-on-the-spot, ready to make prompt delivery. So what in thunder are you talking about?"

For answer J. Augustus Redell drew from his pocket that morning's paper and pointed to the headline of a front-page story. Cappy adjusted his spectacles and read: Bakers Announce Six-Cent Loaf!

"Hum-m-m!" said Cappy.

"You bet! And it's a smaller loaf, by the way. Doesn't that argue that there is something doing in wheat, when the price of bread goes to six cents for a half portion?"

"Well, there might be something in that, Gus. Crack along and tell me some more."

"Until the identity of the real culprits is fixed, Cappy, we must blame the war in Europe for the six-cent loaf; likewise for the fifteen-dollar shoe that formerly cost our wives six or seven; for the eleven pounds of sugar for a dollar, when twenty to twenty-two pounds was the standard in the good old days. Europe is too busy fighting to pay much attention to farming; the wheat farmers of Canada are somewhere in France instead of being at home 'tending to business; and it has been up to Uncle Sam and the Argentine Republic to feed the world, you might say. Naturally speculators have seized upon this condition to shoot the price of wheat to the skies, and in desperation the millers have been casting about to buy cheaper wheat. Investigation discloses the fact that Australia has an enormous quantity of wheat on hand; some of it is the surplus of the 1915 crop. Of course she has exported all she could to England; but, at that, she has been handicapped."

"How?"

"Because when a ship sails from Liverpool with goods for Australia, it is a rare case when that same ship promptly loads with Australian goods and puts back to Liverpool. She takes a cargo of coal, say, from Newcastle up to Manila; a general cargo from Manila to Seattle or San Francisco; thence to a West Coast port with a general cargo; thence to New York with nitrate; thence to Europe with foodstuffs or munitions. Australia hasn't had the tonnage to export her wheat and it's been piling up on her. Now they've simply got to sell something to get some ready money."

"This is perfectly re-markable!"

Redell took a document from his pocket and gravely handed it to Cappy, who examined it and discovered the same to be a charter party, consummated the day before between the West Coast Trading Company, owners of the barkentine *Mazeppa*, and Messrs. Ford & Carter, a well known export and import firm whose principal business was done in grain. Cappy read the charter party carefully and even verified the signatures, with which he was familiar. The vessel was to carry a cargo of wheat from Melbourne to San Francisco at a freight rate that fairly shrieked the word "Dividend."

"Re-markable!" Cappy declared. "Preposterous!"

"Seeing is believing. Call up Ford & Carter, and they'll jump over themselves to give you a cargo of wheat for your *Mindoro*."

"Im-possible!"

"Well, I'm telling you. Why, it stands to reason, Cappy! Canada and the United States are so much nearer Europe than is Australia that it has been cheaper to use our wheat, and the result is we've been cleaned out; and the newspapers are filled with dismal stories of the sufferings of the poor due to the increased price of bread."

"Come to think of it, Gus, there *has* been a lot of that stuff in the papers lately. But, of course, when a fellow's stomach is full and he isn't in danger of being attached for debt, he never thinks of the less

fortunate brother. Yes, Gus, I dare say the demand
for our wheat now exceeds the visible supply."

"Is it any wonder, then, that this condition of affairs
should come to the attention of the Australian ex-
porters? Just because Australian wheat has never been
shipped into the United States is no reason why it
shouldn't be shipped—particularly when the price of
flour goes up daily. Why, we pay two and a half
dollars for the fifty-pound sack of flour that formerly
cost us a dollar and a quarter! Eggs are up to seventy
cents a dozen—by jingo, Cappy, what's going to become of us?"

"God knows!" Cappy answered dismally.

Redell had him hypnotized. Already Cappy could
see the gates of the poorhouse opening to receive them
all. Redell's voice brought him back to a realization
of his peril.

"You'll find, Cappy Ricks, that for months to come
every sailing vessel that carries lumber to Australia
from the Pacific Coast will come back with a cargo
of wheat while these war prices are maintained."

"Great Jumping Jehoshaphat! How'd you get next
to all this, Gus?"

"The early bird gets the worm, and success comes
to the man who creates his own opportunities. I
thought it all up out of my own head, Cappy, and then
tried it out on Ford & Carter. It knocked 'em cold for
a minute; but that was only because the proposition
was so unusual. When I explained the situation to
them, however, and gave them time to digest it, both
offered to take me out to luncheon. You can see for
yourself they've chartered our *Mazeppa* at a fancy
freight rate."

Cappy licked his lips.

"The *Mindoro* is sound, tight and seaworthy," he murmured. "She could carry wheat."

"Come on in, Cappy. The water's fine!"

"I'll do it! Gus, you're a mighty good fellow, if I do say it that shouldn't. I have five windjammers en route to Australia this minute, and, by the Holy Pink-Toed Prophet, if I can get wheat charters for all of them on the return trip I'll accept, if it costs me money. Gus, something has got to be done about this high cost of living or we'll all go to hell together. There comes a time in a man's life when he must put aside the sordid question of 'How much is there in it for me?' and ask himself: 'How much can I put in it for the other fellow?' Gus, it's our Christian duty to furnish tonnage to import this wheat. We should, as patriotic citizens, make it our business to boom Australian wheat in the United States and give these doggoned pirates that gamble in the foodstuffs of the country a run for their money. Food prices should be regulated by this Government. The Chicago Pit should be abolished by legislative enactment——"

"Well, they won't do it this year, Cappy," Redell interrupted dryly. "Still, it occurred to me that I saw an opening where two high-minded philanthropists— to wit, Alden P. Ricks and J. Augustus Redell—might strike a blow for freedom and at the same time give these wheat speculators a kick where it will do them the most good. When one cannot annihilate his enemy the next best thing is to take some money away from him; and you and I, Cappy Ricks, can take a young fortune away from these fellows, while at the same time depressing the price of wheat and doing our fellow

countrymen a favor. Are you prepared to volunteer
under my banner? If so, hold up your right hand."

Cappy held up his right hand.

"Out with it, Gus," he ordered; "out with it! This
is most interesting."

"Ah! You're interested now, are you? Well, bearing in mind the fact that your specialty is lumber and
ships, I will give you an opportunity to withdraw before it is too late. Besides, it occurs to me that I
have already done enough for you today."

"Don't be greedy, Gus. Remember there is an exception to every rule. Besides, I'm getting old and—er—
ahem!—hell's bells, boy, I've got to have my fling every
once in a while. Come now, Gus! Out with it! I
believe your proposition embodied the coupling of
both our names in the betting, did it not?"

"It did, Cappy. Still, come to think of it, I really
ought not to come in here and tempt you into speculating——"

"How much money do you want?" Cappy shrilled im-
patiently. "Cut out this infernal drivel and get down
to business. Unfold your proposition; and if it looks
to me like a winner I'll take a flyer with you if it's the
last act of my sinful life."

"On your own head be it, Cappy. Here goes! However, before laying my plan before you, perfect frank-
ness compels me to state that my visit to you was not
born of an overweening desire to do you a kindness or
make money for you. Philanthropy is not my long suit
—in business hours; and my interest in you today is
purely a selfish one."

"Go on; go on, boy! Am I a child in arms?"

"I have made a ball, Cappy," Redell continued, "and

I want you to fire it. I have a splendid prescription to make a clean-up in December wheat——"

"Give me your prescription."

"Well, sir, my prescription lacks one small ingredient to make it a standard household remedy. You can supply that ingredient—to wit, cash of the present standard of weight and fineness. Every spare dollar that Live Wire Luiz and I can get our hands on is working overtime in the legitimate business of the West Coast Trading Company; every loose asset with a hockable value has been hocked, and we dare not strain our credit with our banker by borrowing money with which to speculate. If I apply for a sizable loan, without putting up collateral, he'll ask me what I want to do with the money—and if I answer truthfully he'll throw Luiz and me and our account out of his bank. And I never was a very successful liar. Therefore, in consideration of the valuable information I can furnish, I suggest that you carry me for a quarter of a million bushels of December wheat."

"How much will that cost me?" Cappy queried warily.

"We'll operate on margin. I think a margin of ten cents a bushel will do the trick; of course, if wheat should go up a point you'll be asked to come through with more money. However, I have a sneaking notion that a well-known heavyweight like you can place his order with any of the local brokers without having to put up a single cent; at the most they might ask you for five thousand or ten thousand dollars. But they know you're good for any engagement you may make; they'd be tickled to death to have your promissory note. I suggest that you get in touch with a sound brokerage house in this city—one that is a member of the New

York Exchange and the Chicago Board of Trade—and
sell, for my account, two hundred and fifty thousand
bushels of December wheat at the market."

"What'll I do for myself?"

"Go as far as you like. You know your own limita-
tions. I'm desirous of selling a quarter of a million
bushels at the market; and, as I am furnishing the
plans and specifications for this raid, I suggest that
you sell at least a quarter of a million yourself."

"Funny business!" Cappy murmured. "Selling a
quarter of a million bushels of wheat you do not own
and never will! Hum-m-m! Ahem! Harumph-h-h!
Then what?"

He bent his head and gazed very severely at Mr.
Redell over the rims of his spectacles. For reply Mr.
Redell took from his pocket thirteen sheaves of paper
and handed them to Cappy, who investigated and discovered them to be thirteen forty-eight-hour options
on thirteen sailing vessels bound to Australian ports
with lumber, and not as yet provided with a return
cargo to the United States.

"By to-morrow morning I shall have exercised those
options and closed for thirteen cargoes of wheat,"
Redell explained. "You have five vessels bound to
Australia also. Give me an option on them for their
return cargo and that will make eighteen."

"Yes, yes. Then what?"

"I will charter all of the eighteen to Ford & Carter,
who will load them with Number One white Australian
wheat for Pacific Coast ports. Before doing so, however, Ford & Carter will have closed contracts with
Pacific Coast milling companies for the sale of every

grain of it, in order to protect themselves against a falling market."

"Naturally. And the market is——"

"December wheat closed in the Chicago Pit yesterday at $1.89½, and the market has been very stiff for quite a while. The bulls are right on the job."

"Will not the advent of all this Australian wheat depress the market?" Cappy shrilled excitedly.

"Not unless the bears happen to find it out, Cappy," Redell retorted gently. "It is our job to bring the matter to their attention, for it so happens that Alden P. Ricks and J. Augustus Redell are the only two people in the United States who happen to know about it. Ford & Carter know; but they are very conservative, and I doubt that the tremendous possibilities of this information have occurred to them. At any rate, we'll probably be first aboard the lugger."

Cappy nodded sagely.

"Are you sure, Gus, my dear young friend, that we are not too conservative in selling but a quarter of a million bushels each? There's such a thing as playing 'em too close to the vest, you know."

"We'll try selling half a million bushels first; if that doesn't depress the market we'll just keep on selling until something happens. That's right, isn't it?"

"I think so. The bulls will probably grab that first half million bushels to hold up the market; they may even absorb a million. We'll try 'em, at any rate. What next?"

"Having sold all we can at the market, Cappy, our next move will be to kick the market to pieces."

"How?"

"Publicity! We'll tell all we know to the bears. The

bulls will get panicky; the bears will take heart of hope, and with Number One white Australian wheat they'll beat the brains out of the market and in all probability kick it down to $1.85, at which figure we promptly buy as much wheat as we have previously sold. Thus we cover our shorts, and the difference between $1.89½ and $1.85, less brokerage and interest—if any—will be, roughly speaking, four cents. Four cents on a quarter of a million bushels is ten thousand dollars— not a great deal, truly, in these days of swollen fortunes, but, nevertheless, a nice piece of velvet—eh, Cappy, you sporty boy?"

"It isn't so much the money we make," Cappy replied sagely. "It's the fun we have making it, my boy; the joy of putting over a winner. The instant a man begins to love money for money's sake he's a knave and a fool. Kill him! But—er—ahem—as you say, my dear young friend, ten thousand each is not to be— er—sneezed at."

"Then you're coming in on the deal?"

"I should tell a man!"

After the fashion of the West they shook hands on it and went to luncheon at the Commercial Club.

CHAPTER XLII

Directly luncheon was over and Cappy Ricks had returned to his office, J. Augustus Redell moved into action. He called on Messrs. Ford & Carter, talked the situation over with them, and showed them where they, having the necessary tonnage in hand with which to guarantee delivery, could bring a couple of million bushels of fine Number One white Australian wheat to the Pacific Coast, cut the price a cent, and doubtless unload every kernel of it at a fair profit. There was every probability that wheat would go to two dollars. For his part in producing this profit Mr. Redell desired a commission of five per cent on all sales of wheat imported in the bottoms he had under option and which he stood ready to turn over to Ford & Carter without profit, since the owners of the vessels would pay him the customary broker's commission on the freight money earned on the voyage. Ford & Carter said they would think the matter over; so Mr. Redell tactfully withdrew, stating that he would call up the following day for an answer.

He knew Ford & Carter would promptly dispatch a long cablegram to their agent in Australia, instructing him to get a forty-eight-hour option on the wheat, with a guaranty of delivery to the vessels as they arrived from time to time. Meantime, Ford & Carter would quote every milling company in the West, subject to prior acceptance and their ability to deliver Num-

300

ber One Australian wheat at a price that would be
of interest.   If the milling companies accepted this
rather nebulous quotation and telegraphed orders, and
Ford & Carter's Australian agent could purchase at a
satisfactory price the wheat to fill these orders, then
Ford & Carter would make formal acceptance and
purchase the wheat.   If, on the other hand, their agent
in Australia failed to get the wheat, then Ford & Carter
had an "out" with the milling companies who desired
to buy the wheat from them, and the entire matter
would be off, with Ford & Carter merely out a couple
of hundred dollars in telegraph bills.   That was the
bet they had to make to put their fortune to the touch;
and right cheerfully did they make it.

J. Augustus Redell gave them all the time he could.
His forty-eight-hour options on the vessels then en
route to Australia had cost him nothing; that was a
courtesy which one shipowner always extends to another, free of charge, unless the vessel happens to be
on demurrage at the time the option is given.   When
his options were within two hours of expiring he called
on Ford & Carter.

"We'll take 'em all," Carter almost shouted at him.
"They'll be arriving with sufficient time elapsing between arrivals to guarantee us immunity from any
undue delay or embarrassment in loading them.   We've
bought the wheat and sold it; now give us the tonnage
to freight it, Redell, and we'll all be happy, and a little
richer than we were the day before yesterday."

Redell took up the telephone and called each shipowner, in turn, to inform him that he would exercise his
option on the latter's ship, and for the owner to pre-

pare charter parties and send them up to his office for signature.

"I will have no difficulty in getting the owners to agree to an assignment of these charters to you," he advised Carter. "You and Ford are brothers in good standing, I take it. However, if they insist on doing business through me, in order that they may hold me responsible, I'll simply recharter to you at the same rate."

"Lovely!" cried Messrs. Ford & Carter in unison.

Ten minutes later J. Augustus Redell burst into Cappy Ricks' sanctum and wakened the old gentleman from his afternoon siesta.

"The trap is set," he announced. "Come on, Cappy! We're going up to the broker's office now and give the order to sell our December wheat. I can't go alone, you know. There wouldn't be an odor of sanctity about the transaction if I did."

"We'll have Gregg & Company attend to it for us," Cappy announced. "You remember Harry Gregg, don't you? Used to be in the steamship business years ago. Gosh, that boy knows me! He'll take a stiff finger bet from Alden P. Ricks."

Together they motored uptown to the office of Gregg & Co., where Cappy's card gained him instant admittance to the broker's private office. Redell remained in the anteroom on pretense of speaking to an acquaintance, and the instant Cappy disappeared into Gregg's office Redell stepped out into the hall, where he waited until Cappy had booked his order and came hunting for him.

"Well, I've sold my two hundred and fifty thousand bushels at a dollar-ninety," Cappy announced.

"How much margin?" Redell demanded.

"Oh, Gregg didn't sting me very hard. Ten cents a bushel. It seemed like a good bet to him. He looks for a drop in December wheat."

"Met a pest out here and couldn't seem to get away from him," Redell explained. "Take me in and introduce me to Gregg, and I'll give him an order to sell a jag of wheat for me."

Cappy complied and Redell gave the broker his order.

"It will take about twenty-five thousand dollars to margin this trade, Mr. Redell," the latter remarked easily as he wrote out the order and handed a copy to Redell.

"Nonsense!" Cappy struck in. "Mr. Redell is one of our most delightful, trustworthy and popular young men, and to ask him for twenty-five thousand dollars today would prejudice his standing with his banker. I guarantee him, Harry. Treat him as you'd treat me. I guarantee him up to a hundred thousand dollars."

"Your guaranty goes with me, Mr. Ricks," Gregg answered promptly, and shoved the copy of the order he had just booked over to Cappy, together with the fountain pen. Cappy wrote: "O. K. Alden P. Ricks." Redell gave his check for ten thousand dollars margin and the deal was closed. When the scheming pair returned to Cappy's office the latter gave Redell his check for ten thousand to reimburse Redell for margining the trade, in accordance with Cappy's verbal agreement to provide the sinews of war.

"Now then, Cappy," Redell announced as he stuffed Cappy's check into his pocket, "the next move is to return to my office, close those charters with the

owners and turn the ships over to Ford & Carter.
That matter attended to, I shall, with eighteen charter
parties in my pocket, drift casually over to the Merchants' Exchange. There I shall find the market reporters for both of our sunrise sheets; if they are not
there I shall wait until they arrive. These gifted young
men I shall draw to one side; to them I shall, with
great gusto, relate a tale of Number One white Australian wheat, shortly to descend upon the United States
of America in no less than eighteen vessels, now chartered for that purpose, with more to follow. In proof
of this statement I shall exhibit the charter parties;
and then——"

"Front-page story!" Cappy declared, interrupting.

"Not yet—but soon. To get on the front page a
story must be rather unusual. A perusal of our daily
rags will convince the most skeptical that the sensa-
tional, the unusual, the bizarre are what appeal most to
the men who make the newspapers. The unusual thing
about our deal lies in the fact that this is the first time
in the history of Australia or the United States that
the former country has exported wheat into the latter
—the first time the latter has ever had to call on an
outsider for help. Then, Cappy, it will be a front-page
story—and how those boys will hop to it! Why, we'll
get a column about Australian wheat invading the land
of the free whose rapacity threatens the very food
that goes into the mouths of little children! Little
children and their mouths is good stuff! I'll use that
line when slipping the story to the boys. They might
overlook it if I didn't. I'll remind them of the six-cent
loaf of bread, the sufferings of the poor, and how far

the importation of Australian wheat will go to knock
the Chicago wheat barons for a goal."

"Here, here! You're too precipitate," Cappy cautioned. "Don't tip this story off to both reporters.
That's coarse work. Tell it to one only. Put him under
obligations to you by seeming to give him a scoop.
Tell him you won't say a word to his competitor, and
he'll tell his city editor the story is exclusive; then
they'll be certain to play it up big."

"Cappy, you're the shadow of a rock in a weary
land! Who'll tip off the other reporter?"

"I will, of course. Leave it to me. A man doesn't
go through the mill of Big Business without knowing
the way of that singularly useful individual, the newspaper man."

Redell sat down and laughed until the tears ran down
his merry countenance. Cappy thought the outlook
sufficiently cheerful to warrant that laugh, and suspected nothing. He even joined in the laugh.

"And to-morrow morning, when that story appears,
the local brokerage firms will be calling up Ford &
Carter to verify it," Redell continued presently. "Of
course it will be verified; then—bingo! the story will
be wired on to Chicago. It busts, first, in the Wheat
Pit and, second, in the afternoon editions. The bears
will leap on the market and kick it to pieces; the bulls
will get panic-stricken and hesitate about supporting
it; all the little fellows who have been going long on
December wheat will get cold feet and throw their
trades overboard; and before the smoke clears away
December wheat will break four or five points."

Cappy Ricks put his old arm around his young

friend and gave him a paternal hug. He winked wickedly.

"My dear boy," he suggested, "suppose you and I go out and pin one on? Hey? How about you, boy? A pint of '98, in order that we may properly drink confusion to the wolf of want and damnation to dull care!"

CHAPTER XLIII

Late that afternoon Cappy Ricks graciously summoned the Chronicle reporter to his office and told him in detail all he knew about the Australian wheat invasion.

"Of course," he added, "this may be mere street gossip; but I think there's something in it, my boy. At any rate, I thought you might care to be tipped off to the situation. It looks like a corking story to me. I suggest that you call up Ford & Carter and see what they have to say about it."

"I wonder whether the Examiner reporter has a tip on this?" the Chronicle man queried hopefully.

"Not from me. This story is for you, young man. That's why I called you down to my office."

About the same hour J. Augustus Redell might have been seen at the press table on 'Change, unfolding a similar story to the market reporter of the Examiner, who thought it was a humdinger of a story, and so declared.

"All right. Glad you think so," Mr. Redell replied, beaming upon him. "And just to show you I'm right, I'll not breathe a word of it to the Chronicle man."

Having planted his journalistic bomb, Mr. Redell glanced at his watch. It was exactly eleven o'clock. "I still have time," he murmured, and departed immediately to the office of Gregg & Co., where he placed an order to sell for his account up to half a million bushels

of December wheat, but to cease selling the instant the
market hesitated to absorb it or the price broke a
point.   At the same moment, in another brokerage
office, Cappy Ricks was issuing a similar order.   Before the market closed, Cappy had succeeded in selling a hundred and eighty thousand bushels, while Redell had disposed of a hundred and thirty.   Evidently
the bears took it as it came, for the market closed
strong at $1.89.

Neither Cappy nor Redell reported at his office the
following day.   At the hour when the market opened
in Chicago both schemers appeared on the floor of the
Merchants' Exchange and bent their gaze upon the only
blackboard on 'Change they had not heretofore honored
with their scrutiny—the board in back of the Grain
Pit, which carried the quotations on the Chicago Board
of Trade, already beginning to come in by wire.

For an hour the trading was inactive.   Then suddenly the price broke half a point as somebody tossed
a lot of fifty thousand bushels on the market.   Cappy
and Redell each wondered whether he might not be the
responsible party; and while they pondered somebody
unloaded a hundred thousand bushels at $1.88.   Cappy
gasped as the quotations appeared on the blackboard.

"Something doing, Gus!" he whispered; Redell nodded.

And now commenced a period of wild trading.   The
price crept back to $1.89, only to be assaulted and
beaten back to $1.87; then, fraction by fraction and
point by point, the price fell; and J. Augustus Redell
wagged his head approvingly.

"They have received our message," he said.   "The
riot is on!"

When the price had been beaten down to $1.83 Cappy turned to his associate.

"I'm through!" he said. "Time to cover my shorts." And he trotted away to a telephone booth.

As for Redell, he would not intrust his fortune to a telephonic order, but sprang into his runabout, parked at the curb outside the Exchange, and scorched uptown to Gregg & Co.'s offices, where he learned that he had sold four hundred and ten thousand bushels of December wheat. One hundred thousand had been sold at $1.90, two hundred and eighty thousand at prices varying from $1.89 to $1.88⅛, and the remainder at $1.88.

"Buy me four hundred and ten thousand bushels at the market," he ordered.

Before he left the office the sale had been confirmed and Mr. Redell's shorts had been covered at a price ranging from $1.83 to $1.83⅝, whereupon he closed out his trade and received a check for his margin and his profits. An hour later he met Cappy Ricks again on 'Change.

"Well, Cappy?" he queried.

"I cleaned up, thank you," the old gentleman informed him. "Sold, bought, and got the money. This is one time it rained duck soup and I was there with a bucket."

He prodded Mr. Redell playfully in the short ribs and the incident was closed. They had made a profit of more than twenty thousand dollars each; and when each returned to his office he forgot all about December wheat until half past five that evening, when both met on the deserted floor of the exchange to scan the blackboard. December wheat had closed that day at $1.83!

Two days later J. Augustus Redell called Cappy Ricks on the telephone.

"That you, Cappy?"

"Yep!"

"Redell speaking. Read the story on the front page of the Chronicle this morning?"

"No; what was it?"

"The British Government has placed an embargo on the exportation of wheat from Australia; so all those eighteen charters I negotiated with Ford & Carter are knocked out."

"You don't say so!"

"Surest thing you know, Cappy."

"Well, say! That makes it hard on Ford & Carter, doesn't it? All those ships on their hands and no wheat! They'll have to hustle like the devil to dig up new business for them."

"Not at all! There's a clause in the charter parties that saves them. You know, Cappy—that line about fires, floods, strikes, lockouts, the acts of the public enemy, and other causes beyond their control. Consequently the ships are back on their owners' hands. I wish you joy with your five, Cappy."

"Well, that's all right. Considering my winnings in December wheat I won't hold it against Ford & Carter; so you needn't inject that note of malice into your conversation. Those boys are stuck hard enough as it is, I dare say. They've contracted to deliver a lot of Australian wheat to various milling companies; they can't do it, and I'll bet they'll be sued out of house and home for breach of contract."

"Oh, no, they won't! They hedged on their quotations when making them; all those telegraphic orders were placed with Ford & Carter subject to Ford & Carter's ability to make delivery and to prior sale. Before Ford & Carter could make them firm orders and get in over their heads, I tipped them off to the possibility of this government embargo."

"You tipped them off! How did you know the British Government was going to clap an embargo on Australian wheat?"

"Why, I didn't know," Redell confessed. "I just guessed it would; so I advised Ford & Carter to lay low a day or two and await developments. Said developments appear to have arrived according to schedule, so everybody's happy. I have even reimbursed Ford & Carter to the extent of a two-hundred-and-eighty-five-dollar telegraph bill they incurred. You see, Cappy, I gave them the wrong steer, and I knew it was wrong when I gave it to them; consequently my conscience wouldn't let me rest until I'd squared myself."

"You in-fer-nal scoundrel! Well, you didn't give me the wrong steer; and I'm surprised at that. For once in your life you were on the level."

"Don't cheer until you're out of the woods. Do you remember that German steamer, the *Valkyrie*, that you skinned me out of last year?"

"Ah!" Cappy chuckled; "you bet I remember that! Maybe after a while, my dear young friend, you'll get enough of this funny business and lay off on the old man."

"I'm off you now. I've had enough of you, Cappy Ricks. I've made fifty thousand dollars off you in the past week; and that satisfies me."

"Gus, don't lie to me! You didn't make a cent more

than I did—and I made a trifle more than twenty-four thousand dollars."

"Is that so? Well, listen to me tell it: When you and I cashed in that day our deal was closed wasn't it?"

"Yes."

"And I'd played fair with you?"

"You certainly did, Gus."

"Then I was freed from any further obligations to take you into partnership with me, was I not?"

"That's how I figure it, my boy."

"That's how I figured it also, Cappy. Consequently, being morally certain that the British Government would place an embargo on the exportation of Australian wheat—Cappy, you must admit that the British Government would have been absolutely crazy if it hadn't—I just called on Gregg & Co. and bought another half million bushels of December wheat at $1.83 to $1.84 a bushel. Then I sat tight and waited for that embargo story to break. Cappy, do you know that story just raised hell on the Chicago Pit today? The bears were caught napping; and the bulls got busy and kicked the price up to $1.90 again, at which figure I unloaded and took my profit."

"You amazing rascal! Why didn't you tip your partner off to that deal?"

"We were no longer partners. You admitted that a moment ago. When I first outlined this scheme I didn't have a dollar to spare with which I could speculate. Every last cent was tied up in the business of the West Coast Trading Company. So I schemed to take you in as a partner on one-half of the deal; and you not only financed me but guaranteed me to the broker!

Your introduction was all I wanted. After that my credit was as good as December wheat; in consequence of which, without a cent invested, I was actually enabled to carry a trade for half a million bushels! Much obliged to you, Cappy. You're a fine old sport, and I like you—I wouldn't be surprised if you laid off on me after this—eh, Cappy?"

"Gus," said Cappy Ricks, "one of these days the Democratic party is going to wake up and discover that America isn't where they left it the night before! And when that happens they're going to ask you about it, you—you—infer-nal——"

The phone clicked. J. Augustus Redell had hung up.

"Drat it!—— God bless him!" murmured Cappy Ricks—and hung up, too.

CHAPTER XLIV

WHENEVER Cappy Ricks made up his mind that his Blue Star Navigation Company ought to add another vessel to its rapidly growing fleet, he preferred to build her; for a few bitter experiences early in life had convinced him that the man who buys the other fellow's ship quite frequently is given a bonus in the shape of the other fellow's troubles—troubles which have the unhappy faculty of tilting the profit-and-loss account over into the red-ink figures. In order to avoid these troubles, therefore, Cappy would summon his naval architect, whom he would practically drive to distraction by fussing over the plans submitted before giving a final grudging acceptance. The blue prints approved, Cappy would spend a week picking holes in the specifications, and when there was no more fault to find Mr. Skinner, his general manager and the president of the Ricks Lumber & Logging Company, would send a list of the timbers, planking, and so on required, to one of Cappy's sawmills in Washington; for Cappy had a theory—the good Lord knows why or where acquired—that Douglas fir from the state of Washington was better for shipbuilding purposes than Douglas fir grown in Oregon. Perhaps he figured that the Columbia River, which separates the two states, made a difference in grade.

The woods boss would then be adjured to select his trees with great care. No tree would do that sprouted a limb within eighty feet of the butt, and the butt had to be at least six feet in diameter, in order that it might produce fine, clear, long-length planks that would not contain "heart" timber—the heart of a log having a tendency to check or split when seasoned. When the material was sawed a Blue Star steam schooner would transport it to San Francisco Bay, and it would be stored in Cappy's retail lumber yard in Oakland, to be seasoned and air-dried; following which Cappy Ricks would let the contract for the building of the vessel to a shipyard on Oakland Estuary, and sell the builder this seasoned stock at the price of rough green material, even though it was worth two dollars a thousand extra —not to mention the additional value for the extra-long lengths furnished specially. Cappy's ancestors, back in Maine, had built too many ships to have failed to impress upon him the wisdom of this course; for, on this point at least, initial extravagance inevitably develops into ultimate economy.

Following the laying of the keel, Cappy would come out of retirement and become an extremely busy man. He had the vessel's engines to consider; and for two weeks his private office would resound with the arguments and recriminations of Cappy and his port engineer. There would be much talk of pistons, displacement of cylinders, stroke, reciprocating engines, steeple compound and triple-expansion engines, Scotch boilers, winches, compressors, dynamos, composition and iron propellers and the latest developments in crude-oil burners. And on the day when the port engineer, grown desperate because of the old man's opposition to some detail, would fly into a rage and resign, Cappy would know that, at last, everything was all right;

whereupon he would scornfully reject the resignation
and take his port engineer to luncheon at the Commercial Club, just to show he wasn't harboring a
grudge.

In the meantime the port captain would be making
daily visits to the shipyard to make certain that the
builder was holding rigidly to the specifications and
not trying to skimp here and there; and on Saturdays
Cappy would accompany him and satisfy himself that
the port captain wasn't being imposed upon. Finally
the ship would be launched; and as she slid down the
ways Cappy Ricks would be standing on her forecastle
head, his old heart fluttering in his thirty-six-inch
chest and his coat-tails fluttering in the breeze, one
arm round the port captain and the other round the
port engineer. As the hull slipped into the drink he
would say:

"Boys, this is the life! I love it! By the Holy
Pink-Toed Prophet, there's more romance in ships than
you'll find in most married lives!" Then he would wave
an arm up Oakland Estuary, which prior to the great
war was the graveyard of Pacific Coast shipping, and
say with great pride: "Well, we've done a good job on
this craft, boys; she'll never end in Rotten Row!
Every sliver in her is air-dried and seasoned. That's
the stuff! Build 'em of unseasoned material and dry
rot develops the first year; in five years they're punk
inside, and then—some fine day they're posted as
missing at Lloyd's. Did you ever see a Blue Star
ship lying in Rotten Row? No; you bet you didn't
—and you never will! I never built a cheap boat and
I never ran 'em cheap. By gravy, the Blue Star ships

are like the Blue Nose that owns 'em! They'll be found dead on the job!"

Quite early in 1915 the Blue Star Navigation Company had found ample opportunity, due to a world scarcity of tonnage, to dispose of several of their oldest and smallest steam schooners at unbelievably fine prices.

"Get rid of them, Matt," Cappy advised his son-in-law, Captain Matt Peasley, whom he had made president of the company. "You have the permission of the president emeritus to go as far as you like. Big boats for us from now on, boy. Slip the little ones while the slipping is good. These high prices will not prevail very long—only while the war continues; and at the rate they're slaughtering each other over in France the war will be over in six months; then prices will fall kerflump! Then we'll build a couple of real steamers."

So Matt Peasley promptly sold five steam schooners, following which he made up his mind that the world still had two years of war ahead of it. Accordingly he urged the letting of contracts for two seven-thousand-five-hundred-ton steel freighters immediately.

"Nothing doing!" Cappy declared. "Why, it's rank nonsense to think of building now at wartime prices. If our recent sales have pinched us for tonnage we'll have to charter from our neighbors and worry along as best we can until the war is over."

"You're making a mistake, Cappy Ricks," his son-in-law warned him.

"Ask Skinner if I am. Skinner, let's have your opinion."

Mr. Skinner, always cautious and ultra-conservative

promptly advised against Matt Peasley's course; but
Matt would not be downed without a fight.

"I know prices for ship construction are fearfully
high just now," he admitted; "but—mark my words!—
they're going to double; and if we place our contracts
now, while we have an opportunity to do so, we'll be
getting in on the ground floor. I tell you that war
hasn't really started yet; and the longer it continues
the higher will prices on all commodities soar—but
principally on ship construction. Father-in-law, I
beg of you to let me get busy and build. Suppose the
boats do cost us a quarter of a million dollars more
each than we could have built them for in 1914. What
of it? We have the money—and if we didn't have it
we could borrow it. I don't care what a ship costs
me when freight rates are soaring to meet the advance
in construction costs."

Nevertheless, Cappy and Mr. Skinner hooted him
down. Three months later, however, when Cappy
Ricks had changed his mind, and Mr. Skinner was too
heartbroken to curse himself for a purblind idiot, it was
too late to place the contracts. Every shipyard in
the United States and abroad was loaded up with
building orders for three years in advance, and the Blue
Star Navigation Company was left to twiddle its corporate thumbs. Matt Peasley was so angry that he
almost speculated on the delight of being at sea again,
in command of a square rigger, with Cappy Ricks and
Mr. Skinner signed on as A.B.'s; in which condition of
servitude he might dare to call them aft and knock their
heads together. However, he managed to have his
revenge. Every time nitrate freights went up a dollar
a ton he told them about it with great gusto, and the

day he chartered the *Tillicum* for Vladivostok, with
steel for the Russian Government at seventy-five dollars
a ton, he had poor Cappy moaning in his wretchedness.

"Just think how nice it would be," he taunted his
aged relative, "if we had only placed contracts for two
big boats when I urged it. By the middle of summer
I'd have them both on the Vladivostok run—perhaps at
a hundred dollars a ton; and long before the war is
over you could do what you've been trying to do for
the past ten years."

"Do what?" Cappy queried.

"Retire!" Matt retorted meaningly.

"In-fernal young scoundrel!" Cappy was angry
enough to commit murder. "Out of my office!" he
shrilled, and pointed to the door.

CHAPTER XLV

For once in his busy life it was, figuratively speaking, raining duck soup, and poor Cappy was there with a fork! When he had recovered his composure he sent for Matt Peasley.

"Matt, my dear boy," he confessed miserably, "this is certainly one occasion upon which father appears to have overlooked his hand. However, none of us is perfect; and if we're caught out without an umbrella, so to speak——"

"We?" Matt reminded him witheringly. "Cappy, it's all right to use that 'we' stuff when you're talking to Skinner, but trot out the perpendicular pronoun when you're talking to me. I hate to say 'I told you so'; but——"

"Lay off me!" Cappy pleaded. "I'm an old man, Matt; so be easy on me. Besides, I don't make a mistake very often, and you know it."

"I do know it. But when you blocked me on that building scheme you certainly made up for lost time. Really, Cappy, you mustn't make me play so close to my vest in these brisk times. If I'm to manage the Blue Star Navigation Company I mustn't have my ideas pooh-poohed as if I were a hare-brained child."

"I know, Matt; I know. But I built up the Blue Star Navigation Company and the Ricks Lumber & Logging Company by playing 'em close, and it's a hard habit to break.

"However, let us forget the past and look forward with confidence to the future. Matt, my dear boy, since we cannot get a shipyard to build a steamer for us, I'm going to break a rule of forty years' standing and buy one in the open market. I guess that'll prove to you I'm not so hide-bound with conservatism as you think. Go forth into the highways and the byways, Matt, and see what they have for sale."

"How high do you want me to go?"

"As high as they hung Haman—if you find it necessary."

"That's certainly a free hand; but I'm afraid it comes too late. I doubt if there is an owner with the kind of steamer we want who is crazy enough to sell her."

"Tish! Tush! All things are for sale all the time. Scour the market, Matt, and you'll find Cappy Ricks isn't the only damned fool left in the shipping business. My boy, you'd be surprised at the number of so-called business men who are entirely devoid of imagination. Dozens of them still think the war will end this fall, but I'm willing to make a healthy bet that the fall of 1917 still finds them going to it to beat four of a kind."

"You said something that time, father-in-law," Matt replied laughingly.

Then he roughed the old man affectionately and went forth into California Street, where he wore out much shoe leather before he located what he considered a bargain and reported back to the president emeritus.

"You're right, Cappy!" he declared. "You aren't the only boob in the shipping business. I've located another."

"That's what you get by taking father's advice,"

Cappy retorted proudly. "Have you bought a steamer?"

"No; but I'm going to buy one this afternoon. She's going to cost us half a million dollars, cash on the nail, and I have an option on her at that figure until noon today. Skinner has a lot of lumber money he isn't using, and I'm going to borrow a quarter of a million from his company on the Blue Star note at six per cent. Don't want to run our own treasury too low."

"Dog-gone that Skinner! That's some more of his efficiency. I own both companies, and it's just like taking money out of one pocket and putting it into the other; but Skinner's a bug on system. Just think of making me pay myself six per cent interest! However, I suppose we must have some kind of order. What's the name of the steamer?"

"The *Penelope*."

Cappy Ricks slid out to the edge of his chair, placed one hand on each knee, and appraisingly eyed his son-in-law over the rims of his glasses.

"Say that again, Matt—and say it slow," he ordered.

"I said *Penelope*—*P-e-n-e-l-o-p-e*. Maybe you call her the *Pen-elope!*"

"Are you buying her as is?" Matt nodded. "To hear you tell it, Matt, one might gather the impression that half a million dollars is about what we give the janitor at Christmas. Boy, half a million dollars is real money."

"Not in the shipping business these days, Cappy. Why, you have to wave that much under an owner's nose before he'll look up and show interest enough to ask you who you are and who let you in."

"Well, the man who would, in cold blood, consider paying half a million dollars for the *Penelope* is certainly ripe for a padded cell," Cappy jeered. "That fellow Hudner, of the Black Butte Lumber Company, owns her, does he not?"

"Yes, sir."

"Then you know exactly the condition she's in. I'll bet a cooky her bottom plates are rusted so thin from lack of an occasional coat of red paint that if you were to stand on her bridge and toss a tack hammer down her main hatch you'd punch a hole in her. She's a long, narrow-gutted, cranky coffin—that's what she is; and the worst-found ship in Pacific waters. Why, let me tell you something, young man: she can't get by the inspectors this minute."

"She has just gotten by them," Matt contradicted. "Passed yesterday."

"What does that signify? When her skipper has her up for inspection he scours the water front like a hungry dog, borrowing a boathook here, a sound lifeboat there, some fire buckets elsewhere, a hose from the fire tug, and a lot of engine-room tools wherever he can get them. As for life preservers, he rents them for ten cents each from a marine junk dealer. So, when the inspectors arrive, the *Penelope* is a well-found ship; as soon as they pass her the skipper returns the equipment, with thanks. As for paint—why, the only painting she ever gets is when Hudner lays her alongside some British ship to discharge a foreign cargo of lumber into the lime-juicer; then her mate steals all the paint in the Britisher's lazaret. The poor, unfortunate devil! He has to do something to make a showing with the *Penelope's* owner! I tell you, Matt, I know this man Hudner! He's as thrifty as an Armenian and as slippery as a skating rink. He's laying to stab you, boy. Mind your step!"

"Even so, Cappy, she's a bargain. I expect to spend fifty thousand dollars putting her in first-class condition after we get her."

"You expect to spend it! Why, how you talk! Hudner is the one that should spend that money. For the love of trade, what is he selling you? A ship or a hulk?"

"I don't care what she is; we can make her pay for herself and earn half a million or a million extra before this war ends. And she won't be such a bad vessel after she's shipped a couple of new plates. She has a dead weight capacity for six thousand tons and was built at Sunderland in 1902. When she went ashore off Point Sur, in 1909, Hudner bought her from the underwriters for five thousand dollars and spent more than half her original cost repairing her. That, of course, made her tantamount to a ship built in the United States, and under American registry she can run between American ports. And that's what we want. She'll be just the thing to carry lumber to New York, via the Canal, when the war ends and the nitrate harvest is over."

Cappy Ricks threw up his hands.

"You see before you, my boy," he said mournfully, "a dollar-burdened, world-weary old man, who for ten years has been trying to retire from active business, and cannot. The reason is he dassent; if he dassed, this shebang would be in the hands of the sheriff within a year. Now, listen, young feller! I know all about the *Penelope*. Before the war she had repaid Hudner, with interest, every cent she cost him, and since the war I suppose she's made half a million dollars. Now when Hudner finds he has to spend a lot of money fixing her up, he figures it's best to get rid of her and saddle somebody else with the bill. Her intrinsic value is just about one hundred and twenty-five thousand dollars, and when Hudner asks half a million for her he expects to get four hundred and fifty thousand. In order to play safe, go back and offer him four hundred thousand dollars; presently he'll come down fifty thousand and you'll come up fifty thousand, and the trade will be closed on that basis. Meantime I'll sit here and weep as I reflect on the cost of putting that ruin in fit shape to receive a Blue Star house flag. I tell you, Matt, I wouldn't send Pancho Villa to sea in her as she is now."

Matt Peasley, like Cappy Ricks, was a Yankee; when he did business he liked to chaffer; and, after all— he thought—there was a certain shrewd philosophy in what his foxy father-in-law had said. At least Cappy had supplied him with ammunition for argument; so he went back to Hudner's office and argued and pleaded and ridiculed, but all to no avail. He returned to Cappy Ricks' office.

"I fought him all over his office," he complained, "but he wouldn't come down a cent. I think we'd better take a chance and give him half a million."

"Fiddlesticks! Stay with him, Matt. I know Hudner. He acts like he's full of bellicose veins, but anybody can outgame him. Let your option expire; then to-morrow meet him accidentally on 'Change and talk with him half an hour about everything on earth except the S. S. *Penelope*. Just before you leave him he'll grab you by the lapel of your coat and ask if you're still interested in the *Penelope*. Then you say: 'Why, yes—moderately; but not at half a million.' Then you make him a firm offer—for the last time— of four hundred and fifty thousand dollars; and he'll say: 'I'll split the difference with you'—and before he can crawfish you accept. You're bound to make at least twenty-five thousand by following my advice, Matt."

Matt Peasley ran his big hand through his thick black locks.

"By jingo," he declared, "we'd make twenty-five thousand dollars while we're dickering with Hudner!"

"I know, my boy; but then I don't like Hudner, and it's awful to do business with a son of a horsethief you don't like and let him put one over on you. That's the thrill of doing business, Matt. Though I'd hate to have anybody think I'm in business for fun, still, if I thought I couldn't get some fun out of business I'd go right down to Mission Street Wharf and end all."

"Nitrate freights are up to thirty dollars a ton," said Matt later that day. "They were twelve a year and a half ago. Cappy, we can't risk the delay; and I'm sorry I took your advice and let my option expire. I insist on buying." He reached for Cappy's desk 'phone. "I'm going to tell Hudner to prepare the bill of sale—that I'll be up in fifteen minutes with the check. He who hesitates is lost, and——"

The door opened and a youth stood in the entrance.

"Mr. J. O. Heyfuss is calling," he announced.

"Show him in immediately," Cappy ordered, glad of the opportunity to delay Matt's telephonic accept-

ance of the vessel at Hudner's price. "Hold on a
minute, Matt," he continued, turning to his son-in-law.
"Heyfuss is a ship broker; maybe he has a ship to
sell us; she might prove to be a better buy than the
Penelope . . . Howdy, Heyfuss? Come in and sit
down."

Mr. Heyfuss entered smilingly, saluted both satellites
of the Blue Star and sat down.

"Well, gentlemen," he announced, "wonders will never
cease. Every day I'm seeing, hearing and doing wonderful things in the shipping business. Day before
yesterday I bought the old barkentine *Mayfair*. She'd
been laid up in Rotten Row for seven years, and for
at least four years the tide has been rising and falling
inside her. She cost me seven hundred and fifty dollars,
and I sold her the same afternoon to Al Hanify for a
thousand. Not very much of a profit; but then it
was Saturday and everybody closes up shop at noon,
you know. So I felt the day wasn't a blank, anyhow.

"And what do you suppose Al did? You'll laugh.
He called up Crowley & Son and got Tom Crowley on
the line. At first Tom wouldn't listen to him; but
when Al told him the *Mayfair* had good oak ribs still
left in her carcass Tommy said he'd take a chance,
and bought her, sight unseen, for fifteen hundred
dollars. The next morning, being Sunday, Tommy had
nothing particular to do; so he took Live Wire Luiz,
of the West Coast Trading Company, over to the
Boneyard and showed him the prize lying on her beam
ends in the mud. That little Peruvian parrakeet actually paid Tommy two thousand dollars for her;
and now Live Wire Luiz and J. Augustus Redell, his
partner in the West Coast Trading Company, have

her out on Hanlon's Marine Way, putting a new bottom
in her. They're going to spend twenty thousand dollars on her; and when she's ready for sea Redell has a
cargo of fir for Sydney waiting for her.

"She'll come back with coal and make her owners at
least fifty thousand dollars."

"That's all very interesting to outsiders, but commonplace stuff to us," Cappy reminded his visitor.
"Have you got a commission to sell a ship for somebody?"

"Want one?"

"Surest thing you know!"

"All right. I'll sell you the *Alden Besse*. She's an
old tea clipper, built in the forties; but she's sound and
tight. Been a motion picture ship for the past five
years. I can deliver her to you for forty thousand
dollars."

"No, you'll not. I sold her to the motion picture
people for fifteen hundred," Cappy countered, "and
I don't want her back at any price. I send my boys
to sea to earn a safe living, not to visit Davy Jones'
locker."

"Well, I think I might get you the old Australian
prison ship, *Success*. She was built at Rangoon in
1790, of teak, and will last forever. Perhaps you saw
her when she was exhibited at the Exposition last year.
Might get her for you kind of cheap."

"Nothing doing. Heyfuss, we want a steamer."

"Sorry, but I haven't a thing in steamers. Just sold
the last one I had ten minutes ago—the *Penelope*."

"The what!" Matt Peasley and Cappy cried in
chorus.

"The *Penelope*. Sold her to a big Eastern powder

company. She goes into the nitrate trade, of course. These munition manufacturers must have powder, and to get powder they must have nitrate, and to get nitrate they must have ships, and to get ships they must pay the price. I got Hudner a million dollars for that ruin of a *Penelope*."

Matt Peasley gently seized J. O. Heyfuss by the ear and led him to the door.

"Out, thief!" he cried. "You can't sell us anything; so we don't want you hanging round this office. You might steal the safe or a roll-top desk, or something."

Heyfuss departed, laughing good-naturedly, and Matt Peasley turned to confront Cappy Ricks. The latter had shrunk up in his chair and was looking as chopfallen and guilty as a dog caught sucking eggs. He favored his big son-in-law with a quick, shifty glance, and then looked down at the carpet.

Matt folded his arms and stared at him until he looked up.

"Don't you go to pick on me!" he warned Matt furiously. "I'll not be picked on in my own office, even by a relative."

Matt threw back his head and chanted,

> "*There was I, waiting at the church,*
> *Waiting at the church*——"

"I was right!" Cappy shrilled. "My mode of procedure was without a flaw."

"Absolutely! The operation was a success, but the patient died."

"But a feller just has to haggle!" Cappy wailed. He was almost on the verge of tears. "It's the basic principle of all trading. Why, I've made my everlasting fortune by haggling. Drat your picture, don't you know that the very pillars of financial success rest on counter-propositions?"

"Listen, relative, listen: I haven't said a word to you, have I?" Matt replied.

"No; but you looked it, and I'll not be looked at."

"All right, Cappy, I'll not look. But I can't help thinking."

"Thinking what?"

"That it's about time you quit talking about retiring—and retired!"

CHAPTER XLVI

With this Parthian shot Matt himself retired, leaving Cappy to shiver and bow his head on his breast; in which position he remained motionless for fully an hour.

"I guess the boy's right," he soliloquized finally. "I think I'd better retire, after pulling that kind of a deal twice in the same place. The pace is getting too swift for me, I think; I can't keep up . . . Well, I guess they've got the goods on me this time. Matt was certainly on the job twice, and I blocked him both times . . . Oh, Lord! I'll never hear the last of this . . . By the Holy Pink-Toed Prophet, I've lost my punch! Matt didn't say so; but he thinks it. And I don't blame him a bit."

The door of Cappy's office opened and again the youth stood in the entrance. "Mr. Redell is calling; there's a gentleman with him," he announced.

"Tell 'em I'm busier'n a cranberry merchant," Cappy snarled. "And unless you're figuring on hunting a new job, my son, don't you come in here again today."

The youth retired. However, he knew from experience that Cappy Ricks never discharged anybody save for insubordination or rank incompetence; hence, he did not hesitate to disobey the old gentleman's edict.

"Mr. Redell says his business is very important," he announced, presenting himself once more at the door.

"All right! No rest for the weary. Show them in."

J. Augustus Redell entered, accompanied by no less a personage than the British Consul. Cappy greeted them without enthusiasm and bade them be seated.

"Well," J. Augustus Redell announced cheerily, "It's plain to be seen that Little Sunshine hasn't been round this office recently."

Cappy grunted.

"What's gone wrong, Cappy?"

"Everything! Been going wrong for years and I never realized it until this afternoon. Ah, Gus, my dear young friend, how I envy you your youth, your capacity to think, your golden dreams, your boundless energy, your ability to make two-dollar bills grow where one-dollar bills grew before, thus making an apparently barren prospect as verdant as a meadow in spring. But make the most of your opportunity, young feller! The day will come to you, as it has come to me, when everything you do will be done twenty minutes too late; when every dollar you make will be subject to a cash discount of one hundred per cent; when every competitor you held cheap will suddenly develop the luck of the devil, the brains of a Demosthenes, and the courage of a hog going to war."

"I should judge that you have recently suffered a great bereavement."

"I have, Augustus, I have. Through my indecision I have just lost a bank roll a greyhound couldn't have jumped over. Suppose it was a paper profit? I grieve just the same."

"Forget it, Cappy! Life is real, life is earnest, and you have a bank roll of real profits a giraffe couldn't reach the top of."

"Oh, it isn't the money, Gus. Money is only a vulgar symbol of my bereavement. The trouble is—I've lost my punch! I can't think, Gus; I can't act promptly. I'm out of touch with my times. I remind myself of nothing so much as the old rooster that suddenly discovered he had been elected to furnish the dinner the following Sunday. His hens cackled and called to him that they had found some worms, but he wouldn't pay any attention to them; just leaned up against the wire netting in the poultry yard and said to himself: 'Oh, hell! What's the use? Today an egg—tomorrow a feather duster!'"

"Don't be pessimistic, Cappy. Don't! It doesn't become you, and I don't believe a word you're telling me. You're still the old he-fox of the world; and I've come to you for help on a deal that's going to mean a whole lot of money to both of us if we can only put it through."

"I'm sorry, Gus, but I'm not interested. As a matter of fact, I've retired."

"Nonsense! Nonsense! I know where there's a beautiful ten-thousand-ton, net register, steel steamer to be bought for three hundred thousand dollars——"

Cappy Ricks threw out an arm and pressed his hand against Redell's mouth.

"Sh-h-h!" he warned. "Sh-h-h! Hush!"

With the agility of a man half his age Cappy ran to the door, bolted it on the inside and returned to his desk. He was rubbing his hands and his eyes were aglow with interest.

"What are you sh-h-h-ing about?" Redell demanded.

"Matt Peasley and that cowardly Skinner. Not a word of this to them, Gus! Not—a—whisper!" And he winked one eye and twisted up the corner of his mouth knowingly. Mr. Redell nodded his promise and Cappy went on: "Now Gus, my dear young friend, start in at the beginning and tell me everything. I assume, of course, that this is real business and not another of your jokes on the old man. Word of honor, Gus?"

"Word of honor, Cappy."

"All right; blaze away! Come, come! What have you got to offer?"

"I have a condition and I offer you a half interest in it if you can suggest a plan to circumvent His Royal Highness, Kaiser Wilhelm——"

"Hum-m-m! Enough!" Cappy interrupted, and turned to the British Consul: "This is an international affair, eh? See if I don't state the proposition in a nutshell—if I may be pardoned the bromide. This steamer is a German, and the proposition is to get her under the American flag so firmly that she'll stay there; then, I suppose, we're to charter her to the British Government, or one of Britain's allies—Russia, for instance."

J. Augustus Redell and the British Consul exchanged admiring winks.

"What did I tell you, Mister Consul?" Redell declared triumphantly. "Mr. Ricks knows the story before we have told it. And yet he's complaining about the loss of his punch!"

Cappy looked slightly self-conscious; it was plain the compliment pleased him.

"Well, Gus, my boy," he answered, "I have lost my punch, though at that I'm not exactly a pork-and-beaner. Hum-m-m! Ahem! Harumph-h-h! This must be a hard order to fill, Mister Consul, when Gus Redell has to come to me for help. That son of a gun can move faster and go through more obstacles than quicksilver. Gus, what's gone wrong with you? Have you lost your punch too? And at your age?"

"Looks like it, Cappy. I've thought and thought until I'm desperate, and not an idea worth while has presented itself. That's why I've come to you."

"Well, I don't guarantee a cure, my boy. But I'll say this much: If you and I can't put this thing over, then it just isn't put-overable. Fire away, Gus!"

"Have you ever heard of the steamer *Bavarian?*"

"Of course! She belongs to Adolph Koenitz and flies the German flag. Since the war started she's been interned down in Mission Bay."

Redell nodded.

"Adolph Koenitz never became an American citizen, despite the fact that he had lived in San Francisco twenty years and operated three steamers out of this port. He was a reserve officer in the German Navy; and when the war broke out he interned his ships, placed his entire estate in his wife's name and reported for duty. He perished in the Battle of Jutland, both his boys were killed at Verdun, and now his widow would like to sell the *Bavarian* and get some cash. She had a large income from an estate in Germany, but the war cut that off.

"Also, it appears that Koenitz was rather heavily involved, and the expense of maintaining those interned steamers, with their German crews aboard, has his widow badly worried; in fact, she has reached the point where she finds it necessary to sell one of the steamers in order to hang on to the other two. She has tried to raise a mortgage on the *Bavarian,* but nobody cares to loan money on an interned German steamer."

"Naturally," Cappy replied sarcastically. "And I'm amazed that you should consider me boob enough to consider seriously buying the same steamer outright! Gus, I'd have about as much use for that steamer as I would have for a tail. Even if I should buy her now, and not use her until the war is over, I should be risking my money; for the German Government, if you remember, issued an order in 1915 forbidding its subjects to sell their interned ships without the consent of the said government. And, even if Mrs. Koenitz can procure the Kaiser's consent, I fail to see the wisdom of tying up three hundred thousand dollars in an idle investment."

"Ah, but under those circumstances she wouldn't be an idle investment."

"Yes, she would, my boy. Great Britain issued an Order in Council in 1914 notifying all neutral nations that she would not sanction the transfer of registry of any German vessel. A few daring devils took a chance—and what happened? The British Navy overhauled the ships at sea and took them into a British port where a British prize court confiscated them. There is the case of the *Mazatlan,* for instance. She was German owned and flew the German flag; her owner put her under the Mexican flag, and subsequently she was sold at a bargain to one of our neighbors, who put her under American registry. Do you know where the *Mazatlan* is now? Well, I'll tell you: She's freighting war munitions for Johnny Bull—and our optimistic neighbor isn't collecting the freight money either."

"Quite true, Mr. Ricks; quite true—in ordinary cases," the Consul told him smilingly.

"By the Holy Pink-Toed Prophet! I smell a mouse. Hum-m-m! That simplifies matters. We-l-l! If you are in position, Mister Consul, to give me your word of honor as a gentleman and an officer of your king that the British Navy will turn its blind side to the *Bavarian* when she puts to sea, I'll buy the *Bavarian* so fast it'll make your head swim. In return for this favor, of course, I am to charter the ship at the going rates to——"

"Our ally, the Russian Government, Mr. Ricks. And you have my word of honor, which is all I can give you; for a deal like this, as you know, cannot be made in writing. I have had the matter up with the Admiralty, however, and permission has been granted me to give the verbal assurance of my government."

"I'll make a finger bet with your government, Mister Consul. As for Kaiser Bill's consent to the transfer— *heraus mit 'em!* We'll get along without that. Wilhelm doesn't cut much ice with me these days and I'm willing to wager the price of the *Bavarian* that such ice as he does cut will blame soon melt. Gus, you say Mrs. Koenitz wants to sell?"

"Yes."

"And she doesn't care who buys?"

"Not a particle! She's sore on the Kaiser; it's been thumbs down on Wilhelm ever since Adolph and the boys lost the number of their mess. She says to me: 'Herr Riddle, dot Kaiser orders war like I order beer!' However, there's an 'if' to the transfer. While we

know the British Navy will not bother us should we
buy the steamer, still enthusiastic Britishers all over
the world will have their eyes on the *Bavarian* and
clamor for her capture. Great Britain cannot publicly
—or, at least, obviously—make any exceptions to her
Order in Council, and we'll have to mess up that
steamer's title and nativity to save John Bull's social
standing. Ye must make a bluff at deceiving him.
If we can show some sort of legal transfer to another
flag J. B. can play blindman's buff with dignity and
honor; otherwise nix!"

Cappy Ricks' eyes sought the ceiling.

"What have I done to deserve this?" he demanded
of an invisible Presence. "Why am I afflicted thus?
Job had his boils; but you and I, Augustus, are covered with a financial rash, bleeding at every pore, and
with no relief in sight."

"I told you this was a tough one, Cappy. I've
pondered the situation until my brain is addled like a
last year's nest egg, and finally I've come to you as
a last resort. If you can't cook up an airtight scheme,
then there is no help; and I'm going to forget the
Bavarian and attend to some business more profitable
and less debilitating."

"There must be an out, Gus. It's too good a thing
to abandon. Suppose you and the Consul go away
and give me time to concentrate my thoughts on this
problem. It's a holy terror; but—— Well, I've seen
dogs almost as sick as this one cured."

"God bless you!" Mr. Redell murmured fervently.
"Consul, let us depart and leave Mr. Ricks to himself.
Call me up, Cappy, when you see a ray of light. Two
heads are better than one, you know."

CHAPTER XLVII

When his visitors had gone Cappy Ricks gave orders that he was not to be disturbed on any pretext whatever. Then he locked himself in, swung his legs to the top of his desk, slid low in his chair until he rested on his spine, bowed his head on his breast and closed his eyes. The battle was on.

One hour later J. Augustus Redell entered breathlessly in response to a telephonic invitation from Cappy.

"Gus," the latter began, "am I right in assuming that you possess a reasonable amount of influence with that hair-trigger partner of yours, Live Wire Luiz?" Redell nodded. "And is Luiz absolutely trustworthy? Will he stay put and keep his mouth closed?"

"He is my partner, Cappy. He's mercurial, but a gentleman. I'd trust him with my life, and I always trust him with my bank roll. He requires no watching."

"Good! Gus, send Live Wire Luiz down to Guaymas and have him incorporate the North and South American Steamship Company there, under the extremely flexible and evershifting laws of the Republic of Mexico. Luiz is a Peruvian and speaks Spanish, and knows the Mexican temperament. He can easily procure three Mexicans to act as a dummy board of directors; his own name, of course, for obvious reasons, must never appear in connection with this company. A thousand dollars ought to cover this Mexican expense."

"Consider that point attended to, Cappy."

"Fine! Now then, when this corporate vehicle is in running order and has opened an office in Guaymas, Live Wire Luiz will write your company, The West Coast Trading Company, saying that his company has been referred to you by some mutual friends in Guaymas. Of course Luiz doesn't sign this letter. It is signed by the North and South American Steamship Company, per the dummy secretary or president. The letter goes on to say that the latter company is in the market for a steamer, the general specifications of which, singularly enough, fit the *Bavarian*. The vessel is to be used for transporting troops up and down the west coast of Mexico and for freighting munitions from Japan; and in a delicate way it might be hinted that the de facto Mexican Government is the real buyer. A commission of five per cent is offered you for buying the vessel for them, said commission to be split fifty-fifty with the North and South American Steamship Company; this being the Mexican way of doing business, as you know."

"Consider that matter attended to also. I'll write the letter myself before Luiz starts for Guaymas, so I'll be certain the job will be done exactly right."

"As soon as you receive this letter you get busy and wire the North and South American Steamship Company that you have just the vessel they want, price three hundred thousand dollars. Live Wire Luiz will then cause a reply to that telegram to be sent, advising you that his clients would not balk at paying half a million! That, of course, is hint enough for you.

Right away you see the old Mexican graft sticking out, and you say to yourself, 'Why not?' And you do! You reply to that telegram, saying you erred when naming the price in your first telegram; that it is five hundred thousand instead of three. Then you come down to me and I hand you three hundred thousand dollars in currency; for in such a transaction as this, checks, with their indorsements, provide a trail that may prove embarrassing. You take that money and deposit it in escrow in any local bank against a bill of sale of the *Bavarian* from Mrs. Koenitz to the North and South American Steamship Company, of Guaymas, Mexico. Before doing so, however, have Mrs. Koenitz place the vessel under Mexican registry. She can do that through the Mexican Consul for the de facto government; and when the bill of sale is turned over to you, record it promptly with the Mexican Consul. Later you will record it in Mexico.

"The vessel is now the property of the North and South American Steamship Company; and the North and South American Steamship Company is the property of Cappy Ricks and the West Coast Trading Company, per Señor Felipe Luiz Almeida. But we must never admit this. To have the North and South American Steamship Company transfer the vessel to us would be very coarse work indeed; so we must avoid that."

"How?"

"I'll get to that presently. The steamer is now in our possession, and you will already have notified her German skipper and crew to hunt a new residence. You will then put an American skipper in charge and ship American engineers and a crew of parrakeets;

and on the very day the sale is consummated, just before the customhouse closes, have the skipper clear the
vessel for Guaymas and put to sea that night. Since
she carries no cargo the collector of the port will not
stop you; the risk of going to sea is all our own—if we
care to take it.

"The next day the newspaper boys will be hot on
the trail. An interned German merchantman has suddenly transferred to Mexican registry and put to sea!
Now! Inquiry at the customhouse and at the Mexican
consulate shows that the vessel has been sold, and the
trail leads straight to the office of the West Coast
Trading Company. You are interviewed—and say
nothing; and that day, when I appear on 'Change,
these baffled journalists drive me into a corner and ask
me what I think about it. And I'll tell them it's just
another case of the lowly Mexican peon being horn-
swoggled by the foxy Americano. The Mexicans
wanted a ship and asked the American to buy one for
them. He did—only he forgot to tell them she was a
German. She was such a good buy they snapped her
up without asking questions, though in all probability
the poor devils had no knowledge of Kaiser Wilhelm's
edict that no German ships shall be sold without the
consent of the German Government. I will say that
it looks to me as if the ancient rule of *caveat emptor*
applied, and that the Mexicans are stung and have
no comeback. Then, again, it may be a shrewd German
trick to put something over.

"Well, they make a snorting story out of what I
give them; the frau's friends read it and think she's
done something smart. Nobody feels sorry for a
Mexican. Next morning you come out with a blast of

righteous indignation and admit that you cannot or will not deny that the vessel was sold to parties representing the de facto Mexican Government. You deny, however, that you sold them a pig in a poke; and the papers print a copy of your letter to the North and South American Steamship Company specifically advising them that the vessel was a German and liable to prove an embarrassment. This, of course, clears you, and the blame for the graft is placed where it belongs—on the shoulders of the North and South American Steamship Company, which has deliberately stung the de facto government!"

"Cappy," said J. Augustus Redell admiringly, "you're immense!"

"I accept the nomination. Upon her arrival in Guaymas the *Bavarian's* name is changed to *La Golondrina*, or *Sobre las Olas*, or *Mañana*, or *Poco Tiempo*—whatever's right. I think we may safely gamble that she will arrive in Guaymas in the light of what the British Consul told us; and, in view of her departure unannounced, no British warship on the West Coast can get so far north as Guaymas in time to intercept her.

"Well, having changed her name, she picks up a general cargo and comes back to San Francisco, where she goes on dry dock and is cleaned and painted, has her gear overhauled, fills up with fuel oil and stores, and—but that's enough. Now comes the blow-off.

"Strange to relate, you haven't received a cent of that five-per-cent commission due you from the North and South American Steamship Company for buying the *Bavarian* for them. The issue is in dispute. They claim you are not entitled to any commission, because

you stung them with a German vessel; and you claim
you told them she was a German, but that they needed
her so badly they would take a chance. Also, the fact
that she went to sea that time in such a hurry, and
forgot to pay for her fuel oil and stores, looks rather
suspicious; so, when the vessel comes off dry dock, with
about ten thousand dollars' worth of bills against her,
you decide to protect your claim for the commission—
and, by the Holy Pink-Toed Prophet, Gus, you libel
her! The news breaks into the papers, and next day
every creditor of the ship files a libel on her, also, to
protect his claim. Gus, she'll have so many plasters on
her she'll look like a German coming home from the
war."

J. Augustus Redell leaped from his chair and picked
little Cappy Ricks up in his arms and hugged him.

"Oh, Cappy! Cappy!" he yelled. "You're the
shadow of a rock in a weary land—a cup of cool water
in the suburbs of hell!"

"Are you game?" Cappy gurgled.

"Does a cat eat liver? Cappy, you've solved the
problem! Naturally the North and South American
Steamship Company does not directly or indirectly
make any attempt to lift these libels and get the vessel
to sea. Why? I'll tell you—or, rather, I'll tell the
newspaper boys and they'll tell everybody. It will
appear that as soon as the Mexican Consul here got an
inkling of the apparent plan of the North and South
American Steamship Company, of Guaymas, to sting
Don Venustiano Carranza by slipping him a steamer
with a clouded title, he must have wired Don Venustiano
to round up the directors of the said company and
give them the *ley fuga*. Fortunately for these culprits,

however, they got next in time to get out from under. Mounting swift steeds, the entire board of directors fled north and east, never pausing until they had joined Pancho Villa; and we learn from some Border gossips that all three subsequently were killed in action. But, before leaving Guaymas, they left their tangled steamship affairs in the hands of their attorney——"

"Nothing doing, Gus! They left their tangled steamship affairs in the hands of my attorney, and they gave him an absolute, ironclad, airtight power of attorney to sell the ship, receive and receipt for all money due the company, and so on, and so on, ad libitum, ad infinitum; said power of attorney being nonrevocable for five years."

"Great stuff! In due course the libelants sue in the United States District Court; your attorney appears for the defendants and confesses judgment, but pleads for a ten-day stay of execution until he can raise a mortgage on the vessel. But, strange to relate, the ten-day stay expires and the judgments against the steamer are not paid; so the judge of the United States District Court orders the steamer sold at public auction on the floor of the Merchants' Exchange to the highest bidder, to satisfy the claims of the creditors. Thirty days later the United States Marshal conducts the sale, and a gentleman named Cappy Ricks buys her in. The United States Marshal gives the said Ricks a bill of sale for her, which the said Ricks thereupon records in the United States Customhouse, and——"

"*Und Hoch der Kaiser! Und Hoch der* John J. Bull! We've finally got that clear American title we've been looking for. It makes no difference what the nationality of a vessel is; the minute she enters the territorial

waters of the United States of America she is amenable
to the laws of the United States of America, one of
which reads thusly: 'Thou shalt pay thy bills; and if
thou dost not, then *poco tiempo* thou shalt be made to
pay them, even unto the seizure and sale of thy ship.'
And with the purchase of that ship, under an order of
sale issued by the United States District Court, she
becomes a United States ship; we register her as such;
and the United States simply has to stand back of the
bill of sale it gave us. Germany knows that; England
knows it; Austria knows it; and from the jackstaff of
the late *Bavarian*, now renamed the *Alden M. Peasley*,
in honor of my first grandson, there floats——"

J. Augustus Redell raised his index finger, enjoining
silence:

"Now then! One, two, three! Down, left, up!

"O-ho, say, can you see, by the dawn's early light,
  What so-ho pro-houdly we hailed at the twilight's last
    gleaming?"

Cappy Ricks sprang to attention. Presently,
through the partition, his cracked old voice reached
Mr. Skinner:

"Then conquer we must, when our cause is so just;
  And this be our motto: 'May we nev-er go bust!'"

"What's doing here?" Mr. Skinner demanded, bang-
ing at the door, which was locked.

"Go way back and sit down!" Cappy shrilled. "I'll
show you and Matt Peasley where to head in, yet—see
if I don't!"

"Two million dollars!" cried J. Augustus Redell.

CHAPTER XLVIII

Cappy Ricks and J. Augustus Redell arrived at the Merchants' Exchange promptly at one o'clock on the date of the sale of the S. S. *General Carranza*, as the *Bavarian* was now called. Just inside the door they paused and looked at each other.

"Whe-e-e-ew!" murmured Cappy Ricks. "All the shipping men in the world are here to bid on our property, Gus."

Mr. Redell whistled softly. "This," he said, "will be some auction!"

Cappy chuckled.

"There is only one thing that a shipping man in this country has more respect for than an Order in Council—and that is an Order in the United States District Court!"

"Naturally. It's backed up by our army and navy."

"By the Holy Pink-Toed Prophet, somebody's sporting blood is going to be tested today; and something tells, me, Augustus, my dear young friend, that it's going to be Matt Peasley's."

"What makes you think so, Cappy?"

Again Cappy chuckled.

"Having used German methods to bring about this auction sale," he confessed, "I concluded to steal a little more of this Teutonic stuff; so I established a system of espionage in Skinner's office and another in Matt Peasley's. Gus, I got a lot of low-down informa-

tion on those two young pups; they're trying to slip
something over on the old dog."

"Well, they'll never teach him any new tricks,
Cappy."

"You know it! I observe that, as usual, Jim Searles
will conduct the auction. He's climbing up on the block
now, and, by the Toenails of Moses, Matt Peasley is
on the job! Look, Gus! You can see his black head
sticking up out of the heart of the riot."

As Cappy and Redell joined the crowd Jim Searles,
by acclamation the auctioneer of the Port of San
Francisco, rapped smartly with his little gavel, and
a tense silence settled over the crowd.

"This," Mr. Searles announced, "will be a fight to
a finish, winner take all. In accordance with an order
of the United States District Court I am about to sell,
at public auction, to the highest bidder, the Mexican
Steamship *General Carranza*, ex-German Steamship
Bavarian, to satisfy the following judgments: Mr. J.
Augustus Redell——"

"Cut it out!" roared Matt Peasley. "We've all
read the list of creditors, and you're only gumming
up the game. Come down to business Jim."

"Good boy, Peasley! Sure! Cut it out, Jim! Get
busy!" A dozen voices seconded Captain Matt Peasley's motion and Jim Searles rapped for order.

"How much am I offered?" he cried.

"One million dollars!" roared Matt Peasley.

On the fringe of the eager crowd Cappy Ricks leaned
up against his friend Redell and commenced to laugh.

"The young scoundrel!" he chortled. "He never
said a word to me about this auction; he was afraid
I'd butt in and block his purchase; so, for his impu-

dence, I'll teach him a lesson he'll never forget. Bid,
Gus! Bet 'em as high as a hound's back."

"Captain Matt Peasley, representing the Blue Star
Navigation Company, bids one million dollars. Chicken
feed! Won't some real sport please tilt the ante?"
Jim Searles pleaded. "Don't waste my time, gentlemen.
It's valuable. Let's get this thing over and go back to
our offices."

"One million five hundred thousand!" called J.
Augustus Redell.

"I called for a sport and drew a piker," Jim Searles
retorted. "Mr. J. Augustus Redell, of the West Coast
Trading Company, bids a million and a half."

Young Dalton Mann, representing the Pacific Mail
Steamship Company, raised his hand and snapped his
fingers at the auctioneer.

"And a hundred thousand!" he shouted.

"And a hundred thousand!" Matt Peasley retorted.

"And fifty thousand!" Mann flung back at him.

Matt Peasley eyed his antagonist belligerently.

"That's doing very well for a young fellow," Searles
complimented the last bidder. "Skipper Peasley, are
you going to let this landlubber outgame you? He
has bid a million and three-quarters. Think of the
present high freight rates and speak up, or remain
forever silent."

The bidding had so suddenly and by such prodigious
bounds reached the elimination point that every piker
present was afraid to open his mouth in the presence
of these plungers. Matt Peasley licked his lips and
glanced round rather helplessly. He knew he had
about reached the limit of his bidding, but he suspected that Mann had reached his also.

"And ten thousand!" he shouted desperately.

"Cheap stuff! Cheap stuff!" the crowd jeered good-naturedly.

Cappy Ricks nudged J. Augustus Redell as Mann waved his hand in token of surrender. "One million seven hundred and sixty thousand I am offered," the auctioneer intoned. "Any further bids?" He waited a full minute; then resorted to three minutes of cajolery, but in vain. There were no more bids.

Jim Searles raised his hammer.

"Going—once!" he called—and waited. "Going—twice!" Another pause. "Going——"

"Two million dollars!" cried J. Augustus Redell; and a sigh went up from the excited onlookers.

"Ah! Mr. Redell is a sport, after all! Two million, flat!" Searles looked down on Matt Peasley. "Die, dog, or eat the meat ax!" he warned the unhappy young man.

"Let him have her," Matt growled; and, very red of face, he commenced to shoulder his way through the crowd.

"Beat it, Cappy; he's coming!" Redell warned the president emeritus.

Cappy Ricks, dodging round the flank of the crowd, fled through the side entrance of the Merchants' Exchange; and he was tranquilly smoking a cigar in his private office when Matt Peasley dropped in on him an hour later. Cappy eyed him coldly.

"Is Skinner back from luncheon?" he demanded. Matt nodded. "Tell him to come in here. I want to see him," Cappy continued ominously. "And you might stick round yourself."

Mr. Skinner made his appearance.

"Close the door," Cappy commanded.

Mr. Skinner looked a little startled and surprised, but promptly closed the door.

"You wanted to see me, Mr. Ricks?" he queried.

Cappy Ricks edged forward until he was seated on the extreme edge of his chair. Then he rested a hand on each knee, bent his head, and glared at the unhappy Skinner over the rims of his glasses. After thirty seconds of this scrutiny he turned to his son-in-law.

"Well," he said, "I hear you've been attending an auction sale and making a star-spangled monkey of yourself bidding a million seven hundred and sixty thousand dollars on that Mexican steamer. Matt, have you taken leave of your senses?"

"No, sir—not quite; but Gus Redell has. He bought her in for two million dollars. Of course he was acting for somebody else, because every cent he has is working overtime in the West Coast Trading Company."

"Oh!" Cappy murmured. "Then you didn't get her, after all?"

"No, sir! So perhaps you'd better not holler until you're hit." Matt sighed. "By Neptune," he declared, "I'd give a cooky to know the name of the crazy man who paid two million dollars for that steamer!"

"Behold the lunatic, Matt! Grandpa Ricks, in his second childhood! Gus Redell was bidding for me, sonny."

Matt Peasley sat down rather limply and stared at the president emeritus.

"Cappy," he said presently, "you sent a boy to do a man's work. I had the boat bought for a million seven hundred and sixty thousand! For heaven's sake,

why didn't you tell me you wanted her? And I would
have laid off. For the love of heaven, why did you
go bidding against me?"

"Why didn't you tell me you wanted her, you big
simp?" Cappy retorted. "You never said a word to
me; and naturally Redell thought you were acting for
somebody else. He had orders from me to get her
and damn the cost—and he fulfilled his orders."

"'A comedy of errors, truly!" Mr. Skinner observed
witheringly.

Matt Peasley raised his huge arms and clenched his
great fists in agony.

"Oh, Cappy! Cappy!" he pleaded. "Won't you
please retire? You're just raising hell with the organization!"

"All right, Matt; I'll retire. But, before I do, I'm
going to give Skinner a piece of my mind. Skinner,
what the devil do you mean by going up to the Marine
National Bank and borrowing a million dollars on the
credit of the Ricks Lumber & Logging Company? I
admit I have given you entire charge of the lumber
end, and you were quite within your rights when you
negotiated the loan and signed the note as president;
but how did it happen that you didn't consult with the
old man, if only as a matter of common courtesy?"

"I—I—that is, I—well, I didn't mean to be dis-
courteous, Mr. Ricks. Oh, I wouldn't have you think,
sir——"

"No; you'd have me be a dummy if you could. Why,
you almost put the skids under me; because, when I
went up to the Marine National to make a little personal loan in a spirit of preparedness, I discovered
that the loan you had been given on my assets had

jazzed my personal credit all to glory! I used to be
able to borrow a million dollars on my bare note; but
I'll be shot if they didn't make me dig up a lot of
collateral this time! Skinner, I wouldn't have thought
that of you. After trusting you as I have done for
a quarter of a century, to find you giving me the
double-cross just about breaks my heart. Great Godfrey, Skinner, how could you be so false to me? I expect that sort of thing from Matt—those one loves the
best always swat one; but from you—— Skinner, I
don't know what prevents me from demanding your
resignation here and now, unless it be because of your
previous splendid character and loyal service."

"Oh, Mr. Ricks, Mr. Ricks!" Poor Skinner held up
his hands appealingly and commenced to weep. "Please
do not think ill of me. I swear——"

"You loaned the Ricks Lumber & Logging Company's million dollars to Matt Peasley to help buy that
steamer for the Blue Star Navigation Company; and
he, the son of a pirate, went to work and borrowed it
from you, well knowing he had no business to do so.
What are you paying the Marine National for that
money?"

"Five per cent," Skinner sniffled, for his heart was
broken.

"What are you soaking the Blue Star Navigation
Company for it?"

"Six," Skinner confessed miserably.

"That's all right, Skinner, my boy. Cheer up! I
forgive you. That little profit of one per cent saves
your bacon, boy. I guess there's some good left in
you still; and I'm happy to have this evidence that,
though I own both companies, you have not forgotten

you are responsible for the profit-and-loss account of one of them, and Matt Peasley for the other. You did quite right to claim that one per cent jerk from Matt. Business is business!"

"Yes, you bet it is!" Matt Peasley struck in. "And I want you to lay off on Skinner, because what he did was done in fear and trembling, and under duress. We were both afraid you'd block the purchase; so we agreed to keep our plans secret from you, because— Well, somehow I did want that bully big boat the very worst way."

"And that's exactly the way you set about getting her, Matthew. However, you're young—you don't know any better; so I forgive you. Of course I realized you wanted that steamer, boy. I knew your heart was set on seeing our house flag floating from her main-truck; so I—Well, I just thought I'd get her for you, to sort of square myself for those two bonehead plays I pulled earlier in the year."

"Oh, but you shouldn't have paid two millions for her, Cappy! Business is one thing and sentiment is another."

"Why, I didn't pay any such price for her! Originally I bought her, as a German, for three hundred thousand dollars; in addition to that I've spent about ten thousand dollars improving her, and maybe five thousand more fussing up the trail of my operations so no smart secret-service operative could come round and hang something on me." He reached into his coat pocket and drew forth the United States Marshal's bill of sale. "Here, sonny," he announced, "is your Uncle Sam's certificate of title. Hustle up to the customhouse and get it recorded; then make out a bill

of sale for a one-third interest to the West Coast
Trading Company and record that also. Then change
her name to *Alden M. Peasley*, in honor of your first-
born, and put her under these two flags."

He jerked open a drawer in the desk and brought
forth a bright new edition of Old Glory, followed by
the familiar white muslin burgee with the blue star.

"Skinner!"

"Yes, Mr. Ricks."

"The United States Marshal has paid all the debts
of the *Alden M. Peasley*, and this afternoon he'll send
his check for the proceeds of the sale still remaining
in his hands to my lawyer, who holds a most ungodly
power of attorney from that dummy Guaymas corporation Live Wire Luiz organized to buy the ship
for us. Our attorney will cash that check and send the
cash down to you. Please bank it to my credit and
take up that note I gave the Marine National; then
get the securities I hocked and tuck them back in my
safe-deposit vault. As for the interest at five per cent,
which the Ricks Lumber & Logging Company will have
to pay on that million you borrowed to help Matt
Peasley hornswoggle father, you just charge that to
your personal account as a penance for your sins. As
for the six per cent you pay the Ricks Lumber &
Logging Company for the money loaned your Blue
Star Navigation Company, Matt Peasley, just charge
that to your personal account as a penance for your
sins."

Both culprits nodded dazedly.

"Now," Cappy continued, "I'll tell you something
else: The *Alden M. Peasley* belongs to the West Coast
Trading Company and Alden P. Ricks; they own one-

third for bringing the deal to my attention and furnishing some labor, and I own two-thirds, or the lion's share, for doing a lion's work—to wit, putting up the cash and promoting the deal to a clean title. Consequently, though you two boys own a nice little block of stock in the Blue Star Navigation Company, you don't own a red cent in the *Alden M. Peasley*, because she doesn't belong to the Blue Star Navigation Company, but to the president emeritus thereof. However, as I am about to retire for keeps this time, I'll tell you what I purpose doing with my two-thirds of the *Alden M. Peasley:* Skinner, my dear boy, I kidded you into tears. Bless you, boy, it broke your heart when you thought your old boss figured you'd quit being Faithful Fido, didn't it? Skinner, loyalty like yours is very, very precious; and your affection is—er— Skinner, you human icicle, you can't bluff me! I'm on to you, young feller! Matt, you prepare a deed of gift for one-half of my two-thirds interest to Skinner, and take the other half for yourself; and when the *Alden M. Peasley* has earned what I put into her, credit my account with it. After that, you and Skinner and Gus Redell and Live Wire Luiz can collect the dividends."

"Oh, Mr. Ricks! This is too much," Skinner began.

"Tut, tut, sir! Not a peep out of you, sir! How dare you argue with me? Now just one word more before you fellers go: The next time you boys go bidding on a ship at auction, take a leaf out of Cappy Ricks' book and bid against yourself! You can always scare the other fellows off that way; the sky is the limit—and you're bound to get your money back. So you should *Ish ka bibble.*

"Now you two young freshies go back to your desks and try to learn humility. Thus endeth the first lesson, my children."

Matt Peasley came close to Cappy and put his big arm round the little old man.

"Cappy," he whispered, "please don't retire!"

"All right, son," Cappy answered; "but get that infernal cry-baby, Skinner, out of my office. He's breaking my heart."

If J. Augustus Redell had been content to sue for peace following his deal with Cappy in Australian wheat, all would have been well for that young man. Alas! As we have already stated, he was young—and there is an old saying to the effect that youth must be served. J. Augustus Redell, like Oliver Twist, desired more. His triumph over Cappy in the wheat deal merely whetted his desire for more of the Ricks blood, and in the end the ingenious rascal evolved a plan for making Cappy the laughing stock of the Bilgewater Club for a month of Sundays.

CHAPTER XLIX

CAPPY RICKS entered his office at the unheard-of hour of eight-thirty. On his way to his sanctum at the end of the long suite of offices Cappy paused in the lair of Mr. Skinner, who looked up, amazed.

"Hello!" he saluted the president emeritus. "What brings you down on the job so early this morning, Mr. Ricks?"

"I've got a hen on," Cappy replied briskly. He glanced at Skinner and rubbed his hands together. "Skinner, my dear boy," he continued, "this is a one-horse concern."

"Three sawmills with a combined output of a million feet a day on a ten-hour shift—not to mention a billion feet of stumpage—isn't my idea of a one-horse concern," Mr. Skinner retorted with some asperity.

"Tut, tut, Skinner! I'm not referring to the lumber end at all; so don't get touchy. I'm referring to the Blue Star Navigation Company. It's a dinky proposition."

"Forty-two vessels—windjammers, steam schooners and foreign-going freighters——" began Mr. Skinner; but Cappy cut him short:

"Foreign-going grandmothers! We've got the *Narcissus* and the *Tillicum.*"

"How about my boat—the *John P. Skinner?*"

358

"Oh, yes! That one we scraped up off the bottom of Papeete Harbor," Cappy answered maliciously. "Well, that makes three; and really the *Skinner* and the *Narcissus* are the only vessels built to go foreign. Remember, Skinner, we built the *Tillicum* for the coastwise lumber trade, even though she's so big our competitors thought when we launched her we were crazy to build such a whale for that trade."

"Well, Mr. Ricks?"

"We ought to have more big bottoms, Skinner. We'll have hell-cracking freight rates during the war and for a long time thereafter—and here we sit round like a lot of dubs, too conservative to help ourselves to the gravy. Why, you and Matt Peasley ought to be knitting socks in an old ladies' home, for all the progressiveness you're displaying."

"I am not in charge of the shipping end, Mr. Ricks."

"No; but you've got a tongue in your head, haven't you? You were practically in charge of the Blue Star for more than six months—during the entire period Matt was at sea in the *Retriever* and we thought he was a goner. Why, dog-gone you, Skinner, even when you thought Matt was dead you didn't suggest increasing the fleet. I'm surprised, Skinner, my boy, that in my old age, after gathering a lot of young fellows round me to carry on the business, I've still got to be the bell mare!"

Mr. Skinner had nothing to say to this; if he had it is doubtful whether he would have said it, for he had been too long with Cappy Ricks not to know the signs when the old gentleman took the bit in his teeth and declared for a new deal.

"I'm going into my office to do some tall thinking,

Skinner," Cappy continued. "Remember! No visitors until I've threshed this whole business out to my satisfaction. I'm not in to anybody."

Cappy retired to his office, sat down on his spine in his upholstered swivel chair, swung his thin old shanks to the top of his desk, bowed his head on his breast, and closed his eyes. Scarcely had he done so when the door opened and Matt Peasley thrust his head in.

"Well, Matt?" Cappy queried without opening his eyes.

"I have an offer of forty thousand dollars for our old bark *Altair*, Cappy. What do you think we ought to do?"

"Take it!" Cappy shrilled. "You jibbering jackdaw! Grab it! She's been a failure since the day I built her; never balanced, always burying her nose in the seas, and drowning a sailor about once a year. If we keep that ship much longer she'll sail herself under some day and we'll be out the forty thousand. *Altair!* Fancy name! Skinner got it out of Ben Hur. He'd been in the shipping game ten years then and hadn't learned that was the name of a star! We should have called her the *Water Spaniel*. Sell her, Matt, and we'll put the money into a steamer that can run foreign."

"If you can tell me where we can buy, even at three times her intrinsic value, a steamer that will run foreign, I'm willing to consider selling the *Altair*. Just at present she's earning big dividends; and until we can find a place to invest her selling price, the money will earn six per cent instead of sixty, as at present."

"Clear out and let me think!" Cappy commanded,

and Matt Peasley retired to Mr. Skinner's office.

"Have you noticed the old gentleman lately?" he inquired of Skinner. "Ever since his grandson arrived grandpa has been paying attention to business."

"He's dissatisfied with his own and our efforts thus far. He thinks he's been a piker and that you and I are his first-assistant pikers. He has ships on the brain."

"He's getting pretty cocky," Matt agreed; "but, at that, I guess he has a license to be."

"I've been with him twenty-six—yes, twenty-seven—years; and I know him, Matt. He's cooking up something prodigious—and it will soon be done."

The door of Cappy's office opened and Cappy stood in the entrance.

"Skinner," he ordered, "get me a letter of credit for about twenty thousand dollars. I'm going travelling."

"Where?" Matt and Skinner queried in chorus.

"To Europe."

"You're not!" Matt Peasley declared. "You're liable to be torpedoed en route."

"I know, but then, too, I'm liable not to be; and if I am, why, I'm an old man, and I'll only be cheating the devil by a few years or a few months. Come in here, you two dead ones."

They followed him into his office.

"We need some steamers," Cappy announced. "Every shipyard in the United States that could build the kind of steamer we want is full up with contracts for the next three years; so I'm going to Norway or Sweden or Denmark, or some non-belligerent European country, and see whether I can't place some contracts there for a couple of real freighters. Then, too, I may be able to pick up good vessels over there at a reasonable price. Under the Emergency Shipping Act we can get them provisional American registry—and that's all we need. Before a great while Uncle Sam is going to turn his antiquated shipping laws inside out, and any foreign-built boats we may acquire now will be given the right to run in the coastwise trade also."

"See here, Cappy," Matt reminded the old man; "you're retired and I'm in charge of the destinies of the Blue Star Navigation Company. I don't want you working yourself to death."

"You mean you don't want me butting in. Nonsense! What's the use of having a grandson if a fellow doesn't hustle up something for the boy to sharpen his teeth on when he grows up? Here I've been living from day to day, just marking time on the road to eternity and figuring life wasn't worth while because the stock was going to die out with me. Up until recently I was content with a little old one-horse business; but now, by the Holy Pink-Toed Prophet, boy, we've got to get out and shake a leg! Freighters! That's what we want. Big, well-decked tramps, flying the Stars and Stripes in every port on earth. Why, what kind of a nation are we getting to be, anyway? We're a passel of mollycoddles, asleep on the job. We haven't half enough ships to coal our navy. In the event of war it would take us a week to dig up ships enough to transport the New York Police Department. I tell you, Matt, when I'm gone you'll have to have something for that grandson of mine to do or he'll grow up into one of these idle-rich, ne'er-do-well, two-for-a-quarter dudes. You bet I've been doing a deal of thinking lately. We can't send that boy to college, and spoil him before he's twenty-five. We'll run that young man through high school; just about that time he'll begin to get snobbish and we'll take that out of him by sending him to sea as a cadet on one of our own ships. We'll teach him democracy—that's what we'll teach him. When he's twenty-one he'll be a skipper like his forebears and you'll be only about forty-six. Good Lord! To think of you two young fellows running my Blue Star ships—and not enough ships to keep you busy! Preposterous! I can't consider—— Well, Hankins, my dear boy, what's troubling you?"

Mr. Hankins, the secretary, had entered.

"I wanted to see Mr. Skinner a moment. I'll wait. Didn't know you were busy."

And he started to retire. Cappy checked him: "Finish with Skinner, Hankins. He'll be in consultation here with Matt and me for an hour yet."

"I just wanted to know, Mr. Skinner, whether all those cablegrams to Captain Landry, of the *Altair*, are to be charged to general expense, Captain Landry's personal account, or to the *Altair*."

"It seems to me you should charge them to Captain Landry, Hankins," Mr. Skinner spoke up. "It isn't ship's business and it isn't Blue Star business. If he wants this office to cable him every day about his family——"

"Here! What's this you're talking about, Skinner?" Cappy interrupted.

"When Captain Landry sailed for Callao his wife didn't accompany him——"

"Lucky rascal! He told me he was expecting an heir."

"And he's still expecting that heir."

"Naturally," Mr. Hankins explained, "he's been anxious for news; and ever since his arrival in Callao he's cabled us every other day——latterly every day—asking whether the baby has been born, and whether it's a boy or a girl."

"A very pardonable human curiosity, my boy. Proceed."

"Unfortunately the baby appears to be held up on demurrage and I think we've spent at least fifty dollars cabling to Landry that the youngster has failed to report. I imagine the skipper has spent twice that sum inquiring for news——"

"Of course! It's his first baby, isn't it? You must allow for human nature."

"I thought we would—for the first half dozen cablegrams; but after it became a habit it appeared that Landry ought to pay for his fancies."

"He should," Mr. Skinner declared firmly. "Charge the cablegrams to Landry."

"Nothing doing!" piped Cappy. "Charge 'em to general expense. Dang you, Skinner, I despair of ever breaking you of that habit of operating on the cheap!"

"Oh, very well, sir—only the expense is getting to be quite an item."

"I'm just about to send him another cablegram," Mr. Hankins declared fretfully. "The *Altair* is due to sail from Callao and the baby is still unborn; it will be two months old, at least, before the skipper gets any further news."

"Let's see your cablegram," Cappy ordered, and Mr. Hankins passed it over. Cappy read it. "Holy suffering sailor!" he cried. "Why this concern isn't in the hands of a receiver is a mystery to me." He looked up at Mr. Hankins with blood in his eye. "Here you are, Hankins, trying to saddle a bill of expense on a poor, heartbroken, anxious, embryo parent-to-be. Knowing full well that he only makes a hundred and fifty dollars a month, you admit to an endeavor to stick him for fifty dollars' worth of cablegrams from this end, not to mention those from his end. If you had spent your time, sir, figuring out a way to cut down that cable expense, instead of discovering a rotten way to get rid of it—— Why, look here! You can use your code book and save a couple of dollars."

"Code book!" Mr. Hankins protested indignantly. "Why, who ever heard of a code book for cabling on baby business?"

"Use your shipping code. Here; hand me that code book. There's bound to be something to fit the occasion—there always is. Hum-m-m! Ahem! Harumph-h-h! Let us see what we shall see under the head of cargoes; Loading! Discharging! Demurrage! Ahem! That won't do. He'd be liable to confuse it with the ship's business. Harumph-h-h! Arrivals. Now we have it. Landry has been asking of an expected arrival, hasn't he?" Cappy ran his index finger down the page. "Here you are, Hankins. Hum-m-m! Afilamos— meaning no new arrivals. Naturally Landry will say to himself: 'Well, for heaven's sake, when will that child arrive?' We should enlighten him on that point."

"We cannot."

"Very well, then. Say so. Here you are. Affumi-cata—meaning: We cannot guarantee time of arrival. Hankins, have you talked with Mrs. Landry's physician in order to get the latest ringside reports?"

"Yes, sir."

"What does he say?"

"Well, he says he thinks it will be twins, in a couple of days at the most."

"Good news! Here you are. Afilaba—meaning: Heavy arrivals expected shortly. Now then, Hankins, he'll want some news of his wife, won't he? How about her?"

"She went to the hospital this morning."

Cappy closed his eyes and pondered; then once more took up the code book. Followed a silence. Then:

"Bully! He'll understand perfectly, being a sailor. Desdoble—meaning: Is now in dry dock. And, of course, Landry will want to know whether his wife is in any danger. Danger! Danger! Ships are sometimes in danger. When? When they're wrecked, of course. Let us look under the head of wrecks . . . No; nothing seems to fill the bill. Wreck, wrecked, worse, writ, write, wrong—ah, I have it! Wohlgemuth —meaning: There is nothing wrong." He looked up at Mr. Hankins. "Now there's the kind of cablegram to send—even on baby business. Those four code words translated mean: No new arrivals; heavy arrivals expected shortly; is now in dry dock; there is nothing wrong. Literally translated it means: Baby not born yet; twins expected shortly; your wife now in hospital; everything lovely! I suppose, Hankins, you have carbon copies of all these cablegrams you've been sending?"

"Yes, sir."

"Code them all, so far as possible, and ascertain how much money you might have saved the Blue Star by the exercise of a little common sense; then charge the cablegrams, on the coded basis, to our general expense, and charge to your personal account the sum you might have saved by the exercise of the ingenuity and efficiency I have a right to expect of a man who draws down as fat a salary as you do."

CHAPTER L

Mr. Hankins withdrew, greatly crestfallen, and the despot of the Blue Star office turned to his trusted lieutenants.

"Well," he declared, "one after the other you have to come to the old man to be shown. I guess I've proved to you two boys this morning that I'm to be trusted with buying a few ships and letting contracts for a few more, haven't I?"

"I don't like the idea of Cappy Ricks on a steamer that's likely to be torpedoed. I don't want you to go to Europe alone——"

"I'm not going alone. Captain Mike Murphy, our new port captain, is going with me. I wouldn't think of buying a steamer unless that splendid fellow O.K.'d the hull. And Terry Reardon, our new port engineer, will accompany me also. Terry has to O.K. the engines. Between the three of us, it's going to take a smart trader to sell us any junk, I'm telling you!"

"I ought to go with you," Matt suggested.

"You have your work at home, attending to the fleet. It isn't much of a fleet, I'll admit; but such as it is it requires some attention. I'll be the chief scout of this organization and see whether I can't rustle up some major-league vessels from some of those bush-league European owners."

"I've had a fine time getting good men to take their places in the *Narcissus* since you promoted Mike and

Terry in my absence!" Matt complained. "Mike and Terry know her well—and she's such a big brute to handle."

"Where is the *Narcissus*, by the way?"

"Loading nitrate at Tocopilla and Antofagasta, Chile. This is her last voyage under the old charter."

"Got any new business in sight for her?"

"I won't have the slightest difficulty getting another nitrate charter and at a rate double what she's been getting."

"Every vessel taken off the nitrate run stiffens the freight rate in these days, when they have to have so much nitrate in the manufacture of war munitions," the astute Cappy declared. "If I were you, Matt, I'd find her a good outside cargo or two, and then slip her back in the nitrate business again. Freights may have advanced in the interim."

"I have a mighty profitable cargo offered me this morning, Cappy. An agent of the British Government called on me and offered a whopping price for carrying a cargo of mules and horses from Galveston to Havre. I think I shall turn the proposition down. It's too dangerous, Cappy."

"You mean we might have our ship blown up by a German submarine?"

Matt nodded.

"Well, we'd collect our freight in advance, wouldn't we? And the British Government will guarantee to reimburse us if the ship is lost, will it not? Well, then, where's the risk?"

"There's the danger to the crew."

"Any man that goes to sea knows he has to take a chance. Bet you Mike Murphy could take that cargo

of livestock across and bring another cargo back.
He's luckier than a cross-eyed coon. And another
thing, Matt: If you accept that business we can kill
two birds with one stone—yes, three—because Mike and
Terry and I will cross over on the *Narcissus* and save
the price of transportation from here to New York,
and from New York to Liverpool. Then, while the
Narcissus is discharging and taking on another cargo,
we'll go scouting for available steamers."

"It might be done, though I hate to think of it
Cappy. If we lose the vessel they'll pay us a million
and a half for her, of course—and she cost us less than
three hundred thousand a year ago. And, as you say,
we'll collect the freight in advance. They're very anxious to get the *Narcissus*. She's a whopping big boat,
and that's the kind of a vessel they need for a horse
transport."

"Yes; and, by the Holy Pink-Toed Prophet, it will
be a bully vacation, and a bully vacation is something
I haven't had since the night of the big wind in Ireland. Moreover, I combine business with pleasure,
which is always desirable; and, if that isn't excuse
enough, I want to tell you it's cheaper to travel dead-
head on our own boats than to pay for three round-
trip tickets to Europe on a Cunard liner."

"But suppose a German submarine——"

"Matt, all my life I've played a quiet, safe, sane,
conservative game. I've always longed for adventure
and never had it. Why, just consider a moment what
a tiresome thing life would be were it not for the
prospect of death at any moment! That's all that keeps
us hustling, my boy—trying to put over a winning
run before the game is called on account of darkness.

Hell's bells! Don't try to scare me with a sheet and
the rattle of old bones. Suppose they do blow us up?
We don't lose a dollar; in fact, we make money—and
we can take to the boats, can't we?"

"They only give you fifteen minutes——"

"We'll have the boats swung overside, provisioned
and ready, two days ahead."

"But they don't care how far out to sea they leave
you. I spent two weeks in an open boat once and I
know you can't stand two days. The exposure——"

"When we get down to Galveston," Cappy interrupted triumphantly, "I'll have Mike Murphy buy a
nice, staunch little secondhand motor cruiser, thirty-
eight or forty feet long, with plenty of power and comfortable living accommodations for half a dozen people.
Mike will arrange for extra oil and gasoline tankage,
and we'll swing this cruiser in on the main deck and
let it rest there in a cradle, with the slings round it,
ready to lift overside with the cargo derricks at a
minute's notice. I'll be as snug in that little cruiser
as a bug under a chip—and we'll tow the lifeboats.
So that settles it—and if it doesn't I'd like to know
who's the boss of this shebang, anyhow!"

Mr. Skinner glanced covertly at Captain Matt Peasley and shook his head almost imperceptibly, as who
should say: "Better give in to him, Matt. I know
him longer than you do; he'll have his way if it kills
him." And Matt took the hint, with the result that
some six weeks later Cappy Ricks, accompanied by
his faithful port captain and his equally faithful port
engineer, cleared for Galveston aboard the Sunset
Limited. And at Galveston began the only real vacation Cappy Ricks had ever had.

CHAPTER LI

To begin, there was the task of superintending the installation of the accommodations for the cargo of mules and horses. Cappy was particularly interested in the ventilating system below decks, for he was fond of horses and had resolved to deliver the cargo without the loss of a single animal. Of no mediocre turn of mind mechanically, he, assisted by Terry Reardon, made a few suggestions that the British veterinaries in charge were very glad to accept.

The real enjoyment of the trip, however, Cappy found down at the breaking corrals where the horses were detraining. They were all young and full of life, and fully ninety per cent of them had only been halter-broken. In the lot was many an outlaw whose ancestors had run wild for generations in Nevada; and as the delivery contract specified that a horse to be accepted must be broken—God save the mark!—as Terence Reardon remarked after seeing one passed as broken, following five minutes of furious pitching and squealing—Cappy Ricks was one of the first at the corral and the last to leave. Perched on the topmost rail, he piped encouragement to the lank, flat-bellied border busters who, a dozen times a day, risked life and limb at five dollars a bust.

Mike Murphy and Terence Reardon, who had ridden more than one China Sea typhoon and West India hurricane, marvelled that men should take such risks

372

for any amount of money. Privately they considered
Cappy Ricks an accessory before the fact, inasmuch as
Cappy hung up at least five hundred dollars in small
prizes for the vaqueros. Whenever they had a "bad
one" they could always induce Cappy to offer ten
dollars for staying two minutes and five dollars a minute
for each minute over the limit—which seldom reached
two minutes. Also, Cappy was willing to furnish two
silver dollars whenever some adventurer thought he
could put a dollar between each leg and the saddle and
have the dollars there when the horse surrendered. They
ran in a couple of trained buckers on Cappy and de-
pleted his bank roll considerably before he began to
smell a rat.

To these plainsmen, charged with the destinies of the
mounts for the young British soldier, Cappy Ricks
was known familiarly as Cap. Before the last of the
horses had been passed as broken and hustled aboard
the big *Narcissus,* Cappy knew each horse wrangler
by his first name or nickname, and had learned the
intricacies of many hitherto unheard-of games of
chance that flourish along the Rio Grande. He was
an expert at cooncan, and Pangingi fascinated him;
then they taught him Mexican monte, and one worthless
individual stole an ace out of the deck, whereupon all
hands had a joyous hack at Cappy, who, when informed
privately by his friend, Sam Daniels, foreman of the
outfit, that he was in bad company and being skinned
alive, went uptown and bought some specially constructed dice, which he introduced brazenly into a crap
game, thereby more than catching even. He was the
last man in the world a gang of wicked cowboys

would suspect of guile; all of them, quite foolishly, thought he had more money than brains.

Eventually, however, the *Narcissus* was loaded, Cappy moved into the owner's suite, and his new-found friends bunked in a temporary deck house forward when they weren't busy below decks playing chambermaid to the cargo. And with Cappy's motor cruiser swung in the cradle, ready for launching from the main deck aft, the *Narcissus* slipped out of Galveston and went snoring across the Gulf of Mexico, bound for Le Havre.

Mike Murphy was not happy, however. He resented Cappy Ricks, who would persist in going below to inspect the cargo and in consequence smelled like a hostler. Moreover, Michael was the port captain of the Blue Star Navigation Company now and not the master of the ship; and the *Narcissus* wasn't out of sight of land before Mike made the discovery that the boatswain of the ship was absolutely inefficient, that the cook was wasteful, that the first officer was too talkative, and the skipper too easy-going.

And these conditions, on a ship he had once commanded, irked Murphy exceedingly. Terence Reardon was in much the same state of mind. Being port engineer, he investigated the engine room and found that his favorite monkey wrench had been lost; there were two leaky tubes in the main boiler; the ash hoist was out of kilter; his successor in the *Narcissus* was carrying ten pounds of steam less than Terence used to carry; and there was something not quite right with the condenser. The engine room crew Terence characterized to Mike Murphy as a gang of "vagabones," and hinted darkly at sweeping changes when the ship should get back to the United States. Once he went so far as to state that he might have expected as much when, upon leaving the *Narcissus* to become port engineer, he had given her to his old first assistant; since he had never known a first assistant, barring himself, to make a good chief!

CHAPTER LII

On the very day the *Narcissus* left Galveston the German submersible V-14 left her base at Zeebrugge, with oil and torpedoes sufficient to last her on an ordinary three weeks' cruise, and promptly headed for that section of the Atlantic where information and belief told her commander the hunting would be good. And it was—so good, in fact, that to the very great disgust of her crew she had just two torpedoes in stock when the man on watch at her periscope reported a large freight steamer to the west. Promptly the V-14 submerged and proceeded on a course calculated to intercept the freighter, which presently was discovered to be the U.S.S. *Narcissus*.

The captain of the V-14 almost licked his chops. He had heard of the *Narcissus*. The neutrality laws of the United States had prevented him from hearing of her by wireless when she cleared from Galveston, but he had been on the lookout for her, just the same, ever since a Dutch steamer from New York, with an alert German chief mate, had touched at Copenhagen, from which point the dispatches that mate carried had gone underground straight to the office of the German Admiralty. The information anent the *Narcissus* had been brief but illuminating: She had been chartered to carry horses for the British Government from Galveston to Le Havre, and the word to get her at all hazards had been passed to the submarine flotilla.

376

Captain Emil Bechtel, of the V-14, did not possess
an Iron Cross of any nature whatsoever, and as he
studied the oncoming *Narcissus* through the periscope
he reflected that this big brute of a boat would bring
him one, provided he was lucky. He remembered he
had but two torpedoes left, and under the circumstances he paused to consider.

Clearly—since the *Narcissus* was laden with horses
and mules for the enemy she was carrying contraband
—she must not escape. On the other hand, there had
been a deal of unpleasantness of late because President
Wilson had been protesting the sinking of vessels without warning—and the *Narcissus* was a United States
steamer. Consequently if he torpedoed her without
warning the temperamental Kaiser might make of
Captain Emil Bechtel what is colloquially known as the
goat; whereas, on the other hand, should he conform
to international law and place her crew in safety before sinking her, there was a chance that her wireless
might summon a patrol boat to the vicinity—Bechtel
had sighted one less than an hour before—and patrol
boats had a miserable habit, when they sighted a periscope, of shooting it to pieces.

Then, too, it was just possible that the perfidious
English had mounted a couple of six-inch guns on her
after getting to sea—and the German knew a six-
inch shell, well-placed, would send his vessel to the
bottom. Moreover, it was sunset; in half an hour it
would be twilight; he had no knowledge of the speed of
the *Narcissus* and she might try to make a run for it,
thus forcing him to come to the surface and shell her
should he miss with his torpedoes. Further, if he
attacked her and she escaped, there was an elderly

gentleman with whiskers back in Berlin who would do things to him if the Kaiser didn't.

There was, however, one course open to the German. To his way of thinking, during the exciting diplomatic tangle with the United States, he would be damned if he did and damned if he didn't; but if he did, and nobody could prove it, old Von Tirpitz would ask no questions.

"I'll let her have it," Captain Emil Bechtel concluded; and he passed the word to get ready.

A minute later Cappy Ricks, smoking his after-dinner cigar on the bridge of the *Narcissus* with her skipper and Mike Murphy, pointed far off the port bow.

"There's a shark or a swordfish, or something, breaching," he said. "I can see his wake."

Mike Murphy took a casual glance in the direction Cappy was pointing, while the master of the *Narcissus* reached for his marine glasses and lazily put them to his eyes.

"Shark be damned!" yelled Murphy. "It's a torpedo or I'm a Chinaman! Hard-a-starboard!"

He leaped for the engine-room telegraph and jammed it over to Full Speed Astern; then dashed into the pilot house and commenced a furious ringing of the ship's bell, summoning the crew to boat drill, the while his anxious eye marked the swift progress of the white streak coming toward them. What wind there was happened fortunately to be on the vessel's port counter, and as the helmsman spun the wheel the big vessel fell off quickly and easily, while the rumble of her shaft, suddenly reversed, fairly shook the ship. To Cappy Ricks it seemed that the vessel must be brought

up standing, like one of the broncos he had seen ridden
with a Spanish bit; but a big ship under full headway
is not stopped very abruptly, and the *Narcissus* swept
on, turning as she went in order to offer as little target
as possible to the torpedo.

"Will we make it, Mike?" Cappy Ricks queried in a
very small, awed voice.

Mike Murphy turned and found his owner at his
elbow.

"I hope it hits her forward," he replied. "That
motor cruiser is cradled aft and we might save it. They
never hailed us—ah-h-h, missed!"

The torpedo flew by, missing the big blunt bow by
less than three feet.

"I guess they'll get us just the same," Mike Murphy murmured quietly; "but we're going down fighting."

And, disregarding the master of the *Narcissus*, who
was staring vacantly after the flying torpedo, he rang
for Full Speed Ahead, and called down the speaking
tube to the chief to hook her on for all he had; then,
with his helm still hard-a-starboard, he swung the
ship in as small a circle as possible and headed her at
full speed back over the course so recently traveled
by the torpedo.

"That was a beautifully timed shot—that last one,"
he informed Cappy Ricks admiringly. "If we'd sighted
it thirty seconds later——"

"Where the devil are you going, man?" Cappy yelled
frantically.

"I'm going to give that fellow a surprise," Murphy
growled. "He expected us to run for it after that first
one missed—and I'm running for him! He may not

get me with the next one if I come bows on—and I
might ram him! I'll take a chance. Keep your eyes
open for his periscope."

Aboard the V-14 Captain Emil Bechtel said nothing,
but thought a great deal—when he saw that his first
torpedo had missed its prey. He was in for it now;
he had started something and he had to go through.
And, anticipating that the *Narcissus* would show him
her heels and steer a zigzag course, he immediately
launched his last torpedo as the horse transport lay
quartering to him.

To his disgust, however, the steamer, having avoided
the first torpedo, did not run as he had anticipated.
Instead, she continued to turn round on her heels,
each revolution of her wheel lifting her out of the
course of the second torpedo, since the submarine had
fired slightly ahead of the vessel, knowing that if she
continued for two minutes on the course he expected
her to take she would steam fairly across the path of
the huge missile. So he missed again—the torpedo
slid under her stern—and here was that demon horse
transport bearing down on him at full speed and with
a bone in her teeth.

"The jig is up," murmured Bechtel, and gave the
order to submerge deeper, for he would not risk showing his periscope to the keen eyes on that bridge.

For ten minutes he waited, while the submarine
scuttled blindly out of the path of the onrushing transport; then, concluding that the *Narcissus* had passed
him, he came up and took a look round. He was
right. A cable length astern and another off his port
quarter the steamer was plunging over the darkening

sea, and Captain Emil Bechtel knew he had her now; so promptly he came to the surface.

Mike Murphy, glancing off his starboard quarter, saw her periscope come swiftly up; then her turret showed; then her turtle deck flashed for a moment on the surface, like a giant fish, before she rose higher and the water cascaded down her sides.

Cappy Ricks' anxious face turned a delicate green; he glanced up at his bully port captain as if in that rugged personality alone could he hope for salvation. Murphy caught the glance, shook his head, walked over to the engine-room telegraph and set the handle over to stop.

"No use, sir," he informed Cappy. "That Dutchman is out of torpedoes, so he's coming up to shell us. We'll heave to and save funeral expenses." He turned to the master of the *Narcissus*. "Captain, I'll stay on the bridge and conduct all negotiations with that fellow; get your mates, round up everybody and prepare to abandon the ship in a hurry. Get the motor cruiser overside first."

As the captain hurried away, Terence Reardon came up on the bridge. The port engineer's gloomy visage portended tears, but through his narrowed lids Cappy Ricks saw not tears, but the light of murder. Terence did not speak, but thoughtfully puffed his pipe, and, with Murphy and Cappy Ricks, watched the booby hatch on the submarine's deck slide back and her long, slim, three-inch gun appear, like the tongue of a huge viper.

Heads appeared round the breech of the gun; so Michael J. Murphy seized a megaphone and shouted:

"Nein! Nix!" accompanying his words with wild pantomime that meant "Don't shoot!"

Captain Emil Bechtel was vastly relieved. He was not an inhuman man, even if, on occasion, as has already been demonstrated, he could, for the sake of national expediency, sink a ship without warning. Having missed with both torpedoes, he could now, in the event of national complications, enter a vigorous denial of any affidavits alleging an attempted breach of international law, and his government would uphold him. This knowledge rendered him both cheerful and polite, as he hove to some hundred yards to starboard of the *Narcissus* and informed Captain Michael J. Murphy that the latter had just fifteen minutes in which to save the ship's company; whereat Michael J. proved himself every inch a sailor, while Terence P. proved himself a marine engineer. If there was a word of opprobrium, mundane or nautical, which the port skipper didn't shout at that submarine commander, the port engineer supplied it. In all his life Cappy Ricks had never listened to such rich, racy, unctuous abuse; it lifted itself **above** the level of the commonplace and became a 'work of art. Cappy was horrified.

"Boys! Boys!" he pleaded. "This is frightful!"

"What do you expect from a German, sir?" Murphy demanded. "Frightfulness is his middle name."

"I mean you two—and your language. Stop it! You'll contaminate me."

"Well, sor," Terence Reardon replied philosophically, "I suppose there's small use cryin' over spilt milk— musha, what are they up to now?"

"They're dragging a collapsible boat up from

below," Mike Murphy declared. "That means they're going to board us, place bombs in the bilges, and sink us that way. They know blamed well we've wirelessed for help and a patrol has answered; so that——"

"No profanity!" Cappy shrilled.

"So he has decided he won't try to sink us by shell fire with such a small gun. It'll be dark in five minutes and he's afraid the flame of the discharge or the reports of the gun may guide the patrol boat here before he's finished his job. Oh, wirra, wirra!"

Murphy's surmise proved to be correct, for he had scarcely finished speaking before the submarine commander hailed him and ordered him to let down his gangway. Terence P. Reardon's eyes flamed with the lust for battle.

"Be the great gun av Athlone," he cried, "if they're comin' aboard sure we can get at them!"

Murphy's rage vanished as suddenly as it had gripped him; he smiled at Terence affectionately, approvingly.

"You with your monkey wrench, eh, Terry, my lad? And they with automatic pistols and wishful of an excuse to use them, not to mention the nitroglycerin and guncotton bombs they'll be carrying—a divilish bad thing to have kicking round in a free-for-all fight?" he queried.

Terry's face showed his deep disappointment.

"They'll see us all in the boats," Murphy continued; "then they'll go below, set the bombs, light a slow fuse to give them time to get back to the submarine—and then——"

"With all these poor dumb beasts aboard?" Cappy Ricks quavered. "Horrible! Horrible! I could kill them for it."

"I could kill them for a greater crime than that," his port captain reminded him. "Didn't they try twice to sink us without warning? Damn them! They're forty fathoms outside the law this minute."

CHAPTER LIII

For the first time in his life Cappy Ricks was in financial and physical danger coincidently. Old he was, and a landlubber, for all his courtesy title; but in his veins there coursed the blood of a long line of fighting ancestors. It occurred to him now that in all his life he had never cried "Enough;" that always, when cornered and presumably beaten, he had gone into executive session with himself and, fox that he was, schemed a way out. In this supreme moment there came to him now the words of the gallant Lawrence: "Don't give up the ship!" They inspired him; his agile old brain, benumbed by the shock of the exciting events of the last quarter of an hour, threw off its paralysis; his little five-feet-four body thrilled with the impact of a sudden brilliant idea.

"I have it!" he piped. "By the Holy Pink-Toed Prophet, it might be done! Mike, the submarine lies to starboard. Tell the mate to lower the port gangway."

Murphy ran out on the end of the bridge and bawled the order. Then he came back, and he and Terence and Cappy Ricks put their heads together while in brief, illuminating sentences Cappy Ricks unfolded the fruit of his genius.

"Tell me," he pleaded when he had finished, "is that scheme practicable?"

"It might be done, sir," Mike Murphy assented.

"I'll thry anything the wanst," Terry Reardon almost barked.

"It means some fighting—probably some killing."

"Sorra wan av me'll feel broken-hearted at killin' the likes av that Dutchman," Terry answered. "Shtill, we'll be needin' some help, I'm thinkin'."

"We'll get it, or I'm no judge of human nature. Mike, pass the word for Sam Daniels, the boss of muleteers and broncho busters. Sam used to be a Texas Ranger."

Accordingly Sam Daniels was sent for and arrived on the jump.

"Sam, my dear boy," said Cappy calmly, "I'm enlisting volunteers to raise hell with that submarine. They're going to put bombs in the bilges and blow up the ship."

"Count me in, Cap," Sam Daniels replied laconically. "Want me to rustle up a couple of the boys?"

"Yes, about three real ones—boys that are handy with a six-shooter."

"I guess most of the boys from the border have their guns in their war bags. I'll go get them together."

He did—in about three minutes; by which time the collapsible boat from the submarine had been launched and was pulling toward the *Narcissus*. While her master directed them to pull round to the port gangway, Sam Daniels slipped down unobserved into Number Three hatch, two of his horse wranglers disappeared with an equal lack of ostentation down the gangway into Number Two hatch, and a third man went forward and down Number One. The trap was set.

A stout young lieutenant clad in soiled dungarees, his uniform cap alone denoting his rank, came briskly

up the companion, followed by four jackies carrying
the bombs. A fifth man remained in the boat, fending
it away with a boat hook from the tall black side of
the *Narcissus*.

"Who commands here?" the German demanded in
most excellent English.

"I do," the master of the *Narcissus* replied, and
stepped a pace forward.

"Then hurry and get your boats overside. We're
going to bomb the ship, and if anybody remains aboard
when those bombs explode it will be his fault, not
ours."

The motor cruiser had already been dropped overboard, and the life-boats, having been for two days
swung out in the davits, were quickly filled and lowered
away. As each boat pulled clear of the ship the man
in charge of it was ordered by the submarine lieutenant
to stay to port of the *Narcissus*, and to pull well clear
of the ship before proceeding to pass the towing
painters to the cruiser.

"Are all your men off the ship?" the officer queried
of the skipper as the latter entered the last boat and
gave the order to lower away.

"All off; I've accounted for all of them," was the
answer.

The German waited until the boat had slipped away
in the gloom before turning to his command.

"Proceed!" he said briefly; and, followed by his four
men, he led the way down the cleated temporary gangway built diagonally down Number Three hatch to accommodate the horses when they had been led aboard.

The better to facilitate their progress, Terence
Reardon had turned on all the electric lights in the ship,

and the detail proceeded quickly to the lower hold, where they set two bombs and piled double-compressed baled hay round them, with the fuse leading out from under the bales.   In addition to blowing a hole in the ship they were taking the added precaution of setting her afire after the explosion.

From the spot where the bombs were set a long alleyway, lined on each side with the rumps of horses, each neatly boxed in a stall just wide enough and long enough to inclose him firmly and hold him on his feet in the event of rough weather, led forward and aft to the bulkheads.   And in one of these stalls, close up against the rump of a horse he could trust, Sam Daniels, the ex-Texas Ranger, crouched, with one eye round the corner of the stall, calmly watching the grim proceedings.   Something told him that, having arranged the bombs in that hold, the enemy would not light the fuses until he had set similar bombs at the bottom of the other hatches; then, all being in readiness, a man would be sent into each hold to light the fuse, scurry on deck, descend to the waiting boat, and be pulled clear of danger before the fuses should burn down to the fulminating caps.

So Daniels waited until the men were about to pick up the remaining bombs and ascend to the deck; whereupon he stepped quietly out into the alleyway, a long-barreled forty-five in his hand, and pussyfooted swiftly toward the Germans, whose backs were now turned toward him.   Halfway down the alleyway, on one of the heavy six-by-six-inch uprights temporarily set in to support the weight of the hundred mules on the deck above, was the electric switch controlling the circuit in that hold—and Sam Daniels reached up and turned

it down. Instantly the hold was in darkness; and
then the horseman spoke:

"Hey, you Dutchies! Stay right where you are! I
want to have a little powwow with you before you go
any farther."

Having said this, the astute Mr. Daniels, out of a
vast experience gained while fighting Mexicans and
outlaws in the dark, promptly lay down. In case the
enemy should become rattled and fire at the sound
of his voice he preferred to have plenty of room
for the bullets to pass over him.

"Who's there?" the lieutenant demanded in English;
and by the firm, resolute voice the Texan knew that
the German was not rattled and that his men would not
fire unless he gave the word.

"Great thing, this naval discipline!" Mr. Daniels
soliloquized. Aloud he replied:

"The fastest, straightest little wing shot with a six
shooter that ever was, old-timer!"

"What do you purpose doing, my friend?"

"I purpose giving you some good advice; though
whether you accept it or not is a matter of indiffer-
ence to me. You will observe that this hold is in comparative darkness. I say comparative, because through
the hatch space a certain amount of light is projected
from the deck above, and you and your men are standing in that light, whereas I am in the dark. I can see
you and you cannot see me. I have a forty-five caliber
revolver in my hand and another in reserve. There are
five of you fellows, constituting a fair target—and I
seldom miss a fair target. I can kill all five of you in
five seconds. Of course some of you may manage to fire
at the flash of my gun and accidentally kill me; but—

make no mistake about it, son—I'll get you and your
gang before I kick the bucket. Now, then, which do
you want to do—live or die? I'm going to be fair
to you fellows and give you some choice in the matter—
which is more than you did when you launched those
two torpedoes at us. Speak up, brother! I'm a nervous man and dislike suspense."

The German lieutenant glanced at his men, who had
not yet touched the other bombs and were looking
stolidly at him for orders. He licked his lower lip and
scowled, sighed gustily—and made a swift grab for
his automatic. A streak of flame came out of the
dark alleyway and the German's arm hung limp at his
side. He had a bullet in his shoulder.

"Told you I was a wing shot!" the plainsman cautioned him pleasantly. "I would have put that one
through your heart if I didn't need an interpreter. I
imagine these roustabouts with you only speak their
mother tongue."

"What do you want me to do?"

"Well, first, I want you to leave that high explosive
right where it is. Then I want you to deposit all your
sidearms on the floor, and have your men do likewise."

The German had had his lesson and arrived at the
conclusion that valor without discretion is not good
business. He slipped his belt off and let it drop to the
floor; at a word from him his men did likewise, whereupon Daniels stood up, threw on the electric switch,
and revealed himself and his artillery to the gaze of the
invaders.

"Forward; in a bunch, up the gangway!" he ordered.

They obeyed. As the Texan passed the little heap
of belts, with the automatics in the holsters attached,

he gathered them up and followed. Just before the procession reached the main deck he halted them and whistled—whereupon Michael J. Murphy, Terence P. Reardon and Cappy Ricks came to the edge of the hatch and peered over.

"Well, look who's here!" Cappy exclaimed maliciously. "Five nice little pirates, who would sink my *Narcissus* without so much as a be-damned to you! Mike, bring the irons. Terence, my boy, restrain yourself. If you use that monkey wrench until I give the word the Blue Star Navigation Company will have a new port engineer. Undress these fellows. Just remove their caps and outer garments—and be quick about it."

"Tell them to molt—*muy pronto!*" Sam Daniels ordered the lieutenant, who relayed the order in a voice that had in it a suspicion of tears.

In three minutes they were undressed and handcuffed together; leg irons were put on them, and they were expeditiously gagged and chained to a stanchion.

"Now then, Terence, I have work for you and your monkey wrench," Cappy continued. "You're about the same size as this officer. Into his dungarees and uniform cap; and don't forget to slip on his belt, with the automatic."

"In two shakes av a lamb's tail, sor. What next?"

"As you run down the gangway to the waiting boat, hold your handkerchief over that Irish mug of yours. Pretend you're blowing your nose. The man in the boat won't recognize you until you're on top of him."

"Wan little love tap—no more!" Terence breathed lovingly.

"When Terence has tapped him, Sam," Cappy continued, "you go down and help to get him out on the landing stage. He'll be off our hands there and the submarine people cannot see what's happened to him. They're still lying on our starboard beam."

Terence and the deadly Samuel disappeared, to return presently and report all well. Thereupon Michael J. Murphy retired to the port side of the house, lit a kerosene torch he had brought up from the engine room and waved it. He waited. Presently, in the gloom off to port, he saw the red and green side lights of the little cruiser. For a moment both lights were visible; then the master of the *Narcissus*, now in charge of the cruiser, ported his helm and showed his red only. Murphy waited, and presently both red and green showed again.

"Starboard now, and show your green," Murphy pleaded.

The red went out and the green alone showed; so Mike Murphy extinguished his torch and rejoined Cappy Ricks, Terence and the ubiquitous Mr. Daniels.

"Sam, my dear boy," Cappy was saying as Murphy came up, "Mike and Terence own in the *Narcissus* and they work for me—hence their alliance. You owe me no fealty——"

"The hell I don't, Cap!" Sam retorted lightly. "You're a fine old sport, and I'm for you till the last dog is hung."

"Sam, I am deeply grateful. Your friendship is very dear to me indeed. I have a twenty-two-thousand acre ranch down in Monterey County, California—don't know why I bought it, unless it was because it was a bargain and ranch property in California is bound to increase in value—and you're my foreman if we ever get out of this with a whole skin. I'll make it the best job you ever had, Sam."

"Thank you, Mr. Ricks!" A moment before it had been Cap. "If you never saw a man fight for a good job before, just watch me!"

CHAPTER LIV

The horse tenders in the other holds were summoned and informed that for the present the *Narcissus* would not be bombed. Quickly two of them, with Mike Murphy and Sam Daniels, donned the dungarees and caps of the prisoners and strapped on their belts containing the automatics in their holsters. In the interim Terence had descended to the collapsible boat bumping at the gangway and fended her off until Sam Daniels, the two cowboys and Mike Murphy joined him; whereupon Terence took one pair of oars, while Murphy handled the other, and the boat crept out from the steamer and headed directly for the submarine, which had been ratching backward and forward under a dead-slow bell, watching the towering black hulk of the *Narcissus* rolling idly. A light showed on the turret of the submarine, outlining vaguely the figures of half a dozen men on her small deck.

The disposition of Mike Murphy's forces was such that the chances of the enemy detecting the substitution of the boarding party before it should reach the submersible were reduced to a minimum. In the bow of the collapsible one of the cowboys sat, facing the stern; Terence and Mike also faced the stern, by reason of the fact that they were rowing; and Sam Daniels and the other cowboy, seated in the stern sheets, were under orders to turn and look back at the *Narcissus* as the boat came within the radius of the meager light from the submarine's turret. Thus they ran little risk of premature discovery.

"For," as Cappy Ricks sagely reminded them just before they pulled away from the *Narcissus*, "the German is both cautious and cocksure. The capture of his bombing party has been effected without a sound; the commander saw our men leave the steamer in the boats; he sees the *Narcissus* now not under command and wallowing; he figures that all is lovely and the goose honks high. Therefore, he will be off his guard, since his suspicions have not been roused. His deck is very dimly lighted by that single light on the turret, and he knows that light is sufficient to guide the boat party back to the submarine. There is no sea running to speak of; so it will not be necessary for him to turn his searchlight on you to light the way for you.

"Moreover, he will not care to use his searchlight, because it may guide a patrol boat to this spot, and Terence has very carefully turned out all the lights on the ship which might be visible from a distance, because that is precisely what that lieutenant would or should have done if we had given him time. And when you row toward that submarine, row like the devil, because that's the way the bombing party would row in their hurry to board the submarine and steam clear of the explosion. It is my guess that the instant you heave alongside you will be snagged with boat hooks by the men on her deck. In the excitement of making a quick get-away nobody will be looking into your faces, anyhow; they'll see your familiar dungaree suits and caps; some of them may even give you a hand to help you when you leap aboard. Do not despise such help; just extend your left hands and before you let

go the enemy's right bend your guns—and you, Terry,
your monkey wrench—over their heads. You'll have
the deck in a pig's whisper! Then, Mike, the rest is up
to you. I've made the ball; now you fire it.

"I take it the submarine will be in such a hurry to get
away that all the men on her deck will reach down
and snake the boat in; once out of danger, they'll plan
on knocking that collapsible down and storing it away
at their leisure. Tackle 'em while they're busy with the
boat—provided you get aboard unsuspected. Terence,
remember to shout the minute you go into action—and
I'll give you fighting light."

Following these instructions, Cappy had very solemnly shaken hands all round and departed for the
bridge, where he removed the canvas covering from
the searchlight, bent the reflector toward the submarine,
and waited, with his nervous old finger on the switch.

In pursuance of Cappy Ricks' instructions, Mike
Murphy and Terence Reardon rowed furiously toward
the submarine—so furiously, indeed, that the harsh
grating of their oars in the rowlocks apprised Captain
Emil Bechtel of their approach some seconds before
the boat was visible. At his brisk command the men
on deck stepped down to the low pipe railing on the
port side of the deck, prepared to snag the boat the
instant she drew alongside. When he could hear the
sound of the commander's voice, Mike Murphy chanced
a quick look over his shoulder, noted the position of
the submarine, and turned his head again.

"Four more strokes, Terry; then ship your oars,"
he cautioned the engineer in a low voice.

At the fourth stroke Terence obediently shipped
his oars; with a deft twist of one oar, Murphy straight-

ened the boat and shot neatly in alongside the submarine, the deck of which was less than three feet
above the water. As Cappy Ricks had anticipated,
the men on that deck promptly snagged the boat at
bow and stern with boat hooks—and on the instant
Cappy Ricks' bully boys leaped for their prey.

As luck would have it, Terence P. Reardon was the
only one offered a helping hand—and he did not despise
it; neither did he forget Cappy's last instructions.
With neatness and ample force he brought his monkey
wrench down on the German's skull; and then to Cappy
Ricks, waiting on the bridge of the *Narcissus,* came
the ancient Irish battlecry of *Faugh-a-ballagh!* For
the benefit of those not versed in the ways of the
fighting Celt, be it known that *Faugh-a-ballagh* means
Clear the Road. And history records but few instances
when Irish soldiery have raised that cry and rushed
without clearing a pathway.

The fight was too short and savage for description.
Suffice it to say that not a shot was fired—the work was
too close for that, for the surprise had been complete.
Even before Cappy Ricks could focus the steamer's
searchlight on the fracas, it was over. Terence P.
Reardon got two in two strokes of his trusty monkey
wrench; Sam Daniels and his two fellow-bronco-busters
each laid open a German scalp with the long barrels of
their forty-fives; and Michael J. Murphy, plain lunatic-
crazy with rage, disdaining all but Nature's weapons,
tied into the amazed Captain Emil Bechtel under the
rules of the Longshoremen's Union—which is to state
that Michael J. Murphy clinched Emil Bechtel, lifted
him, set him down hard on his plump back, crawled him,
knelt on his arms, and addressed him in these words:

"Hah! (A right jab to the face.) You would, would you? (Left jab to face.) You pig-iron polisher! (Bending the nose back forcibly with the heel of his fist.) When I get (smash) through with your (smash) head (smash) it'll be long (smash) before you'll block (smash) your hat again (smash) on the Samson post, you——"

"Out av me way, Michael, lad, till I get a kick at his slats!" crooned Terence P. Reardon, heaving alongside.

"You gossoon! Take care of the scuttle; don't let them close it down, or they'll submerge and drown us. Leave this lad to me, I tell you. He's the captain, and why shouldn't he be killed by one of his own rank?"

Thus rebuked, Terence curbed his blood-thirsty proclivities. Leaving his countryman to beat his devil's tattoo on the submarine commander, Terence leaped to the open scuttle just in time to bang another head as it appeared on a level with the deck.

"Let that be a lesson to you!" he called as the unconscious man slid back down the companion into the interior of the vessel.

Then he sat on the lid of the scuttle, poised his monkey wrench on high over the scuttle, and awaited developments, the while he tossed an order over his shoulder to Sam Daniels:

"Bring me the bum!"

"Which one?" Mr. Daniels queried.

"The German bum, av coorse," Terence retorted waspishly.

"But all these bums are Germans——"

"Not that kind av a bum!" howled Terence. "I mean the bum in the boat."

Thus enlightened, Sam brought a bomb from the boat and handed it to the engineer. In the interim Mike Murphy had polished off his man to his entire satisfaction and joined Terence at the scuttle, while one of the horse wranglers, a cool individual and a firm believer in safety first, collected the weapons from the fallen.

Mike Murphy approached the scuttle and bawled down it to the amazed and puzzled crew below. As a linguist Mike was no great shakes, particularly when called upon to juggle German; but he was a resolute fellow and not afraid to do his best at all times. Consequently his hail took the form of "Hey! *Landsmann!*"

Something told Terence Reardon that Michael was through; so he added his mite to the store and bellowed: "*Spreckels die deutsch*, ye blackguards?"

Then both sat back to await developments. Presently a voice at the foot of the companion said:

"Hello dere! Vat iss?"

"Vat iss? Hell iss! Dot's vat! Listen to me, you Dutchy. I'm the skipper of that horse transport your commander tried to sink without warning, and I'm in command of the deck of this craft, with the scuttle open; and you can't submerge and wash me off, either. When I give the word I want you and your men to come up, one at a time and no crowding. And if you're not up five minutes after I order you up I'll not wait; I'll set a bomb in your turret, back off in the small boat and kill with revolvers any man that tries to come up and see where the fuse is burning in order to put it out. Do you surrender, or would you rather die?"

"Vait a minute und I find oud," the German answered promptly.

It required five minutes for a council of war below decks; then the interpreter came to the foot of the companion and informed Mike Murphy that, considering the circumstances, they had decided to live. In the interim the skipper of the *Narcissus* had arrived, with re-enforcements, in the cruiser, and reported that his crew was getting back aboard the steamer as fast as possible and would have her under command again in a minute. At Murphy's order the unconscious Germans were put aboard the cruiser; later, when the remainder of the submersible's crew came up, one at a time, they were disarmed and lined up on the little deck; whereupon Michael J. Murphy addressed their spokesman thus:

"Listen—you! It would be just like you to have set a time bomb somewhere in this submarine to blow her up after you were all safely out of her. If you did you made a grave tactical error. You're not going to leave her for quite a while yet. You're going to sit quietly here on deck, under guard, while the steamer hooks on to this submarine and tows her; and if my prize crew is blown up, remember, you——"

The spokesman—he was the chief engineer, by the way—yelled "*Ach, Gott!*" and leaped for the scuttle. Mike Murphy followed him into the engine room in time to see him stamp out a long length of slow-burning fuse.

"Any more?" Murphy queried.

"Dot von vas sufficient, if it goes off," the German answered simply.

"All right!" Mike Murphy replied. "I'll take a

chance and so will you. You'll stay aboard and run
those oil engines."

Half an hour later with the submarine's crew safely
under lock and key on the *Narcissus*, the big freighter
continued on her course, followed by the captured submarine, with Michael J. Murphy in her turret and a
quartermaster from the *Narcissus* at her helm. In the
engine room her own engineer grudgingly explained to,
Terence P. Reardon the workings of an oil engine and
the ramifications of the electric-light system—and during all of that period the deadly monkey wrench never
left the port engineer's hand.

Sam Daniels and his comrades were once more back
aboard the *Narcissus*, attending to the horses; and
Cappy Ricks, his heart so filled with pride that it was
like to burst, occupied the submarine's turret with the
doughty Michael J. For an hour they discussed the
marvelous coup until there was no angle of it left
undiscussed; whereupon fell a silence, with Michael
J.'s eyes fixed on the dark bulk ahead that marked the
Narcissus, and Cappy's thoughts on what Matt Peasley and Mr. Skinner would say when they heard the
glorious news.

For nearly an hour not a word passed between the
pair.

Presently Cappy's regular breathing drew Murphy's
attention to him. He had fallen asleep in his seat, his
chin bent on his old breast, a little half-smile on his
lips. And as Murphy looked at him pridefully Cappy
spoke in his sleep:

"Holy sailor! How Mike Murphy can swear!"

Terence P. Reardon came to the foot of the little
spiral staircase leading to the turret.

"Michael, me lad," he announced, "the internal-combustion ile ingin' is the marine ingin' av the future. They're as simple as two an' two is four. Listen, *avic!* Does she not run like a twenty-four-jewel watch? An' this man that invinted thim was a Ger-r-man—more power to him! Faith, I'm thinkin' if the Ger-r-mans were as great in war as they are in peace 'twould need more nor the Irish to take the measure av thim!"

"Irish?" Mike Murphy answered irritably. "Terence, quit your bragging! God knows the Irish are great——"

"The greatest in the wide, wide wur-rld!" Terence declared, with all the egotism of his race.

"Whist, Terry! There's a little old Yankee man aboard; if you wake him up he'll call you a liar."

"The darlin' ould fox!" Terry murmured affectionately, and went back to his engines.

CHAPTER LV

The entire office force of the Blue Star Navigation Company and the Ricks Lumber and Logging Company had assembled in the general office to greet Cappy Ricks, Mike Murphy and Terence Reardon upon their return from Europe, and to hear at first hand the story of their wanderings and adventures. And when the wondrous tale had been told, and business was once more resumed, Matt Peasley, Mr. Skinner, Mike and Terence convened in Cappy Ricks' office for further discussion.

"We sent that half million dollars to New York to be transferred to the credit of the French Government when the bill of sale for that steamer should be deposited with the bank there," Matt remarked presently. "What kind of a vessel did you buy, Cappy? What are her dimensions?"

"What kind of a ship did I buy?" Cappy piped. "Hum-m-m! A ship is good. I bought four; and—believe me!—they're no skiffs, either. All of them are big foreign-going steel tramps, with lots of speed and power."

"Four for half a million dollars?" Matt Peasley cried unbelievingly.

"They would have cost anybody else a million and a half; but—er—well, you see, Matt, I had a stand-in with the right people. The four vessels I bought were all prizes of war—German merchantmen converted into commerce raiders, which had slipped through the cordon of British cruisers and got into the North Atlantic, where French cruisers overhauled them and brought them into port. They were all there and up for sale to the highest bidder when we got there with the horses and our captured submarine.

"I bid half a million for the lot, which is probably about half of what it cost to build them; and there was a Frenchman and an Englishman bidding against me. They each had me topped, and the vessels were knocked down to the Frenchman; but when he found I was a competitor—that I was Monsieur le Capitaine Ricks— that's what they called me, Matt—in command of the party that captured a German submarine, intact and without the loss of a single man on either side—say, Matt, the stuff was all off!

"He and the Englishman went into a conference; and the result was, the Frenchman ran out on his bid and forfeited his ten-per-cent certified check. That left the Englishman the next highest bidder; and he ran out on his bid and left the ships to me! Then the Englishman shook hands with me and the Frenchman kissed me. I thought the least I could do was to make good to them on the earnest money they had forfeited, and they accepted it. Then the President of France heard about it and came down to Brest to see me; and he kissed me, too, and gave me the Officers' Cross of the Legion of Honor. I didn't tell him I was just a private in the ranks. Oh, no! Nothing doing. I was introduced as Monsieur le Capitaine Ricks—and that settled it. I was an officer, for all my courtesy title; and I took the Cross, because I was prouder than Punch to have it.

"Then the Chamber of Deputies met and voted the Frenchman and the Englishman back their forfeited earnest money; and they gave me back my checks, and I wrote new ones for the same amount and split the swag fifty-fifty between the two nations for the care of their wounded. Then I gave a dinner aboard the submarine, and President Poincaré was present. I presented the submarine, with the compliments of the Blue Star Navigation Company, to the Republic of France, and the President accepted, all hands went out on deck and we cracked a bottle of champagne over that submersible's bows and rechristened her."

"What name?" Matt and Skinner chorused.

"The Shamrock—out of compliment to Mike and Terence."

"Fine!" Matt cried. "Then what?"

"Nothing, Matt. Our business was finished and I was anxious to get back on the job; so we engaged skippers and crews to bring our four freighters to New York, and came home.

"Better step lively, boy, and dig up some business for them! Mike will give you the data on their tonnage."

Matt drew Mike Murphy aside.

"Tell me, Mike," he whispered, "did the old man get soused at that dinner aboard the *Shamrock?*"

"Look here, Matt," Murphy answered; "what Monsieur le Capitaine Ricks does outside of office hours is none of my business—or yours, either. And if you don't like that answer help yourself to a new port captain. I'm not telling everything I know, Matt."

CHAPTER LVI

ON the morning of April 3, 1917, Cappy Ricks came down to his office, spread a newspaper on his desk and carefully cut from it the war address of President Wilson to Congress, made the night before. This clipping the old gentleman folded carefully; he placed it in an envelope, sealed it and wrote across the face of the envelope: "Property of Alden Matthew Peasley." Then he summoned Mr. Skinner, president of the Ricks Lumber & Logging Company.

"Skinner, my dear boy," he began, "have you read the President's Message to Congress?"

"I have," replied Skinner.

"I guess that President of ours isn't some tabasco, eh? By the Holy Pink-Toed Prophet, he's just naturally read Bill Hohenzollern out of the party. Bully for Woodrow!"

Mr. Skinner's calm cold features refused to thaw, however, under the heat of his employer's enthusiasm, seeing which Cappy slid out to the edge of his chair and gazed contemplatively at Skinner over the rims of his spectacles. "Hum-m-m!" he said. The very tempo of that throat-clearing should have warned Mr. Skinner that he was treading on thin ice, but with his usual complacence he ignored the storm signal, for his mind was upon private, not public affairs.

"I'm offered the old barkentine *C. D. Bryant* for a cargo of redwood to Sydney," he began. "The freight rate is two hundred and twenty shillings per thousand feet, but the *Bryant* is so old and rotten I can't get any insurance on the cargo if I ship by her. I'm just wondering if——"

"Harumph-h-h! Ahem-m-m!"

"——it's worth while taking a chance to move that foreign order."

"Skinner!" Cappy almost shouted.

Mr. Skinner looked at him, startled.

"How can you think and talk of old barkentines and non-insurable foreign cargoes at this crisis in our country's history?" the autocrat of the numerous Ricks corporations shrilled furiously. "Dad burn your picture, Skinner, are you human? Don't you ever get a thrill from reading a document like this?"—and he tapped the envelope containing the press clipping. "What kind of juice runs in your arteries, anyhow? Red blood or buttermilk? Is your soul so dog-goned dead, crushed under the weight of dollars, that you have failed to realize this document is destined to go down in history side by side with Lincoln's Gettysburg speech? I'll bet you don't know the Gettysburg speech. Bet you never heard of it!"

"Oh, nonsense, Mr. Ricks," Skinner retorted suavely. "Pray do not excite yourself. Suppose war does impend? Is that any reason why I should neglect business?"

"Of course it is, you gibbering jackdaw! I feel like setting fire to the building, just to celebrate. Can't you step into my office on a day like this and discuss the country and her affairs for five minutes, just to prove you're an American citizen? Can't you rejoice with me over these lofty, noble sentiments——"

"Words, words, empty words," warned Mr. Skinner, always a reactionary Republican.

"Skinner," said Cappy with deadly calm, "one more disloyal peep out of you and I shall have no alternative save to request your resignation. I think you're a pacifist at heart, anyhow!"

"Huh," snorted Skinner. "You've changed your tune, haven't you? Who trotted up and down California Street last fall, soliciting campaign contributions for the Republican nominee from the lumber and shipping interests? Wasn't it Alden P. Ricks? Who thought the country was going to wrack and ruin——"

"That was last fall," Cappy interrupted shrilly. "We live and learn—that is, some of us do," he added significantly. "Never mind about my politics last fall; just remember I haven't any this spring. I'm an American citizen, and by the Holy Pink-Toed Prophet, some German or Germans will find it out before I'm gathered to the bosom of Abraham. I have a right to disapprove of my President if I feel like it, but I'll be shot if I'll let anybody else pick on him." And Cappy shook his head emphatically several times like a squinch-owl.

"Oh, I'm for him, now that we're committed to this war," Skinner declared in an effort to soothe the old man.

"Sure! We're locking the stable door after the horse has been stolen. If we'd been for him when the *Lusitania* was sunk instead of being divided in our opinions and swayed in our judgment by a lot of hysterical pacifists and German propagandists we'd have been into the war long ago and saved millions of human lives; we'd have had the war won." He sighed.

"What a prime lot of jackasses we Americans are!"
he continued. "We talk of liberty and demand license;
we prate of democracy and we're a nation of snobs!"

"You wanted to see me about something," Skinner
reminded him.

"Ah, yes; I was forgetting. This envelope, Skinner,
contains the President's address. Take it and put it in
the vault, and when my grandson is twelve years old
give that press clipping to his mother and tell her I
said she was to read it to the boy and make him learn it
by heart. I won't be on hand to do the Americanizing
of that youngster myself, and most likely Matt Peasley
will be too busy to think much about it, so I'm taking
no chances. You rile me to beat the band sometimes,
Skinner, but I'll say this much in your favor: I have
never known you to forget anything."

"Thank you, sir."

Mr. Skinner took the envelope and departed, and
Cappy rang for a stenographer.

"Take a telegram, fast day message," he barked:
" 'His Excellency, The President, White House,
Washington, D. C. Dear Mister President: I did
not vote for you last fall, but your address of last night
makes me ashamed that I did not. I am controlling
owner of the Blue Star Navigation Company, operating a fleet of fifty vessels of various kinds, twelve of
which are foreign-going steam freighters. Am also
controlling owner of the Ricks Lumber & Logging Company, cutting a million feet of lumber daily. Everything I control, every dollar I possess, is at the service
of my country. God bless you, sir! Alden P. Ricks.'

"That sounds sloppy, but it's the way I feel," Cappy
declared. "When a man has a big heart-breaking job

to do and a lot of Philistines are knocking him, maybe
it helps him to retain his faith in humankind to have
some fellow grow sincerely sloppy and slip a telegraphic
cheer in with the hoots. Besides, if I didn't let off
steam today I'd swell up and bust myself all over the
office——"

The door opened and Mr. Terence P. Reardon,
port engineer of the Blue Star Navigation Company,
entered. Mr. Reardon's right eye was in deep mourn-
ing and at no very remote period something—presumably a fist—had shifted his nose slightly to starboard;
indeed, even as he entered Cappy's office a globule of
the rich red Reardon blood trembled in each of the
port engineer's nostrils. His knuckles were slightly
skinned and the light of battle blazed in his black eyes.

"Terence, my dear, dear fellow," murmured the horrified Cappy, "you look as if you had been fed into
a concrete mixer. Have you been fighting?"

"Well, sor," Mr. Reardon replied in his deep Kerry
brogue, "ye might call it that for lack of somethin' more
expressive. I've just fired the chief engineer o' the
Tillicum."

"Mr. Denicke? Why, Terry, he's a first-rate engineer. I'm amazed. He was with us ten years before
you entered the employ—worked up from oiler; in fact,
I must have an explanation of your action in this case,
Terence."

"He called the President a nut. I fired him for that.
Then he said the Kaiser was the greatest single force
for civilization that ever was, an' wit' that I gave him a
lift under the lug an' we wint at it. He's in the Harbor
Receivin' Hospital this minute, an' I'm here to tell ye,
sor, wit' all respect, that if ye don't like the way I've

threated that Dutchman ye can get yerself a new port ingineer, for I'll quit, an' that's somethin' I'm not wishful to do."

Quite calmly Cappy Ricks pressed the buzzer on his desk. The cashier of the Blue Star Navigation Company entered. "Son," said Cappy, "hereafter, when making out Mr. Reardon's pay check, tack onto it twenty-five dollars extra each month. That is all."

"Thank you, sor," murmured Mr. Reardon, quite overcome.

"Get out!" cried Cappy. "You're a vision of sudden death. Go wash yourself."

As Mr. Reardon took his departure Cappy sighed. "If Skinner only had a set of works like that port engineer!" he murmured. "If he only had!"

CHAPTER LVII

It will be recalled that war with Germany was declared on Good Friday. Bright and early on Saturday morning Cappy Ricks arrived at his office and immediately summoned Mr. Skinner.

"Skinner, my dear boy," he chirped, " 'the tumult and the shouting dies.' We're down to brass tacks—at last; and now is time for all good men and true to come to the aid of the party. I'm too old to bear arms, and when I was young enough bantam battalions weren't fashionable; nevertheless, I am enlisting for the war, and I start in this morning to do my part. I won't wear any uniform, but believe me, Skinner, I'm the little corporal who's going to mobilize the Blue Star Navigation Company and the Ricks Lumber & Logging Company, together with all and sundry of their subsidiary corporations. I'm starting with you, Skinner. Are you figuring on enlisting?"

"Certainly not, sir. I'm forty-three years old, married——"

"No excuses necessary, Skinner. Even if you had planned to enlist I would have forbidden the banns. You'd make a bird of a paymaster or quartermaster, but as an enlisted man—well, the other bad soldier boys would toss you in a blanket. So I'll assign you to a job in civil life. Skinner, what do you know about aeroplanes?"

"Absolutely nothing, except that they fly."

"Then learn something! Skinner, the ideal wood for aeroplane construction is clear Pacific Coast spruce. I've been reading up on the subject. Inasmuch as this war must be won in the air, you can imagine the number of aeroplanes the country must turn out in the next eighteen months. Stu-pen-dous, Skinner, simply stu-pen-dous! Try to visualize the wastage alone in the aeroplanes on the battle fronts; consider the thousands of seaplanes that will scour the Atlantic on the lookout for submarines, and then ask yourself, Skinner, what the devil those overworked army and navy officers in Washington are going to do about laying in a supply of clear Pacific Coast spruce before these pirates of lumbermen get next and boost the price clear out of sight. Skinner, what is clear spruce worth at the Northern mills today?"

"About fifty-five dollars per thousand, sir. For years clear spruce never rose in price beyond thirty-five dollars, but purchases by the British Government have shot the price up during the past year."

"Exactly! And purchases by the United States Government will shoot the price up to a hundred and fifty dollars a thousand if you and I don't get busy. Now then, Skinner, listen to me! We have a couple of thousand acres of wonderful spruce timber adjacent to our fir holdings at Port Hadlock, Washington. Wire the mill manager to swamp in a logging railroad to that spruce timber, put in logging camps and concentrate on spruce. The clear stock we'll sell to the Government, and the lower grades will be snapped up by the box factories."

Mr. Skinner nodded his comprehension of the order and Cappy continued: "Wire our mill managers at

Astoria, Oregon and Eureka, California, to log out
all the spruce they come across among the fir. As for
you, Skinner, accept no more orders for clear spruce
from our regular customers, and go easy on accepting
orders for any kind of lumber from our Eastern customers. All those car shipments must be made up of
kiln-dried stock, and we'll want most of the space in our
dry kilns to cook this clear green spruce for Uncle
Sam, because he's going to want it in a hurry, and if
he can't get it when he wants it—why, chaos has come
again and all hell's let loose!"

"What price do you propose charging the Government for this clear spruce?" the cautious Skinner
queried. He owned a little stock in the Ricks Lumber
& Logging Company and already he had a vision of an
extra dividend.

"Absolute cost plus ten per cent," replied Cappy
promptly. "No excess profits at the expense of the
country at war, Skinner."

He gazed upon Skinner contemplatively for several
seconds. "And mind you don't figure the cost too
liberally," he warned him.

"Very well, sir. Is that all?"

"Not by a jugful! You scatter round the market
and buy up every stick of clear two-inch spruce sawed
and on hand at the Northern mills. Buy at the market,
but do not hesitate to go five dollars over the market if
necessary to get the stock. Then place orders for all
the clear spruce the mills can cut and deliver within
the next six months, and we'll have the market hog
tied.

"Got to do it, Skinner. I tell you there isn't a whole
lot of difference between a lumberman and a manufac-

turer or a food speculator. When he gets the public foul, doesn't the public pay through the nose? Haven't we been doing it ourselves in the matter of ship freights? But we must reform, Skinner, we must reform and get down to a cooperative basis, no matter how great the agony. On this spruce deal alone, for instance, we'll save the Government a couple of million dollars. See if we don't."

"We're entitled to a liberal profit," Mr. Skinner protested. "If——"

"No ifs, buts or ands! Obey orders! About the time we have the market on clear spruce well cornered the lumbermen's boys will be in the army and the lumbermen themselves will have begun to realize that they must sacrifice something for their country. And once we're sane we'll be able to work hand in glove with the Government. The United States of America has been money-mad for a long time, Skinner, but this war is going to spiritualize us and show us that there's a lot more in life than dollar-chasing. Hop to your job, P. D. Q., Skinner, my boy; and as you pass out send Captain Matt Peasley in to me."

Matt Peasley came smilingly into his father-in-law's office. "Well, Cappy," he hailed the old gentleman, "I understand you've come out of your retirement."

"You're damned whistling, I have!" Cappy rejoined. "Something doing, boy, something for everybody! Have they told you about it in the general office?"

"Told me about what?"

"About the President asking me if I would cooperate with him to the extent of serving as the Pacific Coast member of the Shipping Board? I guess that isn't some honor, eh? How the devil he ever dug up an old fossil like me is a mystery. I wired him, advising that he appoint a younger man, but he replied that he knew I was the livest shipping man in the country and an American through and through. So, of course, Matt, I have accepted."

"Your forty odd years' experience will be of inestimable value to the country in this emergency," Matt declared heartily. "I'm proud of you."

"Thank you, son. Now then, Matt, to business! The Government's going to need every one of our ships that can run foreign." Matt nodded. "Very well, then," Cappy continued; "as fast as their present charters lapse, decline to recharter except for single trips. We must go on a war basis and be prepared to turn our ships over to the Government on short notice. I'll be too busy to keep my eye on the details of the Blue Star's transactions with the Government, so I'll give you a straight tip now—I want no gouging. Remember that, Matthew, my son."

CHAPTER LVIII

The following day Cappy had a call from Sam Daniels.

"Hello, Sam," Cappy greeted his lanky ranch manager. "What brings you up to town? Not that I'm not glad to see you, for I was on the point of writing you on some matters that had occurred to me."

"I've come up to resign my job," Daniels declared humbly.

"Resign the best job you've ever had, Sam!" Cappy was amazed.

"To resign the best job I ever will have, Mr. Ricks."

Mr. Daniels hitched his chair close to his employer's desk. "Boss," he said, "I'm awful sorry, but I'm goin' soldiering."

Cappy Ricks sprang to his feet with an oath. "You're not!" he shouted. "I won't hear of it. You're too valuable a man to go into the army and get yourself killed—particularly since you can do your share at home. Why, I was just going to write you and give you your orders for patriotic duty. You go back to the ranch, Sam, and get busy. Plant spuds, wheat, oats, barley, corn—plant all you can of it. Raise heifers, sheep, hogs, cows, bulls, calves, turkeys—everything that can be eaten. Raise horses—and in particular, raise mules."

"I'd rather raise hell with a bunch of Germans," Sam Daniels declared feelingly.

417

"Your job is to help produce cereals and canned beef for the hell-raisers," Cappy declared. "The army will want horses for the artillery and mules for the transport. Why, this war may last for years. Sam, you infernal scoundrel, you get back on the farm. You're forty-five years old and you've been shot and whittled enough in your day to last you the remainder of your natural life. Let the young fellows do the fighting abroad, while you and I and the other hasbeens do it at home."

"I'd a heap rather lay off in the brush somewheres an' snipe Germans," Mr. Daniels pleaded. "On the level, boss, if they'll give me a Springfield rifle with telescopic sights I'll guarantee to sicken anythin' I get a fair sight on at a thousand yards."

"In-fer-nal scoundrel! How dare you argue with me! You get back on your job!"

"Boss, I'm going into the army," Daniels announced sadly, but nevertheless firmly. "I'm givin' you a month's notice so you can get a man to take my place."

Cappy surrendered. "All right, Sam. If you survive, your job will be waiting for you when you get back. However, you needn't give me any notice. I'll have another man in charge of the ranch to-morrow, and you can enlist today."

"And you're not sore at me, Mr. Ricks?"

"Sam, I'm proud of you. Wish I were young enough to go it with you. Are you in a hurry to get to France?"

"Certainly am."

"Then join the marines. They always go first. Good-bye, Sam. Good luck to you and God bless you! Draw your wages as you go out and tell the cashier

I said to give you an extra month's wages for tobacco money."

Mr. Daniels withdrew, visibly filled with emotion. Ten minutes later Cappy Ricks, watching at his office window, saw Mr. Daniels cross the street and enter the marines' recruiting office. Immediately Cappy called that recruiting office on the telephone and asked for the doctor.

"Look here, doctor!" he said. "In a few minutes a lanky, battle scarred rancher is coming in to be examined. I don't want him to enlist. He's my ranch manager and worth more to the country in his job than at the Front. You turn him down physically, doctor, and I'll guarantee to send you five fine recruits instead of that old fossil. His name is Sam Daniels, and I'm Alden P. Ricks, of the Blue Star Navigation Company, across the street."

"We need an automobile to send our recruiting sergeant out through the state," the wary medico replied. "Now, if you could loan us one——"

"I'll have my own car and chauffeur over in half an hour, and you keep him as long as you need him," Cappy piped. "Only tell Sam Daniels he's faltering on the brink of the grave and send him back to me."

An hour later Mr. Daniels slouched into Cappy Ricks' office. "Well, Private Daniels," the old man saluted him, "you look downcast. Has something slipped?"

"I should say it has. The doc over to the recruitin' office says I got a heart murmur from smoking cigarettes, which it's a cinch the excitement o' battle brings on death from heart failure, an' then folks would say I died o' fright."

"He's crazy Sam! Tell him to go chase himself."

"I guess he's right, Mr. Ricks. He 'most cried to let me go, an' was for waivin' the heart murmur, but it seems I got a floatin' kidney, an' flat feet. Gosh, I never knew I had flat feet, but then I've rid horses all my life an' ain't never hiked none to speak of."

He was silent several minutes, studying the pattern of the office carpet. Presently he looked up. "Is my successor at the ranch already appointed?" he queried.

"Go back to the fields and the kind-faced cows, Samuel," quoth Cappy gently. "Hurry, or you'll miss the train."

Sam Daniels fled, and hard on his heels came Mrs. Michael J. Murphy, *née* Miss Keenan. It will be recalled that prior to her happy alliance with Michael J. Murphy, Mrs. Murphy had been Cappy Ricks' favorite stenographer. He received her cordially.

"Now then, what's gone wrong, my dear?" he demanded. "Have you and Mike been making a hash of your married life that you should come in here on the verge of tears?"

Mrs. Murphy blinked away a tear or two and sat down. "Some of the boys in the office will be enlisting, Mr. Ricks," she faltered. "I wonder if there might be a vacancy for me—if I might not have my old position back?"

Cappy Ricks was genuinely concerned. "Why, Mike won't let you earn your living," he declared. "Why do you make such an extraordinary request?"

"For Mike's sake, Mr. Ricks. Of late he has been very nervous and distrait; scarcely touches his meals, and thinks, talks and dreams of war. Last night he dreamed he was back in the navy and shouted out an order that woke him up."

"Come to think of it, I believe Mike did spend several years in the navy prior to going into mercantile marine," Cappy observed. "So he has the war fever again, eh? Wants to go back?"

"Ever since he received a letter from the Navy League. They're searching out all the old navy men—gun pointers particularly—and asking them to come back to help train the young fellows just coming into the service. Mike was a gun pointer——"

"Well, what in thunder is he hesitating for?" Cappy piped wrathfully.

"About me. Mike's married to me, you know, and he worries about what will happen to me if he should be killed. He knows I'll be broken-hearted if he enlists—he's afraid I'll not let him go. But if I got my job back and was self-supporting, Mike's conscience would be——"

"Do you want him to go?"

"No, Mr. Ricks, but he must go. I do not want to make a coward or a slacker out of Mike. I've got to do my part, you know."

"My dear," said Cappy feelingly, "you're a noble woman. Go back and attend to your little home; Mike may go whenever he's ready and his salary with the Blue Star will go on while he is in the navy; his job will be waiting for him when he comes back. Good old Mike! How dreadful a crime to hobble that Irishman with a first-class fight in sight."

When Mrs. Mike had left the office Cappy stiffened out suddenly in his chair, clenched his fists and closed his eyes, as if in pain. And presently between the

wrinkled old lids two tears crept forth. Poor Cappy!
He was finding it very, very hard to be old and little
and out of the fight, for in every war in which the
United States had engaged representatives of the tribe
of Ricks had gladly offered their bodies for the supreme sacrifice, and as Cappy's active mind ran down
the long and bloody list his heart swelled with anguish
in the knowledge that he was doomed to play an in-
glorious part in the war with Germany. Mr. Skinner
coming in with a letter to Cappy, observed the old man's
emotion and asked him if he was ill.

"Yes, Skinner, I am," he replied. "I'm sick at heart.
God has given me everything I ever wanted except six
big strapping sons. Just think, Skinner, what a
glorious honor would be mine if I had six fine boys to
give to my country." His old lips trembled. "And you
could bank on the Ricks boys," he added. "My boys
would never wait to be drafted. No, sir-ree! When
they heard the call they'd answer, like their ancestors.

"Skinner, what has come over our boys of this generation? Why don't they volunteer? Why does the
President have to beg for men? Has the soul of the
idealist been corroded by a life of ease? Did the
spirit of adventure die with our forefathers? Is it any
harder to die just because war has become more terrible
—more deadly? Oh, Skinner, Skinner! To be young
and tall and strong and whirled in the cycle of vast
events—to play a man's part in a glorious undertaking
—to feel that I have enriched the world with my efforts,
however humble, or with my body revitalized the soil
made fallow by a ravishing monster. I feel, Skinner—
I feel so much and can do so little."

Nevertheless, he did do something that very afternoon. One after the other he examined all the young men in his employ, discovered which of them could afford the luxury of enlisting and then asked them bluntly whether they were going to enlist. Three of them said they were, and Cappy promised each of them a month's salary the day he should report to him in uniform. Nine others appeared to be uncertain of their duty, so Cappy fired them all, to the great distress of Mr. Skinner and Matt Peasley. Cappy, however, turned a deaf ear to their remonstrances.

"A man who won't fight for his country is no good," he declared; "and I won't keep a no-good son of a slacker on my pay roll. Get married men or men who have been rejected for military service to take the places of these bums who haven't courage enough even to try to enlist."

CHAPTER LIX

The campaign for the Liberty bonds brought Cappy an appointment from the mayor as captain of a corps of volunteer bond salesmen to work the wholesale lumber and shipping trade, and for three weeks the old gentleman was as busy as the proverbial one-armed paper hanger with the itch. He was obsessed with a fear that the bond issue would be under-subscribed by about a billion and a half and result in the United States of America being accorded a hearty Teutonic horse laugh. Consequently he made five separate subscriptions on his own account, and just before the lists closed on the last day he was again overcome with apprehension and subscribed for an additional ten thousand dollars' worth for his grandson! When the result of the Liberty-bond campaign was made known he almost wept with joy and gave a wonderful dinner to his corps of salesmen, after which he went down to his ranch to rest for a week and see what Sam Daniels was up to.

The morning he returned to town, prepared to leap, heart and soul into the hundred-million-dollar Red Cross drive, he had a visit from his port captain, Michael J. Murphy.

"Well, sir," Murphy announced, "I've cleaned up all the little details in my department, your new port captain is on the job, and I'm about to go over to the naval training station on Goat Island and hold up my

hand again. But before I go, sir, I want to express to
you something of what I feel for what you've done for
me and mine."

"Tut, tut. Not another peep out of you, sir!" Cappy commanded. To be thanked for anything always
made him feel uncomfortable. "What branch of the
service do you hope to get into, Mike?"

"I want to get aboard a destroyer, sir, though
they're the divil an' all to live aboard. They offer
the best chance for action. Patrolling the submarine
zone, you know."

"Gosh," Cappy groaned; "everybody's got the submarines on the brain, and I'm tagging along with the
rest. Mike, I swear I can't sleep nights, thinking of
this war. It breaks my heart to realize I'm out of it.
And because I'm a shipping man, naturally my fool
brain runs to submarines and how to control them.
Mike, I have a great yearning to sink a submarine;
the screams of those scoundrels aboard her would be
music to my ears."

"It's a serious problem," Murphy declared soberly;
"but I'm hoping our Yankee ingenuity will solve it."

"Well, we haven't done it to date, and in the meantime all the nut inventors in the world are sending their
nut ideas in to the National Council of Defense. Of
course I have a bright idea too. I'm a great hand at
hatching cute schemes, you know. However, I differ
from the average submarine nut in this—that I want to
try out my theory in practice before submitting it to
an expectant world. Still, I'd need you to help me;
and now that you're going into the navy I suppose
I'll have to forget it."

"I seem to remember a scheme of yours that resulted

in the capture of a submarine last year," Murphy reminded the old man. "That was a bully scheme, and I'm willing to wager that the head which produced it can produce another just as good. Tell me your plan for eliminating submarines, Mr. Ricks."

"My scheme doesn't contemplate a continuous performance," Cappy hastened to explain, "but it might work out once or twice—and in this great international emergency anything is worth trying once. I could demonstrate my theory in about two months—with your help."

"Then," declared Michael J. Murphy, "I'll wait until you give the demonstration before enlisting in the navy."

"Bully for you, Mike! I'll declare Terry Reardon in on the experiment also, for the reason that one of the ingredients required is a chief engineer with courage to spare. Now then, for my scheme: Do you know the *Costa Rica?*"

"That old steamer that used to run to Panama for the Pacific Mail?"

"The same."

"What about her?"

"She's in the bone yard—laid up for keeps, Mike. Her plates are so thin and soft the least jar would punch a hole in her; she's wrecked and strained from fifty years of service; her engines are worn out, her boilers are burned out, her gear is antiquated, and even in these times of abnormal freight rates she's too far gone to patch up and keep running. They kicked her up in the mud of Oakland Inner Harbor yesterday, and there she'll be stripped of everything of value and left to rot. My plan, Mike, is to buy the old *Costa*

Rica for a couple of thousand dollars, turn **Terence**
Reardon and his gang loose on her engines and boilers
for a couple of weeks and take the old coffin out for one
final voyage. She can make eight or nine knots in
good weather, and if she's torpedoed the loss will be
trifling. Will you run the risk and take her out for me,
Mike?"

"Yes, sir. What for?"

"As a decoy."

"I don't understand."

"We'll put a hand-picked crew aboard her, Mike;
we'll arm her fore and aft with six-inch guns, which
we can readily get from the navy now that it's the
fashion to arm merchantmen; and then go cruising in
the submarine zone. You can pick up a few old navy
men for a gun crew and train some of the *Costa
Rica's* crew, can't you?"

"If we can get somebody to give me the range and
manage to get the gun loaded somehow, I'll do the gun
pointing; with half a chance I'll guarantee results."

"And that is exactly what I plan to give you—half a
chance," Cappy declared enthusiastically. "The
Costa Rica isn't worth two hoots in a hollow, but she
still looks enough like a steamer to attract submarines;
and during this fine summer weather we can chance a
final voyage with the old wreck."

"Where do you get this 'we' stuff, Mr. Ricks?" Mike
Murphy queried bluntly. "You're not figuring on
going to sea in that coffin, are you?"

"I most certainly am so figuring. I take my fun
where I find it, Mike, and if I'm to plan and pay for
this experiment—then, by gravy, I'm going to be on

deck to watch it work out if it's the last act of my sinful career."

"But if they fire on us you may be killed."

"We'll be firin' back at 'em, won't we? And if I'm killed in action, won't that be a fitting finish for a Ricks?"

"We may be afloat in an open boat for a week. I don't want you to die of exposure, sir."

"Forget it, Mike! I've been charged off to profit and loss for so many years it makes me ill to think of them. And you remember, my dear Mike,

> " 'To every man upon this earth
>   Death cometh soon or late;
>   And how can man die better
>   Than facing fearful odds
>   For the ashes of his fathers
>   And the temples of his gods?'

Don't argue with me, Mike. My mind is quite made up. I'm going into action in this war, for, as I said before, I'll try anything once—particularly when it isn't very expensive and I can afford the luxury. We're going to buy the *Costa Rica*, take her into the submarine zone and lose her, but, by the Holy Pink-Toed Prophet, we'll take a submarine with us!"

"Not if the German sees us first."

Cappy leaned forward and laid his index finger impressively on Michael J. Murphy's knee. "That's the only way we can hope to win," he declared. "We must make certain the submarine sees us first. Mike, a German is a rabid disciple of law and order; anything out of the usual run of things upsets him terribly; he never makes allowance for the unexpected or for the other fellow's point of view. To be more exact, Mike, I figure that German psychology is the only kind of psychology a German can understand. And to tell you the truth, Mike," he added musingly, "there are blamed few people who can understand mine."

Michael J. Murphy nodded a vigorous indorsement to this last remark, and Cappy went on: "Do you think any proud and arrogant skipper of a German submarine would ever suspect an American citizen of such a harebrained scheme as the sending out of a rusty, creaking old rattletrap of a steamer that can't get out of her own way, for the avowed purpose of destroy ing him and his sub? No sir! His microphones will tell him, while he is still totally submerged, that his approaching prey is a slow poke and cannot possibly outrun him; then he'll come up, take a look and clinch his conclusions—after which he will attack."

"True for you sir. He'll launch his torpedo and dive before I can get a shot at him or correct my range to hit him; then the torpedo will hit us and we'll go up like a shower of mush—probably with half a dozen men killed and nothing accomplished in the way of a return swat."

"That was the program a few months ago," Cappy retorted triumphantly. "Have you noticed, however, that since merchantmen have been armed the submarines are more and more prone, when attacking in daylight, to pursue a steamer at a reasonable distance and rake her with shell fire? If a vessel is fired on and her skipper, looking back, notes the position of the submarine and realizes that he cannot possibly outrun her and that she outranges him, what does he do, Mike?"

"He does the sensible thing. Heaves to to avoid loss of life, gets his men into the boats and abandons his ship to the Hun."

"Precisely! And if the Hun thinks he is not likely to be disturbed for a couple of hours, what does he do?"

"Why," said Murphy, "he comes aboard, removes all the stores he can—particularly engine oil—and strips the vessel of all her brass, copper and bronze fittings. These metals are very scarce in Germany and they need all they can get in the manufacture of munitions."

"Correct! And we must bear in mind, Mike, the fact that a German is naturally thrifty; if he can sink a ship with shell fire or bombs set in her bilges he will not waste on her a torpedo that costs from ten to twenty thousand dollars. Now, will he?"

"Well, I wouldn't, Mr. Ricks."

"Then my plan is absurdly simple. We merely provide a gorgeous opportunity for the enemy; we inculcate in him the idea that he is about to pick a soft one —then: Alas, poor Yorick!"

Michael J. Murphy rose and put on his hat. "Where are you going, Mike?" Cappy demanded.

"I'm going up to the navy yard at Mare Island," the port captain declared, "to see if I cannot pick up a couple of six-inch rifles of the model they used when I was in the navy. They're obsolete now, but I understand them—and while I'm getting the guns I'll pick up four or five old navy men. Leave it to me, Mr. Ricks."

"We'll give 'em hell!" shouted Cappy.

"We will!" quoth Michael J. Murphy with conviction.

CHAPTER LX

Two weeks later the old *Costa Rica*, looking somewhat youthful in a new coat of black paint and with a huge American flag painted on each topside, slipped quietly out of San Francisco in ballast and for the last time turned her nose toward Panama. In the brief period given him in which to overhaul her interior, Terence P. Reardon had accomplished wonders, and an hour after Mike Murphy had taken his bearings from Point San Pedro and laid out his course the chief came into the chart room to announce that the old girl was doing eight knots and, barring unexpected bad weather, would continue to do it without falling to pieces. "If I could have spint two t'ousand dollars more on her," Terence declared, "I believe I could get another knot out av her. Time was whin she could do sixteen."

Cappy Ricks, enjoying his afternoon cigar in the snug chart room, snorted vigorously. "I don't very often take a notion to throw my money into the sea, Terence," he reminded his port engineer, "but when I do get that reckless I limit myself to twenty thousand dollars, and that, in round figures, is what this old ruin will stand me about the time the torpedo blows you up on top of the fiddle. However, that is a trifling investment if we succeed in destroying a late-type German submarine with a couple of hundred thousand dollars' worth of torpedoes aboard. As a sport-

431

ing proposition it's somewhat more expensive than golf, but the excitement makes up for the added cost."

"The old box is alive with rats and bedbugs," Murphy complained.

"If they annoy you, Mike, my boy, comfort yourself with the thought that they're all going to be drowned," Cappy replied gayly.

Slowly the old packet wallowed down the coast, the while her crew, under Mike Murphy's supervision, built gun platforms fore and aft. Following their completion, the two six-inch guns Cappy had succeeded in getting from the navy were lifted out of the hold with the aid of the cargo winch and placed in position, one forward and the other aft. Thereupon the mate took charge of the *Costa Rica*, while Mike Murphy drilled his crew in range finding and celerity in loading the piece. Pointing the gun was entirely up to Murphy and, needless to state, the task was in capable hands, as was frequently demonstrated during target practice as they loafed down the coast.

Upon arrival at Panama the *Costa Rica's* bunkers were replenished and an extra supply of sacked coal was piled on deck, for with her patched-up boilers the old steamer was a hog on fuel. Then the mechanics and carpenters and all men not vitally needed aboard for the remainder of the voyage were put ashore and furnished with transportation back to San Francisco by the regular Pacific Mail liner. Next, the name on the bows of the *Costa Rica* was painted out, the name boards at each end of her bridge removed and the raised-letter record of her identity and home port chipped off her stern; following which Cappy Ricks, Terence P. Reardon and Michael J. Murphy commended their souls to their Creator, and the *Costa Rica* slipped leisurely through the ditch and out into the Caribbean Sea.

Fourteen days later Mike Murphy dropped round to Cappy Ricks' cabin. "We're in the danger zone, sir," he announced. "And from now on we're liable to meet one of the larger type of U-boats that operate a couple of thousand miles from the base at Zeebrugge."

"Very well," Cappy replied calmly. "Whether torpedoed or shelled, your instructions are the same. Forbid the wireless operator to send out a call for help, heave to immediately and get the men into the boats and away from the ship. Terry Reardon will remain on duty in the engine room, provided it isn't wrecked by a torpedo and the engine room crew killed; you and your gun crew will remain aboard and hide in the forecastle if it's action front, and in the auxiliary steering-gear house if it's action rear. I will relieve the quartermaster, take charge of the wheel and direct the action. If I see that there isn't going to be any action we'll put on life preservers, jump overboard and be picked up by our men in the boats. However, something tells me, Mike, that we're going to have a crack at——"

At that very instant something rapped the *Costa Rica* terrifically on the starboard side amidships and tore through her with a grinding, wrenching noise, followed by an explosion.

"There's the crack you were speaking of, sir," Murphy yelled and started for the door. Cappy Ricks grasped him frantically by the arm. "Was that a shell or a torpedo?" he cried. His voice, thin and shrill with age, quavered now with excitement.

"It was a shell," Murphy answered. "Went through the second cabin."

"Then that German belongs to Alden P. Ricks," Cappy declared, and scurried for the pilot house. "Out and into life-boats!" he ordered the quartermaster, and shoved him away from the wheel. "Set her over to slow speed ahead," he called to the mate, who was standing stupidly, gazing at the white puffs of smoke that marked the position of the submarine two miles off the starboard bow. The mate came to life, jammed over the handle of the marine telegraph and, obeying an order bellowed to him by Mike Murphy from the main deck, abandoned the bridge for the boat deck, there to superintend the task of getting the men away from the ship.

His first thrill of excitement having subsided, Cappy carefully drew the little half curtains on the pilot-house window, leaving a small slit through which he could observe the submarine without being observed himself, for it was no part of his plan to disclose to the enemy the fact that the ship was not entirely deserted—and that the submarine commander should jump to the conclusion that she was deserted by all hands was precisely the condition that Cappy desired to bring about.

Down in the engine room the indomitable Terence Reardon, with one hand on the throttle and one eye on the steam gauge, put the *Costa Rica* under a deadslow bell; she seemed scarcely to move, yet she had sufficient steerage way to enable Cappy to keep her pointed in the general direction of the submarine, the commander of which, seeing the crew of the *Costa Rica* scurrying for the boats, contented himself with sending over half a dozen shells for the purpose of hurrying them along; then he ceased firing, and when the boats pulled out from the ship in tow of a motor lifeboat and his powerful glasses showed neither guns nor sign of life upon the *Costa Rica's* decks, he did exactly what Cappy Ricks figured he would do.

He circled warily round his prize, but the absence of frantic wireless calls for help lulled his suspicions, and presently he bore down upon her, hove to two cable lengths abreast the wallowing hulk and watched her fully five minutes for a possible trap, for the absence of any name puzzled him. His suspicions subsided at length, however, the hatch in her turtle deck slid back and men appeared, dragging up a small collapsible boat.

Slowly, slowly—so gradually that it seemed the old vessel was merely drifting, Cappy brought the *Costa Rica* round until her bow pointed toward the submarine. Mike Murphy, standing just inside the forecastle door, kept his glance on the slit in the curtains on the pilot-house window—and presently Cappy motioned violently to him.

"To the gun!" ordered the captain. Followed by his gun crew he dashed out of the forecastle and up the companion ladder to the forecastle head. A jerk at a lever connecting a cunningly constructed set of controls, and the false topsides on the forecastle head flopped to the deck, revealing Mike Murphy's six-inch gun. Cappy saw him deflect the gun while another man traversed it; for five seconds his eyes pressed the sight, and when the gun remained motionless Cappy knew that the hull of the submarine was looming fairly on the intersection of the cross wires in the sight. The range was point-blank!

Quick as were Murphy and his crew, however, the gun crew of the submarine was quicker. Before the *Costa Rica's* gun was properly laid, a shell from the submarine flew a foot over the heads of the Murphyites and burst fifty yards beyond the ship. "Ah, missed!" breathed Michael J. and raised his hand. The gunner released the firing pin and the six-inch projectile with which the gun had been loaded for two days crashed into the submarine at her water line.

A terrific explosion followed the shot. Cappy Ricks, gazing popeyed with horror, saw the submarine disintegrate and disappear in a huge water-spout; when the water settled only a vast and widening smear of heavy fuel oil showed where she had been.

From the forecastle head Michael Murphy yelled to Cappy Ricks. "Well, are you satisfied, sir?" On his part, Cappy, jubilant, even in the instant when he knew thirty new faces were already whining round the devil, dashed out on the bridge, seized the whistle cord and swung on it. A sad, nautical sob from the *Costa Rica's* siren answered him, and ten seconds later Terence Reardon whistled up the bridge. Cappy let go the whistle cord and took up the speaking tube. "Hello," he piped.

"What the divil do ye mean be blowin' that whistle?" roared Terence, thinking he was addressing the mate. "Wit' me alone in the engine room how d'ye expect me to keep shteam up on this ould hooker wit' you blowin' it off in the whistle! Take shame to yourself!"

"Mike sunk the submarine! Mike sunk the submarine!" Cappy shrilled over and over again. "Come

up, Terence, and see the oil. See the oil, Terence, see
the oil! Mike sunk the submarine, Mike sunk it. Bully
for Mike! Oh, bully! Bully! Bully! Mike sunk it,
but I schemed it. Come up, Terence, I'm going to
faint."

And then, with shrill yips of delirious delight he slid
down the companion to the main deck, to be gathered
in Michael J. Murphy's arms and hugged and passed
to the gun crew, who hoisted him to their shoulders and
paraded joyously and blasphemously round the deck.

"I told you he wouldn't use a torpedo if he could
do the trick with shells," Cappy shouted. "I told
you he'd board us if we didn't wireless for help. Ha,
ha, ha! Te-hee!" And he burst into shrill cachinna-
tions. "I out-thought the scoundrel—goin' to get a
patent on my idea—turn it over to the Government—
oh, Mike! Oh, Terence! Get the steward back aboard.
We must have some liquor. They used to serve grog
in the old navy after a victory, didn't they? Yi-yi-yi!"

Terence P. Reardon came up and proffered his
greasy paw, the while his quizzical glance swept the
oily sea. "Well, sor," he remarked philosophically,
"what wit' bein' a Christian I'm a little bit sorry the
Dutchman lost, but back av that again I'm a little bit
glad we won. Michael, do you get those blackguards
o' mine down below as quick as ye can, or we'll be all
day gettin' shteam up agin in this ould brute av a
ship."

CHAPTER LXI

Two days passed uneventfully; then shortly before sunset on the third day the look-out reported a periscope about a thousand yards distant and three points off the port bow. Cappy Ricks' old knees promptly commenced to knock together with excitement.

"Here's where Terence gets that torpedo if he doesn't come up out of the engine room," Mike Murphy remarked laconically, and promptly whistled Terence on the engine room speaking tube. "Come up or be blown up," he yelled.

"Divil a fear! We're comin'," Terence replied.

The chief and his crew had just reached the deck when the black shining turtleback of the submarine broke water.

"They have to come to the surface to discharge a torpedo," Murphy explained to Cappy Ricks.

"Great Godfrey! Here it comes!" shrilled Cappy, and watched, fascinated, the wake of the torpedo as it raced toward them. Just as Terence Reardon and his engine crew came panting up on the bridge, the old *Costa Rica* walked into it. "Me ingine room! I knew it!" cried Terence. Then the explosion came.

From where he lay on his back, half stunned, Cappy Ricks saw water and wreckage fly high in the air. The *Costa Rica* shivered. So did Cappy. Then the débris descended, and Cappy, choked with salt water, dimly realized that Terence Reardon had him in his arms

438

and was carrying him down to the boat deck, where the motor lifeboat swung wide in the davits.

"Here, take the boss from me," Terence commanded, and passed Cappy to a negro fireman, who carried the old man forward and laid him on a pile of blankets, previously placed there for just such an emergency.

Then the lifeboat commenced to drop away from the towering black topside and Cappy was aware of Michael J. Murphy's face—white, anxious, terrified—gazing down at him from the ship's rail.

"I'm just suffering from the shock," Cappy called. "Mike, you 'tend to business. Remember what I told you and tell the crew to keep their mouths shut. He'll do the natural thing and walk into your hand."

Murphy, reassured, waved his hand, and with his gun crew fled aft to the little house that protected the auxiliary steering gear from the weather, where they concealed themselves. In the meantime the other lifeboats had been lowered away; the painter from the third boat was passed to the second, which in turn passed its painter to the motor boat, and the ship's company hauled clear of the shattered, sinking ship. The *Costa Rica* was going down by the head, and Cappy, curious as any human being, sat up to watch his decoy disappear.

The submarine steamed up to them. "What vessel is that?" her commander shouted from the conning tower in excellent English.

"The American steamer *Soak-it-to-'em*, of Rotten Row," Cappy Ricks replied, "carrying a cargo of post holes. She has three decks and no bottom."

"How do you spell the name?" the German bawled.

"Can't hear you," Cappy fibbed. Then, *sotto voce*, to Mr. Reardon: "Kick her ahead, Terry."

"How do you spell the name?" the submarine captain repeated.

Cappy jibbered something unintelligible, and Mr. Reardon added to the puzzle by bellowing the information that the *p* was silent, as in pneumonia. All this time the motor boat was putting distance between itself and the submarine, and the disgusted German, as a last resort, steamed away and circled round the rapidly lifting stern of the doomed *Costa Rica*, confident that there he would find the record of her identity and home port—information which, in his methodical German way, he desired to include in his official report to the Admiralty. And while he ratched slowly past, striving to find with his binoculars that which was not, Michael J. Murphy and his bully boys came aft with a rush, tore aside the tarpaulin that screened the stern gun and expeditiously opened fire. To Cappy Ricks' horror Murphy's first shot was a clean miss, and instantly the big sub started to submerge with a hoarse sucking sound that brought despair to Cappy Ricks' heart. She was halfway under before Murphy's gun was reloaded, but quite calmly the gun was traversed and deflected until the black stern flashed across the intersection of the wires in the sight; then Murphy's hand dropped and the gun roared.

"That'll do nicely, lads," he told his crew. "Tore the stern off her that time; and from this dive she'll not come up. Cappy Ricks was right. He banked on human nature, and if curiosity isn't a human trait then I'm a Chinaman. Overboard with you, and away before the old girl goes under or we'll be sucked down in the vortex."

And overboard they went, to be picked up five minutes later by Terence and Cappy in the motor lifeboat. "You were right, Mr. Ricks," cried Murphy as he scrambled into the boat. "Curiosity killed the cat!"

"Yes, and it's blamed near killed me," Cappy declared feebly. "Some of that débris came down and hit me a slap on the dome——Jerusalem! There goes my decoy—peace to her bones!"

The *Costa Rica* dove to the Port of Missing Ships. Michael J. Murphy, however, did not turn to see her disappear; he was gazing, instead, at a thin red trickle that came from under Cappy's cap band and was running down his wizened neck. "Mr. Ricks," he said anxiously, "you're wounded."

Cappy rubbed the sore spot, and when he withdrew his fingers they were bloody.

"By the Holy Pink-Toed Prophet!" he gasped wonderingly. "You're right, Mike. I've been wounded in action with the enemies of my country! So help me, Mike. I've actually lived to shed my blood for the Stars and Stripes, like any other Ricks."

He gazed wonderingly at Mike Murphy. "Now I can die happy," he murmured. "I've done my bit."

"Yes, begorra," rumbled Terence P. Reardon, "an' if I have my way about it ye're honorably discharged from the service this minute, Misther Ricks. I'll gallivant no more wit' you in ye're ould breadbaskets av shteamers. 'Tis highly dangerous an' no business for a man of family."

Mike Murphy grinned at his colleague. "For all that, Terence," he declared, "you must admit that Mr.

Ricks' scheme for destroying submarines is the only practical one yet devised."

"Thrue for ye, Michael. But shtill, like all fine invintions, the idjea has its dhrawbacks. Now if we could only be sure av a continyous supply av ould ships for use as decoys——"

"I see a smudge of smoke," cried Cappy Ricks.

Mike Murphy followed the old man's pointing finger. "There's only one kind of boat makes a smudge like that," he declared; "and it's a destroyer. Safe and well out of a glorious adventure. Faith, we're the lucky devils; and by this and by that, I'll enlist aboard that destroyer, now that I'm here on the job."

"Do—an' good luck to you!" murmured Terence.

"Amen," said Cappy Ricks, and fingered his trifling but honorable wound. "Gosh!" he murmured. "If Skinner could only know a thrill like this!"

THE END.